# THE VIRGIN QUEEN

## JENNIFER ALLIS PROVOST

Bellatrix Press

BELLATRIX PRESS

# CONTENTS

# PROLOGUE

The legends of that day are great and many, though most are false.

They say that on the Day of Sadness, Asherah's dearest companion, Torim, and then her mate, Lormac, both gave their lives in the Battle for Teg'urnan. Tor, Parthalan's Prelate and direct descendant of Solon, was also listed as having perished, as were his sons. Asherah then captured the renegade king and beheaded him with one quick stroke. Asherah shed two tears, one for each of her loves, then as per Solon's edict she became Queen of Parthalan. Asherah still leads her people to this day.

As sometimes happens in the case of legends, the truth is somewhat different. Torim and Lormac did indeed perish, though neither death occurred during the battle. Tor survived, as did two of his sons; one son went to the south and the other west, though no one knew what became of Tor. And while Asherah had taken the old king's head, it had taken many strokes to sever it. Either way, in the end the king's blood had flowed down the palace steps.

The legend of Asherah shedding two tears is also false. The tear she shed were many, and occasionally some still fall.

Though bereft of her loves, Asherah went on to lead Parthalan. In the beginning, her only strength came from their memory; in time, she discovered her own. A new Prelate stepped into the place of the old, though no one replaced Asherah's mate. In time, her lack of a king gave her a new title, that of the Virgin Queen of Parthalan. Her people worshipped her, and celebrated the peaceful reign of Asherah the Ruthless in song and story.

Long may she reign!

# Chapter One

Asherah held her hand against her brow, shading her eyes from the suns as she surveyed the carnage across the plain. There had been no warning of this attack, led by the *mordeths* Mersgoth and Esguth, no scouts had run to the gates alerting Teg'urnan that demons had been on the move near Teg'urnan; then again, the scouts probably had been the first to die. Yesterday had been a day like any other, almost boring in its sameness to the days that came before, until darkness fell.

Shortly after the child sun went to rest, demons had amassed before the gates of Teg'urnan, an unusual and effective tactic for creatures who shunned the darkness. It was a force Asherah hadn't seen the like of since her army of slaves and elves, the *Ish h'ra hai* led by herself, Lormac, Harek and Tor, had taken the palace from Sahlgren. Since that bloody, tragic day when both Asherah's mate and dearest friend had perished, she had led Parthalan through nearly eight centuries of peace.

Harek...the one time Teg'urnan was attacked since she took the throne, her Prelate, along with all of the *con'dehr,* had been away in the south. He'd been leaving the palace more often of late, and Asherah suspected that the *mordeths* had become aware of his frequent and extended absences. She also suspected that they'd waited until the Prelate and his guards hadn't been in residence before they moved against the palace. She wondered if Harek had been attacked, and if he yet lived. She needed him alive, needed him to return, for she doubted she could set this mess to rights without him.

*No, that's not true. I just don't want anyone else near me to die.*

The queen shoved away her thoughts about Harek's possible demise and brought her ruminations back to the prior evening. Upon the alarm's sounding, the legion and hunters had scrambled to meet their attackers. Even the *sola* had emptied, with each and every *nuvi* grabbing the nearest weapon and mustering in defense of their home. Asherah and her First Hunter, Argent, had been the first outside the gates. As they had called out orders, one of the *mordeths*, Esguth, had taken notice of Argent. Esguth had baited the hunter while Asherah had shouted for Argent to keep his head, for he had been too canny a warrior to fall for a demon's tricks. Or perhaps not. His body had yet to be found, but reports claimed that Esguth had ripped Argent to pieces.

*My Prelate is gone; my First Hunter is dead. Why am I left breathing?* Why Esguth had bothered singling out Argent was a mystery. Argent was First Hunter, and therefore a target of all demons, but she could not recall Esguth having ever having had set eyes on him. Further, Argent had gone into battle clad in simple leather armor that in no way differentiated him from the rest of the hunters. She shuddered as she remembered the look in the *mordeth's* eyes, as if Argent had been his intended prey. Even now, after all the death she had seen and all the demons and men she herself had killed, the malevolence in Esguth's stare made her blood run cold.

A herald approached Asherah and confirmed what she had been dreading: none of the hunters could be found, and each was assumed dead. As queen, Asherah felt the loss of each and every Parthian deep within her being, but her hunters were as special to her as her *Ish h'ra hai* had once been. It had been Caol'nir's idea to have a team of warriors specially trained to fight demons, in much the same way he had taught her and Torim the finer points of combat. She'd wanted Caol'nir to train them himself, but his main concern was to get his mate, Alluria, as far from Teg'urnan, and demons, as possible. Asherah understood, and honored their pact that his name be stricken from Teg'urnan's records, and never had sought them out or spoke, their names. She never knew where Caol'nir and Alluria eventually made their home, but she never gave up hope that she would see them again.

*Gods. If only they'd been here.* Caol'nir had killed seventeen *mordeths* during the Battle for Teg'urnan, but the one who'd gotten away was Mersgoth.  Mersgoth, the beast who had marked Caol'nir's mate and driven them into hiding, the same beast who had led yesterday's charge alongside Esguth. What she wouldn't give to see that creature's head on a pike.

The battle had suddenly ended when the demons scattered, and it was later reported that the lessers had abandoned the fight when Esguth fell. No one knew who killed the *mordeth*, and there was no sign of the demon's carcass near the gates. Asherah now wended her way down the Hill of Rahlle, named for the sorcerer who'd sacrificed his sight for its creation, and across the deathly stillness of the battlefield, desperate for any sign of her hunters. She forged ahead like one possessed, ignoring the sucking noise the blood-soaked ground made against her boots.

*Lormac, if ever you wished to offer your wise counsel, now is the time.* Lormac would have rallied the survivors, issued orders... he would have known what to do. He had always known the right word or action; he who had been her mate, he who she'd lived without for far too long. She sighed, and wondered when she would join him. On days like this, she hoped that day would be sooner rather than later.

The queen wandered on, picking her way among the dead as the sharp incline of the Hill of Rahlle gradually leveled out to the flatness of the plain. She hadn't realized the distance she'd covered from the palace until she spied an individual kneeling before the rocky outcrop on the far side of the plain.

*Is that a survivor, or yet another demon?* As she got closer she saw that it was a faerie man, kneeling with his head bent forward as if in prayer. Scattered around him, as if they'd been flung from a great sack, were the limbs and heads of demons. His back was to Asherah, but as she approached she noted his long chestnut hair, and that his jerkin looked to be blue underneath the gore...

"Aeolmar!" Asherah cried as she threw her arms around the hunter. "Aeolmar, Aeolmar, Aeolmar, I thought those beasts had killed every last hunter." She felt his arms and back for wounds. "Are you all right?"

Aeolmar nodded slightly; Asherah assumed he was in shock. Still searching for wounds, she grabbed his hands, pausing when she saw the sword he held in a white-knuckled grip.

"This is... Is that Esguth's weapon?" she asked incredulously. While she was aware of Aeolmar's excellent swordsmanship, the taking a *mordeth's* sword was nearly unheard of. Not even Caol'nir, arguably the greatest warrior she had ever known, had managed such a feat. She looked again at the heaps of demon limbs, and noted how one arm was so much larger than the rest. *No, he couldn't have, not alone...*

"Did you kill Esguth?" Asherah asked. Aeolmar finally met the queen's gaze, his face as unmoving as stone.

"Yes." He glanced at the destruction he'd caused. "I killed them all."

Asherah stood, awed and slightly frightened of this man who was able to dispatch at least a dozen lesser demons as well as the *mordeth* on his own. In all her days she'd only known a handful of people capable of such a feat, herself being one of them. She pulled Aeolmar to his feet, and hunter and queen began the long walk back to Teg'urnan. Aeolmar kept his free hand on the queen's elbow as he led her around the bodies, his other hand clutching the *mordeth's* sword as if one of the corpses may rear up and attack. After a time, they came upon a man's arm clad in dark green leather, and that was the last either of them saw of Argent. Once they reached the gates, they were told that the other *mordeth*, Mersgoth, fled the battle shortly after Esguth fell, the suspicion now confirmed by a sighting of him east of Teg'urnan. Once again, the demon escaped with his hide intact.

The queen nodded, hardly hearing the detailed account of the demon's whereabouts. Instead, she contemplated the statues of the stag and doe as they leapt toward each other over the dark iron gates of Teg'urnan. Sculpted as representations of Olluhm and Cydia, gods of the sun and moon who were parents to the Fair Folk, they were meant to honor her kind's origin. To Asherah, the statues went far beyond a mere reminder. Olluhm was strong and his justice swift; indeed, tales were told of him setting entire realms ablaze to ensure the safety of his mate and progeny. Cydia, the calm mother goddess, tempered her fiery mate with the compassion that only a mother could possess.

*For this offense there will be justice, swift and sure. Compassion be damned.*

"Aeolmar, you are now my First Hunter," Asherah proclaimed. "What is your first command?"

"Find Mersgoth and kill him," Aeolmar replied through clenched teeth.

Asherah laced her fingers with the new First Hunter's. This new threat would be dealt with, and Asherah wouldn't need Harek's help. No, she and Aeolmar—she and her First Hunter—would have their vengeance.

"As you wish."

###

Harek stood in front of the large window, his hands braced on the ledge. He surveyed the valley before him as if it were his own private kingdom. Indeed, these past few winters he'd spent far more time at this southern residence than in the palace, so much so that he'd had a full manor built to accommodate himself and his *con'dehr*. They'd spent much of the cold season at this home away from home, he and his warriors and no others. There was the occasional complaint over the lack of women, but generally the men bore their isolation well, and Harek needed no reminders of Asherah.

Many speculated as to why Parthalan's Prelate took such frequent leaves from Teg'urnan, though few dared to ask him directly. Officially, he stated that since the old king had hidden away in the south while plotting with the *mordeth-gall*, there was a dire need to secure the region against further threats. That had been reason enough for his presence, but then a routine sweep had revealed a fissure at the desert's edge, belching the all-too-familiar stench of demons. It wasn't large, perhaps the length of three horses standing nose to tail, but its small size had mattered not. Whether by accident or design, there had been a crack in the very fabric of Parthalan that lead directly to the underworld.

"So this is why he went south," Asherah had said when she was told of the fissure, assuming that the source of Sahlgren's betrayal had been at last revealed. Against Harek's advice, she had gone to look at it with her own eyes, though he hadn't let her get too close to the edge. Back then, in the early days of Asherah's reign, she still had worn the Sala, the armband given to her by Lormac that marked her as Lady of Tingu. The four green stones of the Sala had glowed an ominous red to warn her away from the evil sludge that oozed from the crack. Trust the elves to make an object that warned you of impending evil when you were right in front of said evil, not when you were still a league or two off. Foolish, foolish creatures.

No matter, Harek would worry about the elves another day. It had taken nearly a full turn of the seasons to close the fissure, which had first been first packed with rock and assorted rubble, and then with dressed stone as masons fit together an impenetrable wall of granite. Once the masons had completed their work, the royal sorcerers, under Sarfek's direction, had woven a net of spells tightly around the stones. When all was said and done, the area looked like an ordinary hillside, not a gaping chasm where evil once spilled forth.

Harek had never doubted Sarfek's abilities, and had been confident that the seal was sound. Life had gone on in Teg'ur-nan, and as time wore on the queen wore the Sala less and less. Eventually the fog of despair had lifted from Asherah's sparkling black eyes, and those dark gems had settled upon a man. His name had been Brendan, and he was one of the warriors who'd fought in the Battle for Teg'urnan. He had been a kind man, strong and swift and handsome, a man who made Asherah smile again.

A man who wasn't Harek.

Unable to voice his despair, Harek had made up the excuse of ensuring that the fissure hadn't reopened and fled Teg'urnan before the sight of Asherah in Brendan's arms drove him mad. As time continued to flow, Harek stopped citing the fissure as the reason for his long absences, and Asherah stopped questioning him. He wondered if she noticed when he wasn't there.

*Soon, things will be different. Soon, Asherah and I will be close like we once were, and—*

A commotion in the courtyard below interrupted Harek's thoughts. It was a messenger wearing Teg'urnan's silver and blue colors tumbling off a horse that looked as if it would collapse in the next moment. The messenger gasped his missive between breaths, then crumpled to the ground. Harek turned from the window and rushed toward the stairs; his warriors were already running to fetch him. It was Olwynn who spoke, his face bloodless.

"Teg'urnan has been attacked!"

# Chapter Two

Hardly a sennight had passed from what was already immortalized in song and verse as the Battle of Esguth when Harek and the *con'dehr* made their return to Teg'urnan. The warriors gaped at the devastated landscape. What had once been the well-manicured royal concourse was scarred and bloodied, which shocked and unsettled the *con'dehr*. Most had been born during Asherah's peaceful reign, and the stories of the epic battle that marked her taking of the throne were just that: stories, not the daily matter of living. The Battle of Esguth had been the first time a demon had been within view of Teg'urnan since Sahlgren lost his head, and many feared that Asherah's era of peace was finally at its end.

Asherah observed Harek and the *con'dehr's* approach from the balcony overlooking the great square, Aeolmar standing at her shoulder. The new First Hunter had hardly left his queen's side since she found him out on the battlefield, and Asherah couldn't decide if she was comforted or irritated by his presence. It wasn't that she minded his closeness. As First Hunter Aeolmar should attend her often, and if Mersgoth and his beasts attacked again, she'd like to be near a man capable of killing a *mordeth*. However, she found his constant silence more than a bit unnerving. That, coupled with his tall frame and broad shoulders made Aeolmar seem more like a statue than a man. Asherah sighed, and wished he'd go loom over someone else.

Harek met Asherah's eyes as he passed under the gates, and raised his arm in salute. The queen held his gaze, stone-faced, until he looked elsewhere. The queen was not pleased about this most recent journey south, and her cold gaze made her displeasure with the Prelate plain for all to see. Harek barked a few orders to the *con'dehr,* and entered the palace. Asherah moved to enter her chamber and wait for him—and almost bumped into Aeolmar.

"Come, we'll tell Harek of our plans to capture Mersgoth," Asherah said, slightly annoyed as she stepped around the immobile Aeolmar. They entered the chamber as Harek did, flanked as always by several members of the *con'dehr. I remember when their sole purpose was to guard the temple,* Asherah mused as they filed into the room. Like Tor and the Prelates before him, Harek had hand-picked the warriors for the temple guard. Over time, the *con'dehr* had somehow left off guarding the Great Temple and had become the Prelate's personal retinue. She always had wondered if Harek's acquisition of the *con'dehr* had been his response to Asherah's hunters, of which he had wanted no part. Asherah remembered that argument well...

"You don't think a warrior trained in engaging demons is a good idea?" she had asked so long ago. They had that argument many times over the winters, yet Asherah had always hoped Harek would at least concede that her reasoning was sound.

"We had no such training," Harek had reminded her. "Anyone with a sharp blade or heavy cudgel can defeat a demon." Asherah gave him a look that told him how ridiculous she found that statement.

"When one is fighting for one's life, one tends to learn the basics of combat rather quickly," Asherah had stated.

"Remember our first bumbling efforts? I feel that training accomplished in the *sola* is much more desirable than the haphazard way Torim and I learned. If not for the training Caol'nir gave me, I'd be long since dead." Harek had snorted in reply, but Asherah was undeterred. "Speak your mind, Prelate. Why don't you want me to do this?"

"What do you mean to do with these hunters?" Harek demanded in turn. "Run off and track demons on your own?"

Asherah pursed her lips as she recalled that old dispute. None of those arguments had swayed Harek, but she'd established her band of hunters nonetheless. It had been a slow process, made all the slower by Harek's lack of help. She'd begun by filling the *sola* with the best instructors—one came from as far as the mortal realm, and another was rumored to be from Ysr—then Asherah had extended personal invitations to the finest, most accomplished warriors in Teg'urnan's legions, asking them to join in her new endeavor.

Many warriors ignored the invitation, while others refused outright. Asherah understood their reticence; one who has devoted one's life to killing demonic vermin constantly seeping up from the underworld usually was not the most refined sort, and warriors did tend to be a prideful lot. Asherah suspected that the problem was her, and her lack of royal blood. Many saw her as a mere usurper, a semi-redeemed slave who should have remained in the north, far from Teg'urnan.

*I am no longer just Hillel,* she'd told herself. *I am queen, and I will protect my people.*

Asherah had persevered, and in time, her hunters not only had resided in Teg'urnan, but four full contingents had created outposts at Parthalan's borders. Still, the hunters had been laughed at—and not always behind the queen's back. That laughter had died off when fewer villages were attacked, when crops stayed in the field long enough to reach harvest and livestock wasn't stolen from the pasture. The people of Parthalan had then lauded the queen's demon-catching warriors, and these long centuries of calm and serenity owed her hunters no small debt.

That peaceful era had ended abruptly, shattering to pieces as Esguth led his attack. And now Asherah would do exactly what Harek feared: deal with the *mordeth* without him.

"Where is Argent?" Harek demanded.

"Dead," Asherah replied. She had long ago grown accustomed to Harek's moods; normally they bothered her a great deal, but she wasn't going to let him affect her. Not today. "You've been away for three moons," she continued. "Why so long?"

"We had matters to attend to," Harek replied. "The dark fae—"

"Are leagues away from where you were," Asherah finished. Her gaze flicked toward the far wall, on which hung a map of Parthalan and the surrounding kingdoms; the map was spelled to represent the true borders of the realm and would instantly reflect the slightest change, be it the result of battle or politics. In fact, it was the only way Asherah learned that Leran had reclaimed Nugt for Tingu.

"Have our dark brothers managed to extend their kingdom without my or Leran's knowledge?" Asherah approached the map and traced the edge of the dark fae's lands. "No, it appears to be where it has always been." She gazed thoughtfully at the map, then turned to capture Harek and all the *con'dehr* in her royal glower. "While you fools were attending to some *matter* leagues away from Teg'urnan, we were attacked by two *mordeths* and scores of lessers. All of the hunters are dead, save Aeolmar. All of the *nuvi* perished, and more than half of the soldiers." Asherah went on to give Harek the horrible, soul-numbing details of the attack. Normally, she would have omitted certain facts, such as how the gatekeeper's mate, heavy with child, had been found without her head or her babe, or how the girls who'd left to pick brambleberries the afternoon prior to the attack had been discovered partially eaten but alive, though they'd been driven to madness by their ordeal and would likely be sent to asylum. No, Asherah spared him nothing, just as her people hadn't been spared.

"We will set out after the escaped *mordeth*," Asherah concluded. "I mean to send a clear message to Asgeloth. We fae have enjoyed peace, yes, but it has not made us soft, and I will not abide an attack upon my home."

Harek nodded; since Ehkron's whelp came of age they had waited for the new *mordeth-gall* to show his hand. "We will be ready by morning."

"No."

Harek glared at the queen. "No to what, Asherah?"

"I need you and the *con'dehr* to remain here as Teg'urnan's defense. Aeolmar and I will track the *mordeth*."

Harek's gaze settled upon Aeolmar, the first time he had acknowledged the man's presence. "Aeolmar?" Harek stared at the hunter, who didn't flinch under the Prelate's icy glare. "You now prefer to hunt demons with this Aeolmar?" Asherah's conviction wavered briefly; had it not been for Harek and his arrogance toward their captors, might have died a slave. Since that fateful day when he brought salve and bandages for her, and water for Torim, Harek had been her most loyal supporter...until a few winters past, when his brother died.

*No, it was long before Sarfek's death.* She recalled Harek's face when he had learned that she'd taken Argent as her lover, how he had set his jaw and turned away as if her words stung him. While Harek never had spoken against Argent, it had been plain that he had not approved of Asherah's choice—not that he'd approved of those before Argent, either.  But then, Asherah hadn't been making these choices to please anyone but herself, and her choice had never—and would never—be Harek. She'd made that plain long ago, not that Harek had chosen to hear her.

Asherah had lived like a spinster after Lormac died, so much so that songs were still sung about the Virgin Queen of Parthalan, and it had taken her many winters to invite a man to her bed. Harek hadn't liked that first man, Brendan, either, and when he had eventually tired of the queen and left Teg'urnan without so much as a farewell, Asherah had wondered if Harek had given him a fat purse and had sent him on his way. She'd never asked, not knowing if it would make her feel better knowing that Brendan had left because he was unsatisfied with her, or worse, because his affection could be so easily bought and sold.

Other men had come into her life; one by one, they had all left and Asherah had been alone again. Then Argent arrived at Teg'urnan with his arrogant tongue and brash swagger, and Asherah immediately had been drawn to him. She never loved him, but she had found a measure of comfort in his arms.

Shortly before Harek had learned about Asherah and Argent, his brother Sarfek had been ambushed by a band of rogue sorcerers in the western region of Parthalan. Harek had been close to tears as he recounted the tale of Sarfek's death, and Asherah immediately had granted him the resources necessary to avenge his brother. The *con'dehr* had managed to locate and execute those responsible, but instead of expressing gratitude for her support, Harek had begun spending more and more time away from Teg'urnan. She and Harek had once discussed every aspect of their lives, yet within a few seasons of Sarfek's demise the distance between them had become as vast as the whole of Parthalan.

Asherah hadn't confronted Harek over his frequent journeys to the south or called him on his excuses, which ranged from watching over the long-sealed fissure to pursuing the dark fae. Instead, she'd assumed that he needed both time and space to properly grieve for his brother, however long that might take. She understood well how grief could sink its talons deep into one's being, but he had been gone when Esguth and Mersgoth attacked.

*And Aeolmar was here.* Asherah didn't know if she could forgive Harek's for his absence—or if she wanted to. *No, I don't think this is the time for forgiveness. The time has come for Harek to respect his queen.* With that, Asherah squared her shoulders and faced the Prelate. "Aeolmar is now my First Hunter," Asherah informed Harek. "It is a hunter's place to track a demon, not a soldier's."

"What?" Harek shouted as he leapt to his feet. "Why him?"

"He killed Esguth," Asherah said flatly. An interested murmur rolled over the *con'dehr;* if not the Prelate himself, then his men were certainly impressed by Aeolmar's actions.

"You appointed him as First because he is the only hunter left alive," Harek yelled.

"I am queen, and I will appoint whomever I wish," Asherah shouted, slamming her hands on the table so hard an inkpot tipped over and created a sea of black upon a map of the eastern border. "Or have you forgotten who rules Parthalan from stars to sea?"

"If not for me, you wouldn't have this throne," Harek growled. Asherah's black eyes flamed like coals; nothing incensed her more than when Harek belittled her in front of the *con'dehr*. Before she could lash out, Aeolmar spoke.

"Why she rules is not in question," Aeolmar said. "What matters is that she is our queen, and you are beholden to follow her."

For the first time since Asherah had met him, Harek was speechless. He twisted the heavy gold ring he wore on his left hand. While Harek would never admit to a weakness, he was the only Prelate in Parthalan's long history who wasn't descended from Solon, and his lack of a blood affinity with the god made him feel more than a little inadequate. *That, and other things*, Asherah had remarked to herself when he first showed her the ring, struck with an image of the child sun as if Solon himself had approved of the new Prelate.

That ring hadn't made Harek's tongue any more eloquent, and for a moment, he was too furious to respond. When at last he spoke, his words were dark and clipped.

"You dare to speak to me so?" Harek demanded, his low voice rumbling across the room. "You, naught but a hunter?"

"*First* Hunter," Aeolmar corrected. He took a step toward Harek, putting his body between the queen and Prelate, "and I will speak to you however I wish."

"I am Prelate," Harek shouted, but Aeolmar spoke over him.

"What you are is a little man disrespecting our queen," Aeolmar said. "Now go, and do not return unless you mean to beg the queen's forgiveness." Aeolmar looked down at the much shorter Prelate. Harek opened his mouth, then clamped it shut as he turned on his heel and left.

Asherah dismissed the *con'dehr* with a gesture; each bore a look of utter befuddlement since no one, not even the queen, had ever chastised Harek in such a manner. Once they were gone, the exhausted queen sank into a chair, and Aeolmar strode to the door. Asherah assumed he meant to follow Harek, but Aeolmar merely threw the bolt before returning to her side.

"Why did you do that?" Asherah asked.

"So he won't come back before you're ready," Aeolmar replied. Asherah sighed as she propped her elbows on the table, narrowly avoiding the spilled ink, and rested her forehead on her palms. She doubted a season's preparations could ready one for Harek on a rampage.

"You shouldn't speak to him so," Asherah admonished. "He does outrank you."

"I care not for ranks and titles," Aeolmar snapped, then softened his voice as he took in Asherah's bowed head, the tired slant of her shoulders. "Forgive me my outburst. I don't have the best control of my temper."

Asherah nodded, then looked toward to her bolted door. "It matters not that you locked the door. There's another entrance in my private rooms, of which Harek is well aware." Aeolmar raised an eyebrow, but Asherah waved away his insinuation. "Not like that, you fool. On occasion, we discussed strategy and matters of the land late at night."

Aeolmar frowned at her explanation, but accepted it. "If you'd like, I'll charm the door so he cannot enter on his own."

It was Asherah's turn to arch her brow. "You're a sorcerer as well as hunter?"

"Sorcerer, no," he replied, "But my mother taught me a few tricks."

"She was a magic handler?" Asherah asked as she rose and led him through the rooms in which she conducted what passed for a private life, hidden away from the eyes and ears of the court. First they traversed her sitting room, of which an entire wall was occupied by an imposing green marble hearth. Before the hearth was arranged sumptuous furniture in which no one ever sat. The wall opposite was comprised of arched glass doors that led to her private garden. Asherah glimpsed her pale hair and skin reflected in the rippling glass; her coloring was unusual for a faerie, and coupled with her inkblack eyes and ruby lips, she had quite a striking appearance.

Asherah glanced at Aeolmar, who'd hardly acknowledged the trappings of royalty as he followed Asherah into her bedchamber. The first thing she'd noticed about him was his eyes, deep blue like sapphires heated in a forge, more than able to pierce one's soul. He wore his chestnut hair long, rarely restrained by thong or braid, and it gleamed like a shining fall of light. That, coupled with his tall, well-muscled frame and features worthy of a god, made Asherah suspect that Aeolmar received no small amount of invitations to bedchambers, and was thus uninterested in hers.

*Like as not, he's the last man that will see this room for a time,* Asherah mused, then shoved away the rising tide of guilt and pain. Argent had been her lover, but not her love. Even so, she did not relish the thought of beginning again with yet another man who would only leave her, by death or other means.

"Here is the doorway," Asherah said once they reached the far side of her bedchamber. Aeolmar laid his hand upon the pale wood for the barest moment, then he straightened and proclaimed the task complete. "That's it?" she asked dubiously.

"What had you been expecting?" he asked.

"Something more," Asherah murmured, unsure if that something more was as simple as a mere ripple of magic or if she'd expected sparks to fly from Aeolmar's fingertips. "Now, it will only open for me?"

"And myself," Aeolmar said. "I don't know how to cast the charm without allowing myself admittance."

"I suppose I can live with that," Asherah said, appreciating his honesty. "Speaking of which, there's something else I wish to show you," she said, pitching her voice low. The queen led Aeolmar up the steps to her bed and drew back the silk curtains, but he remained on the floor as she maneuvered around the many cushions.

"My lady," Aeolmar protested, but fell silent when she drew back the tapestry behind her bed and revealed yet another door.

"Now, don't dawdle," she called over her shoulder as she plunged into corridor, the darkness hiding her smile. Leading Aeolmar toward her bed in such a manner was a cruel jest, but she had so few opportunities for games. Argent had never appreciated her playful nature, and Harek was as humorless as stone.

If Aeolmar was offended he made no mention, not that she expected anything from him other than silence, and they soon emerged in a set of apartments easily as large as Asherah's own. "I would like you to have these rooms," she said with a sweeping gesture.

Aeolmar looked about the well-appointed chambers; a crofter's cottage, and a wealthy one at that, would have fit inside with room to spare. Three sides of the chamber were a solid expanse of the smooth gray stones ubiquitous to Teg'ur-nan, as were the steps leading to a sleeping platform that rivaled the queen's in luxury. The chamber was on the far side of the tower and therefore did not overlook the courtyard, so there was no balcony. Instead, the fourth wall was glass surrounded by an ornate fretwork of carved wood, and offered an expansive view the southern plain.

"Why give me such chambers?" Aeolmar asked, his eyes settling on the passage that emerged next to what would become his bed. "These were not Argent's rooms."

"They were not," Asherah agreed. She did not mention that the rooms were meant to house the queen's mate, the king she had long ago resigned herself to living without. "I feel…" She fell silent, remembering Lormac's chamber at the Seat. These rooms had always reminded her of his, but that was something else she wasn't mentioning. "The Prelate and I have grown distant of late, and if I need to discuss a matter of some import in the small hours of the night it should be with my First Hunter, not my *saffira-nell*."

"Then I am most honored," Aeolmar said with a bow of his head. Asherah smiled at her First Hunter, then reentered the passageway with Aeolmar following close behind. Mostly to fill the silence, she prattled on about his belongings, first saying that they should be relocated by nightfall, then deciding that the task should wait until they returned from tracking (and, hopefully killing) Mersgoth. Finally, she asked Aeolmar when he would prefer to move into the chamber.

"Whenever you wish it done is fine with me," Aeolmar replied as they emerged in the queen's bedchamber. His eyes moved about the chamber and settled upon the hearth; it was also carved from green marble, the smaller twin to the one in the outer chamber. Asherah fell silent as Aeolmar approached the small niche above the hearth, his attention having been drawn by her most prized possessions.

"This is the Sala?" he asked, overlooking the golden cuff that lay beside it, the cuff once worn by Torim. *But then, he wouldn't know it was hers. To him, it's just a piece of metal.*

"It is," Asherah affirmed, reaching out to stroke the heartstone. It had remained a deep red, even these many centuries since Lormac's death. *And I don't love you any less*, she silently proclaimed as she remembered her mate. "It marks me as Lady of Tingu."

"Why don't you wear it?" Aeolmar asked.

Asherah sighed; for her to explain why she refused to wear the Sala would require her to not only bare her soul to Aeolmar, but also be honest with herself, and she wasn't of a mind to do either. Tingu hadn't fared well in the years following Lormac's death, and by the time his son, Leran, came of age, the elf kingdom had fractured into seven distinct lands. All the work Lormac's father, and then Lormac himself, had done to keep Tingu's borders strong seemed to have been for naught.

But Leran was nothing if not his father's son, and he kept Tingu, itself, free from invaders, not only from the neighboring elf lands who wished to claim it for themselves, but also from the dark fae's continuous attempts to visit retribution against the grandson of their conqueror. Leran had been tenacious, even ruthless at times, and had gone so far as to reclaim two kingdoms as his own. She hoped that he would be able to reunite the elf lands under Tingu's banner and preserve Lormac's legacy.

Asherah had sent him the aid of her legion many times. Each time they had returned without engaging in battle, Leran having refused their assistance without so much as an explanation. Asherah knew exactly why. Leran still blamed her for his father's death. What Leran did not realize was that Asherah blamed herself, as well.

"I leave the elves to manage their own affairs, as I manage mine," was Asherah's reply. Aeolmar didn't press her for details, for which she was grateful. "Come, let us finalize our plans to track this beast."

# Chapter Three

As Aeolmar had suspected and Asherah had known, Harek returned to the queen's chambers later that evening, sulking like a dog with his tail between his legs. It had ever been this way with them, even during their long-ago closeness; Harek would lose his temper and storm off, while Asherah patiently waited for his apology.

When Harek found the queen she was sitting on the clipped grass in her garden, drinking the strong elfin brandy that Lormac had been so fond of. She had never much cared for it, preferring instead the cool sweetness of wine, but as it burned a path to her belly she imagined that the ensuing warmth was created by Lormac's touch. That made her miss Lormac all the more, so she had the Sala laid before her, her lone companion in the garden. The armband, and his bones, were all that remained of her mate.

Harek grunted at the queen drinking alone as he took an uninvited seat on the grass. "You mourn him still," he observed.

*How did he get in?* Asherah wondered, then remembered that Attia, her *saffira-nell*, had retired a short time ago, and Asherah hadn't bothered to bolt the door behind her. "Of course I mourn him still," Asherah said bitterly. "He was my mate, my love. I'll mourn him until I join him in death." Asherah threw back more of the brandy, then stroked the edge of the Sala.

"I ran after Tor," she said quietly. "I was so intent on capturing Sahlgren that I ran blindly after Tor, and Lormac died behind me. If I'd stayed with him, he would have lived."

"Asherah, there's no way to know if he would have survived," Harek soothed. "What if the demon that killed him had killed you as well?"

"Then we would be dead together," Asherah said blandly.

"It was not for you to die that day," Harek insisted, reaching for her hand. She evaded him, spilling brandy on her lap in the process.

"How can you know that?" Asherah railed. "How can you be so sure that Lormac was meant to die? Run through like a...like a..." She covered her face with her hands as she remembered Lormac's body on his funeral pyre, wrapped in that brown cloak she hated so. It had been unevenly woven and longer on one side than the other, but he'd always insisted upon it and no other, all because his son made it for him. "You forget, on that day I lost not only my mate but my son as well."

"You weren't bound to him," Harek stated. "You could take another mate."

"I want no other," she said wearily. "No one will ever compare to Lormac."

"That is just as well," Harek said.

Asherah dropped her hands from her face; she'd gotten brandy on her cheek as well, and her hair stuck to the sticky liquid. "You really believe that?"

"You are too long in your reign to take a mate," Harek replied. This was yet another subject they had discussed often. Harek believed that Asherah should remain a solitary ruler, strong in her own right and needing no king. *Only, I'm not strong*, Asherah lamented. *I need someone to lean upon, and that someone is not Harek.*

"Why you still bother with Leran is beyond me," Harek continued.

"He's all the family I have," Asherah mumbled. "He may hate me, and rightly so, but I can't think of him as anything other than my boy." She poured herself another measure of brandy, but her gut lurched and she offered it to Harek instead.

"You have your people," Harek said. "We still see you as our savior." He drank the proffered brandy, then reached for Asherah's hand. "Deliverer."

She snatched her hand away. "Don't call me that," Asherah snapped. She stumbled to her feet and moved a few paces away from Harek, whom she had once considered her dearest and only friend. Without his support, she doubted she would have survived those first few days as queen, so soon after Torim and Lormac were both taken from her. Then the days became years, and the years had stretched into decades. Somewhere along the way Harek, once her stoic pillar, became her petulant child, always pouting when he didn't have Asherah's full attention.

In fact, she was well aware that his last journey south was born of Harek's jealousy over her relationship with Argent. She had elected to spend that day outside the palace with her hunter rather than cloistered in her chambers while Harek rattled on about the growing, and mostly imagined, threats to Parthalan's safety. Harek and the *con'dehr* had left before she returned, and Argent dead before Harek again passed through Teg'urnan's gates.

"Do you even care that Argent is gone?" Asherah demanded. "Or does it please you that you no longer need to vie with him for my attention?"

"Asherah." Harek approached her, standing so close she could feel his breath on her neck. "I only want you to be happy."

Asherah laughed. The first time he'd claimed to want her happiness was when she caught him spying on her and Lormac making love. Harek had pledged himself to Asherah on that day and had kissed her before melting back into the trees. For not for the first time, she wondered at Harek's true motives.

"What is your definition of happy?" she spat. "Are you happy, Prelate?"

"You know what would make me happy," Harek replied. "I wish we were close, like we once were."

"When was that? While you watched demons destroy my body? Or later, when you skulked around after Lormac and me?" she demanded. "Or later yet, on those nights you tried to garner an invitation to my bed?"

"After Sahlgren was dead, and Tor and his boys left, and it was just you and me in Teg'urnan," Harek said. "I wish we could return to those times, when you and I looked after the good of Parthalan together."

"Those days were the worst of my life," Asherah said hoarsely. "I would spend the rest of my days in a *doja*, just for one more night in my mate's arms." *Or to hear Leran call me Mama once more.*

"Asherah, you cannot live in the past," Harek began, but her mirthless laughter drowned out his words.

"*I* do not live in the past," Asherah said. "*You* live in the past, still harboring the misconception that there is something between us."

"We had—"

"We had nothing!" Asherah shouted. "Get out of my garden!"

"Asherah," Harek pleaded, "please listen to me!"

"I have heard enough. Leave, or I will remove you myself." Asherah grabbed the Sala before walking deeper into her garden, and did not watch her Prelate's exit.

# Chapter Four

## Asherah Speaks

*The day after I threw Harek out of my garden, Elkin, commander of the Northern Contingent of hunters, arrived with five hunters to assist Aeolmar and me in the pursuit of Mersgoth. Riding at Elkin's side was an unfamiliar woman, and I assumed she was a prospective hunter. At least, I hoped she was a prospective hunter. if Elkin had brought her along for any other reason, I would wear his skin as a hat.*

*I said as much to Aeolmar, who remained silent. That in itself was not unusual, since the man seemed determined to utter as few words as possible, but his tense shoulders became markedly tighter when I mentioned Elkin's name. At this rate, he'd snap his own spine. "Have you had occasion to meet the Northern Commander?" I inquired.*

*"Elkin and I are well acquainted," Aeolmar replied, his words clipped, then delved back into silence. Well, that was unproductive. Perhaps he'd taken a vow of silence or an oath to continually behave in the most infuriating manner possible. I was thinking the latter.*

*We watched the hunters dismount, and Elkin was clearly surprised and pleased to see Aeolmar standing beside me. I couldn't fathom when the two of them had met, since the last time Elkin had come to Teg'urnan was while Aeolmar had been assigned to the Eastern Border, and the time before that was long before Aeolmar had first arrived at the palace. Could they have known one another in their youth?*

*I must admit, I was intrigued at the prospect of learning more about Aeolmar. Twelve winters past he had arrived in Teg'urnan with nothing more than the gear on his back and two swords, one so battered I had feared it would crumble at any moment, the other wrapped in oilcloth and hidden from the eyes of others. He had demanded an audience with me and Argent, his tone so urgent we had hurried to the great hall to hear his plea. I remember well the first time I set eyes upon Aeolmar, with his fine features and length of shining hair in stark contrast to his dusty and well-worn leathers. He'd claimed to have spent the last few decades tracking demons and had boasted in excess of one thousand kills, and he had the unprecedented audacity to demand that I name him a hunter. Argent nearly had driven him from the palace, but I appreciated the fire in Aeolmar's eyes; it had reminded me of myself before I became queen, when the tracking and killing of vermin had been my only joy. So I had acquiesced to this strange man's request, and Aeolmar was promptly sent to the Eastern Border, where he proved his claims many times over.*

*I glanced at him as we entered the chamber, marveling that so little had changed. He had a new sword and better gear, but he still kept that other sword hidden from view; the commander of the Eastern Contingent once told me that Aeolmar had nearly come to blows when another hunter dared to touch his secret weapon. I knew almost nothing about him, and other than our shared hatred of the* mordeth-gall *we didn't seem to have a thing in common. Although, few have anything in common with me, what with me being a former slave girl turned queen. I am somewhat unique in that respect.*

*While I considered Aeolmar's life before Teg'urnan, and our lack of common ground, we settled at my map table and*

*I selected a depiction of the western region. Aeolmar's gaze darted to the map but (of course!) he remained silent. If I remembered correctly, he hailed from the west. Then Elkin made his entrance, and I wondered if he held a few of the answers I sought about my First Hunter.*

*"Aeolmar, old friend," Elkin greeted upon seeing the new First Hunter; yes, apparently they did know one another. Elkin gave me a formal if belated greeting, which I didn't mind. I'd rather he kept on questioning Aeolmar.*

*"When the messenger told me the new First Hunter's name, I hardly dared hope it would be you. When did you come to Teg'urnan?" Elkin grinned as he clapped Aeolmar on the back.*

*"Twelve winters past," Aeolmar replied, "but I've been at the border until recently."*

*Elkin seemed unaware of Aeolmar's reticence to speak, or perhaps he was accustomed to his long silences, and went on asking after Aeolmar's family.*

*"You two knew each other as boys?" I inquired during a rare lull in Elkin's chatter.*

*"Aeolmar's father taught me to handle a sword," Elkin replied. "He taught every child within three day's walk, such was his skill."*

*"Your father was a warrior?" I asked.*

*"A farmer," Aeolmar answered, his tone making it clear that he would speak no further on the matter. Elkin was a bit confounded, but decided to leave it for another time and turned his attention to the task at hand.*

*"My lady, it has grieved us all to learn of Argent's demise," he said gravely. "I pledge to you that we will avenge his death and the deaths of all who fell at the Battle of Esguth. To that end I have brought you Innetha, the greatest tracker in Parthalan."*

*With a grand sweep of his arm, Elkin indicated the un-known woman—well, now known to be Innetha—and she halfheartedly bowed in my direction. In spite of her doe eyes, she was most certainly not a faerie; based on her golden complexion and sturdy yet voluptuous form I assumed she was a sylph, or maybe a nymph. When Elkin introduced her to Aeolmar her eyes lingered on him for far longer than was polite, and I felt an absurd pang of jealousy. Not only was Aeolmar not mine to be jealous over, Argent had perished less than a moon past.*

*I sighed as I thought of Argent, his placating smile and his rough voice, and I recalled that I had never once felt jealous over him. He had always made a polite effort to hide his drinking and whoring, and I pretended not to listen to the rumors about his latest conquests. He and I were a match of convenience, nothing more, and I daresay we both wished to find our comfort elsewhere.*

*Aeolmar finally noticed Innetha's heavy gaze and deliberately shoved back from the table as he avoided her eyes. I felt a small triumph; even though my First Hunter had not chosen me, neither had he chosen her.*

*Our meeting with Elkin and Innetha was brief because we had already decided to leave on the morrow and follow Mersgoth eastward. Innetha was confident to the point of arrogance as she described her tracking skills, and she stated that the* mordeth *would not long be ahead of us. Luckily, she had arrived on her own horse and our plans did not need to be altered for her presence; little did she know that if she or Elkin had exaggerated her skills I had no qualms about leaving her behind. Or him, for that matter. Once she and Elkin departed, I bade Aeolmar linger for a few moments.*

*"Tell me again how you are acquainted with Elkin," I said when he asked why I wanted him to remain.*

*"I don't like to speak of my past," Aeolmar said.*

*"Then speak of Elkin's," I suggested. I retrieved two cups and my flagon of elfin brandy—my, but the level had gotten low of late—and poured two measures. "To loosen your tongue," I said, sliding the cup toward him. He wasn't pleased with me, but he accepted the cup regardless as he told me of Elkin's youth.*

"Elkin's father was a cobbler," he began. "As far back as I can remember, Elkin did everything he could to avoid learning the craft. It wasn't that he found such things beneath him, but he had a wanderlust that was difficult to ignore."

"Did you also feel your feet itch and burn with the desire to see all the realm?" I asked.

"No," he replied, staring at the amber liquid. "I loved my home."

Well and so, we weren't going any farther down that path. I smiled at him, an apology for pushing him. Then I pushed in a different direction. "You must have lived in a large village for it to have its own cobbler," I observed.

"Elkin and I are not from the same village," Aeolmar clarified as he glared at me, well aware of my tricks to extract information from him. By way of a second apology, I refilled his cup; I assumed the smile would only work the one time. "His village was a day's walk from my home."

"So he was one of the children who ranged far and wide to learn swordplay at your father's knee," I surmised, and Aeolmar nodded. "Perhaps your father should teach in the sola. If your skill is any indicator, he is an excellent teacher."

"Yes." Aeolmar now stared toward something in the far reaches of his memory. His wistful expression of pain and longing squeezed my heart, and I regretted my attempts to pry.

"Forgive me," I said. "I'm only curious. I don't wish for you to think on things you'd rather not."

Aeolmar smiled tightly. "I think on them all the time," he said quietly. "It's a wonder they haven't driven me mad."

I knew well the madness he spoke of, for I had been trying not to succumb to it for nearly all of my life. "May I help?" I reached across the table and squeezed his forearm, and he covered my hand with his own.

"Help me find Mersgoth," he said fiercely. "Help me kill him. Once he's dead, I'll be able to breathe again." His deep blue eyes, bluer that the priceless gems mined in the north, shone *with fury and hurt, and something in his voice touched me on a primal level.*

*"We will," I promised. "We will."*

# Chapter Five

In spite of both the queen and First Hunter's doubts, Innetha proved that her reputation as a tracker was well-earned, and not one of Elkin's tall tales. As such, within a few days of their departure from Teg'urnan the hunters were little more than a day behind Mersgoth. Innetha's task was made easier since the *mordeth* was wounded during the battle, a detail that neither Asherah nor Aeolmar had been aware of. The wound, which Innetha suspected was to his lower leg, slowed the beast's progress as he headed due east. He made few attempts to hide his blood trail, which confounded the queen as much as the direction of his progression.

"Innetha claims the beast is heading east," Aeolmar told the queen after they had established camp on the fourth day of their hunt.

"Interesting." Asherah and Aeolmar were in her tent, discussing strategy after their evening meal. Since demons rarely travelled at night, the pursuers were confident that little time would be lost during their short rests. Asherah had once wondered why demons went to ground once the suns set, but brushed it off as one of their many oddities. "In all my time as queen, they have usually gone north, toward the cold. Yet this beast has led us nearly to the Eastern Border." Aeolmar leaned over the map, spread on the tent floor between the two, and squinted in the dim light.

"Before I came to Teg'urnan, I had much success against demons here," he said, indicating a region to the north and east of Parthalan where Grelk, the troll king, made his dens. "Perhaps the *mordeth-gall* has moved."

"Perhaps," Asherah murmured. She chewed her lip as she examined the map. The place where Aeolmar claimed to have killed the most demons was less than a day's ride from the Seat of Tingu. Less than a day's ride from Leran, and by all accounts Mersgoth was getting closer to him every day. "If Asgeloth's plan is to move his efforts east, I like it not."

"Then we will kill him," Aeolmar said simply. Asherah ignored his arrogance; normally she would have taken such conceit to task, but Aeolmar had proven time and again that he did not brag about his skill. That, and he was still carrying the sword he'd wrested from Esguth.

Asherah leaned closer to the map, struggling to make out a minute detail in the darkened tent, when she was suddenly awash in light. She looked up and saw the lamps blazing, but Aeolmar had not moved to light them.

"Another trick of your mother's?" Asherah asked, arching her brow at the hunter. He mumbled an affirmation, and Asherah continued, "I should like to meet this woman. She seems useful, what with locking wayward doors and lighting lamps from afar."

Aeolmar said nothing; Asherah was more than accustomed to his silence, though she hadn't grown to appreciate it. He took his leave of the queen shortly afterward. Asherah briefly wondered if she'd offended him, but needn't have worried. The next morning she awoke to find her lamps lit, and Aeolmar waiting outside her tent. Normally she would have admonished such needless attention—nothing irritated her more than others leaping to assist her in the most basic of tasks merely because she was queen—but she understood his urgency. That, she appreciated.

***

As a result of Aeolmar's desire to capture the *mordeth*, camp was swiftly broken and they were on their way before the elder sun crested the Eastern Ridge. Shortly thereafter, Innetha announced that she had Mersgoth's trail. They followed it for a time, until the tracker dismounted and placed her hands against the ground.

"What is it?" Asherah asked, dismounting to stand beside her.

"He has been joined by at least twelve, maybe fifteen lesser demons," Innetha replied as she worked the brown earth between her fingers, then raised worried eyes to Asherah. "They now far outnumber us. This seems like a trap. Is it folly to pursue them?"

Asherah fought the urge to fire off a sharp response to Innetha. They were following a clutch of demons, led by the most despicable *mordeth* left alive. Of course he would try to trap them. He'd also try to kill them, and suck the marrow from their bones.

"How long will this trail remain?" Asherah asked. "Can you find it again?"

"I can tell you every foot that has touched this ground in the past season, and in what direction they went," Innetha stated.

*Gods, I am surrounded by the prideful,* Asherah mused as she swung herself into her saddle. She hoped that folly did not accompany the pride.

"Then we will keep on the trail," the queen said. "We are less than a day from the Eastern Contingent. We will implore upon Brynne to lend us her five best hunters, and then we shall be a force for Mersgoth to reckon with."

***

The queen and her hunters arrived at the Eastern Contingent before the child sun went to rest. By the time he rose again, they had returned to the *mordeth's* trail with their numbers nearly doubled. Among the six who joined them was the commander of the Eastern Contingent, a gruff woman called Brynne, who had held the outpost for the last hundred winters. Every aspect of Brynne had an edge, from the sharp lines around her mouth, to her yellow braid drawn taut as a rope, to her harsh, gravelly voice. She might have been beautiful once, but her beauty had waned as her time at the border increased. It was her success against her foes and the intensity of her personality that drew others toward her, not the vestiges of her long-departed youth.

The hunters that accompanied Brynne were each as rough—or, as Innetha put it, barbaric—as their commander, and Asherah speculated that they'd all been out too long at their remote outpost, so very far from Teg'urnan. Neither the climate nor the terrain was hospitable; the winters were frigid and the summers short but sweltering. The surrounding landscape was comprised of bare mountains and sharp-edged cliffs, the whole of it worn barren by the harsh winds. Yet hunters who were sent to the Eastern Contingent often elected to remain long after their initial assignment had been completed. Asherah could not imagine how such a rough existence attracted so many.

Asherah sighed, then glanced sidelong at Aeolmar; he had been a member of Brynne's contingent for nearly ten winters before Argent had ordered his relocation to Teg'urnan. Brynne had regularly advised the queen and Argent about Aeolmar's many successes against their foes, which was why Argent had added him to the palace contingent. Asherah had thought Argent rash to do so, for they had not observed Aeolmar with their own eyes and had been only relying upon Brynne's reports; a place in Teg'urnan's guard was reserved for only the best hunters. After the Battle of Esguth, Asherah had been glad that Argent had not paid her more heed.

Tired of the unending, unchanging view that rolled away from either side of the road, Asherah watched Aeolmar as he gazed stoically ahead. *Stoic, now that is a good word for him.* She wondered if Aeolmar's indifferent nature was a help at the border, and if those walls that surrounded him, high and thick and mortared in silence, were intended keep him from acknowledging that he was a singularly efficient killer. While she had no reason to draw such conclusions, save her own intuition, she sensed that Aeolmar was a much kinder soul than he would have others believe. Why such a man would chose a life of battle and death was no small mystery.

At length Aeolmar acknowledged that Asherah was watching him—or perhaps he had grown tired of ignoring her—and met her eyes. Times past, Asherah's gaze would have darted away, but her timid nature had gone the way of her modesty long ago. She smiled at Aeolmar, and to her utter surprise and delight, he smiled in return. Thus emboldened, Asherah sidled her mount next to his. He didn't speak, but she hadn't expected him to, and they kept quiet company until the suns went to rest and they made camp. Asherah exhaled heavily when she finally entered her tent, and resigned herself to yet another cold night, alone.

# Chapter Six

"Aeolmar?"

Aeolmar looked up from polishing his sword and saw Brynne, the last woman he wanted to see directly before retiring, or any other time of day or night. She held aside the tent flap, her eyes expectant. *Gods, what does she want?* he grumbled inwardly, but kept his voice polite. "Yes?"

"I brought you something hot to drink," Brynne said as she stepped the rest of the way into his tent, bearing a steaming bowl of tea. "It's not usually so cold this early in the season," she added unnecessarily. It annoyed Aeolmar that Brynne had assumed an invitation into his private space, and that she was babbling on about the weather. Most of all, he hated tea.

"Why are you really here?" he asked wearily. He was tired, his bones creaked and his muscles were sore, and he wanted nothing more than to finish cleaning his weapons, and then drift off to sleep. Alone.

"Where did you get this?" Brynne asked, effectively changing the subject as she picked up a second sword. It was a crude piece, certainly not the smith's finest effort. The hilt was cracked and crazed, the iron blade pitted from years of neglect.

"It was Esguth's sword," he replied. "During the battle, I lost my own weapon."

"So you took a *mordeth's?*" Brynne asked incredulously. He saw the same fear-tinged awe reflected in her eyes that he'd seen in Asherah's, and allowed himself a small measure of pride. *Father, you taught me well.*

"And then I killed him with it," Aeolmar concluded. "I thought it would be fitting to kill Mersgoth with the same sword." Brynne nodded as she replaced the sword, her eyes falling to the untouched bowl.

"You haven't had your tea," she said. Aeolmar put aside the sword he'd been polishing and rose to his feet; he was taller than any man he'd ever met, save his father and brothers, and he glowered down at Brynne.

"I ask again, why are you here?" he demanded.

"I thought you might crave some company," Brynne said, now daring to step closer to Aeolmar. She reached out to him but he evaded her touch, his mood having gone from annoyed to furious.

"Not this again! Woman, how many times have I refused you?" he demanded.

"Your refusals were because I was your commander, but now we're equals," she said, her rough voice catching on the smooth words.

*Your rank had nothing to do with me not wanting you.* Aloud, he clarified, "We are not equals. You are my subordinate."

"I will submit to you, if you wish it," Brynne said, but Aeolmar had had enough.

"Get out!" he yelled as he pointed toward the open tent flap, but in his fury he misjudged the distance and struck the tent's pole with the back of his hand. He bellowed as he clutched his hand to his chest, certain he had broken it. Brynne used his distraction to approach him yet again.

"Are you all right?" she asked, reaching out to stroke his arm. Aeolmar grabbed her wrist with his uninjured hand, squeezing it until he felt her bones grind.

"Touch me again, and it will be the last thing you do," he growled, discarding her wrist as if it were garbage. "I will never bed you, Brynne. The sooner you accept this the better it will be for the both of us."

"I refuse to accept," she said, defiantly crossing her arms.

"Believe what you will," Aeolmar grumbled as he stormed out of his tent and into the night. He heard Brynne follow—crashing about so loudly he wondered how she had ever culled a demon unawares—and he plunged into the nearest tent to avoid her. That tent happened to be Innetha's. She sat straight up in her bedroll, clutching a fur blanket to her breast.

"What's happening?" she gasped, rubbing sleep from her eyes. "Are we being attacked?"

"No, no," Aeolmar replied. "Forgive me; I did not realize this was your tent. I did not mean to disturb you." He moved to leave, but Innetha turned up the flame of her lamp and bade him to remain.

"Would you like to tell me whatever's bothering you?" she asked softly. When he remained silent, she added, "Obviously, something is."

He glanced over his shoulder, and noted that Innetha wasn't possessed of the same wild-eyed passion as Brynne; indeed, her doe eyes seemed to harbor a genuine concern. *What harm could a few words do?* Aeolmar sighed as he accepted her invitation, and sat at the foot of her bedroll.

"I'm avoiding Brynne," he said at length.

"Brynne? You mean the commander of that forsaken border outpost?" Innetha asked, and Aeolmar nodded in reply. Innetha was unimpressed with the hunters from Eastern Contingent and their foul-mouthed leader, and she had declared loudly that no amount of gold or glory could make her live like a common sow, rutting in the mud. That remark had earned her a round of scathing insults from Brynne, which Innetha completely ignored. "She's been out there at the edges of civilization for too long and resembles her men more than a woman ought to," Innetha continued, and Aeolmar laughed. Brynne was certainly not very feminine.

"It's much worse in the winter, once it gets too cold to bathe," Aeolmar said, and Innetha wrinkled her nose.

"Can't you just order her to stop?" Innetha asked.

"If only she would listen," Aeolmar replied. "It has ever been this way with her. I was sent to the border when I was first named, and she chased me almost from the day I arrived. Now I command her, and she still pursues me. I have always been very clear in that I've no interest in her, yet she seems to think she can sway my will."

"You must have made quite an impression on her for this chase to last so long," Innetha observed.

"I've no idea how," he grumbled. Aeolmar leaned back on his hands, flinching when he put weight on his injured hand.

"Are you hurt?" she asked, reading his pained expression.

Aeolmar rubbed his eyes with his other hand, and wondered if he would ever attain his goal of sleep. "I may have broken my hand."

"Here," Innetha said, tucking the fur underneath her arms as she reached for his hand, "let me have a look at it." Aeolmar stared at her for a moment; Innetha was naked in her furs, all dark curls and creamy shoulders, and unless she intended to bandage his hand with those same furs, she had no means to help him.

But her eyes... Her eyes were entrancing. He'd thought they were brown, but he now noticed swirls of green and a dusting of gold flecks. Aeolmar was reminded of a passage in the troll king's forge that ran parallel to a vein of emeralds, and how the uncut gems glowed and danced in the flickering torchlight. Mired somewhere between a waking dream and pleasant memory, Aeolmar let her take his hand.

Innetha stroked her fingers across his knuckles, then his palm, until she located the fracture. It wasn't a bad break, hardly more than crack in the small bone on the outer edge of his hand; she murmured as much while she began to work. Aeolmar sat awestruck as Innetha whispered and coaxed the pieces of bone back together. He felt the unmistakable shimmer of magic, rippling up his arm and spilling over him as she plied her art.

"Elkin...did not mention this," he said hoarsely.

"Elkin does not know," she replied.

Aeolmar looked up and was once again mesmerized by her gaze, filled with kindness and warmth and healing. He felt their souls meet, and he remembered—*how can I remember if it happened to her?*—when Innetha was cursed by a woman she'd once served. The curse weighed upon Innetha's soul like a stone anchor, and she was fated to heal the pain of others at the price of drawing that pain into her own body. Aeolmar couldn't discern why she'd been cursed, but watched as Innetha was doomed to eternally endure the pain of those she cared for.

He blinked, trying to come back to himself, when he saw her expression change. In her eyes, he saw reflected his worst memory, his terrible pain for which he could never atone. Innetha's brow wrinkled as she tried to make sense of the memory and decipher the horrible scene. She looked as if she'd cry out and Aeolmar, desperate to break their connection, wrenched his hand free of her grasp. As he did so, the lack of pain surprised him.

"You really healed me," he marveled as he stared at his hand, clenching and unclenching his fist. He looked back to her, and smiled. "I can't believe it. Thank you, tracker."

"You are welcome, hunter," Innetha replied, returning his smile. Aeolmar's gaze traveled lower and saw that the fur she had so carefully tucked around her bosom had fallen to her waist. The lamplight imparted a golden glow to her skin; her breasts heaved from the aftereffects of the healing.

"Innetha, your fur," he began, "it's fallen." Instead of covering herself, Innetha rose up on her knees and leaned forward, the fur slipping past her thighs as she caught his arm.

"Aeolmar, you don't need to go," she said as she stroked his forearm. "Let me heal you."

For a moment, Aeolmar entertained her offer. Innetha was beautiful, and the notion of sharing her bed was enticing. In his youth, he wouldn't have thought twice about joining her, consequences be damned. But he knew what she wanted to absolve him of, the pain she would try to heal as they lay together, and that was something he could not allow.

"What you ask, I cannot give," he said, dropping his gaze from her lovely form. "You cannot heal the burden I carry."

"Let me try," she pleaded. "I can take away your pain."

Aeolmar caressed her cheek and asked, "But at what cost to you?" Innetha, too startled by his refusal to speak, merely watched as he pressed her fingers to his lips, and left her.

Once outside, Aeolmar momentarily berated himself for his actions. *I am a fool,* he thought, *a fool for disturbing her, and a fool for letting her heal me.* He began the short walk back to his tent, halting when he saw a light emanating from within. He wondered if he had left a candle burning when he realized that the light most likely meant that Brynne waited for him, either to offer some sort of an apology or throw herself at him yet again. Not being in the mood for either scenario, he abruptly turned and walked in the opposite direction, blindly making his way through the camp until he stood before the queen's palatial blue silk tent. He plowed into the tent, not deigning to announce himself or even knock.

The First Hunter found Asherah the Ruthless reclined upon her bedroll, clad in a sleeveless white gown with her pale hair loose about her shoulders. She looked about as ruthless as a lamb in springtime. She'd been studying a scroll, likely a map for the queen did love her maps, and took no offense at his sudden entrance.

"Aeolmar?" she asked, glancing up from her scroll. "Is something wrong?"

"No," he replied, cursing his agitation that caused him to forgo what little manners he possessed. "Forgive me, I didn't mean to disturb you. I'm avoiding Brynne."

"Has she been chasing you about?" Asherah asked, arching her brows while she tried not to laugh. Aeolmar frowned and gritted his teeth, but he had to admit that the image of Brynne chasing the First Hunter throughout the camp was quite amusing.

"We fought earlier, and while I was shouting at her I struck the tent pole and broke my hand," Aeolmar explained, feeling more than a bit foolish as he related this altercation to the queen. "Then I went to Innetha's tent, but I had to leave."

"She wouldn't shelter you?" Asherah inquired.

"She tried. She healed my hand," Aeolmar replied.

"Innetha is a healer?" Asherah asked, surprised.

"Evidently, she is." Aeolmar sat on the ground and rubbed his eyes. "All I want to do is sleep, and instead I have Brynne throwing herself at me, and Innetha working her strange magics on me. It makes me wonder if every woman in Parthalan has taken leave of her senses." Realizing what he'd said, he mumbled, "I do not include you in that statement, my queen. I mean no offense."

"I take none." Asherah regarded him for a moment before she continued. "Would you like to stay here?" Aeolmar dropped his hand and looked sharply at her, unsure if he'd heard her correctly. "Come, there is a chill in the air. We can warm each other."

"Didn't Argent once warm your bed?" Aeolmar asked carefully.

"On occasion," replied the queen.

"Is this a privilege of the First Hunter?" he pressed.

Asherah sighed as she rolled up the scroll. "No, it is not. I do not command anyone to stand at my side or to share my bed. If you would like to stay, you may. If you choose to depart, so be it." With that, Asherah blew out the candle and turned on her side, leaving the First Hunter staring at her back.

Aeolmar remained seated for a moment, considering his options. He would have preferred the solitude of his own tent, but he had no way of knowing if or when Brynne would return. While he had no problem yelling at her, or beating her to a bloody pulp for that matter, he was exhausted. Perhaps he should go sleep in a tree; he'd done that often enough before he'd become a hunter, when he was nothing more than a lone killer. The bark and knobby branches tended to leave one sore, but he would be alone.

But to lie down with the queen... it was an honor to be invited to Asherah's bed, even if the offer was for nothing more than sleep. More, he wondered what the ultimate penalty would be if he left. For all that he was lacking proper manners, Aeolmar did not want to risk insulting her.

*Gods, I'm being a fool. Just lie down and get some rest.* Having made his decision, Aeolmar pulled off his boots, and then his shirt, lastly unbuckling his sword belt and positioning the weapon within easy reach. He drew back the furs and lay next to the queen, careful not to touch her, and before he knew it, he was asleep.

# Chapter Seven

*Aeolmar glanced overhead, the position of the suns telling him that it was long past midday. He hadn't meant to remain at the bathing pool for so long, but then he hadn't known that fair Ishlia would happen upon him during his swim. His heart beat a little faster as he recalled how the water droplets had clung to her lashes, the feel of her firm hips under his hands, her soft lips. He was so enthralled with these recent memories, he nearly bumped into a tree.*

*He shook himself free of his reverie and continued the short walk back to his family's home. As much as he looked forward to his times with Ishlia, brief though they were, Aeolmar loved above all else the tiny cottage full to bursting with his parents and siblings. He didn't mind the hard labor of working in the fields or the mill, and midday, when his mother's delicious bread came hot and fresh from the hearth, was his favorite time of day. Unfortunately, his pleasant dalliance with Ishlia meant that the bread was now long out of the hearth, and like as not stone cold. Worse, his brothers might have already eaten it all.*

*When Aeolmar emerged from the forest and caught sight of his home, the unnatural stillness told him something was amiss. No smoke wafted from the chimney, and by now his mother should have been well into preparations for their evening meal. His younger sisters should have been in the barn, tending the livestock, yet he couldn't hear their laughter. Nor were the older girls in their usual seat next to the cottage door, mending his family's well-worn clothing. By the time he looked to the fields, desperate for a glimpse of his brothers or father, he was running toward the cottage, calling out their names with silence as his only reply. Aeolmar burst through the door, and recoiled in horror at the scene before him.*

*In Aeolmar's young life, he had rarely seen violence and never a dead body, nor a wound that was the result of more than a mishap at the mill. He even turned away when livestock was slaughtered. Now, death surrounded him, its thick scent filling his nose. His family was dead, every last one of them, their bodies covered with cruel wounds and strangely shaped burns. His father lay just inside the entrance, still clutching his sword. His brothers, Tor and Fiornacht, flanked him; they had perished trying to keep whatever did this from his mother and sisters. Behind them lay his oldest sister, Brida, her head twisted around at an unnatural angle while she clutched Linnea's lifeless body. He made his way past the entrance and saw Nessa, splayed out on the kneading table in such a brutal and undignified way he couldn't bear to approach her. Aeolmar covered his face with his hands, unable to move or even think under the onslaught of despair.*

*"Aeolmar?"*

*The weak voice came from the far corner of the room, so faint he hardly heard it. Aeolmar rushed to the area and found his mother, lying on her side with a curved sword impaled in her gut and one of those odd marks scorched onto her back.*

*"Mama!" Aeolmar shouted, relieved to find her alive. He tried to help her sit up, only to have her gasp in pain.*

*"Leave me here," she rasped, "I don't have much life left, anyway. Enna..." Alluria raised her hand toward the hearth. "I hid her."*

*Aeolmar went toward the hearth and found his youngest sibling behind the woodpile; she bore a mark, like the rest, this one burned over her tiny heart. He picked up her limp form and held her to him, brushing golden hair back from her face.*

*"She's gone," Aeolmar said. He held Enna tightly against his chest, remembering how she had bounded into his arms only that morning. "Who did this?" he asked as he knelt at his mother's side.*

*"A demon, a* mordeth, *called Mersgoth," she replied. "He finally found us."*

*"Why would a demon be looking for you?" he asked, and realized that he had been at the bathing pool when the demon attacked his family. "I should have been here," he said bitterly. "I could have defended you."*

*"And died yourself?" Alluria asked gently. She tried to stroke her son's hair, but she could no longer raise her arm that high. Aeolmar lay on the floor next to her, still holding his sister, so she could reach him. "No, Aeolmar, it was not for you to die this day. You are meant for great things, my son." Her hand moved from his cheek to her throat, and she touched the only item of jewelry she owned. It was a blue teardrop pendant strung on a silver chain, given to her by his father long ago.*

*"Take off my pendant."*

*Aeolmar obeyed, and she pressed it into his hand.*

*"Keep it with you."*

*"What?" Aeolmar asked. "Mama, no, it's yours. It belongs with you."*

*"You are to put it around the neck of your mate, your soul's true mate, as your father did to me." She stroked her son's cheek, understanding the confusion in his eyes. "You will know her, when you meet her."*

*"Is it Ishlia?" he asked, confused and distraught and wondering why they were talking about mates while their whole family lay dead around them.*

*"If you need to ask, then she is not." Alluria tangled her fingers in her son's hair, his hair that was so like hers, and smiled. "Aeolmar, my Aeolmar, my only child who took after me. I love you my son, my perfect boy. Never forget that."*

*"Mama, don't leave me," he implored as he grasped her hand. "I can't go on without you, with all of you gone. You need to stay."*

*"I need to join your father." Alluria's sapphire eyes settled on Enna's golden curls. "Let me hold my baby, one last time."*

*Aeolmar placed his sister's form against his mother's breast, carefully wrapping Alluria's arms around her youngest child. He in turn wrapped his arms around them both, mindful of his mother's wounds, his tears falling on Alluria's cheeks.*

*"I love you, Mama," he whispered, but she didn't hear him. Alluria was already gone.*

# Chapter Eight

## Aeolmar Speaks

*I hauled myself out of the dream the way one would haul oneself out of a tar pit: slowly and painfully, gasping for breath as if I had climbed the whole of the World's Spine in a day. Only it hadn't been a dream, but a remembrance of the worst day of my life. I hadn't seen their cold, dead faces behind my eyes for so long I'd hoped that I would finally able to sleep in peace, but Innetha had done a fair bit of poking about in my mind. I don't know if she was snooping to further her own end, or if that intimate touch of her soul to mine was a necessary part of the healing process. Nor did I care about her true motives, since I'd already resolved to keep my distance from the healer-witch.*

*I shoved my hair back and found it damp with sweat. Many winters had passed since my family was murdered in their home, yet I felt their loss as if it had happened only yesterday. Worse yet, Mersgoth, the most despicable member of that foul race of vermin, was still alive and well. Yes, we were tracking him and yes, he was supposedly wounded, but I knew better than to hope he was near his end. I had been tracking him too long, and come close to killing him too many times—only to see him slip through my fingers—to believe his death was imminent. When I cleaved the head from his body I would celebrate his death, and not a moment sooner.*

*The sweat dried upon my skin and I shivered. I yanked the fur coverlet up to my shoulders and rolled onto my side, inhaling a mouthful of Asherah's hair in the process. I had forgotten she slept beside me, forgotten everything save the sight of my mother dying before my eyes. I tried to keep my sputtering to a minimum, but if I woke Asherah she made no sound or movement, which was just as well. She lay on her side with her back to me, so I couldn't see if her eyes were open. It was awkward enough lying alongside the queen, and I didn't want to explain why I was panting and sweaty.*

*Carefully, I gathered up her hair and twisted it into a loose rope. Her hair was very long and soft, nearly reaching her waist when she wore it unbound. And the color...I'd never seen another with the nearly-white tresses that Asherah bore, save for a few mortals nearing the end of their days. Of course, there was nothing mortal or mundane about the Faerie Queen. I ran my fingers through her hair for a few moments. I was taking ungranted liberties by doing so, but it had been a very, very long time since I'd been in bed with a woman, never mind a woman as lovely as the queen.*

*As I smoothed down the long strands my thoughts returned to my earlier encounter with Innetha; her dark curls had tumbled over her shoulders and hadn't hidden a bit of her. Now she was lovely, quite possibly the loveliest woman I had ever seen, and for a moment I considered returning to her tent. Since she had practically dragged me into her bed, I couldn't imagine she would be anything but pleased if I came to collect on her offer. While I concentrated on the image of Innetha's bare breasts, I unlaced my leggings; not only was the leather uncomfortable to sleep in, but they'd become a bit tighter while I imagined folding myself into Innetha's embrace...*

*No, no, I couldn't do that. I was the First Hunter of Parthalan, on a mission to track a* mordeth, *no longer a randy youth intent upon bedding all the women in the village. Besides, hadn't I resolved to avoid her? As I resolved to work on my resolve, I remembered Asherah's hair in my hands and laughed into the darkness. In an attempt to keep one woman from my bed, I nearly ended up in bed with a second, and was now lying next to a third. My brothers would have approved.*

*I moved closer to Asherah and tucked the length of her hair against her back. In doing so my fingers grazed her shoulder and I felt the puckered skin of a scar. Being fairly familiar with scars from my own exploits, I could tell that she had sustained a deep and terrible wound. I traced its path as it arched over her shoulder and toward her spine, easy enough to follow through the thin fabric of her shift. It met another scar, and then another.*

*Now my palms were flat against her back as I felt the cruel wounds, my mood hovering between anger at whoever had done this and amazement that Asherah had survived such torture. I followed the scars as they curved over her hip, and learned to my horror that the torture hadn't been confined to her back. I'd imagined she'd been whipped, but where they were leading argued against mere punishment. Rage got the better of me, as it often does, and I flung Asherah onto her back as I called for the lamps to ignite.*

*"Who did this to you?" I demanded. Asherah blinked rapidly; she really had been sleeping. I'd just repaid the kindness of her granting me a spot to sleep by bellowing in her face.*

*"Did what?" she demanded in turn.*

*"This. These scars." I dragged my fingers across her hip, following the marks as they curled up and around her naval. "How did this happen?"*

*For a moment, I thought Asherah would cast me from her sight, and rightly so. She was the queen and I was no one to her, certainly not one she needed to divulge her secrets to. Hells, I kept plenty of my own. But then the anger bled from her features, and she sighed.*

*"When I was a slave, I was used by demons," she said softly. "The scars are from their claws, and their teeth."*

*"Then the legends are true?" I moved from my position above her and lay on my side, propped up on my elbow while my fingers traced the marks across her belly. I knew that I shouldn't keep touching her, but I couldn't break contact with her soft, yielding flesh. "You killed your captors, and then led the resistance?" While I knew the tales as well as any Parthian, the queen looked as if she had been born into nobility and spent her life cosseted by* saffira. *That this delicate woman had managed to escape a prison and kill scores of demons was unreal to me.*

*She laughed shortly. "They call that a legend? It was only Torim and I, struggling to stay alive. Hardly the stuff of legend."*

*"How did you endure such torment?" I asked. I'd found the edge of yet another scar, and dragged my fingers up the length of her breastbone, feeling the raised line through her thin shift.*

*"I wouldn't have survived without my Lormac, or Torim... They were my strength." My hand remained upon the scar, and I pushed down the edge of her shift to feel it directly. I followed it until it met a scar that ran close to her throat, but Asherah had had enough of my groping. She swatted away my hand as if it'd burnt her. "If I disgust you, you're free to leave," she hissed.*

*"Forgive me," I said, "I mean no disrespect." I lay flat on my back and rubbed my eyes; the image of little Enna still hadn't left me. "You don't disgust me; far from it. I think you're strong, and courageous, and I wish I could be half the person you are."*

*"Aeolmar, you are—"*

*"Demons killed them," I interrupted. If I hadn't blurted it out, I never would have told her. I'd grown comfortable—too comfortable—in my isolation, and I needed to tell Asherah something of my pain, if for no other reason than because she would understand. "Demons... Demons led by Mersgoth killed everyone I have ever loved."*

*"Then we do have something in common," she murmured. I felt her lean against me, then brush back my hair. "I would say*

*that I'm sorry, but we both know such words are inadequate," she said as she stroked my forehead. "We thought Mersgoth was killed during the Battle for Teg'urnan, but he surfaced again a century afterward. Now, more than ever, I wish we'd finished him."*

*I dropped my hand from my eyes and leaned on my side, my face a finger's breadth from Asherah's. "During that battle you lost many that were dear to you, didn't you?"*

*"Yes," she replied, her voice hardly a whisper. "Many were dead by Mersgoth's hand, and at the hands of others. A great many."*

*"How did you manage to go on, to do so much without them? After so much was done to you?" Her body was so enticing I put my hand on her yet again, this time stroking a scar that ran the length of her collarbone.*

*"It wasn't easy," she admitted. "In the beginning, all I felt was pain. Those that hadn't been killed left Teg'urnan, and Harek was all I had left. He helped me through those days, more than he will ever know."*

*"The Prelate was a comfort to you?" I couldn't imagine Harek comforting anyone, with the possible exception of himself.*

*"He was, once." She arched her back toward me, and I moved to caress her neck. "Where you're touching me, there are no scars," she said.*

*"Forgive me. I'm saying that a lot, aren't I?"*

*"You are," Asherah replied, a smile tugging at the corner of her mouth. "You seem to have many scars, yourself, perhaps as many as I do." I felt her fingertips upon me as she traced a mark across my ribs. "But I think you wear most of your scars upon your soul." She was beautiful in the low light, the lamplight reflecting silver on her pale hair. Her only garment was thin, so thin I could see the outline of her body beneath it, save where the fur was pulled up to her waist. Again, I wondered how I'd managed to find myself in the Queen of Parthalan's*

*bed. Then I noticed more cruel marks upon her outstretched wrist, the scars fanned out like fingers.*

*"May I?" I asked, my hand hovering above her skin.*

*"You may," she replied with a glint in her black eyes. I traced each of them in turn, enjoying the slick, almost wet feel of them, then I pressed her slender wrist to my lips and kissed them, one after the other. I don't know why I did it—no, that's a lie. I couldn't not kiss her. Asherah let me nudge her onto her back, and I followed the line of her arm up to her shoulder. There was yet another scar along her hairline, and I kissed that one too, then I nuzzled her alabaster neck. Her back arched, pressing her body against mine, and I pressed my face into her hair. She smelled fresh, and soft, and desirable. Just how a woman should smell.*

*"Do you have many others?" I asked.*

*"Yes," she breathed.*

*"May I see them?" She nodded, and I tugged aside the neck of her shift and caressed the mark that lay along her collarbone. My fingers followed the scar until I reached the edge of her garment, then to where it was laced together over her heart, but as I made contact with the thin skin another memory raged to the surface of my mind.*

*"Are you marked?" I asked hoarsely.*

*"No," she replied to my relief. If I'd found a* mordeth's *hand-print upon her form, I don't know how I would have react-ed, other than badly. "I remember many that were. When a* mordeth *claimed you, they left the marking here, as a warning to others." She placed her hand on the inside of my thigh, squeezing me close to my groin. Gods. "And if you bore a whelp—not just a demon whelp but a* mordeth's *heir—you were marked here." Her fingers crept from my thigh to my belly, her mouth quirking when she found me already half-unlaced. "Were you planning something?" she asked as she traced a handprint onto my belly, a hint of mischief in her tone.*

*"I wasn't earlier,"* I truthfully replied. *I dragged my hand from her breastbone to her neck, then buried my fingers in her pale hair.*

*"And now?" she pressed as she unfastened me the rest of the way. Then she put her hand on my cock, and I couldn't take it any longer. I kissed her, long and hard, so hard that when we parted we both struggled for breath. I claimed her lips again almost immediately, scrambling to touch her and taste her and know her. My hands returned to the laces of her shift, but she stayed me.*

*"What's wrong?" She had me all but naked, and I meant to return the favor.*

*"There are more."*

*"More what?" I asked stupidly.*

*She meant that there were more scars waiting to be revealed under her shift, and obviously some heartless bastard, likely Argent, had made Asherah feel inferior only because she bore a few marks of battle. Well, I would change that. See? I was already improving my resolve. I kissed her lips again, then worked my way to her jaw, down her lovely throat and finally to her breast. When I reached the edge of her shift I pulled at the laces, but she again stayed my hand.*

*"Leave it on," she implored, but I ignored her as I pulled the wispy ribbons from their eyeholes; only a queen would pack such a fine sleeping garment while on a mission to track demons. "Aeolmar," she began, but too late. Her bodice was undone, her lovely breasts bared. They were covered by a multitude of scars, so many it seemed that she'd walked naked into a spider's web and somehow the pale, silvery strands were imbued onto her skin.*

*"Rihka," I murmured as I caressed her breasts with my mouth, "please don't hide your beauty from me." At last her shift was gone, and I followed the path of her scars from her breasts to her belly, and then to her thighs. The scarring was much more pronounced surrounding her womb, and I worried*

*that those who abused her had destroyed her capacity for pleasure.*

*"Can you still feel?" I asked as I stroked the ruined skin of her thighs, thick and puckered with scars.*

*"Yes," Asherah replied, shuddering at the feel of my breath on her bare skin. I resumed learning the path of every scar, laving every wound, relishing the soft sounds she uttered as she writhed under my touch. Then I gripped her buttocks and buried myself in her, pleased to find that her scars did not reach this most delicate area. I took my time with her, enjoying every sigh and moan that escaped her lips, but when I had her at the very edge I stopped. Asherah stared at me in mingled passion and disappointment, but I wasn't done with her yet. Far from it.*

*"Patience," I said against her moist skin. I meant to pleasure her completely, and once I set my mind to a task, my conviction never wavered. I retraced my earlier journey, tormenting Asherah with my lips and teeth and tongue, until I returned to her breasts and caressed one with my hand, the other with my mouth. Asherah arched her back and cried out in mingled pleasure and frustration, demanding release. I laughed softly; she muttered a rather unkind response but was silenced when I kissed her deeply.*

*"Now?" I asked when we parted.*

*"Now," she insisted, and at last I gave in to her desires. Asherah cried out as I entered her, but I was careful to hold myself back; it was plain that not only had her body been hurt by her captors but her spirit by those who came later. I did not want to be yet another inconsiderate lover. I nibbled her neck, the line of her jaw, treating her as carefully as I would a virgin until my own need became too great and I sheathed myself to the hilt within her. She cried out again as I thrust into her, whether the unintelligible sound was supposed to be my name or some other epithet I never knew. My own release came a moment later.*

*I nestled her against me and buried my face against her neck, breathing in the sweet scent of her sweat. For the briefest of moments, nothing existed save Asherah and the happiness she brought me, and I was able to forget.*

# Chapter Nine

## Asherah Speaks

*I was awake for a time before I realized such, convinced that I was ensconced in one of my frequent dreams of Lormac. I still dreamed of him often, and he was as alive and vibrant in my dreams as he had ever been; the many years since his death hadn't reduced my love for him in the slightest, nor my grief. Looking back, I suppose I was being foolish, holding on to his memory as tightly as I did. Perhaps I even sabotaged my own happiness, choosing the memory of my mate over a flesh and blood man time and again. I wonder what Lormac would have thought of my behavior.*

*But the arms around me were solid and warm, and I realized that Aeolmar had remained with me, and—gods!—but if he wasn't holding me in the exact same manner Lormac had: my back to his chest, his face buried in my hair. I used to tease Lormac, saying his love for me would eventually suffocate him, but apparently it was just something men did. I took Aeolmar's hand from where it rested against my belly and stroked his long fingers, enjoying his impossibly soft skin. His palms should have been riddled with calluses, testament to his skill with a sword, but they were softer than my own. Much softer than mine had been in some time; I remember learning how to wield a sword after our escape from the* doja, *and how mine and Torim's hands had blistered and bled until our skin grew thick and tough.*

*Torim... The memory of her embrace was alive in me as well. She had been softness where Lormac was hard lines, yielding where he was strong... As I remembered my dearest companion, it occurred to me that Aeolmar's velvety skin was more like Torim's than Lormac's. I nearly laughed aloud at the comparison of my First Hunter, self-proclaimed slaughterer of demons, to my most feminine of friends.*

*I rolled over and faced him—none too carefully, but he didn't wake at my movement—and regarded his sleeping face. He wasn't just handsome, he was lovely, his features far too fine to belong on the face of a warrior. My fingers traced his jaw, the arc of his cheekbone, then tangled in his sleek hair which should have been mussed after last night but lay as straight and shiny as if he had brushed it for hours. I decided I wanted to be the one brushing his hair for hours. As I contemplated this, Aeolmar opened his eyes.*

*"I hadn't expected you to remain," I said, because it was true.*

*"I find it difficult to leave you," he replied. "Do you wish I had gone?"*

*"No," I replied. His words both surprised and gladdened me; Aeolmar had hardly ever glanced in my direction, much less behaved as if he had the slightest interest in me. "I didn't think you'd want to stay."*

*"I don't often find myself in bed with a beautiful woman," he said as he smoothed back my hair.*

*"I find that hard to believe." Especially since just the evening prior women were throwing themselves at him.*

*He laughed shortly. "My life of tracking and killing leaves me precious few moments for pleasure," he said. He kissed my forehead and tucked my head under his chin. I rested in his arms for a time, feeling more content than I had in longer than*

*I cared to dwell on. Then my old fears came creeping back. "You won't have to behave differently around me," I said. "I won't hold you to anything."*

*Aeolmar turned my chin up, his brow furrowed as he spoke. "Is that what you want?" he asked. As he held me with his gaze, I wondered if anyone could look into those deep blue eyes and tell a lie.*

*"I don't want you to have to pretend it meant something," I said quietly. "I understand if it didn't."*

*"Argent didn't take very good care of you, did he?" he asked. Well, nothing like getting right to the heart of the matter. I laughed inwardly as I remembered my encounters with Argent, which in the beginning were so infrequent we could hardly be called lovers. In time, the frequency increased, but never the passion.*

*"I fear our relationship was more one-sided than I was willing to admit," I said at length.*

*"Then Argent was a fool."*

*I rose up on my elbow and looked down at my bedmate. "You call him a fool often."*

*"Because the term fits," he said, then he leaned up and kissed me. Until the moment Aeolmar claimed my lips, I hadn't given myself the luxury of hoping he would kiss me again, but he did. I may have been a fool myself, but I thought he was kissing me as me, not as the Queen of Parthalan but only Asherah. I'd never felt this way with Argent; in fact, I strongly suspected that every man I had been with since my dear Lormac was only there to make love to the queen.*

*Not Aeolmar. He made love to me.*

*And from the way he was kissing me, I got the impression that he wished to repeat last night's performance. I climbed on top of him and found him more than eager to prove himself a better lover than Argent (which he had already done). I couldn't help the moan that escaped my lips, nor did I want to. Argent had never made me feel so free, so alive, and as I let*

*Aeolmar carry me away I dared to wonder if I could love him like I did Lormac...*

*There was a crashing sound near the entrance of the tent, followed by a stifled gasp. I looked over my shoulder and saw Brynne standing there with her mouth agape, a platter and bowl at her feet. She must have taken it upon herself to bring me my morning meal. How nice of her. Aeolmar, ever mindful of his queen's modesty, moved to cover my breasts with the fur but in doing so it slipped away from our hips, lest Brynne had any doubts about what we were doing.*

*"Brynne," I began as Aeolmar again tried to wrap the fur around me, but I may as well have said nothing. She didn't hear me, hardly even saw me as she stared at Aeolmar, the hurt on her face indescribable. "Brynne!" I repeated, and she tore her gaze from Aeolmar and met my eyes, then she turned and fled. I fell back to the cot and exhaled in frustration.*

*"I wish she hadn't seen us," Aeolmar said as he drew me against his chest. "I...I didn't want to hurt her." I took in Aeolmar's guilty face and understood that he truly meant his words. While he would admit to disliking Brynne to the point of hatred, he would still put himself between her and harm.*

*"You're a noble man," I said.*

*"I am nothing of the sort," he said bitterly. "You would do well to avoid men like me."*

*I found his hand beneath the fur, and as I laced my fingers with his, I considered my time with Argent, and the men that came before him, and decided that Aeolmar was wrong. He was exactly what I needed*

# Chapter Ten

Aeolmar stared straight ahead as he rode, ignoring everyone around him. It had been five nights since Brynne's maddening pursuit had broken his hand and driven him out of his own tent, five nights since Innetha healed that hand and tried to claim him as a bedmate, and four mornings since Brynne walked in on him with Asherah. He would see the lot of them on the plains of hell if they thought he was going to offer explanations or apologies for his actions. While hadn't wanted Brynne to catch him in bed with the queen, he was not ashamed. Not to mention, he had been refusing Brynne's advances for more than twelve winters. If she hadn't gotten the hint by now, well, that wasn't his fault.

The only bright spot in this mess was that Brynne had given up her pathetic attempts at seduction, but now Aeolmar was forced to deal with her pensive stares and silent acquiescence to his every order. That silence was far louder than her shrill voice had ever been. He had initially thought the changes in her behavior were nothing more than a figment of his over-worked paranoia, but Elkin confirmed Aeolmar's suspicions later that evening.

"Poor Brynne, her heart has been shattered to bits," Elkin told him. Their party had come upon a village and was spending the night at the inn. While Aeolmar always preferred sleeping under the stars to a roof, he felt the need to sample the tavern's cold ale and offered no objection to a night's lodging. "I never would have thought her capable of such emotion, but she was in tears over you."

"How do you know?" Aeolmar asked. "Did Brynne sob on your shoulder?"

"Innetha told me," Elkin said, seeming surprised that Aeolmar hadn't guessed the source of his information. "We were having a moment, and she told me afterward."

"A moment?" Aeolmar asked with a raised brow. He swept his gaze across the other hunters in their party, and found many of them staring at Innetha as if she were a fruit ripe for picking. *How many moments is the healer-witch having?*

"She's quite free with her love," Elkin replied with a satisfied grin. "Most nymphs are." Elkin leaned forward and added, "She told me about your encounter. I recommend that you drink from the stream, my friend, for the water is sweet."

"Gods, man, we're supposed to be tracking a *mordeth*, not making notches on our belts," Aeolmar grumbled as he took a long draught from his tankard. When he lowered it he was met by Elkin's all too knowing gaze.

"Strong words coming from the man bedding the queen," Elkin observed.

"That was only once," Aeolmar clarified. *Twice*, he silently amended, with a satisfied smile of his own. Elkin, in that maddening way of his, immediately challenged him.

"Judging by your face, you will seek her again. And well you should; the queen could use a man like you." Elkin paused as he emptied his tankard and gestured to the innkeeper for a refill. "The entire court knows that Argent only used her."

"He did?" Aeolmar asked, and Elkin proceeded to relate every obscure bit of gossip concerning Asherah and the former First Hunter that he'd ever heard. *His tongue wags like a gossip monger's,* Aeolmar thought disgustedly, but he paid close attention nonetheless. Those tales of Argent so thoughtlessly using Asherah's affections for his own ends incensed

Aeolmar. With a heavy heart he remembered Mena, a sweet, delicate *nuvi* who'd had the misfortune of catching Argent's eye. Argent had pursued her relentlessly, so much so that she'd feared sleeping in the open dormitory of the *sola* and had ended up going to Aeolmar for help.

Aeolmar hadn't been able to act against his commander, nor had he wanted to accuse Argent of accosting a *nuvi* without more evidence than Mena's word. He'd done the next best thing and had begun taking the girl to his chamber. Aeolmar never touched her, but once word had gotten around that Mena slept with him instead of the in the *sola*, Argent had let her be.

It was Mena's death at Esguth's hands that had so infuriated Aeolmar. His rage fueled his sword arm as he struck down the *mordeth*, and then took the beast's own sword as spoil.

"So what do you think?"

Aeolmar blinked; Elkin had finished his tales of courtly lust and jerked his head toward the stairway. Aeolmar followed his gaze and saw Asherah, poised to ascend to her room for the evening. She paused at the first step and glanced over her shoulder, giving Aeolmar a look that left little doubt as to whether or not she wanted him to follow.

"Ha!" Elkin exclaimed, clapping Aeolmar on the back. The queen's intentions had been clear to Elkin, as well. "You're nothing if not a shorter version of Fiornacht!"

Aeolmar tried not to flinch when Elkin said his dead brother's name. "Elkin, I don't speak of my past. I came to Teg'urnan to create a fresh start. I would appreciate it if you didn't speak of it, either."

While he did not go so far as to issue a command, Aeolmar did manage to summon the authority of the First Hunter with his words. Elkin mumbled his understanding, and Aeolmar rose from the table. "Now, I will seek my bed. Alone."

Once he was inside his tiny, airless room Aeolmar leaned back on the door, exhausted in both body and spirit from his brief conversation with Elkin. It pained him to hear Elkin mention his family, it pained him that they were gone, and most of all, it pained him that Mersgoth still breathed.

Aeolmar's hand moved to the inner pocket of his jerkin, feeling the small lump within; he had worn his mother's pendant next to his heart every day since her death. He withdrew it and watched the blue gem catch the light, and briefly contemplated giving it to Asherah. But he remembered his mother's words: *Place it around the neck of your one true mate*. Could he say that he loved Asherah? He considered the queen's lovely face, her supple body, her sharp wit and sweet laugh. He could certainly envision spending a great deal of time with her, and he felt that he may grow to love her. Yes, he could love the queen.

Then he recalled Elkin's tales of Argent, how the heartless bastard had used the queen's sweet nature against her while he furthered his own agenda, making Asherah believe that he cared for her when in reality he pursued anything with breasts. Aeolmar knew Argent's false claims of affection had hurt Asherah, much more deeply than she was willing to admit.

Of course, there was also Lormac's memory to contend with. All of Parthalan knew the tale of the elf king who had fallen in love with a faerie woman, only to die before he could see her claim the throne, and of the queen's great sorrow. He wondered if Asherah had ever truly recovered from the loss of her mate, and if such a recovery were possible. Aeolmar sighed as he replaced the pendant. He did not love Asherah, and the last thing he wanted was to be just another man trampling upon her heart. That he cared for her was not in question, but he couldn't lie just to fulfill his mother's wish. His mother would want to see him happy, and would want him to wait for his true mate rather than leap toward the first hint of affection.

As he reclined on the hard, musty-smelling cot, he stared at the stars through the tiny window. His mother once told him that the spirits of the dead resided alongside Cydia in the night sky, and he wondered if his family was there now, looking down upon him. He hoped they were, and he hoped they were happy with his decisions. His mission was to avenge his family, nothing more, and matters of mates and love would just need to wait until after Mersgoth's death.

"I will avenge you," Aeolmar said to the sky. "I will find that *mordeth,* and nothing short of my death will keep me from killing him."

***

First dawn arrived far too quickly for Aeolmar's liking. Unwilling to face the accusing stares just yet, he ordered Elkin to oversee preparations for their departure, then he retreated to the farthest corner of the stable to brush his horse. Only when he was certain that there was nothing left for him to do did he emerge with what had to be the best groomed horse in Parthalan.

Once they set out, Aeolmar rode at the rear; if anyone had bothered asking he would have said that he was scanning for any tracks that Innetha may have overlooked, but no one dared to approach him. His foul mood, clinging to him like a rank fog, kept the other hunters well and truly at bay.

While his dark mood kept the others from questioning him directly, it did nothing to alleviate their backward glances. At length, the glances were accompanied by murmurs and outright speculation until Aeolmar couldn't bear the lot of them craning their necks to get a look at his misery, so he relocated himself to the very point of the procession. As he passed Asherah, he briefly met her eyes. It pained him to avoid her along with the rest, but he would explain his actions once they returned to Teg'urnan. The idle gossip that now flowed as freely as cheap wine threatened to drown him, and he refused to take the queen along in his descent.

"They separated here," Innetha announced, rousing Aeolmar from his dour thoughts. "They've also doubled back a few times, trying to muddle the trail. They must know that we're following them."

Aeolmar inhaled deeply of the dry air as he took in their surroundings. Their pursuit of Mersgoth had led them to the edge of the High Desert. As the packed dirt gave way to the much softer sand, the demons were unable to fully obscure their tracks. It wasn't a bad plan, one that Aeolmar himself had employed on occasion. It was also a tactic Aeolmar knew how to conquer.

*Yes, splitting your force and doubling back is a sound strategy, but that doesn't mean I won't catch you.* Aeolmar dismounted and examined the ground, mainly because it irritated Innetha when he checked the tracks himself. The tracks did indeed break apart and follow separate paths, with the bulk of them headed toward high ground.

"Which path did the *mordeth* take?" he asked.

"Over the rocks," she replied, indicating the direction. "He likely thinks I cannot track him without footprints, but that's his mistake," she added. Aeolmar nodded, and then pointed to two of Elkin's hunters.

"Follow the trail over the rocks," he commanded. They set out at once, and Aeolmar turned to Brynne. "Take your four best, and follow the lower trail," he ordered.

"Why are you sending five after the lessers, and only two after the *mordeth*?" Brynne snapped.

Aeolmar ignored her tone. For once, he was willing to overlook her behavior, though he had much preferred her silence. "If Mersgoth is aware that we're tracking him, the upper trail is probably a decoy." Brynne crossed her arms and stared at Aeolmar, and the small bit of patience he had afforded her was gone.

"Do you question my methods? If you have a grievance with me or my command, air it now, Brynne," he said.

Aeolmar glared at Brynne as he dared her to accept his challenge. Stubborn and peevish she was, but she hadn't survived as the leader of the Eastern Contingent for well over a century because she was foolish. Brynne broke his gaze and silently indicated which hunters would accompany her.

"Follow the trails for no longer than half a day, then return here and report upon what you've found," Aeolmar said to the four attentive hunters, and Brynne. "Do not engage any demons, be they lessers or the *mordeth*, unless you have no alternative."

Having uttered more words than he had in days, Aeolmar led his horse toward the sound of water and found an oasis. It was an island of calm in more ways than one, and Aeolmar tried resting his thoughts. His horse slurped from the pool while Aeolmar replenished his waterskin, but the nearby snapping of a twig alerted him. The sound was deliberate, for the one who made it knew better than to so carelessly announce her presence.

*Solitude. The most elusive of pleasures.* Aeolmar blew out a lungful of air, and met Innetha's gaze.

"Sending away the one you discarded," Innetha purred. "Does this mean you'll no longer ignore the queen?" Aeolmar ignored her as he drank from the skin, then bent to fill it once more. Undeterred, she persisted with her taunts. "Asherah worries that she displeased you. Perhaps I should—"

Aeolmar spun around and grabbed Innetha's throat. "Perhaps you should be silent for fear of losing your tongue," he growled. He released her and Innetha stumbled to the ground, wheezing and clutching her neck. Aeolmar left her by the water's edge and stalked back toward the others but stopped short of rejoining them. Innetha's words rang in his ears, and he hoped that she was only trying to bait him. He had been avoiding Asherah, that much was true, but he was doing it in attempt to spare Brynne further torment and to preserve the queen's dignity. The notion that Asherah had displeased him in any manner was ludicrous.

But did Asherah realize that it was ludicrous? He considered Elkin's tales of Argent, and of how the entire land seemed well aware of his indiscretions. Then he remembered waking with Asherah in his arms, warm and soft, and what she'd said: *I don't want you to have to pretend it meant something. I understand if it didn't.*

Of course it meant something! How could it not mean anything when a woman gave her body and soul to a man, when she helped him forget his painful, agonizing past if only for a few moments... How would she feel if that man hadn't spoken to her unless it was absolutely necessary since he woke beside her?

Aeolmar felt like striking himself. He had handled this badly, even for him, but he meant to set things right.

Thus emboldened, he strode in to the clearing and saw a few of Brynne's hunters sparring to pass the time. They dropped their weapons at the sight of the First Hunter, but he mumbled that he had no problem with such diversions as he approached the queen. Asherah stood on the far edge of the clearing conversing with Elkin. Elkin took one look at Aeolmar's determined jaw, and found somewhere else to be.

"Is something wrong?" Asherah asked, clearly taken aback by his approach.

"You do not displease me," Aeolmar said in a rush. "You have brought me nothing but pleasure."

"Really?" Asherah asked with a bewildered smile. "May I ask what has inspired such a declaration?"

"Innetha said," Aeolmar began, then out of the corner of his eye, he saw the she-weasel slink behind Elkin and smile. Angry red marks encircled her throat, and he wished he had squeezed harder.

"Innetha said what, exactly?" Asherah prompted.

"Innetha is lucky to be breathing," Aeolmar said flatly, glaring at her for another moment before returning his attention to the queen. "Are you upset that I haven't come to you?" he continued in a softer tone.

"I thought you were being discreet," Asherah replied, her black eyes downcast. Aeolmar's frustration was rapidly becoming self-loathing. He'd wanted to spare Asherah the embarrassment of every member of their party knowing that he'd bedded her, and not only had their tryst become common knowledge, his lame attempts at discretion had only hurt her. He moved so his body obscured the queen from the others and caressed her cheek.

"Perhaps too discreet," he murmured.

"It has been cold without you," she teased. His fingers danced across her soft skin from her cheek to the nape of her neck, but he knew where she was softer yet. He was about to kiss her, discretion be damned, when a shout from those sparring captured his attention.

"I will not!" The voice belonged to Leuvlyn; he had won the bout and the loser was goading him to challenge the best swordsman among them, which happened to be Aeolmar. "Why would I challenge him if I know he can beat me?"

"You may get lucky," Asherah called over Aeolmar's shoulder. "Let's find out if our First Hunter is truly first among us!"

At the queen's insistence Aeolmar accepted the challenge, and after a few maneuvers he had taken Leuvlyn's sword. One by one the rest eagerly stepped forward, and one by one they lost their swords to the First Hunter. Elkin, likely since he'd also been taught by Aeolmar's father, put forth a valiant effort, but soon lost his weapon as well. By the time the elder sun had moved a hand's breadth across the sky, Aeolmar stood in the middle of the clearing, hardly panting while the pile of won swords reflected the midday light behind him.

"There is another," Innetha called out when Aeolmar, thinking he'd defeated the lot of them, leaned against a tree.

"You, my lady?" Aeolmar asked. He would enjoy having her at the end of his sword.

"Why, no. The queen," Innetha replied. "The First Hunter may have conquered his fellow warriors, but can he hold his own against Asherah the Ruthless?" Asherah arched a graceful brow at Innetha as she waved away the challenge, but the beaten hunters cheered for their queen. Hesitantly, she looked at Aeolmar.

"Will you lower yourself to spar against a woman?" she inquired.

"I promise I won't embarrass you," he jibed, "too much."

"I accept the challenge," Asherah said as she drew her sword with a flourish. "And I'll make you kneel for your insolence."

Their audience laughed and cheered, so much that any response from Aeolmar would have been lost to the din. As it was, he had no opportunity to speak, for Asherah used the distraction to lunge toward him. Her sword shone in the noonday glare, and her blows were so quick it appeared to be a flashing silver arc. She was better than the others were, but Aeolmar easily parried her strikes. Despite her skill, he was confident that he would add the queen's sword to the pile behind him. Indeed, he had never lost, not to anyone but his father.

He was also enjoying himself far too much to take a quick victory. Every thrust, every lunge showcased Asherah's lithe form, and Aeolmar couldn't help but imagine the coming evening with her. Perhaps he would take her back to that inn, and he would atone for these last few nights she slept alone, that and more. Then she had him in a close struggle, their sword hilts locked together. At the last moment he let het twist out from under him only because he enjoyed watching her smooth reflexes. Then her tongue darted out to wet her lower lip, and Aeolmar had had enough foreplay.

Aeolmar resolved to disarm her with his next lunge and then carry her off to the oasis for the remainder of the afternoon. It wasn't as private as a room at an inn, but he remembered a few trees along the far side, and he could be quiet if need be. Though he didn't know if Asherah could bite her tongue... Perhaps he would bite it for her.

His face split by a wicked grin, the First Hunter planted his feet to deliver the strike that no one, whether they be fae or elf, orc or demon, had ever managed to evade. His father had taught him the strike, one of the plays he reserved for his children and no others. Aeolmar grinned in anticipation as he brought down his sword, for in just a few moments Asherah would be sprawled before him. He lunged...

And she caught his sword with hers and deftly flipped it into the air.

Aeolmar stood dumbfounded as Asherah caught his sword with her free hand, holding it aloft while the hunters cheered for their ruler. Never, not once in three centuries, had that play failed him. "How did you block me?" he asked.

"You aren't the only one who had a good teacher," she replied. "Now kneel." Aeolmar dropped to his knees, and Asherah sauntered up to him and stroked his cheek with the flat of his sword. "Tell me, what will you do to earn back your sword?"

A hundred—no, a thousand—acts of penance crossed Aeolmar's mind, but he never had the chance to reply, drowned out as he was by the crazed shouting from the ridge. The queen turned and Aeolmar stood; in the next moment, Brynne and her hunters galloped into the clearing at a thunderous pace.

"The *mordeth* is in the village!" Brynne cried.

# Chapter Eleven

Finlay ran to the back room of his father's shop, caught his foot on the threshold, landed on a pile of gently worn rugs, and choked on the resulting cloud of dust. The storeroom was full of used carpeting, along with other items ranging from scraps of leather to chipped crockery, the sort of things that brought plenty of coin but just weren't attractive enough to have in the front room with the rest of the merchandise. Regardless of the fact that Cadogan was a tiny village on the edge of the High Desert, and therefore received precious few affluent customers, the quality goods were prominently displayed where such an affluent customer would first look. Now, as Finlay tore through the items they actually sold, he wished he'd been more practical.

*Weapon, weapon, weapon,* he chanted to himself as he dug through bolts of fabric, serving platters, and various other sundries. He had no idea what manner of demons had descended upon his village, nor did he particularly care, but he would see them all upon the plains of hell before he allowed them to damage to his shop. His family needed the shop; they were merchants, not farmers or smiths or cobblers, and if they lost their goods they would lose their livelihood.

With a triumphant cry, he grabbed what he thought was a sword, the cry fading to a groan when he realized that it was a windmill blade. *It will have to do*, he decided as he rushed back to the front of the shop. The demons were raging across his village, leaving nothing but heaps of rubble in their wake. Finlay stood outside the shop's entrance, planted his feet in his best approximation of a warrior's stance, and raised the battered metal. *Let them come.*

***

Asherah's heart was in her throat as she and her hunters raced toward the village, one of her worst fears having come to pass. She'd wanted to intercept Mersgoth before he could cause additional harm, and not only had they failed to capture him, they'd driven the *mordeth* straight to a group of innocents.

The queen leapt from her horse once the dwellings came into view, not bothering to tether it as she hurtled down the steep slope. She glanced about and saw the others do the same. Only a fool would bring a horse into a battle with demons, since horsemeat was among the vermin's favorite foods. Asherah hoped someone had the presence of mind to round them up; without their horses, they would have a long walk back to Teg'urnan.

Terrified screams ripped through the air, and Asherah scanned the area for their source. The scream sounded again, and Asherah saw a villager beating a lesser over the head with a washboard. The demon was small and likely close to death, but Asherah stabbed it anyway; the villager seemed unhurt, but ran for shelter before the queen could ask after her. *If she can run, she can live*, Asherah observed as she yanked her sword free of the body.

At last, Asherah reached the village's center, only to skid across a patch of mud and land flat on her back. She groaned as she rolled to her side, and saw that she was beside the common well. Someone had dropped a water jug, and broken shards of pottery poked her back and hips. Before she could right herself, yet another demon was upon her.

*Blessed Cydia, they just appear out of nowhere.* Asherah thrust her sword into its gut and rolled so the body wouldn't land on her, but she couldn't evade the cascade of caustic blood that poured over her back and neck. She cursed softly as she got to her feet; she hated blood burns with such passion she would have gladly taken a slice to the belly instead. The blood burns reminded her of her time as a slave, when the *mordeth* who was her captor had cut his own flesh and had bled onto hers as part of his twisted games.

His games had ended when Asherah had buried her blade into the base of his spine and burnt the *doja* to the ground.

A shout reached the queen's ears, and she saw a lone man with a head of dark curls beset by three lesser demons. *What is that he's holding?* she wondered as she ran towards him. The man was flailing about with a flat piece of metal, attempting to swat away demons with what looked like a sword that the blacksmith had forgotten to give a hilt. Or an edge.

***

The dust billowed around Finlay, making each breath gritty and thick like quicksand. He coughed and retched, bringing up dust and blood in a vain attempt to clear his lungs. His shoulders shook with each hacking breath, so violently he could hardly hold his makeshift sword before him. He learned all too quickly that while it was called a windmill *blade* it wasn't capable of slicing through an overripe plum, much less through demon flesh. Still, he'd managed to keep the first one at bay by whacking it with the flat part of the blade.

Then two more arrived, scuffling with the first and kicking up the fine sand that blanketed Cadogan. A cold lump lodged in Finlay's gut, matching the lump in his throat, as he realized that they were arguing over who would get his marrow bones. He understood that he was outnumbered, and more than a little outmatched, but they would need to kill him before he would allow them near his shop. He drew another gritty breath and thought that the dust would do him in before the demons had their chance.

Suddenly, a demon fell dead, and another turned toward the street. Finlay saw these events, but he needed to concentrate on the third demon; it was far larger than the other two, and had cracked, yellowed talons. Those talons were deadly sharp, as proven by the burning laceration across Finlay's back. The wound made his arm shake as he gripped his weapon, then another bout of coughing took hold and he nearly doubled over. The demon sneered, raising its arm for the killing blow. Finlay shut his eyes as he silently apologized to his family for the loss of the shop, and thanked whatever powers that were listening that his parents and sisters were away. At least they would live. He didn't open his eyes until he realized that he wasn't dead.

Instead, all three of the demons lay dead before him, the largest having been run through from back to gut. The gaping wound bled across the threshold and onto the fine white marble floor of his shop, but for the first time in his life the normally fastidious Finlay could care less about the imminent hours of scrubbing. He sucked in another lungful of dusty desert air, the sweetest breath he had ever taken.

"You live?"

Finlay turned toward the voice and saw a warrior standing over him; he rubbed the gritty sweat from his eyes and saw that the warrior was a woman, not just any woman but one of rare and singular beauty, with black eyes that glittered like the finest gems. Her brown hair was bound in an elaborate plait, and her lips were full and red, redder than the blood that was smeared across her graceful neck.

"You're bleeding," Finlay said.

She touched her neck, then studied the blood on her hand. "I'll survive," she said as she extended that same hand to Finlay and pulled him upright. He flinched as the movement stretched the wound on his back, then she turned him around and yanked up his tunic.

"You'll survive, as well," she declared after a careful prodding of his wound. "Clean it well, and keep it covered. If an infection sets in, you'll wish for death." She turned to leave, but halted when Finlay caught her arm.

"You cannot face so many," he said. His fingers completely enveloped the width of her forearm, so delicate were her limbs. He went on, declaring that he would see to her wounds and offering to protect her from this onslaught, when his eyes fell to the dead demons at their feet. Dead by her hand, not his.

"I'll be fine," she promised as she touched his cheek with her bloody hand; the blood didn't burn, so it was either hers or Finlay's own, and not a demon's. The warrior maiden smiled sweetly and ran from him, disappearing into the fray.

***

Aeolmar prowled the village streets, ignoring the lesser demons for they were not whom he sought. Most of the lessers fled from the very sight of him; long before he had become a hunter, Aeolmar had earned his reputation as a slaughterer of demons many times over, first in the westlands of his birth, then in the frozen north when his skills had been hired by Grelk, the king of the forge. After Aeolmar had rid the troll lands of orc and demons alike, Grelk had proclaimed Aeolmar the most fearsome warrior to walk Parthalan's soil since Solon had descended from the sky. As payment for his service, Grelk had promised Aeolmar a fine sword, the equal of that he had forged for the god himself. Someday, Aeolmar would make the time to return to Grelk's lands and claim his prize.

A bone-rattling yell shook the very ground he stood upon and Aeolmar broke into a run. In the center of the village he found Mersgoth, bellowing as he crushed a woman's torso in his massive hand. Black hair matted with blood and gods knew what else whipped about his colossal head and down his back and legs. The stench arising from him was putrid, and Aeolmar almost gagged as he reached for the dagger hidden away in his boot. Aeolmar flung the blade without breaking stride, sinking it deep in Mersgoth's forearm. The *mordeth* bellowed again, then flung the woman aside as he faced his attacker.

Aeolmar couldn't spare a glace toward the woman, but he prayed that she still lived. He drew Esguth's sword from the sheath across his back, planting his feet wide as he faced the demon. He had waited so long for this moment, and he wanted Mersgoth to know who was about to kill him, and with what. Mersgoth rumbled a low noise that might have been laughter when he recognized the weapon.

"You think to kill me as you killed him?" Mersgoth growled in his guttural voice, so low Aeolmar could hardly understand him over the din. Aeolmar thrust his sword at the beast but in his crazed state he struck wide. Mersgoth easily swatted the blade away. Aeolmar gritted his teeth as he readied for another blow; since his family's death Aeolmar, had wanted nothing save ending Mersgoth, and that event was finally within his grasp.

*At last, he falls.*

The First Hunter swung again, this time making contact with Mersgoth's shoulder. Cold iron sank in Mersgoth's flesh and the beast howled in rage and pain, but he managed to kick out with his great hoof of a foot. That hoof made contact with Aeolmar's torso; he absorbed the impact and rolled, then regained his feet in an instant. He jabbed at the hoof with his dagger, drawing blood and sending Mersgoth falling backward into the dirt. The beast sniffed the ground, and a low growl emanated from his throat.

"You smell like her," Mersgoth rumbled.

"Who?" demanded Aeolmar.

"The one who was to be mine," Mersgoth replied as a slash appeared across his face, baring his jagged, bloodstained teeth in the demon equivalent of a smile. "The one I killed."

Aeolmar screamed as he rushed the demon; a small part of his mind realized that Mersgoth wanted him to attack in haste and thus wildly, but he didn't care. All he wanted was Mersgoth dead. Aeolmar slammed the hilt of Esguth's sword onto Mersgoth's head, dazing the monster as he bellowed a curse in the demonic tongue. As Aeolmar raised the sword for the killing blow, the *mordeth* spoke again.

"What of your queen?" he growled.

Aeolmar's gaze flew to Asherah, hardly visible where she battled four lesser demons. The queen had proven that she was easily as good with a sword as Aeolmar, if not better, and he watched her kill a lesser. Confident in her safety, he pressed Esguth's sword to the *mordeth's* throat, smiling wickedly when the thick hide resisted the dull blade.

*Dull blades are painful and slow.* Aeolmar didn't care; he'd spend the next moon sawing off the beast's head if that was what it took. The hide split and black blood oozed forth... then Asherah screamed. Aeolmar whipped his head around, but he was unable to find the queen. Asherah must have fallen, and the lessers crowded between her and Aeolmar.

Fear wrapped its icy fingers around Aeolmar's heart, and he made a decision he'd never planned. He cracked Mersgoth's skull with the hilt of Esguth's sword, rendering the beast unconscious, and ran to his queen's side. He beheaded two of the demons while calling Asherah's name, then turned and watched her bury her sword in the third.

"What of the *mordeth?*" Asherah asked as Aeolmar helped her stand. Aeolmar turned toward where he had laid out the beast, but Mersgoth was nowhere in sight. Aeolmar spat a few words that would have made even Brynne blush.

"I had him, but he's gone," Aeolmar replied when he stopped cursing.

"Gone? How is he gone?" Asherah demanded.

"You needed aid, and I came to you," Aeolmar replied, but was met by the queen's mirthless laughter.

"Aid? I needed no aid," she snapped. "Eight centuries I have wanted that beast dead and you let him get away!"

"You needed me," Aeolmar bellowed. "Should I have let you die?"

"If it meant killing him, then yes," she shouted back. "My life is not worth letting a *mordeth* live!"

Aeolmar moved toward the queen, his fury such a palpable force that Asherah stepped back. His fierce gaze bored into the queen's eyes, then he flung Esguth's sword aside and walked away. He heard the demon blade shatter as it struck the ground, but he ignored it.

# Chapter Twelve

## Asherah Speaks

*Fool! Rushing to defend me as if I was nothing more than a simpering maiden, as if I hadn't killed scores—hundreds!—of demons long before he was a twinkle in his father's eye. Doesn't he understand that we may never again have the upper hand on Mersgoth, the right hand of the* mordeth-gall, *wise and crafty that he is?*

*I was still muttering away when I spoke with Innetha later that day. While she truly was a tracker without equal, her lovely face and honeyed tongue also made her the ideal ambassador. She had managed to quell the local lord's outrage over the demon attack. He'd first taken us for a band of mercenaries who had inadvertently flushed a knot of demons into his village, which we'd learned was called Cadogan after the ancient family that founded it, though they hadn't lived there for some time. Names, it seems, are the most tenacious of things.*

*Once Innetha had the lord as calm as he could reasonably be, she informed him that his so-called band of mercenaries was led by the queen and First Hunter, and that he had* referred to Aeolmar and myself as little more than common thugs. Well, that got the man worked up all over again.

"You enjoyed his misery," I accused. We had just declined the lord's offer of lodging, since it was far too hot to sleep indoors, but had accepted the proffered food and stepped out of the way of his saffira as they bustled about readying our meal. Since it wouldn't be ready for some time, one suggested we visit the bath house. A most excellent idea, that.

"He deserved it," Innetha replied as we entered Cadogan's bath house, which had been emptied for our privacy. "We defended his home and people from the mordeth, and all he could do was complain that we dirtied his square." Her hands moved to the laces of her vest, then paused. "Do you mind if I bathe with you?"

"Not at all," I replied as I shed my gear, heavier now with sweat and blood. I moved toward the inviting bathwater, but a naked Innetha blocked my path.

"Sit," Innetha commanded, indicating a bench alongside the pool. "Your hair will foul the water."

I did as I was told, and Innetha began unplaiting my hair, loosening hard chunks of mud in the process. I couldn't imagine how I'd gotten so dirty, then I remembered the fall I'd taken near the village well.  No wonder the lord thought we were mercenaries.

Innetha brushed my hair until most of the dirt and other detritus had crumbled away, and only then did she allow me to plunge myself into the pleasantly warm water. I assumed that those who lived in the hot desert would take cold baths, and I was happy to be wrong.

Innetha situated herself behind me and worked soap into my hair, taking her time as she drew my long tresses between her fingers. Suddenly, she reminded me of Torim.

"You don't need to be my attendant," I said.

"I'm not," she replied. "I think your hair is lovely, and I'm selfishly enjoying it. Now be silent and enjoy yourself as well."

*Again, I did as she commanded and let Innetha's nimble fingers massage their way across my scalp and neck. Normally I would have closed my eyes and given myself over to such luxury, but I couldn't get Mersgoth's escape, or Aeolmar's idiocy, out of my mind. I reached for a small brush and began cleaning under my nails.*

*"You're still angry with him, then?" Innetha asked. I asked why she assumed I was angry with anyone, but she nodded toward my hand. I had been scrubbing away so hard my skin was pink, and close to bleeding.*

*"Can you really find no trace of Mersgoth?" I asked her for the hundredth time.*

*"I cannot," she replied. "It confounds me as to why. I've never had trouble finding a trail in the past, much less a fresh one from such a big and lumbering creature. It's as if he stepped out of this realm entirely."*

*"He must have used a portal," I concluded. A portal, which his kind had been supplied with in times past, that would leave no track or trail to be found. "Gods, I wish Aeolmar had just killed him."*

*"He couldn't leave you in danger." Innetha's fingers moved to dance across my spine, and I wondered if this impromptu massage was meant to defuse my anger. "After all that has happened to him—"*

*"What do you mean?" I demanded, standing up and facing her so those blasted magic fingers weren't distracting me. Innetha merely adjusted her position and continued the massage while facing me.*

*"He shares his bed but not his heart?" she purred, reaching forward and kneading my shoulders. An icy glare from her queen made her to drop the coy act, and she related the vision she'd had while she healed Aeolmar's hand: it was a memory of his, and a horrible one at that. He'd been holding a dead child in his arms as he wept over a woman's body. Innetha's voice faltered; apparently, the memories she usually came across weren't so painful.*

*"The woman must have been his mate," Innetha said quietly, "and the child their daughter. Both of the females were marked."*

*My heart lurched in my breast, for I knew all too well the pain one felt upon losing a mate. But if they'd been marked... I had understood and encouraged Aeolmar's single-minded determination to eradicate Mersgoth at all costs. I believed, as he did, that nothing was more important that the beast's death, save perhaps the death of the* mordeth-gall. *Yet he had let his prey go. For me.*

*I left Innetha to finish her bath alone and searched Cadogan for Aeolmar. He wasn't enjoying the food with the others (not surprising), nor was he in the stables or anywhere in the lord's abode. Finally I found him at the oasis we passed by earlier, sitting next to the pool. His long hair hid his face, but I didn't need to see his eyes to understand how he felt. I understood more than I wanted to. He said nothing as I knelt beside him, and continued staring at the water.*

*"Innetha told me what she saw, when she healed you," I said at length. "I didn't know that your mate and child perished."*

*"Is that how Innetha interprets my memories?" He shook his head, then drew up a leg and rested his forehead on his knee. "I have never been so blessed as to have a woman choose me as her mate, and I have no children."*

*"Then, who was that woman?" I pressed.*

*"My mother," he said softly. "Innetha saw my memory of finding her near death by Mersgoth's hand, his mark scorched across her skin."*

*Gods. If anything could have been worse than finding your mate dead... I touched the back of his neck; his flesh was cold and clammy, despite the warm night. "You should not have come for me," I said. "You should have killed him. It's your right."*

*Aeolmar at last turned to me, his deep blue eyes so mournful I nearly wept. "Don't you see?" he asked, his voice hoarse. "I've lost everything. I can't lose you, too."*

*I wrapped my arms around Aeolmar, my anger having been replaced by a deeper emotion. Indeed, he held onto me as if I was all he had. "I'm right here," I said. "You won't lose me. You won't."*

# Chapter Thirteen

Finlay stared up at the suns while he leaned on the broomstick, then exhaled heavily and resumed sweeping out the shop. The day had gone from hot to sweltering long before midday, and it was easily hotter than it had been yesterday when the demons had attacked. His modest shop had been all but deserted for days prior, what with the denizens of Cadogan reticent to venture out in such heat for anything less than essential. That day, Finlay himself hadn't had done much more than down a few cool beverages in the shade out back. But then the alarm had been raised; it had been so long since a demon had been sighted in Cadogan, he was surprised anyone remembered they had an alarm.

He then had learned that windmill blades, while called blades, are not the most formidable weapon against a demon. Or anything else, for that matter. Finlay had stood if not fearlessly, at least bravely before the shop's entrance, planted his feet and resolved that if he were to die that day he would have at least died with valor. Then he'd closed his eyes and swung wildly at his foe...

But he hadn't died. He'd instead been rescued by his warrior maiden. She had laughed off his concern while chiding him for his lack of a proper weapon, and then she'd disappeared, plunging headlong into the raging battle.

The battle ended soon after Finlay's encounter with the warrior maiden, he and the shop only a bit worse for wear. When he began the onerous but necessary process of cleaning up, he found that the memory of her made his tasks somewhat lighter. He couldn't stop thinking about her lithe body as she stood over him, clad in dark leather that fit like a second skin, or her smooth movements as she ran back to the fight. Finlay had searched the village for her, but his warrior maiden was nowhere to be found. He hoped that she had made it through the battle unharmed, and he'd decided that he would seek her out at the queen's encampment. After the shop had been put to rights, of course.

The shop's door creaked open, rousing Finlay from this pleasant contemplation about his mystery woman. He quickly wiped the dust from his hands, splashed some cool water on his face and pulled a fresh tunic over his head before exiting the store room, pausing to grab a waiting tray. It held a pitcher of watered wine and two goblets; a customer was much less likely to make a purchase with a dry throat.

"Greetings," Finlay called out as he swept the curtain aside. He saw that his patron was a lone woman with long, pale hair. Her back was to him as she studied the wall of portraits, most of which featured the queen. "Not many are about in such heat," he continued as he filled the goblets. "I daresay you're the first who's come in today."

"You're certain it's the heat that's scared away your customers?" she asked. "Not the demons?"

Finlay nearly dropped the pitcher when he heard her voice, melodious yet strong and oh-so-familiar. He turned around and saw his warrior maiden wearing that same wicked grin as when she'd rescued him. She was no longer clad in the dark leathers and heavy boots from the battle, but was wearing a white linen tunic over riding breeches, her delicate feet wrapped in fine woven sandals. His trained merchant's eye noticed that while simple, her clothes were exceptionally well made, with exquisite embroidery edging the sleeves and neck of her tunic. Her footwear was likely worth as much as his entire shop's inventory. He also realized that she was far, far lovelier than he remembered.

"I thought your hair was brown," he blurted out.

"Was I that filthy?" She smirked, then waved away his apology. "I suppose I was. Tracking demons tends to make one rather unpresentable."

Finlay opened his mouth, then clamped it shut before he said she was the most beautiful woman he'd ever seen, filthy or clean. No, a woman of such breeding would have little patience for a babbling shopkeeper. Instead, he offered her a goblet of the cool wine.

"Did you come to browse our paintings?" He joined her before the portrait gallery.

"I came to find out if you'd found yourself a proper sword." She smiled over the rim of her goblet.

"We don't normally stock weaponry," Finlay replied, almost apologetically. "My father is against it."

"He is a pacifist?" she inquired.

"No, he doesn't believe that weapons turn a good profit." Finlay indicated the battered piece of metal propped up by the entrance. "The closest item we have to a sword is that old windmill blade."

"Your father doesn't think he can make sufficient coin with weapons, yet you stock windmill blades in the windless desert?" she asked, arching a delicate eyebrow.

"Just the one," he replied as he returned her smile.

"I should like to meet this shrewd merchant," she said. "Is he about?"

"Unfortunately not," Finlay replied. "He, and the rest of my family, left some days ago to trade at the western market."

"Then you're all alone here?"

"Me, alone." He realized that he was staring at her—how could anyone not stare at such a vision?—and again turned his attention to the paintings. "Do you enjoy portraits?" he asked. She looked at him quizzically, so he continued, "This one is of our queen, Asherah the Ruthless. It was done quite early in her reign."

"Indeed it was." She moved to examine a piece of glassware that caught her eye. Finlay eagerly followed, pointing out rare and expensive items he thought might suit her fancy, for she was certainly from an exotic location far, far from Cadogan. Her appearance told him as much; though the shade varied from rich to pale, the residents of his village all bore dark hair along with pale eyes, and the dusky skin typical of desert dwellers. Finlay himself boasted a head of curls that he cursed more often than not on hot days such as this one, an eye color that was paler than most but still the requisite blue. Years of arranging and rearranging the shop had sculpted his form rather well, something the unashamed girls in the village enjoyed pointing out.

Finlay surreptitiously examined his warrior maiden as he followed her about the shop, trying to glean the slightest clue about her origin. Her hair was as pale as a spider's web; no, it was more like starlight, and her eyes shone like polished onyx. In fact, she was complimenting the selection of carved onyx idols (the most expensive items they carried, kept in the rear to guard against accidental breakage) when the door creaked again. Finlay turned around, and found a hunter standing at attention.

"My lady?" the hunter inquired of Finlay's warrior maiden. "The First Hunter would like to know how long you will be."

"I'll be along directly," she replied as she crossed the room and said something too low for Finlay to hear. The hunter bowed and disappeared, then the warrior maiden returned to Finlay's side.

"Are you a commander in the legion?" he asked.

"Something like that," she replied, her eyes once again full of mischief. "We must depart soon, but before we go I want to commend you on your actions yesterday. You fought with much bravery."

"If only I had the skill to match," Finlay said as he cast his gaze downward. "If not for you I'd probably be dead." To his surprise, she touched his chin and turned his face up to hers.

"Skill can be learned, fortitude and valor cannot," she said softly. At that moment the hunter returned bearing a sword, complete with a sheath and belt. "To that end I bestow this sword upon you, Finlay of Cadogan."

"How do you know my name?" he asked as he accepted the offering.

"I asked who the sweet boy was, the one that defended the merchant's shop with an edgeless weapon as if his life depended on it," she replied as she leaned forward and drew the belt about his waist. She fastened it with the practiced dexterity of one who'd done the action many times. *Yes, surely she's a commander, perhaps a general.*

"Everyone answered that it must have been Finlay," she continued, "for who else would do something so foolhardy, or so valiant?"

Her dark eyes sparkled, and he found himself laughing with her. Finlay was about to ask her name, where she was from, if she liked the desert and would stay here with him until the end of time, when a tall man lacking manners burst into the shop. Finlay noted that the man was clad in black leather from head to foot, and wondered how he didn't collapse from heatstroke.

"Why did you request a sword?" the newcomer demanded of Finlay's warrior maiden.

"I wanted to give one to Finlay," she replied coolly. "He fought quite well yesterday, in spite of lacking a proper weapon." The man glanced at Finlay, sizing him up as if he was a bug to be waved away. "Finlay's family owns this shop. Yesterday he set himself in the doorway and fought off three demons."

The man snorted. "Three. Not bad."

"I don't know how much credit I can take," Finlay admitted, then he extended his hand. "Good to meet you, man."

"Finlay, this is Aeolmar, First Hunter of Parthalan," the warrior maiden said.

Finlay's eyes widened, but only briefly. "My lord," he acknowledged with a bow of his head.

Aeolmar nodded, then began detailing the state of the hunters and their readiness to return to Teg'urnan, adding a short rant about the village arbiter's demand for a tax abatement to pay for repairs to the well and square. *Leave it to Goltheim to let his life be saved, then expect payment for his troubles*, Finlay mused.

Apparently, the First Hunter had dissuaded Goltheim from pursuing the matter, but before he had finished yet another hunter entered the shop. Finlay realized that his maiden must be quite important, possibly one of the elite *con'dehr*, for all these warriors to be at her beck and call. This latest hunter proclaimed that all tasks had been completed, and that they would depart on her orders.

"Very well, Brynne" she said, "I'll be finished here in a moment. Please inform Innetha that I'd like her to ride alongside me."

"As you wish, my queen," the hunter said as she bowed and departed.

"Queen?" Finlay repeated, and his gaze darted to the portrait gallery. Gazing serenely from the wall was a woman wearing a silver and sapphire crown, with hair as pale as starlight, yet much more blonde than white, and black eyes set above high cheekbones...

And a much more beautiful version of that image stood in the flesh before him.

"Forgive me for not knowing you, my queen." Finlay dropped to his knees. "I am sorry; as I said, we do not have any recent portraits of you," he blathered, only stopping when the queen crouched before him.

"How can you be expected to recognize someone you have never met?" Asherah asked, her black eyes now soft. "But I must say, your portraits aren't all that flattering."

"I'll burn them all," Finlay proclaimed, and the queen laughed.

"That is not necessary," she said, "and I imagine your father would miss the coin they would bring." She rose to her feet, indicating that Finlay should as well, and continued, "I meant what I said, Finlay. You acted with much bravery, and you did impress me. I don't hand out swords to just anyone, only to those who I believe will wield them with honor." Finlay bowed his head, suddenly bashful and wishing that Aeolmar would just leave the two of them alone for a moment.

"You have well and truly honored me, my queen," he said. "Will I ever see you again?" he asked, daring to meet her eyes.

"I certainly hope so," she replied. "Perhaps, when next we meet, you'll be in possession of skill that matches your valor."

Finlay couldn't help the grin that bloomed on his face. He knew he must look foolish—the First Hunter's bored expression told him as much—but he didn't care so long as Asherah was smiling back at him. Asherah took Aeolmar's arm, and the queen and hunter left his father's shop.

"You can't possibly ride while wearing those sandals," Aeolmar said.

"But they're so pretty," Asherah countered. "Why can't I wear pretty things and ride?"

Aeolmar snorted. "You've been out in the sun too long. It's time I took you home to Teg'urnan."

Finlay heard Asherah's laugher as she and Aeolmar walked toward their camp. He leaned on the door to the shop, gazing toward Asherah long after she disappeared from view.

# Chapter Fourteen

Aeolmar galloped through the dark gates of Teg'urnan, ignoring the gatekeeper's salutations as he was wont to do. The whole of the palace was well aware of the First Hunter's temperament, and the gatekeeper was no doubt glad to be spared a few coarse words. No one else offered him any sort of greeting, not that it would have pierced the foul mood that surrounded Aeolmar like a moth-eaten cloak. He had been away from Teg'urnan for the past moon, chasing whispers and rumors of Mersgoth's location, and had naught but his tired bones to show for his efforts.

The royal stable was deserted of all but its hoofed residents, with nary a groom or *saffira* to be found. Aeolmar looked up toward the moon, her position high above the palace telling him that it was well past midnight. In his haste to return to Teg'urnan, Aeolmar had ridden longer and harder than he realized. Humbled by his horse's fortitude, he patted Myrnnhe's strong neck.

"Forgive me, old friend." Aeolmar swung down from the saddle and walked Myrnnhe to his stall. Every horse Aeolmar had ever owned was called Myrnnhe, which meant mule in *ahm'ri,* the old language of faerie. They all shared a name in homage to the patient beast on whose back Aeolmar had learned to ride. He laughed silently, remembering his initial terror of the great gray monster, and his brother's insistence that mules were truly the gentlest creature in all the realm. Well, that wasn't exactly true, but they'd spent many afternoons together, Aeolmar and Tor and the indignant mule. Eventually, a fine gelding replaced that first Myrnnhe as Aeolmar's preferred mount.

*That Myrnnhe would have refused to walk another step had I pushed him this hard.* Not wanting to bother waking a groom, Aeolmar stripped the tack by himself, brushed his horse down, and then hauled over a measure of feed. Myrnnhe plunged his nose into the feedbag, his enthusiasm bringing a smile to Aeolmar's face.

It was the first time he'd smiled since he had embarked on this foolhardy mission. During these six long winters since the Battle of Esguth, Aeolmar hadn't been able to uncover the slightest clue about where Mersgoth had holed up to lick his wounds, which was as maddening as it was unusual. Before Aeolmar became a hunter, he'd always been able to glean a few bits of information about the *mordeth*; hells, even when he had been stationed at the Eastern Border for ten winters, he'd heard news of the demon's whereabouts. Then he'd confronted him in Cadogan—and had let him escape in order to rescue Asherah. It was as if the beast had stepped out of this realm and into nothingness.

Asherah... She had been so angry with Aeolmar for leaving his fight with the *mordeth* in order to save her—and rightly so. Three lesser demons were hardly a challenge for the queen, and if he hadn't leapt to her defense, Mersgoth would now be dead, the desert sands having long since stripped the rotten flesh from his bones. But Aeolmar had no way of knowing if Asherah would have only faced three lessers, for what if a second *mordeth* had... Aeolmar shook his head, unwilling to confront the emotions that welled up inside him at the thought of losing yet another that he cared for.

He entered his chamber, dark and cold and a bit dusty from lack of use over the last moon, and called for the candles to light. Their gentle flames burned away some of the dampness, and he dropped his gear, piece by piece, on the way to his bed. He wanted nothing more than to burrow into the furs and ignore the rest of the world for another moon. He only paused to remove his mother's pendant from his jerkin and place it in the special niche he'd had hollowed out behind a tile—a secret place where his father's sword also rested, away from the prying eyes of others—and then the leather garment hit the floor along with the rest of his clothes. Aeolmar no longer kept the pendant on his person at all times; too often, Asherah's slender fingers had danced across his chest and questioned the small lump over his heart. One could really make only so many excuses, and eventually, he resolved that when he was home in Teg'urnan, the pendant would be safely hidden away in his bedchamber.

Something else Aeolmar was not willing to confront quite yet was his aversion to placing the pendant about Asherah's neck. They had remained lovers since that day in the desert, and Aeolmar admitted that he cared for her deeply. And yet...

And yet, he did not feel that he loved her. He remembered his mother's words, that if he had to ask if a woman was his one true mate, then she was not. While he could well imagine being with Asherah until the end of his days, and would never forsake her for another, he couldn't claim to be in love with her. His lack of love for the queen pained him, and he felt that it pained Asherah all the more, but he would not pretend to feel something that he did not. No, he wouldn't, not even for her.

So they kept up their relationship, as discreetly as one could in the bustling madness that was Teg'urnan. Asherah pretended not to care when Aeolmar announced that he would be away from the palace for a time; he knew that his absences hurt her, even though she wanted Mersgoth dead nearly as badly as he did. Just the same, he was well aware that when he went to The Swan, that tavern frequented by hunters and soldiers alike, she assumed that he wanted a new girl for the night. While he received many offers, he never collected, but he didn't tell Asherah. Somehow, Aeolmar thought it would be easier for Asherah to someday move on if she thought he'd been unfaithful.

Aeolmar exhaled heavily as he affixed the tile over the niche, the pendant and sword hidden away yet again, and wondered where his soul's true mate was. His periodic missions to track Mersgoth, which he always undertook alone save for Myrnnhe, had an ulterior motive: Aeolmar held on to the hope that he would somehow stumble across the woman who was meant to be his beloved. During this most recent mission, he'd spent a sennight in a small village by the sea, staring out at the waves. He imagined his mate frolicking in the sun, her sparkling eyes and how they would light up when she saw him, and of the happy and content life he would give her. As he pulled back the cold bedding, more than ready to plunge into oblivion, he was suddenly overcome with guilt. The woman his mind's eye watched was not Asherah.

*What if it is her, and I'm just too stubborn to notice?*

The candles extinguished with a word as Aeolmar opened the secret door behind his bed. He knew the path well and needed no light to guide the way. Gently, softly, he pushed open the far door and found Asherah's bedchamber lit by a pleasant glow emanating from the hearth. He crawled under the furs, threw an arm around her waist, and blew out the last bit of tension he had been carrying. No matter what he felt or didn't feel for his queen, home, to Aeolmar, was the warmth of Asherah's arms.

"You smell like a horse," Asherah mumbleded from somewhere beneath the furs.

"I missed you, too." Aeolmar drew her tightly against him, winding his fingers in her silky hair. "Let me bring you to the sea," he said, surprising himself nearly as much as he surprised Asherah. Aeolmar was nothing if not methodical to the point of boredom in his routine.

"The sea?" Asherah asked as she blinked sleep from her eyes. "Why the sea?"

"I'd like to watch you among the waves," he murmured. *And, I need to know if you're her.*

"The sea it is," she declared as she tucked her head against his neck. "Promise me you'll bathe first." Aeolmar arranged her in the crook of his arm and kissed the top of her head.

"I promise."

# Chapter Fifteen

*I cannot believe I'm doing this.*

The queen tugged the plain brown hood closer to her face and melted into the palace's morning bustle. Had they known who she was, any of Asherah's subjects would have gladly moved aside to allow her passage, but the queen didn't want anyone—not even Aeolmar—privy to her destination.

She passed underneath the palace gates, grateful the gatekeeper hadn't recognized her, though he claimed the clear and sharp sight of a hawk. Perhaps she'd have him reappointed. But his distraction, whatever it had been, was to her advantage, and she didn't spare a backward glance as she approached the village nestled at the base of the Hill of Rahlle.

It wasn't quite a village. It was more of an accumulation of shacks and huts for those occupations deemed a bit too unsavory for the palace proper, or who were wary their activities would get them tossed into Teg'urnan's dungeon all the sooner. There were a few taverns among the shacks, though wine and ale could be had aplenty in the great hall, and wagering houses to part you from the rest of your coin. Why, one had even taken odds on the Battle of Esguth, four to one in the demons' favor. Asherah would have whipped that scoundrel herself if he hadn't died in the fracas.

Asherah sighed, for he was far from the only scoundrel in this village of ne'er do wells and common pickpockets. Harek periodically directed his anger, or at least a measure of it, toward the village and emptied it of thieves and brutes. A few fines were levied and the dungeons were full for a few moons, yet within a season, the village bustled with activity again. The queen didn't really mind the village's existence; she understood that, from time to time, one needed a change of scenery. A tavern where one might find a night's distraction. A place to throw dice where no one knew you were spending your last coin. To speak to a seer about things a wiser woman would leave unsaid.

It was far from the first time she'd gone to the seer for guidance. In those first few winter's after Lormac's death, Asherah went to her often, and always with the same pleas: *Is Lormac's spirit well, and did he blame her for his death? Does he still love her, and will he visit her somehow?*

The answers were always the same; yes, his spirit was well. No, he did not blame his mate for his untimely demise. Yes, he still loved her; no, the spirits of the dead were forbidden from interacting with those of the living. Those brief sessions had always brought a measure of calm to Asherah, though she realized that the seer was likely a charlatan whose only talent was to tell a grieving woman what she wanted to hear.

Still, it comforted her to hear that Lormac's spirit rested well, wherever he may be, despite the strife amongst those he left behind. One of the first arguments Asherah and Leran had had, once he'd grown to manhood, had been over the resting place of Lormac's bones. Traditionally, the prior Lord of Tingu was interred at The Seat by his successor, but Lormac had lain atop his pyre less than a day after his death. Asherah had stood watch while he burned, and once the ashes had cooled she'd retrieved his bones herself, swaddling the remains of her mate in earth-colored silk to mimic his favorite cloak he always wore; indeed, he had worn it right to his death, and it had burned with him. If she'd had her wits about her Asherah would have saved the cloak in order to shroud his bones, but the silk managed the job quite well. Then she'd entombed Lormac's bones in a location she kept secret from all others, including Leran.

He'd railed at her for refusing to hand over the remains of his father, but Asherah was adamant. Lormac had been her mate, her love, and she couldn't bear the thought of what was left of him being so far away from her. Of course, she hadn't quite worked out how she would manage to have her bones someday lie next to his, short of publicly divulging the location. She had a habit of outliving those she trusted.

Abruptly, Asherah stopped before the seer's cottage; she always forgot, or chose not to remember, how close it was to Teg'urnan. Indeed, it practically abutted The Swan, the tavern where Argent had spent the bulk of his time. After much cajoling she'd convinced Aeolmar to bring her there for an evening, since she just had to see for herself what went on in such a place; he'd only agreed after she donned a dark cloak with a hood that concealed her pale hair, the very same cloak she wore to the seer's hut. She'd found it rather nice, with a kindly innkeeper and hearty, plain food the like of which a queen was never served. Nearly all of Asherah's remembered life had been as royalty, and the sharp ales and homespun clothes she encountered in the tavern reminded her of that brief time when she wasn't Queen of Parthalan or Lady of Tingu, and Torim was still alive—a time when Harek convinced the two of them to go north and seek aid from the elves. Yes, she rather liked The Swan, and so what if the servers' blouses were cut a little low? All the better for earning tips, she thought.

*I'm stalling.* She always did before she shoved aside the door, heavy wood with a poorly-tanned hide nailed to the exterior, either to keep the weather out or whatever the seer conjured in. Asherah understood that it was unlikely that a seer operating out of a half-rotted shed could offer her better insight that the court sorcerers; for that matter, Asherah should really seek this sort of counsel with Atreynha, the High Priestess. But then the priestess and sorcerers would know the sort of information the queen sought, and some things she'd rather keep to herself.

Asherah pushed the hide aside and entered the cottage. The seer, an ancient hag of indeterminate race, was shrouded, as always, in a filthy gray cloak that Asherah suspected had never been laundered. She sat behind a table hewn from one of the massive trees common in the west, where the forests were rumored to be older than Olluhm. It was said that the trees were set in place by a forgotten god of agriculture when the realm was new, long before Olluhm cast the old gods from the sky and took his place as the elder sun. The last time Asherah visited the seer she had asked many questions about the tree's origin, but not today. Today, she needed answers, not a history lesson on the gods.

Today, she needed to know the future.

The queen took her place opposite the seer and waited for her to speak.

"You've the same question," the seer stated in a voice rusty with disuse. Asherah often wondered if she was the seer's lone patron.

Asherah opened her mouth to dispute, then sighed. "Yes."

The seer nodded, and started tossing bits of herbs in a carved bone bowl with a bloodstained interior, some of that blood being the queen's own. The woman was maddeningly slow, whether due to age or the spells she cast Asherah never knew. Once the requisite amounts of herbs were mounded into the bowl, the seer reached for a flint. A single spark fell into the bowl, and acrid smoke that had always reminded Asherah of a funeral pyre wafted around the room.

"You believe you found him," the hag croaked. "Why now?"

Asherah sighed again. It was rare that the seer asked her anything, and she wasn't quite sure she wanted to speak the answer aloud. But Aeolmar had crawled into her bed last night mumbling about sojourns at the sea, and Asherah couldn't help it if his words made her heart leap. She hadn't questioned him about it in the morning, wary of his taciturn nature, choosing instead the far more *practical* route of consulting a woman who burned stinking herbs in a dilapidated hovel. Asherah assumed that she'd finally gone mad.

"I feel... I feel that someone may love me," she answered carefully, omitting Aeolmar's name.

"Many feel affectionate toward you," the seer replied. "But you want what only one man may give you." Asherah nodded, and the seer produced a crude bronze dagger from somewhere within the folds of her clothing. Without instruction, Asherah held out her hand and flinched, not from the dagger's point as it broke her skin but from the hag's cold, bark-like flesh.

The queen watched as the ruby drops of her blood mingled with the smoke and herbs. "He comes," the seer said, surprise evident in her tone. Perhaps everyone, otherworldly forces included, thought that Asherah was doomed to live out her life as the Virgin Queen.

"Comes?" Asherah repeated. "He's not here already?"

The seer squinted into the bowl and waved the smoke toward her nostrils. "Perhaps."

Asherah could hardly contain her joy. She wasn't going to suffer eternity alone; she would love, and be loved. She would go with Aeolmar to the sea, and they would be happy there. There, and for the rest of time.

"Thank you," she said emphatically. "You have given me more than I'd hoped. Thank you." The seer nodded and said nothing, but Asherah hadn't expected her to. Asherah left a heavy purse on the table, bowed her head, then hurriedly stepped outside. A light rain began falling, but Asherah didn't care. It would take much more than a few droplets of water to dampen the queen's ecstasy.

***

The seer poured oil over the smoldering herbs; the morass of dead plants briefly flamed, then extinguished itself. She didn't need the herbs in order to find answers to her patrons' questions, just a few drops of blood. However, a bit of a show now and then never hurt anyone.

"Why did you tell her that someone comes?"

The voice came from behind her, and the seer wondered how long he'd been standing there. She didn't bother turning to answer him, since he likely hadn't dropped the illusion that allowed him to enter unawares. "Because it is what I saw."

"Who?" he demanded.

"That, I do not know," she replied in the same bland tone she used with her patrons. "I saw a face; I did not hear a name."

The sorcerer cursed softly, and gradually let his glamour drop. Still, the gray interior obscured the finer points of his appearance; likely, anyone who happened to open her door would be unable to describe him, which was just as well. He was supposed to be dead.

"She now has hope. A hopeful queen is a dangerous queen." He circled the table and stared down at the haggard woman. "If she returns, give her nothing she desires. Tell her she will remain alone for the good of her land. If she asks about the 'he' you mentioned today, tell her he's dead."

The seer nodded; she could not lie about what she saw, but she could choose what she revealed. "As you say, so shall I do, Master Sarfek."

# Chapter Sixteen

Finlay struggled to remain calm as the crowd jostled him about, and adjusted his leather satchel. Normally, he retained his composure in even the most stressful situations, but today was the day he had longed for over the past six winters, and he was a bit more tense than usual.

Today was the day he would again set eyes upon the queen.

He still held the memory of Asherah close to his heart, the image of her standing before the portrait gallery in his shop, and how the painting of her—which was an exquisite work of art—had utterly failed to capture her beauty. In his mind, she laughed gaily, and Finlay could hardly wait to hear that laugh once more.

After Asherah and her hunters had departed from Cadogan, the villagers' lives had returned to normal, all except Finlay's. Unchecked inventory had piled up in the storeroom while the shop's wares had seen a coating of dust for the first time in many winters. The residents of his small desert village, and especially his sisters, had wondered if he'd merely taken ill or a total leave of his senses. Finlay never had been distracted, his shop never anything short of sparkling, but the floor had become dull with tracked-in dirt, and dust and cobwebs had begun to collect in the unswept corners. Try as he might, Finlay just no longer had the ability to concentrate on the tasks he knew as well as breathing. He could think of nothing but Asherah.

Finding the shop in which he'd spent his life too mundane a calling, Finlay had tried to devise a way to bring himself closer to his queen. He'd known that he could relocate to Teg'urnan at any time and continue his work as a merchant. His father would have enjoyed the added revenue. That hadn't been the answer, though; Finlay had wanted to serve Asherah directly, and he'd doubted that she had need of a shopkeeper. For many days, he'd wracked his brain trying to uncover some hidden talent of his that would be of use to the queen until his gaze had fallen to the sword she'd bestowed upon him. It was well known throughout the realm, even in his far corner of the desert, that the queen prized her hunters above all others.

*I will become a hunter.*

Of course, that meant that he would need to learn how to hunt. To that end, he had started questioning his customers about swordplay and where one could be taught the necessary skills to dispatch a demon. Most had laughed, some had thought he'd taken yet another blow to the head, but a few had mentioned a master swordsman who lived in the western woods whose skill with a blade was said to rival Solon's. Supposedly, the man lived like a hermit, and his sanity was called into question by more than one patron, but he had been persuaded to take on students in the past. To Finlay, this crazed warrior sounded like just the man he'd needed.

After Finlay had confirmed that the swordsman was flesh and blood rather than legend, he informed his father of his plan to leave Cadogan, a task which took far more courage than facing down three demons armed with only a windmill blade. His father had not agreed with his son's notions of chasing down demons in the queen's name, but he'd understood the need to make something of oneself, and had sent his youngest son off with his blessing and what few bits of advice he could spare.

For the first time in his life, Finlay left behind the shifting sands of the High Desert for green trees and rolling hills, and went in search of his teacher. He'd located the swordsman living in a cave at the forest's edge. The man had been a surly, wizened fellow who'd refused to grace Finlay with his name, but he had been as deadly as he was eccentric. Finlay had learned quickly, and after two full turns of the seasons the mad teacher had told Finlay that he had learned all he could teach him, and he'd sent him out to complete the last portion of his training alone: testing his new abilities against a demon's tough hide.

This necessitated finding a demon, so Finlay had hired himself out as a guard for the pilgrims that frequented the remote southern temples and shrines. The first two assignments had been noteworthy only for their boredom, but during the third such journey, his party had been attacked by a band of lessers. Finlay never did know how many demons had set upon them that day, but he had managed to kill one and run off the rest. It hadn't been truly a success, since the remaining demons had eaten the pilgrims' horses and Finlay had had to spend all the coins he'd so far earned on their replacements. But he had kept his patrons, a man and his young daughter, alive, and the gratitude that had shone from their faces had been worth more to him than all the gold in Parthalan.

By the end of his fourth winter travelling among priests and pilgrims, Finlay had killed in excess of one hundred demons. He was called Paladin by those that lived in the region, and Finlay felt that he at last had skills that matched his valor, skills worth offering to Asherah.

Ever the meticulous record keeper, for the shop demanded nothing less, Finlay had drawn up contracts with each of his clients in order to document his kills. These scrolls would serve him better than those many registers of used carpets and windmill blades, for queen was far too intelligent a woman to believe him based on his word alone. No, he would present her with proof of his new abilities and then request admittance to the *sola.*

He clutched the satchel of scrolls closer to his chest and craned his neck to peer around the crowds. Today was Reckoning Day, held once every three moons, when Asherah threw open the doors to Teg'urnan and invited all of her subjects to have their grievances heard before the court, whether it be over a matter as pressing as a border dispute or as ordinary as a missing goat. She was kind and just with her people, so much so that most had forgotten she had ever been called Asherah the Ruthless.

The crowd shifted, and Finlay almost sighed aloud when he caught sight of her. Asherah was seated on a silver throne atop a dais wrapped in pale blue carpeting, rich and plush as if it were velvet. The arms and back of her throne were encrusted with gems in varied shades of blue. The dais was positioned so that rays of sunlight illuminated the queen in a pool of radiance, so bright he could hardly see her, with blue-tinged rainbows dancing off the many gems.

The woman who now petitioned Asherah had brought an item to show the queen, so she stood and gracefully descended the dais in order to view the small object. A hum rolled across the great hall, and Finlay himself nearly stumbled at the sight of her. She was clad in a close-fitting gown of white silk, edged with elegant blue embroidery along the high neck and belled sleeves. Her long hair was loose, restrained only by the finely wrought silver crown upon her brow, and even from his distant vantage point, Finlay could see her black eyes sparkle. On occasion, Finlay had questioned his memory of Asherah's beauty, and now he realized just how accurate his recollections had been.

A man bolted down the dais steps after the queen, and Finlay recognized him as the First Hunter. Clad in heavy leather gear and with a sword at his side, he was dressed for battle rather than the relatively tame Reckoning Day. Aeolmar guided Asherah back to her throne, and then resumed his place at her elbow, scowl upon his face. How anyone could spend their days so close to the queen and not be elated was beyond his ken; Finlay was near giddiness just from being in the same room.

The crowd lurched forward once more, and Finlay gave his name and purpose to a *saffira*. The cases queued up before him seemed to drag on, but then he was next. At last, a steward called his name, and Finlay mustered all of his courage as he stepped forward and addressed the queen.

***

Asherah gazed at the crowd filling her hall, and sighed. So few of her Parthians had come to have their cases heard on this Reckoning Day that she wondered if Harek was right and the custom should be discontinued altogether; indeed, most seemed to be spectators, more interested in the feast that followed than in seeking justice. The Prelate was of the opinion that most disputes—and certainly those involving commoners—should be handled locally, not by Asherah herself, and that allowing such trifles to be heard before the court would only dilute her royal authority.

*Of course, if we did things Harek's way he would send the legion to deal with every dispute.* This was the latest ongoing argument between her and Harek, and she knew that once it was resolved, or when Harek became bored with the subject, he would dredge up yet another aspect of Asherah's rulership that he did not approve of. Asherah had been almost happy when Harek turned his displeasure toward Reckoning Day, since it meant that he was leaving her hunters alone, if only for a short time.

She glanced at Aeolmar, who stared straight ahead with his face set as if it were carved from stone. The First Hunter was another of Harek's favorite topics to complain about, for while Argent had easily bent to Harek's will, Aeolmar was stubborn and, unlike prior First Hunters, not the least bit afraid of the Prelate. One of their disputes, which had happened shortly after their ill-fated mission tracking Mersgoth, had been about the number of hunters assigned to the palace contingent.

"Ten is too many," Harek had insisted. "The palace contingent has always been comprised of five hunters, and five it will remain."

"I will not leave our queen so vulnerable," Aeolmar had countered. "Perhaps the *mordeths* Mersgoth and Esguth chose to attack because they knew of the few left to guard Teg'urnan."

"Asherah has the *con'dehr* to defend her! I would not—"

"You were not here," Aeolmar had bellowed, then he'd risen to his feet and had stalked around the table toward Harek. The Prelate had kept his seat and Asherah had watched him tremble, whether in fear or anger she couldn't guess. "You did not watch Esguth rend Argent limb from limb, or Mersgoth as he cut a swath through the *nuvi*! The palace contingent is what was here, *and it was not enough*!"

Normally, Asherah would have quieted Aeolmar, or at least calmed him somewhat, but not that day. Aeolmar was correct in that Teg'urnan's best defense was leagues away to the south, and it was her hunters, not Harek's beloved *con'dehr*, who had suffered the consequences.

"We need military strength," Harek had insisted. "The dark fae—"

"The dark fae are not the threat," Aeolmar had said over him. "The threat to Parthalan was, and has always been, demons."

"You think I know not the terror a demon can visit upon another?" Harek had growled.

"I think you know all too well, which is why you amaze me with your lack of attention to Parthalan's most noble queen,"

Aeolmar had retorted. "What is your purpose, if not to defend her?"

Harek had yelled and yelled, spraying spittle and curses until his face had turned red and blue veins had bulged in his neck and temples. He'd insisted that Aeolmar was guilty of gross insubordination, was disloyal to the Prelate's authority and therefore all of Parthalan, and he had demanded Aeolmar's immediate removal as First Hunter. Asherah had paid no heed to Harek's raving, though she'd ordered him to leave when he'd demanded Aeolmar's banishment. As a result, the distance between the queen and her Prelate had grown ever wider. It had pained her that she and her oldest, sometimes only, friend had drifted so far apart, but as Aeolmar staunchly rose to her defense, Asherah realized that for too long she hadn't been the ruler of Parthalan. Instead, she'd let Harek, and then Argent, bully her until she gave into their whims.

Asherah grimaced at Argent's memory and how he had always taken Harek's side against her; later, he would crawl into her bed, all sweet words and apologies, claiming that if he had agreed with her others would believe that he only did so to curry the queen's favor. Harek had been well aware that the two were lovers, and Asherah understood that he exploited the knowledge to his full advantage. For that reason, Asherah kept her relationship with Aeolmar as discreet as possible, though she knew that Aeolmar would not agree with her just to placate a lover's whim. He had no agenda to further, save killing Mersgoth.

*Would that dealing with demons was my Prelate's main focus.* For the past few seasons, Harek had done nothing but gripe about the ever-growing—and mostly imagined—threat of the dark fae. He claimed that Natraeus, son of their once-ally Drustan the Dark, was conspiring to join Nibika with Parthalan, and that Natraeus' most fervent desire was to unite both races of fae as one. Harek, tactically minded as he was, therefore believed that Parthalan should attack Nibika first. A conquest of the dark fae would mean that Asherah would rule over all faerie and elfin lands, and it would make her queen of more than half the realm. Asherah refused to take such action, since the last thing she needed was to add Queen of Nibika to her long list of unwanted titles.

Those conversations usually flowed to Asherah's ruling of the elves—or rather her lack thereof. While she remained Lady of Tingu, she demanded no tribute or other shows of fealty from her northern subjects. Of course, the elves regularly sent emissaries to Teg'urnan, for each of the elfin kingdoms was acutely aware that Asherah could command their lives—and their deaths—with the mere lift of a finger. Well, six of the elfin lands sought Asherah's favor; Leran claimed that Tingu's interests were better served by Asherah leaving them be. Gods, how she missed her boy.

Asherah was roused from her contemplation by the steward's shrill voice announcing a peasant from the east whose neighbors had accused her of cursing their livestock. The accuser had even brought along a basket of eggs as proof of curse work. Hardly able to see the tiny eggs, Asherah did the practical thing and descended the dais in order to get a better look. The queen ignored the murmur that arose in the hall, focusing her attention on the eggs in question.

"They seem to be only eggs," she said to the woman, while she ignored how Aeolmar sprinted after her and clutched her elbow, "but then, I am naught but a queen. I will have my magic handlers examine them, and they will advise me if a spell has been woven about them or perhaps if there is magic in the nest." Asherah nodded to the steward, who confiscated the possibly cursed eggs while Aeolmar guided the queen back to her throne.

"And what if they had been cursed?" he hissed in her ear.

"In all my days, I have never known a sorcerer to waste a curse on a chicken not yet hatched," Asherah rebuked. She left Aeolmar to his mutterings as she resumed her seat and motioned for the next complainant to approach. It was a dispute regarding what must have been a singularly verdant pasture, but Asherah hardly heard the words. She became distracted by a head of familiar curls.

The queen leaned to the side, ostensibly to better hear the allegation against the supposed poacher but in truth she wanted a better look at the man in the crowd. Aeolmar noticed the path of her gaze and bent to her ear.

"Cadogan," he murmured. "The boy with the windmill blade."

Asherah nodded, wondering what sort of event would cause a merchant to undertake the arduous journey from the High Desert all the way to Teg'urnan. Her curiosity got the better of her, and she decided that the matter of the pasture could wait for another day. The dissenting landowners fell silent when the queen raised a graceful hand and declared that she would consult the maps within the royal archives in order to determine who held the legitimate claim to the land. The grumbling landowners were thus dismissed, and Asherah straightened her back as the man from the desert was brought forward.

"Finlay of Cadogan," Asherah greeted, pleased by the blush that crept up his neck, "I trust my portrait still hangs in your shop?"

"My lady queen remembers me?" Finlay asked in amazement.

"Of course," Asherah replied, "for you are the only man I have ever known to successfully fend off demons with naught but a windmill blade." The color spread to Finlay's ears while Asherah continued, "Now tell me, how fares your family? What news have you brought me from the desert?"

"The shop is well, but I haven't been overseeing it these past five winters."

Asherah's graceful brow arched; the merchant's son intrigued her further. "What have you been doing if not seeing to your family's livelihood?"

"I have been doing as my lady suggested, honing my skill with a sword. You were right; it's much easier to dispatch a

demon with an edged blade than a rusty hunk of windmill."
Asherah smiled at his self-depreciating comment. Thus emboldened, Finlay held out his satchel and Asherah, mindful
of how Aeolmar had chased her down the stairs earlier, motioned for a *saffira* to accept it. As Finlay handed it off he
turned slightly, and Asherah saw that he wore the sword she'd
given him. "I first learned about swordplay and how to track,
and then I ventured forth as a guard for pilgrims amongst the
southern shrines."

"And what will these scrolls tell me?" asked the queen,
rifling among the rolled parchment.

"I recorded the facts of each demon I killed; the number of
them, where they set upon us, and how I dispatched them,"
he replied. "Each patron has signed their respective record."

Asherah nodded and perused the scrolls. Her calm manner
belied her thoughts; there were so many scrolls, and it hadn't
been that long since she'd met Finlay. Is this why her Prelate
was always travelling south? Was the region becoming overrun by demons? Instead of asking that, she observed, "You're
claiming quite a bit of success."

"One hundred and eight kills," Finlay stated, and Asherah's
heart lurched.

"Why do you present this to me now?" Asherah demanded,
unsure if this was some attempt to humiliate her on Reckoning
Day or a plea for help from the southern lords. Or, another
of Harek's ill-conceived plots to make her a stronger queen.
*I need to be a strong woman before I can be a strong queen.*
"What are you after, Finlay of Cadogan?"

"I request that you to allow me entry to the *sola*," Finlay
replied. "As a *nuvi*, I can continue to sharpen my skill. I hope
to someday to serve you as a hunter."

*Well, I wasn't expecting that.* Asherah nodded, then beckoned Aeolmar to her side. "What do you think?" she whispered. "Should we allow him entry?"

"I think we should forgo the *sola*, name him a hunter, and
assign him to the palace contingent," Aeolmar replied. "If he

has killed half of what he claims, he would be a much needed asset."

Asherah glanced back to the boy from the desert. *Man,* she corrected, *if he has killed so many there is nothing boyish left about him.* For all of Aeolmar's insistence that the palace contingent should have no less than ten hunters, no suitable candidates had arisen, save Innetha. Aeolmar had suggested that she be named upon their return to Teg'urnan, and he proclaimed, loudly and often, that he'd regretted it ever since. To date, Innetha ignored him.

No shortage of candidates had entered the *sola* in the six winters since Innetha's naming, but all had yet to be adequately trained. Thus, Aeolmar told Asherah, loudly and often, that Teg'urnan was still not as well guarded as he would like. Harek, ever unhelpful, frequently stated that Aeolmar only needed to call back members of the outlying contingents, but he flatly refused to do so. Aeolmar, and Asherah, understood that Parthalan's border contingents needed to remain strong in order to keep the vermin out. And the dark fae, Aeolmar always added with a sneer, for the First Hunter considered them a threat even less than Asherah did.

Out of the corner of her eye, Asherah watched Finlay, noting how he stood at attention while she spoke with Aeolmar. He exhibited respect and patience while they decided his fate, two traits her Prelate had long forgotten.

"Perhaps he will stand between you and Innetha and keep you from throttling her for a few more seasons," Asherah said with a rueful smile. Aeolmar said nothing as he straightened and resumed his stance at Asherah's side, and the queen returned her attention to Finlay. "I will not offer you a place in the *sola*. However, I will name you a hunter," she proclaimed, enjoying how his dejected expression quickly changed to elation. Asherah glided down the steps from the dais, not chased by Aeolmar this time, and stood before her newest hunter. "I can name you here, or if you prefer we can hold the traditional naming at first dawn, upon the palace steps."

"My lady, it matters not where you honor me, only that you have done so," Finlay said as he knelt.

Asherah placed her hands upon his head, resisting the urge to twine her fingers in his curls. "Finlay of Cadogan, you are hereby my hunter. Rise and go forth to your brother, for you are honored among us."

Finlay stood, and after a gentle prod, he ascended the dais and stood at Aeolmar's right. Asherah smiled at the two for a moment, then turned and addressed those that remained. "We will hear no more disputes today, but remain under my roof and you will be heard on the morrow. I'm of a mind to celebrate our newest hunter."

# Chapter Seventeen

Since Asherah had made the rash decision to name Aeolmar as First Hunter, Harek had stormed out of her receiving chamber nearly every time he'd been in it. Reasoning with the man was like trying to clear a patch of strangleweed with a quill pen, arduous and difficult and an utter waste of time. Harek wished that Aeolmar would finally track down that accursed Mersgoth, and he hoped that the *mordeth* would come out the winner.

Aeolmar's appointment had been but one of Asherah's bad decisions. Honestly, whenever Harek looked away, the woman did something foolish, whether it be placing a cretin at such a high rank or sending off another missive to the ungrateful Leran. Not today, though. Today, for the first time in more winters than Harek could count, Asherah had done something he approved of: sending that blasted Aeolmar to the north for the remainder of the season. Even better, he was taking the useless Innetha with him.

Harek even approved of the mission's purpose, to remind the elves who their true sovereign was. Of course, Asherah's main objective was to obtain news of Leran, but no matter. With Aeolmar out of the way, he'd have the queen's ear again.

She'd listen to his plans, heed his warnings about Parthalan's safety, and realize that only he, her loyal Prelate, truly understood what was in the land's best interests.

*It will be again as it once was*, Harek mused. *Just Asherah and I.*

# Chapter Eighteen

## Asherah Speaks

It was an unseasonably mild autumn day, though summer had become little more than a pleasant memory. But the breeze that stroked my face was warm, and the suns were hot, and the varied flora and growing things that filled my garden seemed untroubled by the coming chill. I sighed and tried to borrow a bit of their serenity. As usual, it didn't work.

I sighed again and leaned on the glass garden door. Looming over me like a silent behemoth was the coming Winter's Eve, which would signify not only a new year, but also a grand jubilee that would be held in celebration of my eight hundredth winter as Queen of Parthalan. Gods, I wish I could just skip over it, but the invitations had long been sent. I was as committed to this feast as surely as if I'd drawn first blood on the battlefield, and all I wanted to do was run and hide behind a tree or perhaps under a rock.

It's not that I don't enjoy a celebration, for I most certainly do, but this coming milestone was more than a bit melancholy. Lormac, my love and mate, had ruled in Tingu for exactly eight hundred and two winters. He once said that the first *eight hundred didn't matter, for he only truly became a king after he met me and I inspired him to do great things.*

*Had he really only been in my life for less than two winters? Now, so far removed from him, it felt like no more than the blink of an eye. Those two winters had taken me from filthy urchin to Lady of Tingu—and then to Queen of Parthalan. I often wonder what would have become of Torim and me without Lormac's generous assistance. Would I have gone on to behead Sahlgren anyway, thus claiming rulership without Lormac's aid? If I had met Lormac later in my life, long after I'd been crowned, would he still have loved me? I believe—no, I know—I would have loved him, regardless of where or when we met.*

*Feeling more than a little entitled to indulge myself with his memory, I wandered out to my garden, lay on the grass, and imagined that my Lormac was there beside me. A Northman through and through, he spent as much time outdoors as possible in total disregard of Tingu's bitter cold, and once he'd gifted me some fur-lined boots and gloves I came to share his appreciation. At times like this, I speculated as to whether he would have liked Teg'urnan, with the warm breezes allowing for more evenings spent under the stars, or if he would miss the brisk northern air.*

*Knowing Lormac, he would have been happier in Teg'urnan, since the mild seasons would mean an increase in outdoor lovemaking. Although, he'd harbored no qualms about stripping down in the midst of a snowstorm if the mood struck him; he once had dragged me out of The Seat during the worst blizzard I have ever experienced. The fact that this blizzard had occurred long after spring began was one of the northern climate's many quirks.*

*"Must we walk?" I had shouted over the howling winds, for he had denied me use of a horse on this little expedition.*

*"The ice isn't good for hooves," he'd shouted in reply.*

*"Nor my feet," I had muttered, but Lormac hadn't heard me over the wind. Or, it could have been possible that he'd ignored*

*me. Whatever the reason for his silence, he soon had ushered me into a cave at the far side of the mountain from which The Seat was carved. After we'd shaken the snow from our cloaks, he'd led me to a sight nearly as wondrous as The Seat itself: hot springs bubbling forth from deep within the rock, emptying their water into a pool. The cave walls were of the same green and purple stone that made up the palace, but rather than worked by masons, they remained in their natural jagged state, with only the floor worn smooth. The front of the pool was sheltered by the cave ceiling, and while it was bereft of the glowing white crystals that lit The Seat there had been plenty of light, since most of it was open to the falling snow.*

*"It's lovely," I'd breathed, entranced by the delicate flakes that had fallen with abandon to the steaming water. It had reminded me of a jeweler's bathing chamber, with the walls covered in amethysts and emeralds rather than more mundane tiles. Of course, the walls of a bathing chamber wouldn't have had a rime of ice that glinted in the gray winter light.*

*"Have I ever brought you anywhere that wasn't lovely?" Lormac had asked as he'd wrapped his arms around me. He had nestled his chin atop my shoulder, and we'd watched the snowflakes melt into the pool for a time. I had been hardly surprised when his hands had traveled to the fastenings of my clothes.*

*"You're joking," I'd said, casting a dubious glance toward him.*

*"I never joke when it concerns pleasuring my mate," Lormac had said as he'd slipped his hands inside my clothes. I had been hesitant, yes, but the combination of his deep voice and gentle hands had been most difficult to resist. Soon enough, he had had me in that wonderfully hot pool and I'd had to admit, making love in the snow had been a pleasant way to spend an afternoon.*

*I cannot say how long I'd been in my garden, joyfully remembering that snowy day with Lormac, when I heard a man's voice call my name. "Lormac?" I called out; it seemed that it would take much longer than eight centuries for me to break that habit. I adjusted my dress and entered my receiving chamber, and found that my newest hunter was seeking his queen.*

*"My lady," Finlay greeted, then his brow furrowed as he took in my appearance.*

*"What is it?" I asked, looking down at my dress. I'd thought I'd smoothed it quite nicely.*

*"There are leaves in your hair, and your face..." He left off, but a quick touch to my face explained his concern: my cheeks were hot to the touch and likely flushed as bright as a hummingbird's throat. My memories of Lormac are intense.*

*"Are you laughing at me?" I accused, seeing him turn away as I picked leaves from my hair. Normally I wouldn't have let them fall to the floor, but what were all these* saffira *for if not to sweep up after me? "And did I get all the leaves?"*

*"There is one more," Finlay said, neither confirming nor denying his amusement over finding his queen... reminiscing in the garden. If he even knew I what I was doing. Hopefully, he assumed I was napping and would leave it at that. I leaned forward for Finlay to pick out the leaf, but he suddenly went bashful on me and directed his attention to the scrolls he carried. After discarding the leaf myself, I invited Finlay to sit at my map table and asked why he'd come.*

*"I thought to report on the* sola," *he began and launched into an intricately detailed account of each and every* nuvi: *how they fared in hand-to-hand combat, who was proficient with which weapons, and who was likely do well in the Trials next summer. By the time we reached the last scroll, I felt that I knew each* nuvi *as well as I knew myself.*

*"I am impressed," I said once he concluded, pleased to see the color return to Finlay's neck. My, but he blushed often for a man. "Indeed, in all my time as queen I haven't heard such a precise report on anything, much less the* sola. *Perhaps your time as a shopkeeper has made your attention to detail sharper than most."*

"It's not that," Finlay said, downplaying his talents.

"Then tell me why you, who have been here less than a full turn of the seasons, have managed to compile more facts and figures than those who have been here many hundreds of winters." There was that flush again, now creeping its way up his neck, though his voice betrayed nothing but confidence when he spoke.

"I understand the nuvi. Not so long ago I was just like them, learning to track and kill vermin, my only goal the opportunity to serve my most gracious queen," he replied.

"And why did you?" I asked. "Decide to become a hunter, I mean. Surely your life in Cadogan was comfortable."

"It was," he agreed. "But after the day we were attacked and I met you, I could think of no greater cause than to serve you." He glanced up, the first time he'd looked at me since I asked him to take the leaf from my hair.

"May I tell you something?" I asked, and he nodded. "I am very, very glad that your life's path has brought you here. To Teg'urnan." I smiled at him, and he returned it with a grin of his own. "You enjoy working with the nuvi?"

"I do," he replied.

"Perhaps you will play the unknown in the next Trial by Combat?" I suggested. "I feel it unfair to send a nuvi against a lunatic like Aeolmar, and Innetha's as likely to kiss them as fight," I said, not adding that Harek's recent distance made me reticent to choose one of the con'dehr, who had traditionally filled the role. I'd expected Finlay to flush again, but no pale redness washed across his cheeks. Instead, he had inquiries of his own.

"Forgive my asking," he began, "but why is there only the one Trial?"

"Do you think the nuvi should undergo the Trial by Combat more than once?" I countered.

"No, once seems to be plenty." He took a deep breath before he continued. "But, isn't there more to being a hunter? Yes, *fighting is the essential skill to master, but not the only skill a hunter should possess."*

*I arched my brow; the man from the desert had intrigued me yet again. "What sort of skills have you found to be essential?"*

*"Stealth, for one," Finlay replied. "I learned the hard way that you can't just blunder about and hope the enemy doesn't notice you." He absently stroked a scar on the back of his hand, and I wondered what he'd blundered into. "And, they should learn how to fight without conventional weapons."*

*"The* nuvi *are taught hand-to-hand combat," I stated, but Finlay shook his head.*

*"No, I mean using things that aren't weapons as such," he said, rather bashfully. Well, I couldn't let that go, now could I?*

*"Such as windmill blades?" I teased.*

*He smiled ruefully. "Yes, such as windmill blades." Finlay dropped his gaze, and I worried that I'd offended him.*

*"I don't mean to demean your ideas," I said. "What you've said is sound. And had it not been for that windmill blade, we may have had a very different outcome in Cadogan."*

*"You mean, I'd have died without your assistance," he stated. Any other man would have been bitter over a woman rescuing him, but Finlay didn't sound the least bit put out. No, he was merely reciting the facts as he knew them. I reached across the table and gave his forearm a gentle squeeze.*

*"Perhaps you would have. But, what matters is that you didn't. You went on to learn the skills you needed, and you're now a valued member of my court." He placed his hand atop mine, his callused palms scraping my knuckles. "Have you shared these thoughts with Aeolmar and Innetha?"*

*"I came to you first. Should I have gone to Aeolmar instead?" He moved out of my reach, the timbre of his words telling me he worried over my offense.*

*"No. I'm glad you came to me." I refrained from detailing my irritation over Harek keeping information from me since Finlay hadn't come to hear his queen rant. I would save that*

*for his second visit. "I would, however, like you to speak with them once they return from the north. Learn what skills have served them best as hunters and report back to me. Then, we will discuss setting up additional Trials."*

*"You want to work directly with me?" Finlay asked. "Not Aeolmar?"*

*"I do," I confirmed. "You are the one with the detailed accounts of the* sola *and the one who has developed such strong relationships with the* nuvi. *It should be you."*

*"I would be honored to, my lady," he said with a respectful nod. "And, I will be honored to play the unknown. You are most gracious."*

*"Only to those who deserve such; otherwise, I'm told I'm quite disagreeable." Cydia knows that's the truth. I looked down at the many scrolls and pushed one towards him. "Now tell me, my stalwart hunter, which of these* nuvi *is most likely to best you in the coming Trial?"*

# Chapter Nineteen

Much to Asherah's relief, Finlay adjusted well to his new life at Teg'urnan and to his role as mentor. She'd worried that his relocation from the desert would be too drastic of a change for him, but he proved to be as skilled a mentor as he was a hunter. He understood how some of the younger *nuvi* struggled with the sword or spear since he had faced those same struggles not very long ago. When a student became frustrated or spoke of leaving the *sola*, Finlay reminded them that a few winter's past his only skills were stacking coins and scratching away at inventory lists. More often than not, his easy nature and sharp wit garnered a smile from the *nuvi,* if not always from their instructor.

Partly because of Finlay's good relationship with the *nuvi* and partly because he had grown to hate Innetha nearly as much as a demon, Aeolmar named Finlay as his second not long after his addition to the palace contingent. Asherah questioned his reasoning, since there were other individuals more qualified to act as Second Hunter who had served longer—Elkin, for instance, though he was comfortable in his command of the Northern Contingent. Aeolmar maintained that he could leave Teg'urnan confident that Finlay would defend the queen as Aeolmar would himself, and for that reason alone, Finlay was the best, and only, choice.

But Aeolmar hadn't considered that as Second Hunter, Finlay would be the one left at the palace when Asherah requested that he journey northward to the elfin lands, which left the only other hunter, Innetha, as the First Hunter's companion.

When Asherah had first taken the throne, she had gone northward every ten winters but quickly learned that the elves did a fine job of governing without any input from their Lady. That, and it was painful for her to visit only six of the seven lands, for she honored her last promise to Leran and would not set foot in Tingu unless he invited her. He hadn't, but then she didn't expect him to do anything but go on hating her.

Despite his continued dislike of her, Asherah still needed to know if the son of her heart was well. To that end, she had begun the practice of sending emissaries to Tingu, rather than making the journey herself, so these ambassadors may learn a few things while ensuring that the queen honored Leran's wishes. Her representatives had fared little better in Tingu than she would have herself; of the scores of fae sent to Tingu over the centuries, less than ten had been allowed entry to the keep, and none had dared to approach The Seat. However, they had all managed to catch a glimpse of Leran, and they told Asherah all she needed to hear: her boy was well and hale.

On this latest journey Aeolmar and Innetha had managed not only entry to the keep, but they had also shared a meal with the Lord of Tingu. Asherah wondered if Aeolmar's outwardly foul temperament found a sort of kinship with Leran or if the Lord of Tingu had been enamored with Innetha; after all, Leran's mother was a nymph and Lormac had been well and truly enchanted by her charms. The First Hunter confirmed the latter while Asherah perused an unexpected gift of gowns that was bestowed on her by the Lady of Thurnda.

"Leran really invited you to his table?" Asherah asked. Innetha had already told her every detail of their time in Tingu, but she needed to hear the tale from Aeolmar as well. She wondered how many times she could convince Aeolmar to tell her the same news; Innetha had balked after the third repetition.

"He was in a strangely hospitable mood," Aeolmar replied. "We were there for nearly an entire day before he reaffirmed his hatred of all things fae. He does send his regards."

Innetha had made no mention of word from Leran, but then Leran probably only said as much to Aeolmar. Men did tend to forget what they were speaking of while in Innetha's presence.

"He does?" Asherah dropped the garments she had been examining and peered at Aeolmar, searching for some hint of sarcasm but his solemn face told her that he spoke the truth. Leran had never once sent word to Asherah, unless it was a request for her to stay out of his affairs. "And, he is well? Does he want for anything?"

"The Lord of Tingu wants for nothing but manners," Aeolmar stated, but Asherah's eyes begged for more. "He is well, as are his lands. He still retains the two kingdoms he has reclaimed and seems to have designs upon Rael."

Asherah laughed to herself; it had been bloody amazing how he tricked old Aish'nn of Nugt into swearing fealty, and his conquest of Urth'nn had been just plain bloody. "He is his father's son."

"Does he know that you've named him your heir?"

Asherah sighed as she turned her attention back to the many gowns. She wondered how Aeolmar came to know that the Lord of Tingu was her heir, but then she remembered the many hours her First Hunter spent in the royal library. She also remembered Harek's opposition to naming Leran as the heir to Parthalan; for once, Harek's reasoning had been sound, since Leran was not a blood relative of Asherah's. But she had been adamant in that naming him was for the good of the land; she would not leave Parthalan without a leader. What if she had no children? What if an assassin slit her throat in the dead of night? What if she died of illness? Or worse, what if some poor woman, sick with grief over the death of her mate, beheaded her on the palace steps...

Eventually, the scribes got the wording right, and if Asherah passed from this plane to reside with the gods—and her dear Lormac—without a successor as defined by Solon's edict, rulership of Parthalan would fall to Leran. Whether he liked it or not.

"Those scrolls you busied yourself with weren't all about demons, were they?" she asked with a rueful smile, referencing the many hours he'd spent in the archives. "I made him my heir so long ago that I doubt he remembers. Knowing Leran, he would refuse Parthalan and leave the land without a leader." She turned her back to Aeolmar, and looked at the many elfin garments spread before her. "Sibeal must have sent every gown she can no longer fit into." Any other woman would be grateful for Sibeal's largess; Asherah, however, had never cared for elfin fashions. The garments tended to be heavy and dark, and all were designed for wearing over many confounding layers of undergarments. It was a wonder there were any elfin children at all. "Her child was born while you were there?"

"Just before we arrived," Aeolmar replied. "She has named him Senan."

"Senan," Asherah repeated, remembering Leran as a boy. He'd loved swimming, and would carve tiny lopsided horses. "I suppose I should at least try these on," she said with a resigned air and unlaced her bodice. Her *saffira-nell*, Attia, indicated Aeolmar's presence with her eyes, but Asherah merely shrugged as she stepped out of her gown while the First Hunter looked on, comfortably reclined on her bed.

"He's already quite familiar with my form," Asherah admonished as she wiggled into a dark green sheath of heavy velvet trimmed in frilly white lace at the neck and wrists; to Asherah, the stiffened lace resembled nothing so much as icicles. While Attia fastened the gown with a buttonhook (for elfin garments had maddening fastenings to match their maddeningly uncomfortable designs), she asked if Sibeal had also been of a mood to hand out weapons, since Aeolmar had returned with a new sword.

"This is the sword Grelk owed me," Aeolmar replied. "I almost didn't make the trek to his den, fearing it still wouldn't be finished." Asherah nodded, for she knew well how troll weapons, prized above all others for their strength and keen edge, seemed to take a lifetime to complete.

"May I?" asked the queen. Aeolmar readily relinquished his blade, commenting that Asherah may unsheathe him whenever she'd like. Attia rolled her eyes. Clearly having had enough of the queen and her lover, she declared that she was needed elsewhere.

"Quite a fine blade," Asherah commented, "good weight to it." She ran her fingers across the swirling patterns etched into the hilt, and she recalled a near-identical sword. "Which smith forged this blade?"

"Grelk made it," Aeolmar replied.

"The troll king, himself," Asherah said. She flipped the sword over and noted the twining vine etched into the blade, the large, sparkling sapphire set into the hilt...if she didn't know better, she would have thought she was holding a sword she hadn't seen for eight hundred winters. "What made you choose this design?"

"My father had a troll sword," Aeolmar answered, "and I wanted something similar. When I described what his sword looked like, Grelk insisted that he make the blade himself. He claims that he's the only one who makes swords in this fashion."

*Your father the farmer had a troll sword made by the king of the forge himself.* "What aren't you telling me?" Asherah asked.

"There is nothing else to tell," Aeolmar said. "My family owned one thing of value, and it was Father's sword. He claimed it was owed to him, and I've never had cause to think that anything other than truth."

"I don't mean to imply anything else," Asherah said. "Perhaps Grelk made your father's sword as well and a merchant brought it to your village. Did you get quite a few traders in Savey?"

"No," he replied, "and I've never told you the name of my village."

Asherah dropped her gaze as she set down the sword, turning toward the mirror while she struggled with the gown. To distract Aeolmar from her fumbling, and her new knowledge of his childhood, she began listing menu items for the Winter's Eve feast. She babbled about roasted birds and stewed fruits while she peeled the green velvet from her form, sacrificing a few buttons in her frustration. Still refusing to look in Aeolmar's direction, she grabbed the next gown on the pile. That garment consisted of a gray lace sheath topped with a red velvet overdress. As she slipped the sheath up over her hips, Asherah's commentary shifted from food to elfin fashion, and how all elves seemed to be partial to the dark, somber colors that she so disliked. The overdress proved more problematic than the green velvet sheath or even the buttonhook, and Asherah fell silent while she struggled to pull on the stiff velvet. When her head emerged, Aeolmar was standing directly in front of her.

"And how is Elkin of the Perpetually Open Mouth?" he asked. He turned Asherah around and set to lacing up the stays, rather tightly she thought.

"Well as ever," replied the queen. "He... Elkin said that he went to visit your family, and found nothing but the burned out remains of your home."

"That is all he would find," Aeolmar said shortly. Having finished with the stays, he grasped Asherah's shoulders and moved her in front of the mirror. She studied her reflection in an effort to avoid Aeolmar's stern gaze. If only she liked what she saw.

"This dress is awful," she declared. "Nothing but a waste of fabric, and fabric that would be better used for draperies, at that." The sheath hugged her from breast to hip; her skin itched where the stiff lace edging scraped. The dark red overdress billowed out from her shoulders like a cape, only to be cinched a hand's breadth below her waist with a narrow gold cord. Each wide, cumbersome sleeve was gathered at her elbow and terminated in a point over the back of her hand, and was topped with a tassel on the back of her hand. Asherah had never thought that Sibeal disliked her, but the dress made her wonder.

"Oh, I don't know," Aeolmar said as he traced the contours of the bodice, "it might be enjoyable to remove." He leaned forward and kissed her neck, then wrapped his arms about her waist. "What else did he tell you?" he asked, his lips against her ear.

"That Savey still mourns the loss of your family," Asherah answered softly. "Apparently, the villagers believe that you also died in the fire."

Aeolmar ignored her comment and continued kissing her neck; Asherah enjoyed his affection, but she knew that he was only trying to distract her. Usually, she let him.

"Why do I need to ask Elkin about you?" she asked pointedly.

Aeolmar clenched his fists and stepped away from her. "Why do you ask after me? There is nothing about me you need to know."

Asherah turned and faced Aeolmar, refusing to let his gallingly stubborn nature dissuade her. *This time, I will have answers.* "I could order you to tell me."

"I could leave this palace and leave you wondering until the end of time," Aeolmar countered. "Gods, Asherah, what are you after?"

"To know you," she shouted. "No one knows anything about you! You are this mysterious man who appeared at the gates claiming to have killed thousands of demons! And now I learn that those who did know you think you're dead!"

"What more do you need to know of me?" he spat back. "I do everything you require of me! I kill whatever you point me at, I travel to lords you don't want to bother with and act as your diplomat, I do whatever you desire in this bedchamber, yet it is never enough!" His words stung Asherah, more so because she knew he meant to hurt her. Her cheeks flushed hot, her fury sharpened by pangs of despair.

"If you do not want to be here, you are free to leave," she said, rage having deepened her voice as it spilled over wetly from her eyes. She turned away from him, hiding the hot tears from he who caused them. Aeolmar reached for her, but she jerked away.

"Asherah, love—"

"Don't you 'Asherah, love' me!" she shot back. "You heart is made of stone, you loveless bastard." Aeolmar put his hands on her waist, but she twisted out of his grip. "Don't touch me," she snapped, but he ignored her and drew her against his chest. She swatted at him, but Aeolmar grabbed her flailing hands in one of his as he nuzzled her neck, murmuring soft endearments in the old language. Once the tension left her limbs, he dragged her with him to the floor, enfolding Asherah into the cocoon of his body.

"I hate how familiar you are with me," she mumbled against his shoulder. Aeolmar always knew how to disarm her, be it with soft words or a gentle caress, even when she would prefer to remain furious. *Most* especially *when I'd rather stay angry.*

"Usually, you like it," he teased, and against her will, she smiled. Aeolmar held her for a time, gently stroking her neck. "You know I don't like to speak of my past."

"I also know that you don't want to be First Hunter," Asherah said quietly. "You hate the politics of court, you hate living within these stone walls... What keeps you here?"

"You do," Aeolmar replied. Asherah raised her gaze to his, and felt the backs of her eyes burn.

"Do I? All this time, I thought it was the prospect of killing Mersgoth." Unable to bear his sapphire gaze any longer, she looked at her hands. "More than seven winters we have been together, yet I feel that I hardly know you."

"You know me better than anyone else in Teg'urnan," he said softly, "I think better than anyone still living." He tilted up her chin and forced her to look at him; as always, Asherah felt as if she was falling into an endless sea of blue. "I've tracked Mersgoth for longer than I care to remember. I can do that from anywhere in Parthalan. I remain here because I want to." He kissed her. "Because of you."

*But you don't love me*, she thought dejectedly. *The seer said that love had come to me, but she lied. She is as powerless as I am foolish.* "I am Asherah, mighty ruler of Parthalan and Tingu, yet I cannot manage to find a companion who loves me," she said bitterly. "Argent never loved me, you never will."

"Argent was a self-centered fool," Aeolmar declared. "He loved his own image so dearly he had no room left in his heart for another."

"And...you?" Asherah asked hesitantly. All she had ever wanted was a companion, like Lormac or even Torim, who loved her. In the beginning of her reign, there was only Harek, who stood so close to her side he nearly suffocated her. Then they drifted apart, and she sought the comfort of another, even if for only one night. She never gave up the hope of finding a companion, if not a mate, and while her bond with Aeolmar was steady, she feared that it was as one-sided as her relationship with Argent had been.

"I lost the ability to love a long time ago," Aeolmar said. "Mersgoth saw to that. I will tell you, my queen, that you are firmly lodged in my heart, and I never want you to leave."

Asherah rested her head on Aeolmar's shoulder and sighed. It wasn't what she wanted to hear, but it was enough. It would have to be enough, since it was all she had. As much as she wanted Aeolmar to love her, she knew that he would never say the words unless he truly meant them, unlike Argent who had professed his undying love for her, loudly and often, along with all his other lies. She was so much happier with

Aeolmar than she had ever been with Argent, and yet... And yet, she wanted love, the one thing her First Hunter could not offer her. The comfort and security she felt with Aeolmar was something she hadn't felt since she was in Lormac's arms, and she was not willing to give that up. It would just have to be enough.

"Why do you always threaten that you'll leave, and never return?" she asked.

Aeolmar chuckled. "My father would say that to my mother when times were lean, as they often were," he replied. "We were very poor, and sometimes she wondered how she would feed all seven of her children, along with herself and Father. Can you imagine nine mouths to feed?"

"I surely cannot." Asherah imagined seven young Lerans running about. She wondered if all those children hadn't made Aeolmar's parents a bit mad.

"At times, it was a daunting task," Aeolmar continued. "Whenever Mother complained, Father said not to worry, and that he would go to the village market and steal whatever we needed."

"His hands could have been cut off for the theft," Asherah pointed out.

"That's exactly what my mother said. So he said he would obtain the goods by whatever means necessary, then take us and disappear to where we would never be found." Aeolmar was silent for a moment, and Asherah sensed that he was remembering the better times of his youth. "He would go on, describing maddening feats such as scaling mountains and swimming across the sea in order to keep us out of the stocks. Father's outlandish, foolish plans always calmed her, and they would talk into the small hours of the night about the new life they would begin." His eyes softened as he gazed at Asherah, and his mouth quirked in that half smile she saw so rarely. "There, I've just told something of my past that I have never shared with anyone."

"Really?" she said.

"Really," he replied as he claimed her lips.

When they parted, Asherah laid her head against his shoulder. No, she wasn't completely satisfied with the state of things between them, but she refused to give up. "What did your father call your mother?" She felt his arms tense, so she added, "Lormac called me his star."

"*Nalla.*" Asherah felt his face stretch into a smile. "He only ever called her *nalla.*"

Nalla. *I'd like to be called* nalla. Asherah took his hand, large and strong and wrapped in his velvet skin, and traced patterns across his palm. "Someday, will you tell me about where you're from and of your family?"

Aeolmar kissed the top of her head. "I promise."

# Chapter Twenty

## Asherah Speaks

*Aeolmar stayed with me long into the night, regaling me with seemingly endless tales of his journey north; thankfully, not all of them centered on Innetha's annoying habits. I was surprised when his words flowed freely as he spoke of his unplanned visit to Grelk. I knew that Aeolmar had once resided with the trolls, but my hunter harbored a genuine affection for the troll king and enjoyed seeing his old friend. Though Grelk had owed him a sword for some time, Aeolmar hadn't expected to collect upon the debt; while Grelk's swords were the finest to be had, he was also the slowest smith ever to swing a hammer.*

*I enjoyed Aeolmar's uncharacteristically loose tongue, even though I knew it was only temporary. This talkative evening was his way of apologizing for the harsh words he had spoken earlier; while I appreciated the gesture, I wished it wasn't born of guilt. In truth, I wished he would finally open his heart and share his true self with me. I longed to know of his childhood, his family, the events in his life that had molded him into the man that shared my life and my bed. That, I was coming to understand, was a wish not likely to be granted. I accepted the bits of himself he deigned to share with me, and for that night, it was enough. As to how long it would remain enough, I could not say.*

*Aeolmar took his leave in the small hours before first dawn, but before doing so he extracted a promise: for the Winter's Eve celebration that evening he wanted me to wear the red and gray gown. "You don't realize how lovely you are in red," he'd said when I complained, and after that statement, I agreed to his request. Aeolmar asked so very little of me, and it gladdened me to think that such a small act could make him happy. And, who was I to question his opinion of me in a red dress? His eyes had danced when I'd agreed, then he'd kissed me in that way of his that left me longing for more.*

*And now I sat atop my throne on Winter's Eve, overseeing a grand feast honoring the eight hundredth year of my reign, clad in that hideous dress as my people toasted to my good health, and Aeolmar was nowhere to be found. I'd nearly eschewed this elfin torture chamber disguised with velvet and silk for a proper fae gown, but I had promised Aeolmar. I have been called many names in my time, but oathbreaker was never—and will never—be one.*

Since he convinced me to wear this monstrosity, at least he could be here to see me in it, *I grumbled inwardly. Aloud, I only sighed, for I knew well how Aeolmar hated crowds, just as I knew that he would arrive eventually. Probably just before the feast's conclusion, but arrive nonetheless.*

*My taciturn lover wasn't the only conspicuously absent guest that evening. Leran had ignored my invitation, just as he had ignored all the others. It hurt—gods, how it hurt!—that he held onto his hatred of me so tightly, and I missed him more than I would ever admit. Publicly, I proclaimed that the Lord of Tingu had many matters to deal with in his own land and could spare neither the time nor effort to journey to Teg'urnan for a mere feast. Privately, I wept.*

*I had just resigned to make the best of my evening, bereft of both my lover and the son of my heart, when Harek approached me. The animosity that flowed between us had been somewhat quelled during Aeolmar's recent absence, and normally I would have welcomed his companionship. If nothing else, Harek was good for keeping unwanted patrons away from my throne. Not on this night, however, for following him, much as a pig follows the one with the slop, was the last person I wanted to speak with: Natreus, king of Nibika.*

*"My queen," Harek called out as he escorted the king of the dark fae before my throne with ill-disguised contempt. "Natraeus has come to celebrate your reign."*

*"My lord Natraeus," I greeted as he climbed the steps of the dais, "I am glad you found the time to attend my simple gathering." One of the larger lies I've told, but no matter. I imagined I was far from the first woman to tell Natraeus an untruth.*

*"For you, my lady, anything." Natraeus bowed low as he kissed my hand, his mouth lingering on my flesh far longer than necessary. Or decent. But then, there was nothing decent about the dark fae, at least nothing I'd ever seen. Natraeus reminded me all too much of his father, Drustan the Dark, and I recalled the many ways he had tried to worm himself into Lormac's affairs. Lormac's father, L'hirre, had conquered the dark fae long, long ago, and they'd never been able to shake the ties that bound them to elfin rule. Well, not until Lormac was gone and I had become the figure of elfin authority.*

*Tingu's political structure had crumbled away while Leran, who had only seen a few short winters with his father, grew to manhood. Somehow, as the elfin kingdoms fractured upon themselves, the dark fae had fallen under my rule. It had been a former Lord of Tingu that had subjugated them, and since I was Lady of Tingu, I suppose it had been only natural. More titles I didn't want, more lands I had never wanted and was responsible for. At times like this, when an oily little man like Natraeus looked upon me as if I was a leg of mutton to gnaw upon, I wished I had remained in Tingu and never attempted my liberation of the fae.*

*Of course, had I stayed in Tingu, Lormac would not have died. Not only would my mate be alive, the dark fae would be his problem.*

*But he had died, and for a time, Nibika had been mine alone to oversee. When Leran came of age I had sent a missive, formally proclaiming him as the ruler of the dark fae, effectively washing my hands of that land. Drustan the Dark hadn't liked that, but he had little choice in the matter. Leran hadn't much liked it either, but because his grandsire was the man who'd conquered Nibika, I felt that a man of Tingu should continue to rule the land. On that, if nothing else, Leran and I agreed.*

*At last, Natraeus released my hand, and I resisted the urge to wipe it on my skirts.* "Have you given any further thought to my offer?" *he asked, with a voice as slimy as his flesh.*

"Offer?" *Harek barked.*

"Yes, my lord Prelate," *Natraeus said,* "I sent a messenger some time ago offering to take our queen as my mate." *Natraeus turned to me and added,* "I received your reply declining, but I do hope you will reconsider."

*Reconsider? Reconsider! I had considered his offer of taking him as a mate for less than one moment before deciding against it. Never would I give myself over to such a disreputable, disgusting, repulsive little man. I, the chosen mate of the Lord of Tingu, would lay down with a filthy beggar before Natraeus.*

*However, voicing such opinions would only ruin my jubilee.* "Our lands have been separate since the gods created us," *I said smoothly, alluding to Nibika'al's treachery in her seduction of Olluhm. To lure a man from his mate's bed is truly an unforgivable act, even amongst the gods.* "Why go against their wishes now?"

"It would not be the first time our royal lines have mixed," *he countered.* "They say your Sahlgren was of the dark fae."

"Was he?" *I inquired with a raised brow. Did this fool really think to seduce me with talk of the man who'd ordered my captivity?* "I never asked after his heritage, but then, I did only have occasion to speak with him the one time. Then he set loose a host of demons within this very room, and I was no longer in the mood for conversation." I gestured about the grand hall, painting a vivid picture of Sahlgren's treachery. I described where the old king had thrown the portal and where the first demon had fallen. "When next I saw him, he'd been dragged from his hiding place and was busy begging for his life from those he'd given in slavery to the mordeths. *Given!* We weren't even worth a few coppers. Then I took his head, and he has remained blissfully silent ever since." My words had the desired effect, and the ever-composed Natraeus shifted uncomfortably. In his lame attempt to sway my heart, he had brought up one of the darkest times in Parthalan's history, not to mention the worst day of my life.

"We have long memories in this land, Natraeus," I continued, "apparently longer than those of our dark brethren."

He began apologizing, tripping over his words in a way I normally would have found amusing, but I had long since tired of his presence. Seeking a distraction, I scanned the gathering over his shoulder until my eyes settled on a head of dark curls. I turned away from Natraeus and requested that my attendant bring the individual forward.

"Lord Finlay," I said as the man in question approached, "I am so very happy you chose to attend." I extended my hand to the confused hunter, and as he pressed my fingers to his lips I again addressed Natraeus. "Natraeus, have you met Lord Finlay of Cadogan?" Natraeus stammered that he had not, and I proceeded to introduce my newest lord to the king of the dark fae. One of Natraeus' advisors leaned forward and whispered in his ear, and that cold, calculating look returned to the dark king's eyes.

"Forgive me, my lady, but we in Nibika have never recognized a province of Parthalan called—what was it? Caddigin?" he said smugly, deliberately mispronouncing Cadogan, but neither I nor Finlay lost our composure. Harek, however, *was throwing daggers with his eyes—and not toward Na-traeus.*

*"Natraeus, do you recall when Teg'urnan was attacked by two* mordeths *some seven winters past?" He nodded, that smirk still plastered across his face. I'd show him a smirk. "One was killed here, by my First Hunter. We tracked the other to a region in the south, called Cadogan.  Finlay's folk demonstrated exceptional bravery when the demons attacked his village, and I bestowed the title upon his father. Naturally, the lordship extends to him."*

*I gazed at Natraeus, mustering the austere calmness of a statue while my heart pounded. Of course he remembered the incident, for his legion was one of those I'd summoned to assist in the defense of Teg'urnan while Aeolmar and I were away. Conveniently, they did not manage the journey until after our return, but my blood raced for a separate reason: Harek. Not only was Finlay no lord, he was one of my hunters, whom Harek hated with his whole being. For all I knew, Harek would choose this most inopportune moment to extract his revenge and call my bluff.*

*Surprisingly, he didn't. Even more surprisingly, Natraeus offered an apology. "Of course, my lady. I meant no offense, my lord," he said to Finlay. "I was merely unfamiliar with your title." Finlay bowed his head, accepting Natraeus's apology as gracefully as any noble would, then he turned his attention back to me.*

*"About that dance you promised, my lady?" Finlay inquired, and I couldn't help but smile at my quick-witted hunter.*

*"Of course. You'll excuse us?" I asked Natraeus, but didn't wait for his reply as I took Finlay's hand. My hunter-lord led me to the center of the hall. The other dancers moved aside for us. Once he found a spot to his liking, Finlay swept me into his arms, and for a man who'd grown up sorting portraits and used windmill parts, he was as graceful as a cob on a still pond.*

*"You dance very well," I said after a few moments.*

"I wouldn't have asked you to dance if I couldn't," he quipped. "Now that I'm a lord, will I often be called upon to rescue you from unwanted suitors?"

"Thank you, for playing along with my ruse." While he said nothing, his blue eyes searched for an explanation, so I continued, "Natraeus is of a mind to join Nibika and Parthalan and had the audacity to suggest that I take him as a mate." I laughed mirthlessly. "Conveniently, his veins are full to bursting with royal blood, while mine have none."

"Does that matter?" There was a turn in the dance, and I let Finlay lead me through the maneuver before I replied.

"There are those who think that one with royal blood should sit upon the throne." A small enclave in the west was administered by remaining descendants of Parthalan's original royal family. Long ago they'd been ousted, a side effect of the beheading of their father, King Markham. Then that usurper king allowed Teg'urnan to be overrun by demons, and Sahlgren drove the demons back to the underworld and beheaded the beheader. He reigned for three millennia—until I beheaded him.

When I'd first been crowned, there had been much talk of me choosing Avinor, Markham's only surviving son, as a mate. That talk had been deafening until Harek proclaimed that since my mate had been killed during the Battle for Teg'urnan I couldn't be expected to take another, royal or otherwise, for quite some time. I longed for the days when my Prelate defended me. "Even a royal blooded mate would lend legitimacy."

"You have reigned for eight centuries, surely no one would question you now. And," Finlay added, his voice softening, "your people adore you."

"Do they?" I tried not to sound like a pathetic, pitiable woman, but I doubt I succeeded.

Finlay, however, was kind enough to overlook my whining. "Surely, we do. You're our savior, our beautiful queen who killed the one who would enslave us all, and sent the demons back to the underworld. How could we not love you?"

*I laughed at his compliments, but felt my cheeks flush nonetheless. Finlay seemed to worry that he had embarrassed me, but I didn't protest as he gathered me against him. "You do look lovely, my lady."*

*"Would you like to know a secret?" I asked, and he nodded. "I absolutely hate this dress. I hate the color, I hate the fabric, and it's laced so tightly I can hardly breathe."*

*"Then why ever are you wearing it?" he inquired. Men have a difficult time understanding the lengths women go to in the name of fashion.*

*"The Lady of Thurnda sent it for me," I said with a strangled sigh. As I said, breathing while wearing a corset is an art I've never learned. "Actually she sent several, but this is by far the worst. Each and every one of them is horrible, all dreary colors and heavy fabrics, but I wanted to wear one before her people to show my appreciation for her gifts." I decided against mentioning that Aeolmar had selected this gown, and why. Instead, I traced the blood red embroidery along the collar of Finlay's gray tunic. "Of course, it does match your finery quite well."*

*"If you'd like, I will tell Natraeus we planned it," he offered, and I laughed again. Thanks to the corset, my laughter quickly became a cough, and Finlay discreetly shielded me while I composed myself. I couldn't remember the last time I laughed with such abandon. It must have driven Harek insane to see me so happy with a lowly hunter such as Finlay. "No matter why you wore it or how much you dislike it, you wear the gown well."*

*The song ended, as they all do eventually, and the musicians took their allotted respite. Still playing the part of a southern lord, Finlay bowed low. When he straightened, he led me to the far side of the hall rather than my dais. A quick glance over my shoulder told me why; the entire retinue of the dark fae and Harek (who heretofore could not stand the mention of the dark fae, but here he was commiserating with them) loitered about my throne.*

*My gallant companion obtained some water at my request; normally I would have requested wine, but with Natraeus skulking about my palace I wanted full use of my faculties. "Thank you," I said when he handed me the goblet.*

*"Of course, my lady," he replied, understanding that my gratitude encompassed more than a cool beverage. We stood together for a moment, idly chattering on about this or that, when a small detail of Finlay's appearance came to my attention.*

*"May I ask what is so amusing?" Finlay asked when I smiled.*

*"Oh, it's nothing. I just hadn't realized that you're shorter than me," I replied with a grin I knew was mischievous.*

*"I am not," he disputed, his voice loud enough to garner a few looks in our direction. You would think I'd called him a desert rat. "If there is any height difference at all, it's due to your shoes," he added firmly and went on about the thick-soled boots women wore in Cadogan. I set down my goblet and lifted the hem of my skirts, revealing the thin slippers I wore. Finlay continued to insist that my shoes were the culprit, until I had had enough and beckoned him to follow me to the rear of the hall, where benches were scattered about for the revelers to rest between dances. Once we were alone in a curtained alcove, I kicked off my slippers and looked pointedly at his boots.*

*"Off with them," I insisted, "we will settle this now." With a minimum of grumbling, Finlay removed his boots and stood barefoot before me. I stepped up to him, so close my billowing velvet monstrosity—oh, I mean my lovely elfin dress—brushed against his chest, and made a point of looking down at him. "You see?" I said innocently.*

*"If you are taller, it's by an eyebrow's width, no more," he stated, and my hand flew to my mouth, hiding my laughter at his indignant tone. That wasn't the best idea, since Finlay noticed how I wobbled. He grabbed a handful of my skirts and yanked them up, revealing that I was balanced on my toes.*

"The queen has been caught in a lie!" he declared as we laughed together. I truly lost my balance and grasped Finlay's arms in order to steady myself. "I should bring this matter to the court's attention."

"You cannot! It's treason to accuse me without proof," I said as I gazed into his eyes. I had never noticed what a bright, playful blue they were. Not the deep, hypnotic blue of Aeolmar's eyes, but they held me nonetheless. "What will you do, stand there and present my shoes as evidence?"

"If I need to," he replied. He caressed my cheek, then drew a tendril of my hair through his fingers; while we danced, I had shared that I'd worn my hair up for the event because Natraeus proclaimed, loudly and often, that he disliked such a style on women. Finlay commented that not only did my up-swept hair aggravate my suitor, but the southern noblewomen wore their hair in a similar manner, thus making the style an excellent choice. And, he said almost without blushing, he found it pleasing, as well.

I could only imagine the successes Finlay had enjoyed with the ladies of Cadogan.

As Finlay's fingers gently brushed against my skin, my breath caught in my throat as it hadn't since my all too brief time with Lormac. I moved closer to my hunter, so close I could feel the heat of his body, but before anything progressed we were interrupted by the noise of a few drunken revelers clamoring around in the alcove abutting ours. Finlay moved a respectable distance from me before taking a seat on our bench, then donned his boots.

I watched him for a moment, trying to make sense of my racing pulse, then decided that the pounding in my breast was nothing more than the result of being startled. I sat next to Finlay with the intent of replacing my slippers, but before I could, he knelt before me.

"May I?" he asked as he took my bare foot; I nodded, and he gently replaced the slippers on my feet, then stood and offered *his arm. "Come along, my lady queen, and I'll return you to your feast."*

*"Perhaps you'll favor me with another dance."*

*There was that flush again. "Perhaps."*

# Chapter Twenty-One

Aeolmar at last entered the great hall, impressed with himself that he'd arrived before midnight. Still, he bore a scowl on his face, for he hated crowds nearly as much as he hated demons. But he had promised Asherah that he would attend, and he was loath to break any promise to his queen. Further, he knew he had hurt her yesterday with his thoughtless words and resolved that he would be her attentive companion as penance for his terrible behavior.

He strode directly toward the queen's dais but halted when he saw those that blocked his path. The repugnant king of the dark fae was lurking around the base, attempting to engage the Prelate in conversation. Aeolmar spun on his heel, hoping that neither of them noticed him, and caught a glimpse of pale hair across the hall. He walked quickly toward Asherah, then stopped as if mired in mud when he saw her take another's arm.

Finlay's arm.

He watched how his second leaned close to whisper in her ear, Asherah's easy smile as she let him lead her in what must not have been their first dance. Aeolmar watched the pair for another moment, then turned away in a hasty retreat. As he left the hall and the revelry behind, he felt sorrow wrap its cold fingers about his heart. He knew well the sort of looks exchanged between Asherah and Finlay, for it was the way he'd once gazed at Ishlia across the bathing pool, the way Asherah looked at him. Aeolmar had always known that his time with Asherah would end, but he had never expected to feel the loss of her so deeply.

*I am going to have to let her go.*

***

Harek stood before the dais as if he were on guard duty, determined to hold his ground until Natraeus left. He was well aware that Natraeus wanted to be the man who walked Asherah up the carpeted steps, and Harek would kill the bastard before that came to pass. It should be the Prelate who escorts the queen to her throne, not the pathetic spawn of men too weak to hold their lands.

The Prelate paced across one corner of the dais, while Natraeus paced at the other. Harek's blood boiled while he watched Asherah, laughing away as if she enjoyed dancing with the boy hunter. All that kept him from losing his temper was Natraeus's growing agitation over the queen's conspicuous absence from her throne. That, he liked.

Then Asherah led Finlay to the rear of the hall, and Harek's heart nearly burst. He knew all too well what went on in those alcoves, and for Asherah to bring a man *there* was almost more than he could bear. A quick gesture sent one of his men after the queen; while the *con'dehr* disappeared among the dancers, Natraeus appeared at Harek's elbow.

"Will she return to her throne?" Natraeus demanded. "Or is she intent upon making a fool of me?"

"You worry that the queen will paint you as the fool? You're accomplishing that quite well on your own," Harek snapped.

"What makes you think that Asherah would choose you as a mate?"

"Oh, I care not about that," Natraeus said offhandedly. "What I really want is to crush the elves."

Harek's eyes darted to Natraeus; he wanted to crush the elves as well. Indeed, he'd wanted it for a very, very long time. "Then, what of the queen?"

"She'll do, as a mate for the king," Natraeus said with a shrug, then he eyed Harek appraisingly. "My mate. There will, of course, be a lucrative position for you in our kingdom."

The *con'dehr* returned and quietly advised Harek that the queen and her hunter only tarried within the alcove for a moment and were once more dancing along with the rest. Harek tried not to let his relief show on his face, but Natraeus wasn't the fool others thought he was.

"Perhaps you'd like to find a mate for yourself?" Natraeus suggested. "I prize loyalty above all else, and I reward my men well." Harek watched Natraeus for long moments, weighing what the dark king had offered. With the elves gone, he could finally expedite the plans he'd made long, long ago. Natraeus didn't need to know that those plans included his removal, as well.

"Thank you, my lord," Harek said, turning to watch the revelers once more. "I look forward to your generosity."

***

Finlay politely ignored the queen's first yawn, and the second, but when she stifled the third he offered her his arm.

"There's no need for you to remain until dawn," Finlay said when she protested. "Let the rest them drink the night away in your name, and we'll have the luxury of clear heads in the morning."

Asherah smiled as she tucked her hand against his elbow, her smile widening when they passed Natraeus and the Prelate; neither party appeared pleased to see the two walking arm in arm. Asherah leaned against Finlay's shoulder as they traversed the near-empty corridors, and murmured that she could not remember the last time she had so enjoyed herself.

"You were a wonderful companion," Asherah told him once they reached her door. "Thank you, for being so kind to me." She placed her hand on his forearm, a simple gesture of affection that made Finlay's heart beat like a hummingbird's wings.

"It was my pleasure, my lady queen," he replied with a shallow bow.

"Please, when we are alone call me Asherah," she said. "Even after all this time, I am still not comfortable with titles and formality."

"As you wish, Asherah." Despite his informal words, Finlay bowed low and pressed her hand to his lips as he bid her good night, then wisely took his leave before he said anything foolish. He looked over his shoulder just once to see the queen watching him, and wondered what he would have done had she asked him to stay.

# Chapter Twenty-Two

## Asherah Speaks

*By the time I'd gotten that velvet and lace prison off my body, I was panting and bloodied as if I'd been in battle. Yes, bloodied; for some unfathomable reason elfin lace is stiffened to create intricate layers of frills and ruffs. This process not only allows the lace to hold its shape, it makes an otherwise soft fabric gritty and rough. As a result, I now bore a series of welts that mirrored the edging of that gray sheath along my wrists and breast; they were a lovely compliment to the scars that already marred my skin. Again, I wondered if Sibeal hated me.*

*After throwing the mess of it to the floor (it only narrowly avoided the fire), I sank into my waiting bath and promptly fell asleep. Cydia must have been smiling upon her wayward daughter since I didn't drown, but I did feel foolish when Attia woke me in the long-cooled water—and even more foolish when I learned that it was nearing first dawn. My teeth chattered as I dried myself while Attia scolded me, but when I spied the silk slippers I'd worn at the jubilee, I remembered dancing in Finlay's arms, and afterward when we were alone in the alcove. The memories warmed me somewhat, and I must admit, he had been an excellent companion.*

At least the Second Hunter danced with his queen. *I was still somewhat perturbed by Aeolmar's lack of presence at my jubilee and his absence from my chamber afterward. Honestly, what if I had drowned? Really, he should have checked on me, if for no other reason than to save me from myself.*

*Once dry, Attia selected a lovely pale green gown for me to wear, but last night's velvets had put me off dressing like a lady. Instead, I donned my favorite riding gear. Then I remembered I was to see Natraeus and his retinue off at noon. Likely, not only the dark king would have a few unkind words over me wearing what they considered man's attire, never mind that I'd worn leggings and sturdy boots while I'd quested to spare Parthalan from becoming a nation of slaves. How soon they forget.*

*Well, since I was already dressed for it, I decided to go riding and spare myself the trouble of dealing with Natraeus and his fool notions. And, since Aeolmar had abandoned me the night before, handling Natraeus without me would also serve at his punishment. I quickly scratched a note addressed to my First Hunter and entrusted it to Attia, my willing accomplice in all schemes. My* saffira-nell *assembled me a lunch fit for travelling, and I packed it and some maps before I slipped out of my chamber toward the stable.*

*And stopped. Why should I ride alone? Cannot the Faerie Queen find a worthy companion to while away the morning with her? I debated waking Innetha, since she was always game for an adventure, but the memory of Finlay's warm arms had me again. Smiling, I made my way to the Second Hunter's chambers. I liked the thought of waking him.*

# Chapter Twenty-Three

In spite of the late hours he kept the prior evening, Finlay was awake long before the elder sun rose. He hadn't really slept at all, but rather lay in the furs remembering Asherah's graceful form, how she had fit so well in his arms, her playful grin, and the way she teased him about his height.

As a result, he dressed while the sky was still dark and busied himself with sharpening his large collection of daggers. During the winters he'd guarded pilgrims as they travelled amongst the desert temples, he had amassed quite the assortment. It was customary for the pilgrims to offer small tokens to those who helped them along their journey, and most assumed that a dagger was the ideal gift for a guard. They had come in handy more often than not.

Finlay had just laid out the blades laid when he heard a knock at his door. A glance toward his lone window told him that the child sun hadn't risen, and he couldn't imagine who would need him at such an early hour. He was further confounded when he opened the door, and found the queen waiting for him wearing not one of her usual elegant gowns, but in simple green riding gear. While Finlay believed that she would look lovely in anything from cloth-of-gold to a repurposed flour sack, the sight of Asherah in that close fitting tunic and leggings made his heart beat somewhat faster.

"Is something wrong?" Finlay inquired, forgetting his manners along with a proper greeting.

"Not at all," she replied, nonplussed. There was that grin again, full of mischief and proof that Asherah was already divining myriad ways to tease him. "After last evening's revelry, I'd like go riding and clear my head. I hoped you would join me."

"You require an escort, then?" he asked.

"I can assure you, I need no escort. You do recall the demons I killed in Cadogan?" Asherah asked, her eyes glinting. Finlay smiled ruefully, for he remembered well the beautiful warrior maiden that had saved him, and how that warrior maiden had turned out to be the Queen of Parthalan. "I would, however, enjoy your company."

Finlay stared at her for a moment, hardly believing his ears. When he'd arrived in Teg'urnan, he'd resolved that he would be happy to serve the queen in any manner she saw fit, be it as a hunter or vegetable peeler. Not only had he been named a hunter, now the woman he had so adored for the past seven winters had come to him, wanting his companionship. "Then I am honored, my lady."

Asherah's smile widened. "Good. Well, let's be off."

They made their way to the royal stables, which bustled with activity despite the early hour. Asherah, ever practical, suggested they saddle the horses themselves rather than wake a groom. Finlay agreed, until he realized that the queen meant to saddle her own horse.

"Absolutely not," he said for the third time.

"Finlay, I'm more than capable of saddling a horse," she insisted.

"Of that I have no doubt, but I'll still do it for you." Asherah crossed her arms over her chest and glared at Finlay. "How would it reflect upon Cadogan if I, its newest lord, let my queen prepare her own horse?"

Asherah's mouth quirked, and Finlay hoped he had won her over.

"I will allow you to do this, on one condition," she stated.

"Name it, my lady queen," Finlay said as he tightened the cinch.

"Call me Asherah, and nothing else."

Finlay glanced over his shoulder; Asherah stood with her arms folded across her breast, but there was laughter in her black eyes.

"As you wish, my—" Finlay caught himself, his ears coloring. "Asherah," he finished, handing her the reins.

"My Asherah," she said as she swung herself onto the saddle. "That, I like."

Finlay hoped she would ignore his obvious embarrassment as he mounted up and followed the queen—no, *his* Asherah—as they rode away from the stable. They left off conversation as they made their way to the gates; Finlay had no idea what to say to her, anyway. As soon as they passed beneath the statues of the stag and doe, eternally leaping toward each other above Teg'urnan's gates, Asherah urged her horse to a trot.

"Race?" Asherah asked.

Finlay grinned. "You'll never catch me."

With that Finlay galloped ahead, Asherah laughing as she followed. They skirted the base of the eastern foothills, alternately racing and giving chase to one another, and ultimately came to rest upon the Hill of Torim. By then, the elder sun was high in the eastern sky and the child sun hurried to catch him.

"Shall we rest a while?" Asherah asked.

"An excellent idea," Finlay said. He quickly dismounted and stood ready to help the queen from her saddle, though he resisted offering to unsaddle her horse. Once the horses received a quick rubdown, the queen and her hunter reclined in the tall grass, still holding on to its green in protest of the coming cold.

"This is one of my favorite spots in all of Parthalan," Asherah said as she lay back, nearly hidden among the tall blades, and gazed wistfully toward the crest of the hill. "The last time I spoke to Torim was here, as she lay dying in my arms." She fell silent, her face turned away from Finlay. "It was the night before we took Teg'urnan. I wanted her to remain with me, but she wanted me to have time alone with Lormac... And then she sacrificed herself for me, even after I'd forsaken her. She was so happy when Lormac and I were mated... She spoke often of wanting me to have a mate, someone to help me in the days ahead. I've always wondered if she knew that she was going to die that day." Asherah lay on her back and watched the clouds scurrying across the sky.

"Do you see her face?" Finlay asked. "In the clouds?"

"I wish I did," she replied.

"It seems that everyone tries to obtain a king for you, whether you'd like one or no," Finlay commented.

"She was always worried for me," Asherah murmured. "On that night, she worried that I would find the burden of ruling too great. How she knew that I would rule, I have never understood...ah, gods." The grass rustled as Asherah shifted and rubbed her eyes.

"When you say that you wanted her to remain with you, what do you mean?" Finlay asked carefully. Asherah rolled onto her side and waited for Finlay to look at her before she replied.

"You're asking if she was my lover?" she countered.

"Forgive me for prying," Finlay began, but Asherah waved his words away.

"Know this: you are my hunter and may ask me anything," Asherah said. "Whether I choose to answer is another thing all together, but you may ask what you will."

"Thank you," Finlay said; to be given leave to ask the Queen of Parthalan whatever one wanted to know was a great honor, indeed. "All the stories claim that she was your companion, nothing more."

"Oh, she was so much more than my companion," Asherah said. "Torim was everything. When we were slaves, we shared a cell in the *doja*, and we fought our way out together. You know, I only hatched that mad escape plan to keep the demons from harming Torim."

"You did?" Finlay asked, and Asherah nodded. "Then it seems that every faerie and elf owes her a debt of gratitude."

"I've always felt that way," Asherah said with a smile. "So she was my cellmate, my first and sometimes only companion. I loved her in a way that defied all sense and reason, and I spent every night in her arms. Well, every night until Lormac went and put the Sala on me. Funny, Torim once made me promise to never forsake her, yet she all but pushed me into his bed."

"Pushed into a king's bed." Finlay shook his head. Many women had suffered far worse fates. "He was the Lord of Tingu, yes?"

"Yes," Asherah answered as she closed her eyes. "I can still see his merry eyes, his craggy brow that was so like a mountainside. Lormac would have made a wonderful King of Parthalan," she continued quietly. "He had ruled for many, many winters in the north, and if it wasn't for his aid, I don't know if we would have prevailed over Sahlgren."

"You loved him a great deal, didn't you?" Finlay asked softly.

"Yes, I did. I still do. But then he died, as do all that I love." Asherah laughed shortly, and went on, "And so I've become the Virgin Queen of Parthalan, long may I reign!"

"In all this time, you've found no one else who could be your king?" Finlay asked.

Asherah's mirthless laughter spoke of her loneliness, even if her words did not. "I cannot take a king, not this late in my reign. It would be seen as a weakness, or so Harek has advised me, time and again."

Finlay moved to lie on his stomach and absently tore at the grass. "You take his counsel in matters of the heart?"

Asherah wiggled toward him through the tall grass and was nearly nose to nose with her hunter as she said, "Most think the Prelate is devoid of a heart, among other things." Her companion grinned. "Are you hungry? Attia prepared a lunch."

"In the saddlebag?" Finlay asked. "Or satchel?"

"I'll get it," Asherah said, but Finlay leapt in front of her.

"Please, let me." She did, and Finlay grabbed the satchel and brought it to Asherah. Carefully stowed within the satchel was a wineskin, a loaf of bread, and hunk of hard cheese, along with several maps. "Do you always take so many maps with you?"

"I enjoy reading maps," she replied, selecting a scroll and spreading it across the ground. She fished around in her belt pouch for rock, and used them to weigh down the corners. "I'd intended to ride alone today. Sometimes, I find myself a quiet spot to go over them." Finlay offered her the wineskin and sat next to her as he looked over the map.

"So, what are we looking for?" he asked.

"Something familiar." Finlay's quizzical expression asked for an explanation, and she obliged. "Once I freed myself from the *doja*, I realized that I don't know where I'm from, or anything about my kin. My earliest memory is of waking in my cell next to Torim."

"Your captors took your memory?" Finlay asked. In the many tales he'd heard of Asherah, none hinted at this most unusual of afflictions. And for one with no memory to go on to lead Parthalan... Finlay shook his head; the more he learned about Asherah, the more she amazed him.

"They did. If I concentrate very hard, I can remember the *mordeth* bursting through a door and grabbing me..." Her voice trailed off as she squeezed her eyes shut, as if squinting at the past would allow her to catch a few errant details. Her hand moved to massage her temple, and without realizing his action, Finlay reached out and caressed her cheek. Asherah turned toward his open palm, and covered his hand with her own.

"Don't," he said, "not if it's painful for you." He withdrew his hand, for no matter how he addressed her, touching the queen's cheek was much too forward of a gesture. Asherah, however, didn't seem to be of a mind to break contact and replaced her hand on his. Finlay gave her fingers a gentle squeeze as he returned his attention to the map. "Have you found any place familiar yet?"

"No. For the last eight centuries, my true past has eluded me. Oh, many have claimed to be my kith and kin, but if I were to believe each of them I would have eight mothers and a score of fathers." Asherah laughed shortly, then recounted the tale of a man who came forward claiming to be her promised mate. She hadn't believed him either, but for daring such a ruse she'd denounced him before all of Teg'urnan as the man who left his love to rot with monsters. Once the impostor had been well and truly humiliated, Harek had sent him on his way.

"All this time and nothing?" Finlay said. "How could no one have come forward?"

Asherah squeezed his hand a bit tighter. "I'm nothing if not stubborn. I will yet discover my past." She tore off a portion of bread, then pulled the satchel toward her. "Did Attia really not pack any fruit?" she mumbled as she rummaged within.

Finlay left Asherah to her search and thumbed through the maps. He unrolled one, only to shake his head and select another scroll. The second was a map of the southern region, and Asherah watched as Finlay traced a route with his finger; once he found the area he sought, he beckoned Asherah to look as well.

"There's a temple in the High Desert, here, about a day's ride north of the sea, which shares your name." Asherah leaned forward, but there was no notation on the map. Finlay had an excellent memory, though he'd been to the temple only once. "Actually, it isn't really a temple, since no priest resides there. It's more a simple desert shrine."

"It shares my name?" she asked.

"Yes, it's dedicated to one of the old gods, *Ish h'ra*, 'she who delivers from evil.'" Asherah brushed her slender fingers over the blank spot on the map.

"Is it?" Asherah breathed as long-forgotten memories flickered across her dark eyes. She recounted to Finlay how Torim had always told stories of *Ish h'ra* the Deliverer. Ultimately, Torim had renamed her Asherah once she led their escape from the *doja*.

"It's really dedicated to *Ish h'ra*?" she asked again. "How is it I've never known of this?"

"Only one who's familiar with the area would know its dedication. *Ish h'ra* isn't worshipped as widely as she once was." Finlay watched her for a moment, enjoying the fascination and wonderment that played across her features. "Maybe you're of the south, as I am."

"'Of the south,'" Asherah repeated. "Even if I wasn't raised in the south, perhaps Torim was from the desert. She was dark-skinned, like you, and she always did hate the cold." Asherah looked up from the map and fixed Finlay in her dark gaze. "Finlay, you do not know the value of what you have given me."

He flushed, and said, "It's a location on a map, nothing more."

Asherah took his hands. "No, it's hope, and believe me when I say that hope is priceless." She smiled at him, gratitude shining from her dark eyes, and he returned it with a grin of his own.

"If you'd like, I can take you there," he offered. "The way is long, but not difficult."

"You've seen it?" she asked.

"I have," he affirmed. "I've stood within it."

"What does it look like?"

"Wide pillars carved from the local sandstone and a pink granite floor. There's no roof, but the whole of it lies open to the sky," he recounted. "Once, there was a statue of the *Ish h'ra*, but it was lost long ago."

"It sounds lovely," she breathed.

*Not nearly as lovely as you.* "It is."

"And, you will be my guide?" she asked, her eyes wide and beseeching.

*Have I really made her so happy?* "Of course."

"Then I am honored to accept your offer." Asherah smiled brightly as she gazed at him, and Finlay realized that while he had lost his heart to this pale beauty seven winter's past, he had loved her only for her appealing form. Now, as they sat together upon the windswept hill, Finlay learned that she was kind and witty, the sort of woman who attracted a man with her face but held him with her sharp mind and open, loving heart. He debated if he should say as much but was interrupted by the clatter of Teg'urnan's gates as they were drawn back.

"Come," Asherah said, beckoning Finlay to the crest of the hill. Once there, they lay on their stomachs and watched Natraeus' retinue as the dark fae left Teg'urnan.

"You went riding to avoid him," Finlay accused.

Asherah looked over her shoulder, a conspiratorial smile on her lips. "What if I did? Harek and Aeolmar are more than able to deal with Natraeus, and they both despise him. With any luck, they've thoroughly dissuaded him from ever returning."

Finlay shook his head, then he rose and extended a hand to Asherah. "All right, my lady Asherah. Now that the bad man's gone, I'll escort you back to the palace."

"So soon?" she asked. Finlay blinked, and Asherah continued, "The day is young, and I've only talked about myself. I want to hear about you."

"Why ever would you want to hear about me?"

"Why ever not?" Asherah countered.

"I'm afraid my life hasn't been all that interesting," Finlay said with a sigh. He considered the many winters he had spent compiling inventories in the back room of the shop, the careful purchase records he had maintained, the stacks of coins that went unspent, since in Cadogan his family already had everything worth having. Never once had he complained, never had he wanted anything more—not until a host of demons attacked his village and he met his warrior maiden.

"Let me be the judge of that," Asherah said with that smile of hers, that smile that had made Finlay relinquish his quiet existence and hunt down demons in her name. Thus emboldened, he bowed with a flourish and extended his arm. Asherah laughed as she tucked her hand in the crook of his elbow and he led her back to their maps. As they passed the wineskin between them Finlay regaled the queen with his stories of a dusty shop on the edge of a desert.

What neither queen nor hunter saw was the Prelate as he departed from Teg'urnan and galloped after the dark fae.

# Chapter Twenty-Four

"You are certain of this?" Natraeus asked Harek. He and his retinue had sequestered themselves at the edge of the plain behind the tree line, far out of Teg'urnan's view, to await the Prelate's arrival. Some things, Harek had suggested, were best discussed outside the palace walls.

"Of course I am," snapped Harek. "You think I don't know all of Parthalan's nobility? The boy is nothing; he has no land or name to speak of. He is nothing to Asherah."

"Good," said Natraeus. "To think, when Nibika is at last united with Parthalan, we fae will finally have the lands and power we deserve. Then we will crush the elves and make them suffer for our long subjugation."

"You will," Harek lied. In truth, he was bored with Natraeus' posturing and irrational hatred of the elves. A prior Lord of Tingu had conquered them, yes, but the fault lay with the dark fae for being weaker than their foes. Now, instead of strengthening their legion and attempting to wrest control back from the elves on the battlefield as a warrior should, Natraeus had resorted to the pathetic plan of convincing Asherah first to become his mate, then to war against the elves. Anyone could see that such a plan would never succeed, mainly because

Asherah would destroy anything that threatened Leran with her bare hands. But then, Natraeus was nothing if not a fool.

"Continue your pursuit of the queen," Harek went on; one of the first things he had learned as Prelate was that those in power preferred hearing agreement to their outlandish plans rather than the truth of the matter. "Asherah is lonely and has been too long without a mate. She will come to you, of that I am certain."

"What of the hunter?" Natraeus pressed. "She looks to be bedding him."

"He's nothing," Harek assured. "A night's diversion, nothing more."

Natraeus grunted. "I don't like the concept of my future mate rutting like a common whore. I want her free of such filth."

"She is loyal," Harek stated. "Once you've claimed her, she will not waver. On that, you have my word."

Harek returned to Teg'urnan shortly afterward, plans and conspiracies swirling about his mind. He knew not if Asherah had any interest in that young upstart from Cadogan, nor did he care. Even since the Battle of Esguth, Asherah had disregarded Harek's wise counsel and started doing things on her own. No, it was much worse, because she was doing them with Aeolmar.

The Prelate bristled as he thought of this latest First Hunter, and how he'd worked his way into Asherah's affections. Of the four men who had held the position of First Hunter of Parthalan, he liked Aeolmar the least. Aeolmar cared nothing for Harek's authority as Prelate and was loyal to the queen to the point of death. On the few occasions Harek had attempted to sway him from the queen's agenda, Aeolmar had scoffed and then reminded Harek that while the Prelate may outrank him, he only took direction from Asherah herself. Aeolmar's stubbornness and outright lack of protocol made Harek long for Argent in a way he never thought he would.

*Argent, now there was a man I could work with.* Argent had cared for nothing save the adoration of the masses, and once Harek had promised him both wealth and notoriety, he had easily bent to the Prelate's will. Harek had noticed Asherah's near instant attraction to Argent, and had used it to his advantage when he'd suggested that Argent be named as the next First Hunter.

After a time, Harek had learned that Asherah had slept with Argent not just once but many times, and try as he might Harek could not ignore the dull ache in his heart, born of Asherah choosing someone else yet again. Then she had begun to have that happy glow about her... that happy glow that Harek was never the cause of.

No matter. Harek had removed Asherah's lovers in the past, and while he hadn't disliked Argent as a man, he could not have someone else supplanting him in the queen's heart. It had taken him longer than he'd anticipated, engineering the Battle of Esguth so soon after faking his brother's death. Nor had Harek meant for so many to perish, certainly not his soldiers and the *nuvi*, but the demons had accomplished their goal. By all accounts Esguth had done exactly what he'd been hired to do, kill Argent while the queen looked on, helpless to save her lover.

Of course, that was the only aspect of the battle that had gone as planned. Harek hadn't anticipated that Esguth would seek aid from a fellow *mordeth*, and Mersgoth at that. Not to mention that the demons had descended upon Teg'urnan a full sennight earlier than agreed, days before Harek and his *con'dehr* had been due to return from the south. The whole point of the attack had been for Harek to be there by Asherah's side, and he hadn't been. Argent's death had been meant to affect Asherah so deeply that she would turn to Harek for comfort and realize that only her Prelate had always been there for her, only he could care for her.

But no, that damned Aeolmar had not only managed to kill Esguth but *he* comforted the queen in her sorrow, *he* was named First Hunter before Harek and the *con'dehr* had even returned to the palace. Never had Asherah bestowed a title on someone without first consulting with him, and that wasn't the end of Aeolmar's influence upon the queen. He encouraged her to follow her own ideas, to make decisions without her loyal Prelate's input; why, their late night conversations before the hearth never happened anymore. In fact, the last time Harek had seen Asherah alone was that night shortly after Argent's death when she threw him out of her garden.

Worse yet, Harek suspected that Aeolmar's comfort of Asherah went far beyond a shoulder to cry on. Asherah had never directly named Aeolmar as her lover, but the two spent a great deal of time together. They were often seen in one another's company as night fell and again at morning's first light. Also, Asherah had specifically told Harek that she'd had the door to her private room charmed, and that it now opened for the queen and her First Hunter alone. Why would Aeolmar need an exclusive entry to Asherah's private world unless he was rogering her?

Harek set his jaw as he passed through the palace gates; out of habit he looked upward to Asherah's balcony and saw Aeolmar standing there. He hated the First Hunter, hated him with every fiber of his being, but still he nodded an acknowledgement to the man. His plans had not worked out in the past because they had been too rigid, not allowing for unforeseen details, but he had thought of everything this time.

If Natraeus managed to win Asherah's heart, Harek would kill him within the palace, though Harek sincerely doubted that this would come to pass; Asherah may be bedding the hunter, but she had more than enough sense to reject the dark fae. More likely, Natraeus would be so incensed over Asherah's refusal that he would go to war in order to claim Parthalan for the dark fae, and Harek would kill him on the battlefield. He hoped the latter plan came to pass, since he could arrange Aeolmar's death at the same time. It would be easy enough in the heat of battle, just like he had killed Lormac so long ago.

Harek laughed deep in his chest, remembering the Lord of Tingu's face as he'd looked down at Harek's sword lodged in his gut. *By the man he'd called pathetic, no less.* He'd called out to Asherah at the end, but she hadn't heard him and the elf died alone. Harek had always seen that as incontrovertible proof that Lormac was not Asherah's true mate and that she belonged with Harek. Obviously, the gods had put them together for a reason.

The Prelate entered his chamber with a satisfied smile on his face, pleased with the day's events. Whichever way Natraeus and Aeolmar happened to die, Asherah would again see Harek as her staunchest ally, her closest companion, her greatest friend. Soon, Aeolmar would be out of his life, the dark fae would crumble, and Asherah would realize that while her meaningless lovers had come and gone, Harek had always been there for her and always would.

*Then, she will be mine.*

# Chapter Twenty-Five

The elder sun had reached his apex long before Asherah mentioned that they should return to Teg'urnan. She hated to do so, for she found her conversation with Finlay far more entertaining than the court business awaiting her attention. Once the horses were put up and Asherah and Finlay parted ways, the queen returned to her chambers alone. She entered her rooms via her private entrance and found Aeolmar lounging on her bed.

"The hunter who abandoned his queen has returned," she said with a wry smile. "I wore that hideous red dress, *for you,* and you didn't even bother to show up." Aeolmar chuckled at her indignation, and descended from her bed. She let him fold her into his arms and kissed his throat. "It was terrible, removing that dress on my own."

"You're mistaken, my lady," Aeolmar said as he stroked her cheek. "I did arrive at your grand, crowded, loud feast, albeit very late. Finlay seemed to be doing an excellent job amusing you, so I left." He held her with his gaze, those deep blue pools that she felt she could fall into and never swim her way out of.

"He was an excellent companion," Asherah admitted.

"I thought as much," Aeolmar said. "Natraeus was quite upset that you two were so smitten with each other."

"Smitten? We were dancing," Asherah said. "Did Natraeus also mention that he brought up Sahlgren and claimed that, since our former king was of the dark fae, I should take him as my mate?"

Aeolmar's eyes narrowed. "I wish you would let me kill him," he said bitterly. "He wants nothing but to use you against the elves. Getting rid of him this morning was enjoyable. Satisfying, even." He paused just long enough to kiss her. "And where was my queen this morning? I hoped you would still have that dress on." He nuzzled her neck.

"Finlay and I went riding," she began, stopping when Aeolmar chuckled.

"Finlay, eh?" Aeolmar searched her face as he released her from his arms. "You enjoy being with him?"

"He's very nice," Asherah answered. "He's charming and easy to talk to, and... Why are you looking at me that way?"

Aeolmar's face was taken over by a knowing smile as he sat on the steps of the bed's platform. "You *are* smitten with him."

"I am not," she cried, somewhat louder that she'd intended. Asherah nestled herself on Aeolmar's lap and twisted her fingers in his hair. "I'm not," she repeated, much softer than before. "I have you."

"Ah, *rihka*, you should be with someone like him, a man who can love you properly."

"You do love me properly," she insisted, but he touched his fingers to her lips.

"*Rihka,* Finlay adores you." Aeolmar stroked her lower lip with his thumb. "I see it every time he looks at you."

"He does?" she asked, surprising herself with her curiosity.

"He does." Aeolmar held her for a time before he continued. "Asherah, I want you to be happy, and you won't be until you find the sort of man you deserve. What if Finlay is that man?" Her protests continued, and she cited reason after reason why she wouldn't pursue anything with Finlay. When she paused, Aeolmar asked, "Don't you want someone to call you *nalla*?"

"I do." She dropped her gaze from his. Asherah was quite fond of Finlay, that much she was willing to admit, and in other circumstances would not be averse to exploring a relationship with him. However, she was afraid to leave behind the comfort and security of Aeolmar.

"What if he isn't that man?" she asked. "What if he wants nothing to do with me? Then I'll be alone again."

"I'm not going anywhere." When she refused to look at him, he gently tilted her face upward. "I will always be here for you, no matter what. Remember, I can't lose you."

"But you can push me toward another. What if you're wrong? What if Finlay doesn't feel anything for me and you find someone else in the meantime?"

Aeolmar laughed softly. "Come now, you're too wise a ruler to think that way. What sort of woman would love a miserable lout like me?"

Asherah smiled, but he was wrong; her First Hunter was nothing if not compassionate and noble—and any woman would be lucky to have him. She wished he could see that in himself. She laid her head on his shoulder, seeking whatever comfort he would give her, and asked, "Are you saying these things because you've tired of me?"

"I could never tire of you. Please don't ever think that." Aeolmar kissed the top of her head, then tucked her face against his neck. "I want nothing more than for you to be happy."

# Chapter Twenty-Six

## Asherah Speaks

*Having received an urgent message that all but demanded my presence, I made my way from the palace proper to the* sola. *It was slow going, what with denizens of Teg'urnan greeting me at every turn, and I certainly didn't want to brush past anyone. When I first took the throne I vowed to be accessible to my people, not secreted away in a tower the way Sahlgren had always been; but then, he was busily plotting our kind's destruction. I suppose one needed privacy for that.*

*Well and so, since I strove to be a good ruler, the least I could do was listen to my people's kind words. Besides, Aeolmar's message hadn't stated what was so urgent, only that my presence was required. Since he hadn't felt the need to explain himself, I didn't feel the need to rush. I was, however, more than a bit intrigued.*

*Upon reaching the* sola, *I climbed the narrow steps to the gallery that overlooked the training field. It was where* nuvi, *those training to be hunters, were taught the varied arts of war and survival and where the Trial by Combat was held each spring. The legion once trained here as well, but Harek* had moved his soldiers out as my hunters moved in. And the rift grew ever wider...

I sat upon the roughly carved bench, hoping a stray splinter wouldn't catch on my gown, and surveyed the scene below me. Assembled before the First Hunter bearing looks ranging from anxiety to unabashed terror were the sola's instructors, along with a frustrated Innetha and a rather relaxed Finlay. Aeolmar himself was stripped to the waist and had tied back his long hair, something he almost never did. He seemed to be teaching them how to work his fire-calling trick, something else he had never done, and his students were experiencing varied degrees of success. A few of the instructors had lone flames dancing upon their palms, but one bereft of both fire and good sense was arguing with Aeolmar.

"How can this be considered a weapon?" he demanded. "Demons may fear fire, but you might as well carry a flint striker for all the good these bits of flame will do."

The man had a point, but Aeolmar, stubborn as a mule, refused any concession. Instead, he turned his back to the instructor and uttered a few words in the old language. A wall of flames higher than his head sprang to life. The instructor's jaw dropped, and the others looked rather pleased at the man's suddenly wordless state.

I clapped, alerting those below to my presence. Aeolmar extinguished his fiery wall and ordered the others to keep practicing, then leapt toward me and grabbed the gallery floor where it jutted out over the field. Apparently, taking the stairs was either too long or too mundane a route for the First Hunter.

As we watched, Aeolmar swung himself up to the gallery in a feat of agility worthy of an acrobat. For anyone else, such a show of strength would be called boastful, but Aeolmar didn't boast. He was what he was, tightly coiled power that burned away inside a man's form.

"Have you decided to join a circus troupe?" I teased. "Is that why you sent such an urgent demand for my presence, *you wish to tell me you're leaving?" Aeolmar glared at me, panting to catch his breath. Indeed, he looked exhausted, his chest heaving as rivulets of sweat cascaded over hard muscle. Dearest Cydia, if this man ever realized what an appealing form he's been blessed with, we would be doomed.*

*He did catch me staring at his bare chest, and while his mouth quirked, he refrained from commenting. Too bad. I have many witty remarks about scaling walls in my repertoire. "I thought you'd like to see for yourself what your Second Hunter has wrought."*

*"Finlay?" I asked. "It looks like you're the one teaching them to call fire."*

*"I was," Aeolmar admitted, "but this was all his idea." I leaned forward, and Finlay had indeed taken over as instructor. I glanced at my sweaty hunter, and an explanation followed. "He claims that you were receptive to his opinion that the* nuvi *should be tested by more than just the Trial by Combat. After a lengthy and somewhat useless debate, we've agreed to a Trial by Fire and another by Stealth."*

*"The Trial by Stealth was Innetha's contribution?" I asked.*

*Aeolmar nodded. "She isn't very good at calling fire," he said, then muttered something about using this fact as grounds for sending her back to the Northern Contingent.*

*"You complain about her much the same way Harek complains about Attia." That observation earned me a glare so scathing I nearly winced. "Does she merely need additional instruction?" I inquired, changing the subject so he'd stop glaring at me.*

*"It's her blood," Aeolmar said simply. When I stared at him, he realized that I'd no idea what he was talking about. "Fae are born of gods, and we have a measure of their power. Innetha is not a faerie."*

*Hmm. I'd never thought about that before, but it did explain why some of the instructors were having a difficult time with the spell. "What about elves?" I asked suddenly. Lormac had wielded power over earth and stone, yet he hadn't a drop faerie blood to speak of.*

*"I don't know," Aeolmar replied with a shrug. The shrug meant that he didn't like not knowing the answer and was pretending not to care. "Elves have no gods, so they must obtain their magic elsewhere."*

*"Elsewhere," I said. I examined the burning melee below and deduced that it wasn't just scaling the* sola *walls that had resulted in a sweaty and exhausted Aeolmar. Nearly everyone present had shed their jerkins and tunics, save Finlay and Innetha, though they both clearly felt the heat of the flames. Of course Innetha, her sweat-damp hair clinging to her neck, and the two other female instructors would have to remain in their tunics, but Finlay's somewhat bashful nature intrigued me.*

*"Perhaps, since he's from the desert he can tolerate heat better than the rest," Aeolmar suggested. I nodded, then realized that I'd either been rambling on about a half-dressed Finlay or Aeolmar had read my mind, and I didn't care for either situation. The claims he'd made the prior day, insisting that I should explore Finlay's unconfirmed affections for me, still rang in my mind. Ever the suspicious queen, I wondered why Aeolmar had really dragged me out to the* sola. *Before I could question my loyal First Hunter, the Second Hunter captured my attention.*

*"My lady queen!" Finlay called. I nodded an acknowledgement, and a ball of fire burst to life in his palm, followed by another, and then another. By all the gods, then he started juggling them. I wondered what sort of blood coursed through his veins.*

*I laughed aloud at the ridiculous sight before me, so much so that Finlay faltered and dropped his fireballs; well, as much one can drop a blob of mystical fire. Finlay said a few words, and they vanished, then he bowed toward me with a flourish.*

*"He's quite good," Aeolmar said, standing up while I applauded Finlay's impromptu performance. "He seems to ac-*

*complish anything he sets his mind to." I ignored the knowing glance that accompanied his words but allowed Aeolmar to help me to my feet. As he walked with me down the stairs, I cast my own appraising glance over his bare chest.*

*"Do you plan to walk about the whole of Teg'urnan in such a state?" I asked, fluttering my lashes since it annoyed him so. "Surely, you'll be mobbed by maidens and matrons alike."*

*"Eyes forward, woman," he grunted, but I saw the hint of a smile. We emerged into the blinding sunlight, made all the brighter by pockets of fire smoldering away here and there.*

*"So what will it be?" I asked the instructors and hunters as a whole. "Do we teach the* nuvi *fire, then combat and stealth? Or in a different order?"*

*"Combat should remain the first Trial," Innetha said, "since it's the most important. It's useless to sneak up on a demon if you can't manage to kill it."*

*"Agreed," I said. "And, I imagine that calling fire can be taught alongside combat. Who will teach that portion?" The instructors remained silent; I got the feeling that Innetha wasn't the only one having trouble with magic. I looked to Aeolmar, for he was certainly the most adept magic handler in Teg'urnan save the sorcerers, when Finlay spoke up.*

*"I will," he said, a bit sheepishly. "These additional Trials were my idea; it's only fair that I share in the burden of teaching." As if to lend proof to his words, he called forth a few flames to dance on his palm. I gasped at the sudden fire, then quickly composed myself. I needed to acclimate myself to the idea of my hunters sprouting flames whenever the mood struck them. More, I was going to need a few lessons on fire-calling, as well.*

*"That will be very well, Finlay," I said, pleased when he smiled. More intriguing by the moment, this man was. "Now, I want the lot of you to bathe. You all stink nearly as badly as Aeolmar."*

# Chapter Twenty-Seven

The grand hall of Teg'urnan was dark and deserted, save for a warm glow at the rear of the hall. Far from the magnificent pillars and mosaic floors that decorated the front of the palatial room, a knot of people gathered around the smaller hearth. The queen herself was in attendance, seated upon a cushioned bench between Finlay and Innetha. Aeolmar sat on the floor at Asherah's feet, staring at the fire as intently as others stared at the women behind him. Harek sat alone on a bench across from the hunters, with the *con'dehr* surrounding him on chairs they'd dragged over, for only Aeolmar liked sitting on the floor.

Olwynn approached the gathering and noted the Prelate's presence with some surprise; the smaller hearth had long been the exclusive domain of the hunters, and Harek hardly deigned to acknowledge their existence, much less sit alongside them. Of course, Asherah wasn't usually at the small hearth either, and she was likely the bait that had drawn his attention.

"What's happening here?" Olwynn asked one of his fellow *con'dehr* as he dragged a chair up to the rest.

"Harek found a northern minstrel to play for the queen," replied the man called Huon. "Apparently, it's a gift."

Olwynn nodded, his eyes traveling toward a slight man clad in the typical green and red silks of a bard, who was engrossed in tuning his lute. For as long as Olwynn or anyone could recall, Harek had done such things as procuring bards and obtaining other treasures ranging from fine silks to silken brandy in order to please Asherah, and Asherah had yet to notice any of them. Or maybe she had noticed, but she just didn't care.

*He's certainly not the sort of man a woman wants.* In fact, Olwynn had yet to see any woman show an interest in Harek, and he suspected that his rough appearance and rougher personality contributed much to the man's solitary state. The Prelate was small for a faerie, with a stocky build, small club-like hands and coarse hair that resembled a halo of dirty straw. However, within that unassuming form was a military mastermind, for Harek's skill and cunning with regard to the battlefield had garnered him more than a measure of respect throughout the nine realms.

What's more, Harek's tactical brilliance had been instrumental in bringing down the old king. Olwynn had been well and truly ensnared in Sahlgren's plot and had spent the better part of a decade under a demon's thrall, forced to do things that were... horrible. Despicable. The stuff of nightmares, agonizing and brutal, yet without the comforting anonymity of darkness. No, the demons had tormented him and others in the full light of day, each act worse than the last until Olwynn had given up his last shred of hope and had assumed that the demons would either kill him or drive him to madness. Then Harek's brother, the sorcerer Sarfek, had broken the thrall and Olwynn had been Harek's man ever since.

The bard plucked at the strings, and Olwynn's gaze travelled to Asherah. Her experience had been far worse than thrall, for she had been one of the women used nearly to the point of death. He remembered the half-wild girl he'd met all those winters ago in Tingu; any other slave would have shied away from a *doja*, but not Asherah. She not only had led the charge into the prison, she'd single-handedly captured the *mordeth*, Mersgoth, along with the heart of the elf king.

*And now, she is our queen.* Asherah felt his eyes upon her and smiled at him, and Olwynn acknowledged his ruler with a respectful nod. He understood Harek's long infatuation with the queen, for the Prelate was far from the only man who stared longingly after her. Olwynn himself had had his fair share of ruminations about a night spent in her chambers, but Asherah was rumored to prefer her hunters in all matters, and Olwynn would never be a hunter. But he was *con'dehr...* Then the minstrel strummed the lute, and Olwynn left off speculating on the sort of men admitted to the royal bedchamber.

The ballad began, as most do, with the story of Cydia, the moon goddess. The bard sang of her great beauty and of the many men, from gods to paupers, emperors and regents, who tried to claim her. Regardless if they were god or man, Cydia eluded them all and kept her virtue as her own until that fateful night when she walked upon Parthalan's soil in the guise of a doe. At length, she lay down in a green meadow, intending to rest for just a moment before returning to her celestial palace, but she was soon asleep. When Olluhm, the sun god, rose in the east he looked upon Cydia, her naked form bathed in his golden light, and loved her in that moment.

*Olluhm rose and saw her*
*Pale and lovely against the meadow green*
*And the Sun left the sky to know the Moon*
*He became a stag to her doe*
*Hart to her hind*
*And the Moon birthed a Son to the Sun*

Fearing he'd lose his audience to their chambers if he continued on with that well-known ballad on such a chill evening, the minstrel plucked a brighter cadence and launched into the tale of Solon. First born of Olluhm and Cydia, Solon took his place in the sky as the child sun behind his father, and thus Parthalan was warmed by two.

From his vantage point in the sky, Solon watched as the fae lived and thrived, but he never joined them. He preferred to accompany his father along his daily journey until the day demons returned to Parthalan. Solon watched in horror as Teg'urnan was overtaken by the foul beasts; by their very nature, faeries were a peaceful race and had not the means to stand against their foes. Solon was incensed by the defilement of Teg'urnan and descended from the skies to become the fae's first warrior. He drove the demons back to the under-world and reclaimed Teg'urnan for his people and, like his father before him, claimed the loveliest maiden in the land as his mate. She happened to be the faerie king's daughter, and Solon pledged that those of his bloodline would always serve the royal house of Parthalan. Their firstborn became the first Prelate, bound to protect the king with his life.

*Warrior, born of the Sun*
*Solon claimed the fairest maiden as his*
*And she loved him well*
*And bore a Son worthy of the Sun*

As the minstrel sang of that first Prelate's many victories, he nodded indulgently toward Harek, obviously unaware that the current Prelate could not claim descent from Solon. Harek nodded as he twisted his ring, heavy gold emblazoned with an image of the child sun. Olwynn had always speculated that Harek's insecurity over his lack of kinship to Solon caused him to have the ring made, though Harek had no reason to fret over his position. Tor, the prior Prelate and Solon's true descendant, had left Teg'urnan with his sons long ago, only a few days after Asherah had taken the throne. Not only had Tor given Harek his blessing, all three had sworn never to return.

The verse continued and described in blushing detail Solon's love for his mate. After a particularly bawdy passage, Asherah leaned forward and whispered in Aeolmar's ear; he laughed, but continued staring into the flames. Olwynn could hardly understand the man who had risen from obscurity to First Hunter in little more than ten winters and was rumored to be the queen's lover. In Olwynn's opinion, Aeolmar should be content, or at least complacent, but more often than not he was morose. Olwynn, who had survived both demons and *dojas*, hoped to never experience whatever series of events had created such a miserable, depressed man as Aeolmar.

The song changed its tone yet again, and the minstrel recounted Nibika'al's seduction of Olluhm. According to legend, the goddess of night had grown jealous of Cydia's children, being that they were fairer of both form and temperament than her own. Suspecting that Olluhm's bright glow was the cause of their lovely faces and gentle demeanors, Nibika'al conspired to lure the sun from the moon's bed. Time and again Olluhm saw through her schemes and proved faithful to his mate, but Nibika'al would not be thwarted. She slipped him a draught that confused him and put him to bed, where he hovered between wakefulness and sleep for three days and nights. While in his befuddled state, Olluhm recognized only a woman's touch and learned too late that the soft form nestled against him was not Cydia.

*So the Sun*

*Wrapped himself in the Night*

*And the Moon wept*

The draught slowly left Olluhm, and when he saw what he had done, he threw himself at Cydia's feet, swearing that Nibika'al trickery was the sole cause of his infidelity. Cydia railed at Olluhm, for there is no greater offense in all the nine realms than to leave your mate's bed for another. Olluhm tried to sway the moon's heart with song, with sweet honey fresh from the comb, and flowers gathered from the meadow where he first lay with her. At last she welcomed him into her arms once more, but then the full extent of Olluhm's betrayal was known, and Nibika'al birthed Olluhm's children.

"I've always hated this part," Asherah said. The bard faltered on the strings, since he didn't want to continue a tale that would upset the queen. Finlay leaned toward the queen, and because Olwynn was seated closer to them than the rest of the *con'dehr*, he heard what Finlay murmured in her ear.

"Fear not, you will never be so betrayed," Finlay said.

"How can you know that?" Asherah asked. Olwynn noticed that the queen's hand gripped her Second Hunter's and wondered if Harek had also taken note.

"Because I do," Finlay replied. Asherah smiled tightly and squeezed Finlay's hand; thus comforted, she motioned for the bard to continue his song.

*Night bore Day's children,*
*And the Moon wept.*

The legends said that Nibika'al had birthed the stars in one fell act, and that all of them lit the sky at once. Many tales told of how the moon once shone as brightly as the elder sun in the night sky, until the stars came to be and stole a portion Cydia's pure glow. The same happened when Nibika'al bore Olluhm's children, for the race of the dark fae came to be in an instant. When the moon made her nightly journey, she saw a land populated with her mate's children, children that she did not bear, and she wept at the sight. The wicked night laughed, taunting the moon in her sorrow. Cydia cast Olluhm from her bed and her pure light changed from white to red, the color of pain, and has remained so ever since.

Treachery does not beget happiness, not even amongst the gods. Nibika'al's children did not take on the soft demeanors of Cydia's children, but instead retained the characteristics of their mother. As true children of the night, they preferred to act under cover of dark than the day's harsh glare and used sedition and deceit to accomplish their goals.

*Olluhm rides across the skies alone*
*Bereft of mate and lover*
*And still, the Moon weeps.*

The tale ended and the minstrel rested his lute on his knees; normally, listeners would have called for more ballads, but the tale of betrayal cast a somber pall over his listeners. Seeking to cheer the room, and hopefully earn a few extra coins, the bard produced a flute and blew a few soft notes, but when Harek spoke it wasn't to request a song.

"You see, the dark fae were born of treachery," he said as he leaned toward Asherah. "It is imperative that we view them as a serious threat."

"What would you have me do, Harek?" Asherah asked wearily. "Accuse them of untoward acts based on a ballad? No, I don't think that would do."

"We need to be vigilant," Harek insisted.

"We are vigilant," Aeolmar said firmly. The First Hunter rose to his feet and extended his arm to the queen. "If they become a threat, we will deal with them. Until then, I'll not accuse another of treachery based solely on their parentage."

His admonishment of Harek complete, Aeolmar escorted Asherah from the hall; in the next moment, Finlay and Innetha departed as well. The minstrel picked up his lute and strummed away, ostensibly to lighten Harek's mood, but when Olwynn chanced a look, he found the Prelate smiling.

"My lord?" Olwynn ventured. Normally, Harek would have been incensed by Aeolmar's words, but his face was the picture of satisfaction.

"She needed to know what sort the dark fae are," Harek said. "Born of deceit, they will deceive the queen." Harek leaned toward Olwynn and lowered his voice. "Do you know the queen's great failing, Olwynn?"

"I do not," Olwynn replied. Having enjoyed the eight centuries of peace under Asherah's gracious rule, Olwynn felt that she'd failed at nothing.

"Her heart," Harek said, "her kind heart. She believes that no one has ever been born evil. It's how she fell in with the Lord of Tingu; she assumed he'd aid her because it was the right thing for him to do, not because he had an ulterior motive."

"He did aid us," Olwynn said. "He gave his life for Asherah." The small hairs on Olwynn's neck stood on end as he remembered Lormac's funeral pyre, Asherah's ashen face and trembling hands as she set it alight. As someone who had lived through the Day of Sorrow, the Lord and Lady of Tingu's great love for one another was something else Olwynn did not doubt.

"He desired to rule over both Tingu and Parthalan. Few know of this," Harek said in response to Olwynn's disbelieving face, "but that was his ultimate goal."

Olwynn considered that information for a moment. "And you now believe that Natraeus wants the same?"

"Yes. He seeks to use our queen as his pawn. Aeolmar refuses to see it, but no matter." He made a cutting motion with his hand, as if to sweep away Aeolmar's influence. "It is for the *con'dehr* to protect the queen, not a hunter."

Olwynn nodded; he had seen no evidence of Natraeus's supposed treachery and frankly didn't believe that the dark fae were strong enough to mount even a small offensive against Parthalan. In spite of this, he understood that the Prelate was privy to information that Olwynn was not. More importantly, Olwynn had pledged his life to his land, and his queen, long ago.

"Natraeus will not prevail," Olwynn swore. "As long as breath remains in our bodies, we of the *con'dehr* will keep the queen, and Parthalan, safe."

"I am most pleased to hear that," Harek said. His eyes glinted with something more than mere satisfaction, but before Olwynn could pin down the emotion, it was gone. "Bard," Harek called out, "Play something with fire in it, and shake these cobwebs from our souls!"

# Chapter Twenty-Eight

Asherah sighed, rolled over, and kneaded her pillows into a more comfortable shape. She'd been overcome by a strange restlessness these past few nights, and couldn't wait for first dawn so she could leave her bed behind. It was an odd feeling, since sleeping alone had never bothered her in the past; even her evenings with Aeolmar ended, more often than not, with him retreating to his own chamber. Finally, she admitted that she was lonely.

Loneliness itself was nothing new to her. During her first few seasons as queen, Asherah had been certain she'd die of it, and more often than not had wished she had. If not for Harek constantly pushing her toward her throne, she'd have run in the other direction... But then, she had had no place to go, no family to turn to, save a son who wasn't really her son, and who hated her, at that. So she'd stayed in Teg'urnan, and while she'd never managed to fully banish the loneliness from her heart, the sharp edges had dulled with time.

Asherah rolled over again, kicking away at the coverlet that had wound itself around her legs, and admitted that furs and cushions were a poor substitute for warm arms. While she wrestled with her bedclothes, her mind traveled back to the Winter's Eve jubilee and the time she spent with Finlay. She smiled at the memory of being in his arms, and recalled Aeolmar's certainty that Finlay was a good match for her.

*As if Aeolmar has suddenly become an expert on matters of the heart.* Unwilling to give credence to Aeolmar's unsolicited advice, yet far too restless to sleep, the queen rose and dressed quickly to flee her empty chambers. She traversed the dark corridors without direction or destination in mind, and soon found herself standing atop the east watchtower. Asherah leaned on the cold stone and stared at the horizon, already glowing with the promise of first dawn. *At least Olluhm will keep me company this morning.*

"My la— Asherah?" The voice startled Asherah, and she turned to see none other than Finlay ascending the steps behind her. "Am I interrupting you?"

"Not at all," she replied, "Why are you about so early?"

"I come here often." He stood next to her and followed her gaze toward the east. "I like to rise early and find a quiet place to greet the elder sun."

"I do, as well." A gust of wind chilled her, and Asherah rubbed her arms as she silently reprimanded herself for putting on such a thin gown, and forgetting her cloak.

"Take my cloak," Finlay said, and before she could decline or accept he settled the thick wool about her shoulders.

"Won't you be cold?" she protested.

"I must acclimate myself to this frigid air," he replied as he fastened the loop and button clasp against her throat.

"You think this is frigid? In the north, this would be considered a warm day, suitable for a swim." She took in Finlay's clothing, which consisted of a thin fabric tunic and breeches more appropriate for the southern deserts than Teg'urnan in the throes of winter. "If you're to reside in the palace this winter, you'll need to forgo your desert attire."

"I suppose I could always wear heavy battle gear as Aeolmar does, and stalk about the palace, glowering at all who dare cross my path."

Asherah covered her mouth, unsuccessfully hiding her laughter.

"That man acts as if a demon will drop upon him at any moment," Finlay continued, miming claws.

"He is...Well, he does look a bit foolish at times," she conceded. The cold wind swirled around them, and Finlay tried not to shiver. "Here, we can share the cloak," Asherah said as she extended her arm, but Finlay hesitated. "Come now, I won't break if you touch me." Finlay's brow furrowed as he carefully placed his arm about Asherah's waist, then stood as rigid as a statue. "This is better," she said as she nestled herself in the crook of his arm, at last within that warm embrace she'd woken up craving.

"I often think of the morning we spent on the Hill of Torim," Finlay said after a time.

"And what occurs to you when you think on it?" she prompted.

"That I'd like to go riding with you again."

Asherah laid her head on his shoulder, and felt some of his awkwardness melt away. "I would like that, as well."

No sooner had she spoken than another icy gust of wind struck them, so bitterly cold that Asherah wondered if it had blown directly from the World's Spine. Finlay wrapped his arms around Asherah and turned his back to the cold burst, shielding her as best he could. Asherah squeezed her eyes shut and pressed her face against Finlay's neck; even after his many moons in Teg'urnan, he still smelled of the sun and the hot desert sand. When the wind subsided, she pulled back from him, her cheek brushing against his as she did so.

"It's too cold and windy for you here." Finlay smoothed her windblown hair. "Let me bring you indoors."

"I assure you, I'm not nearly as fragile as you think I am," Asherah said, turning her face to the wind and letting it blow back her pale hair. Finlay watched her for a moment, then he cupped her face with his hands and kissed her; slow, tender kisses that made time stop, made Asherah forget that she was standing atop the watchtower in the early morning twilight, forget everything except Finlay.

Once they parted, he held her face close to his and stroked her hair. "I suppose I should have asked you first."

Asherah wrapped her arms around his neck and asked, "What if I give you leave to kiss me as often as you'd like?"

Finlay smiled, but before he could reply, they heard clambering up the steps. Another guard, taken aback at the sight of the queen and Second Hunter wrapped in the same cloak, hardly managed a proper bow to his sovereign. Finlay stepped forward and beckoned the bewildered guard back to the stairs. After a few quiet words were exchanged, the guard again bowed to Asherah and left her and Finlay alone.

"What did you say to him?" Asherah asked when Finlay rejoined her.

"I told him that our gracious queen desires to watch the suns rise and would appreciate her privacy," he replied. "He's agreed to stand watch elsewhere for a time."

"Aren't you the shrewd talker," she said appraisingly.

"A good merchant always is. How else would I buy goods for a low price, and turn them around for a profit?"

She laughed at his comparison, then noted that he now stood several steps away from her. "You no longer want to share the cloak with me?" she asked, holding the length of it out in invitation.

"I did not wish to presume," he replied, looking away, and Asherah wondered how deeply that bashful streak of his ran. *We will have to work on that.*

"You don't want me to be cold, do you?" she asked with a smile. "How would it reflect on Cadogan if their lord let the queen shiver away?" He smiled as he gathered her in his arms, his smile widening as she tucked herself against him. They remained atop the watchtower within each other's embrace until they had greeted the elder sun, and then the child, before Asherah mentioned that she was due to meet with the Prelate. Finlay escorted Asherah to her chambers, but when they reached her door the shrewd merchant had left, and he was again an awkward boy.

"I must cure you of this shyness." She stepped closer to him and twined her fingers into the laces of his tunic. "Are they so proper in the south?"

"They—we—are," he replied. "I am not accustomed to being so close to one like you."

"You were quite comfortable at the tower," Asherah observed. "Imagine that we are still there." She tugged him closer, which was akin to moving a brick wall with a feather.

"You aren't worried about what will be said if the queen is caught kissing a hunter?" he asked, his fingertip tracing the line of her jaw.

"Since I am the queen, I will kiss whomever I like," she replied.

Finlay gazed into her eyes, dark and sparkling as a moonless night, and lightly pressed his lips to hers. She felt his face stretch into a smile, then he brought her hand to his lips. "We are proper, in the south," he murmured against her fingers. "When next you are of a mind to go riding, it would be my privilege to escort you."

"I will call upon you and no other," she promised.

"I await your summons, my lady queen." Then Finlay smiled, a smile as blazingly bright as the elder sun, and Asherah felt her heart flutter. Flutter! She hadn't known that hearts really did that; she'd always assumed it was something poets had imagined.

"I will warn you, I ride often," she said. "Your obligations will be great and many."

"Of that, I'm glad," Finlay said as he squeezed her hand. With that, the Second Hunter left the queen to enter her chamber alone. The heavy door creaked shut and Asherah leaned against it, close to giddiness as she remembered Finlay's rough swordsman's hands that belied his gentle touch, his warm arms, and that endearing bashfulness.

*Well, not too bashful to kiss me.* She pushed off the door and found that the cloak was caught between the hinges. Finlay's cloak. Cursing herself for her clumsiness and for neglecting to return it, she freed the garment and turned to find Harek staring at her.

"You startled me," she said as she brushed passed her Prelate. "How long have you been watching me fight with the door?"

"Long enough," he replied. "I feared the door might prevail."

"It nearly did." Asherah took her usual place at her map table and draped Finlay's cloak across her lap. She did not overlook how Harek eyed the garment but ignored his curiosity. His supposed well-meaning advice what the last thing she wanted to hear.

"Is that new?" he asked, nodding toward her lap. *Of course, he needs to know every move I make.*

"I don't believe so," she replied.

"How can you not know if your cloak is new?" he demanded, an edge to his voice that Asherah didn't care for.

Asherah refused to look at him when she replied. "Because it is not my cloak. If you'd like to discuss court fashions, I will send for a seamstress. Otherwise, please regale me with the latest plots and schemes you've uncovered."

His glare was sharper than his sword, but Asherah didn't care. She was in the best mood she'd been in for a long time, and she meant to make that good mood last. Harek, as if sensing he'd lost this bout, settled into a report of the western provinces.

# CHAPTER TWENTY-NINE

"A moment, my lord?"

Olwynn was standing in the open doorway, and watched Harek look up from his scrolls. Most wouldn't approach Harek without an express invitation, but while he had never bothered with naming him as such, Olwynn had performed the role of the Prelate's second almost from the day he was freed from that *doja* in Tingu. As such, he was entrusted with information Harek shared with few others.

"Enter," Harek boomed, and indicated an empty chair. "Have you word from the northern patrols?"

"I do," Olwynn replied, settling himself in the proffered seat. "They ranged as close as they could to Nibika while avoiding detection. No evidence was found of any threat, but the reports clearly describe that something is amiss near the border."

"Amiss?" Harek rubbed his chin. "Explain."

"The land is still, still as death," Olwynn stated. "The trees are green and the water still flows clear and cold, but..." He pursed his lips, and searched for the proper words to surmise the bleakness that was only hinted at in the many accounts he'd read, but detailed with chilling clarity by those who'd been in the region. "Sterile," he concluded. "Like a barren woman, the land is lovely to look at, but brings forth nothing."

"What of the inhabitants?" Harek prompted.

"There are no inhabitants," Olwynn replied. "Cottages remain scattered about, but all seem to have been abandoned some time ago."

Harek leaned back in his chair, his fingertips pressed together beneath his chin. "So, it is worse than I suspected," he mumbled. "Natraeus' foul plot has reached out into the land, poisoning its surroundings and causing those who make their home in the region to flee in terror. He must be moving forward with his wish to attack Tingu and then usurp Parthalan's throne."

Olwynn carefully arranged his face to appear as if he was in agreement with the Prelate. In truth, he doubted the dark fae's ability to do more than shout obscenities over the border. "Is Natraeus truly so foolish? The dark fae would never prevail against the elves, for one, and if Natraeus raised a sword or even a finger to Leran, Asherah would kill him herself."

"Unless they have assistance." Harek rose, and regarded a map of Parthalan hung on the far wall; he traced the border of Nibika with a stubby finger as he continued. "You say the land seems dead?"

"By all accounts, yes," Olwynn replied.

"I know of only one sort of creature whose very presence destroys the soul of the land: dark sorcerers."

Olwynn made a strangled noise in the back of his throat. Truly, after his ordeal in the *doja* he wanted nothing less than to eradicate all sorcery, malicious and otherwise, but to assume that dark sorcerers had taken up with Natraeus and his ilk would be more unlikely than Asherah taking the dark king as her mate. It was absurd.

Harek noted Olwynn's consternation, and silenced him with a wave. "These sorcerers are much more common than you realize. I did not understand myself how their numbers had grown before my brother fell."

Olwynn, after maintaining a few moments of silence out of respect for Sarfek's memory, asked, "Common, my lord?"

"Yes, they are becoming like a plague upon our soil." Harek paced about the room while Olwynn's mind reeled. He considered the many reports he'd read, the men he'd spoken to...None mentioned sorcery or any hint of magic, though the warriors were each familiar with such things. Could such evil have been hidden so completely?

"Sorcerers must be helping Natraeus," Harek concluded for the second time. "That is the only way he would dare to attempt such an uprising." Olwynn mulled this over for a moment, hardly paying attention to Harek as he speculated about the power that these supposed sorcerers held.

"What of your brother?" Olwynn asked suddenly.

"What of my brother?" Harek snapped, his eyes flashing.

"Would he have been familiar with the darker magics? I'm not implying that he would use such knowledge," Olwynn hurriedly added, "I know that Sarfek's heart was true. I only wonder if the knowledge to wield, and therefore combat, such sorcery may be among his things."

Harek's piercing glare bored through Olwynn's eyes and skewered his soul. Olwynn's heart pounded and sweat ran down his back, chilling him in a way the cold never could. All knew that Harek kept his brother's chamber sealed, and that within, all the trappings of magic were preserved untouched as if the room was a shrine to Sarfek's memory. Truth be told, Olwynn could never understand why a warrior, grieving brother or no, would want a room filled with dusty books and the varied making of spells. Olwynn also couldn't understand why Harek was glaring at him with such suspicion.

Harek blinked, and his confusion was replaced with his usual mask of grief. "I know that you would never speak ill of Sarfek," the Prelate said. "I only wish I could ask him of these matters directly."

"If you will grant me your leave, I will have one of the queen's sorcerers look over his belongings," Olwynn offered. "He may yet help the cause of Parthalan."

"He may indeed," Harek agreed. "I will retrieve the key to his chambers and have it sent over to you. I trust you will oversee any entry into my brother's rooms?"

"Of course," Olwynn affirmed. "Pages will not be turned without my approval."

Harek nodded again, and told Olwynn that he was a true and valued warrior before clapping him on the shoulder and dismissing the stunned *con'dehr*. Olwynn wanted to be wrong, wanted these notions he was having about the Prelate's loyalty to be nothing more that misconceptions. But he had seen it; when he mentioned Sarfek, Harek needed a moment to remind himself that his brother was dead. For a man who had openly grieved his sibling's loss these past winters, that moment's hesitation was a moment too long. As much as he wanted to deny it, Harek's behavior had told Olwynn something no one had ever suspected.

Sarfek was alive.

# Chapter Thirty

The palace's contingent of hunters had gathered together in the queen's receiving chamber. In stark contrast to that day's gray and rainy skies, the mood was a celebratory one, because their numbers were being increased by two. The additional hunters were newly returned from the Western Contingent, brothers who went by the names Bron and Luth. Both had longish hair the color of fallen oak leaves and merry blue eyes, but their similarities ended there. Bron was a mountain of a man with legs like tree trunks and a chest like a barrel, while his brother was as lithe as a jungle cat. Aeolmar wondered if they were true brothers or had merely known each other since their youth.

*No matter, at least they're here now.* With the brothers' arrival, the palace contingent numbered five, which meant its roster was half full. If only Aeolmar could locate five additional hunters who were both skilled and cunning enough to guard Asherah, he might be able to breathe again.

Aeolmar watched Asherah while she addressed the assembled hunters; he noted that her gaze kept travelling to Finlay, and that Finlay's gaze hadn't left his queen for a moment. The emotion they felt for one another was obvious, yet neither had made the slightest effort to spend time with the other, which mystified Aeolmar. Asherah had told him about those few stolen kisses atop the watchtower, and of Finlay's bashful nature which the queen had found so intriguing—and Aeolmar considered more annoying. If Aeolmar wanted to kiss a woman he did, certainly if the woman in question was as lovely as the queen. Asherah thought that there may be something more to Finlay's reticence and was now waiting with uncharacteristic patience for him to approach her. The queen's tactic had resulted in little more than a few furtive glances and many cold, solitary evenings. Gods, if Finlay wasn't going to pursue Asherah, he could at least make it known. Aeolmar was tired of sleeping alone.

Asherah concluded her welcome of the brothers and dismissed the hunters. She held Finlay's gaze for a long moment, but instead of approaching the object of his desire, the man nodded respectfully and turned to leave, colliding with Innetha in the process. On seeing his hasty exit, Asherah dropped her gaze, her disappointment evident.

*No more childish games.* Aeolmar, having had enough of their behavior, pushed his way into the corridor and stared down his second.

"The queen desires a word with you," Aeolmar said, ignoring how Finlay's eyes brightened at his mention of Asherah.

"About what?" he asked.

"She did not say," Aeolmar replied, and then walked away, his heavy heart quickening his steps. Not knowing what else to do with himself, he accepted the invitation of the two newest hunters and retreated to The Swan.

***

Finlay hesitantly reentered the queen's chamber; it was an awfully forward act to walk through her door uninvited, but Aeolmar had said that she wanted to speak to him. Still, Finlay worried while he made his way through the chamber, ultimately finding that Asherah remained seated at her map table. She'd removed the clasp from the nape of her neck, and her starlight hair tumbled over her shoulders while she furiously sorted through scrolls.

*She's busy. Of course she's busy; she's the Queen of Parthalan and has important matters to deal with. I should let her be.* Finlay assumed that Asherah had precious few moments to herself where she could relax and just be herself—not a queen, or even one with responsibility, but her true, wonderful, self. Indeed, it was one of the many justifications he used for not seeking her company.

In spite her apparent workload, Finlay didn't leave, not this time. He wanted to be here with Asherah, even if it was only to help his queen organize a few moldy parchments. He cleared his throat, thus capturing Asherah's attention.

"Finlay," she said with a smile, "I'm glad you're here. Come, see what I've discovered." She indicated that he should sit beside her, and he found himself peering at a crude sketch on one of the parchments.

"What am I looking at?" he asked.

"It is a drawing of the shrine you told me about. The one dedicated to *Ish h'ra*, The Deliverer," she replied, then she reached across the table for a book. Finlay didn't mention that the sketch looked nothing like the shrine he'd visited. The pages were so old they were nearly transparant, and Finlay smelled a musty odor his time in the shop had made him all too familiar with. "And," she continued, "this book tells of its history, why it was built, who built it, and what not."

"So, who is responsible?" he asked, his mouth curling into a smile. He wondered if Asherah remembered his offer to take her to the shrine in question.

"I haven't read it yet," she replied. "It was only found in the archive yesterday." Asherah looked up from the crumbling parchment, gratitude shining from her dark eyes. "I never would have thought to search for this if it wasn't for you. As I said before, hope is priceless. Thank you, for giving me hope."

Her smile shone so brightly Finlay dropped his gaze, suddenly uncomfortable with the intensity of Asherah's emotions—and that he had been the cause of that intensity.

"You're quite welcome, my lady." She cleared her throat, and Finlay realized his transgression. "Asherah. You're welcome, Asherah."

The queen smiled approvingly, and Finlay examined the smelly, mold-flecked pages. Time had had its way with them until they were nearly transparent, and the words were in an archaic version of *ahm'ri*. He was concentrating on sounding out the ancient syllables when he felt Asherah's fingers against his neck, and his skin flushed to the roots of his hair.

"I thought you always kept your hair short." She worked her fingers through his thick hair, which had grown long enough to curl over the back of his neck.

"My neck was cold, so I thought to grow it," he said. "I'll shear it again in the spring."

"I like the curls." Asherah twisted the curls around her fingers before she withdrew her hand, and Finlay hoped she hadn't assumed she was making him uncomfortable. She was, but he didn't want her to know that.

"Why did you return?" she asked. "Is there something you wish to discuss with me?"

"Aeolmar said you wanted to speak with me," he replied, his confusion growing when she laughed.

"Aeolmar needs to mind his own affairs," she said, "but I am glad you're here." Attia chose that moment to enter the room, and inquire if the queen would be taking her midday meal in her chambers. "That depends. Finlay, will you join me?"

His face warmed, and he answered, "If you wish me to."

The day had already proven cold and damp, and Attia laid out a hearty meal of stew and warm bread for the queen and her companion. Finlay relaxed somewhat while they ate, allowing himself to enjoy Asherah's company. Once they had eaten their fill, Asherah disappeared into her private chamber for a moment and returned with a crystal decanter and two delicate glasses.

"It's elfin brandy," she explained, "yet another way to chase the chill from your bones."

At her urging, they left the table and sat before the green marble hearth, but rather than watch the flames Asherah gazed at the cold rain that pelted the windows. "I wish this weather would abate. I would prefer sitting in the garden." Finlay mumbled something about his dislike for the damp climate. Asherah turned to find him staring into his glass, and asked pointedly, "Why do I make you so uncomfortable?"

"What?" he asked, taken aback. "You don't, it's just...ah, gods." He took a large gulp of his brandy, larger than he really should have, and stared into his empty glass as he replied. "I still find it difficult to comprehend that the most beautiful girl to ever enter my father's shop is the Queen of Parthalan."

Asherah laughed softly as she touched his forearm. "I find it difficult to comprehend that the most valiant resident of Cadogan is now one of my hunters," she said. Finlay chanced to meet Asherah's eyes, and saw her gentle smile. "Are you surprised that I think so highly of you? You shouldn't be."

He let out his breath in a great exhale and raked a hand through his hair. "It does," he said at length. "It confounds me."

"May I ask why?"

Finlay got to his feet and paced the length of the room and back. "Things are different here, different than I've ever known. In Cadogan, a merchant's son would court a merchant's daughter, not a woman so far above his class. Yet you seem to have no problem spending time with a man like me, so far beneath you."

"Finlay, I've heard of this class system you refer to, and it is nonsense. If I could abolish it, I would." He abruptly looked up, so shocked by her words he forgot to blush. Not only Cadogan's residents, but all the people of the south followed the strictures of their class and did not act outside of it. If the queen abolished it, there would likely be chaos.

Asherah continued, undaunted, "You must remember that you're a hunter now, and I'm a huntress. I imagine that would make you and I of the same class, if I put any credence in such a system."

"You're not just a maiden kindhearted enough to allow a lesser man to court her, you are *the queen*," Finlay stated unnecessarily.

"So?" Asherah's dark eyes held him fast. "Is that what you'd like to do? Court me?" Finlay stared at the eggshell thin glass in his hands, studying the nearly insubstantial rim. Glassblowers had always fascinated him to a certain degree, what with the many hours spent before the blazing furnace, the patience...

*Stop.* Finlay set the glass aside, and knelt before Asherah. "I would like to... if you find me worthy of you." Asherah laughed softly, and grazed her fingertips across his face.

"If you think you're so unworthy, then why did you kiss me at the watchtower?" she asked, her black eyes glinting.

"I shouldn't have." He brushed his knuckles against her cheek, then let his hand fall. "You... you are difficult to resist."

Asherah placed her arms around his neck and languidly toyed with the hair at the back of his neck. Finlay kept his hands at his sides, his arms burning with his need to hold her, but he waited. After long moments of this unbearably close contact, she kissed him. "I suggest you cease resisting," she said against his lips.

Finlay's only response was to kiss her again, parting his lips over hers. As he drew Asherah into the circle of his arms, he kissed her with all the passion he had carried with him for the past seven winters. He kissed her how he had wanted to that day on the watchtower—no, the very day he met her, his warrior maiden, in the dusty streets of Cadogan surrounded by dead demons. Asherah opened herself up for him, unresisting as Finlay finally let himself act on his desires. He was vaguely aware of someone's arrival behind him, but he assumed it was only a *saffira* tasked with clearing away the remains of their meal, and would soon be on her way.

"My lady?"

The urgent tone in the asker's voice caused Finlay to release Asherah, and she glanced over her shoulder. "Yes, Attia?"

"The Prelate is on his way. Are you and—" Attia's inquiry ended once she turned a corner and saw the queen and her hunter, with Asherah's disheveled hair and Finlay's surprised expression answering more than she was intending to ask. "I see you've finished your meal," Attia said with a smug grin. "Do you require anything further?"

"You may retire," Asherah replied, a hint of annoyance in her voice.

"For the *entire* day?" Attia pressed. "My, but it's hardly noon."

"Go," Asherah shouted. The *saffira-nell* laughed softly as she withdrew.

"Attia has served me for many winters," Asherah said as the door clicked shut. "She thinks I won't beat her for her loose remarks. So far I haven't, but there's always tomorrow." Finlay shook his head.

"You baffle me," he said. "You treat your *saffira* as if she's your sister, you dally with men you'd do well to leave alone...you even saddle your own horse and serve others. Are you truly the queen, or a beautiful shade wearing her face?"

"If I were a shade wearing another's face, how would you know if I was beautiful?" Asherah asked with innocent eyes.

"As long as you're my Asherah, you cannot help your beauty, no matter the face you wear," he declared. He, in turn, had expected another gentle taunt, but her eyes were soft.

"Are you an elf reborn?" Asherah asked as she glided her fingertips across his brow, her tone having gone from teasing to wistful.

"I'm naught but a man from the desert," he replied. He moved to take her into his arms, but was startled by a noise from the outer chamber; someone had just entered Asherah's main chamber, and shut the door with a thud. "Attia?"

"Harek," she answered, rising quickly and drawing Finlay further into her rooms. Surrounded by the rich silks and velvets that covered both the walls and furniture, the merchant in him wished he could take a moment to look around, but he got the impression that Asherah would rather not share the identity of the man in her private rooms with the Prelate. Then he smiled, since he was that man.

"This is my private entrance," she said when they reached a door on the far side of her sleeping chamber. "Very few know it is here."

"Then I'm honored to be one of the few," Finlay said, then took her hands in his. She'd told him that class didn't matter to her, and damn it all, but he was going to hold her to that. "May I see you again?"

"You see me every day," she replied.

"I want to see you alone," he said. "You knew what I meant."

"Did I?" she asked with that coquettish smile. "You overestimate me."

"I believe the trouble lies in underestimating you." Finlay kissed her fingertips. "You are a mischievous girl, aren't you?"

Asherah twined her arms around Finlay's neck, and he tried very hard to ignore the sounds of Harek crashing about.

"If I do see you, alone, will you kiss my face more than my hand?"

In response, Finlay kissed her eyes, then her cheeks, and slowly worked his way to her lips, lingering there the longest. "I can manage that."

# Chapter Thirty-One

## Aeolmar Speaks

*I'd been wasting my day at The Swan, which I now saw with greater frequency than my rooms in Teg'urnan. I suspected that Asherah wouldn't seek out Finlay's companionship if I was nearby, so I'd taken to spending my evenings here, pretending to drink. Well, today I was drinking in fact, but the pleasant oblivion that comes with drunkenness had thus far eluded me. It didn't matter what I imbibed, be it wine, ale, or the stronger liquors that those northern warriors drank, my constitution seemed immune to the effects.*

*Olluhm's Balls. I would greatly enjoy a drunken stupor right about now.*

*"Here you are, my lord," murmured one of the wenches as she placed a fresh tankard of ale before me. "Quite thirsty today, aren't you?"*

*"I am," I replied. She perched on the table's edge as she collected the empty tankards, offering a view of her bosom that left little to the imagination, which was just as well. My imagination frequently led me down paths I'd rather not tread.*

*"Most men are little more than limp rags by now," she purred. "More often than not, I need to help them upstairs. But not you. The First Hunter never needs me," she added with a feigned pout.*

*"Perhaps I will, after this next draught," I said. We flirted often, she and I, and lately I had come very close to collecting on her offers. She wasn't beautiful like Asherah, but very attractive in her way, with skin the color of burnt sugar and tight curls pinned atop her head. If only I could remember her name; I think she was named for a flower. Flaedyne? No. Lover's ease? Obviously not. Maybe I was a little drunk.*

*"Letia!" I all but shouted, inordinately pleased with myself for remembering her name (which had nothing to do with flowers). "Letia," I repeated in a softer tone, "must I be a drunken sot to receive your care?" She glanced over her shoulder, ensuring that the innkeeper wasn't watching, and leaned very, very close to me.*

*"You've only to tell me what you need," Letia breathed. I opened my mouth to—oh, I don't know. List my needs? Proposition her? Yank her from her perch and bring her to one of the filthy rooms upstairs? Unfortunately, none of that happened.*

*"My lord," boomed a man's voice. It belonged to Olwynn, one of Harek's* con'dehr, *arguably the most trusted and steadfast member of that collection of prostrating fools. His story was the stuff of legend: Once a soldier in Parthalan's legion, he had served at the Southern Border for many winters until he was ensnared in the old king's plot. Enthralled to do a* mordeth's *bidding, he was forced to assist demons as they imprisoned and defiled faerie women. He regained his freedom when Asherah, long before she was queen, liberated him and the rest who'd been imprisoned in that* doja.

*Interestingly, the* mordeth *that controlled Olwynn's* doja *was none other than Mersgoth. It seemed that the beast began haunting me long before I'd been born.*

*"Yes?" I turned from the lovely Letia and waited for my eyes to focus on Olwynn's rather unappealing visage. I suppose that I was not so immune to the effects of drink after all.*

*"May I join you?" I waved him toward an empty seat, and Letia produced another tankard of ale before she melted*

*into the background, along with the promise of an evening's diversion. "You're frequently at odds with the Prelate, yes?"*

*I bit back my reply; asking if Harek and I were at odds was akin to inquiring about the source of the stench when you were standing next to the palace sewers. "We do not always see eye to eye," I said at length, pleased by my restraint. Olwynn nodded, seeming to struggle with what to say next. When he finally spit the words out, I understood his hesitation.*

*"I believe he is privy to information that you and the queen are not," he said slowly. "Information that may be harmful to Parthalan."*

*At once, the drunken fog that swirled around me dissipated. "What information?" I demanded.*

*"I believe that he is engaged in clandestine communication with the dark fae," Olwynn said. "According to Harek, Natraeus has obtained the means to conquer the elves."*

*If I was the sort of man to laugh, I would have. To think that Natraeus stood the merest chance against the elves—either one kingdom or all seven, united once more under Tingu's standard—was ludicrous. "Natraeus is nothing more than a rodent, nipping at Leran's heels," I said, pausing to take another long swig of ale. When I lowered the tankard, I was met by Olwynn's disapproving stare.*

*"You do not grasp the gravity of the situation," he said. "I remember when Asherah and Lormac were together, and I remember when she lit the elf king's pyre. To say she was distraught after her mate's death is an understatement; she behaved like she'd died as well. If Natraeus moves against the elves—against Leran—I fear for her reaction."*

*Wonderful. Now, I had one of the* con'dehr *reminding me that I was a stone hearted, loveless bastard. Worse, I agreed with him.*

*"Your point is well made," I conceded; Olwynn was gracious enough not to gloat. "However, you and I both know that Natraeus couldn't hope to prevail against Leran. The elf is a madman when he fights, and not only are the elves*

*fierce warriors one and all, they far outnumber the dark fae."
I raised the tankard again, only to lower it with such force
the ale sloshed out onto the table. There was only one way
Natraeus could attempt such an uprising, and for me to have
taken this long to realize it, I must be drunk. "Who is helping
him?"*

*"I don't know," Olwynn replied, "but Harek does. He sus-
pects a sorcerer has supplied the dark fae with some sort of
assistance, but I don't know how he came by such knowledge.
I think Harek means to stop the dark fae on his own in order
to restore himself to Asherah's favor." Olwynn leaned closer,
and dropped his voice. "Truth be told, I wonder if there is a
sorcerer at all. I wonder if Harek hasn't embellished the threat
to make the queen fear for Leran's safety."*

*I nodded as I reached for my tankard, then thought the
better of it and shoved it away. The way I understood things,
Asherah had only ever favored Harek in his delusions, but I
didn't mention that to Olwynn. We had more pressing matters
before us.*

*Speaking of Olwynn, he was rambling on about how Harek
was a good and noble man, loyal to Asherah above all others.
I let him finish, since now was not the time to argue Harek's
character traits.*

*"I don't doubt you," I said when Olwynn paused for breath.
"You've known the man longer than I. But you're right; if
Harek fails, and Leran is compromised, it may be too much
for Asherah."*

*"Should we confront Harek?" Olwynn asked. Ha. Should
we confront Harek? Which really meant shouldn't you, First
Hunter that you are, go make an ass of yourself before the
Prelate? No, I think not.*

*"No, I think not." Now I was repeating my every thought.
Had Letia spiked the ale? "Watch him, but from a distance. If
we confront him without proof, he'll likely deny any involve-
ment. And if Natraeus does mean to move against the elves,
I'd rather catch him like the rat he is."*

*Olwynn nodded, then grasped my forearm across the table. "Agreed. I will watch the Prelate, and we will stop both him and Natraeus. I am loyal to my queen, and to you, First Hunter."*

*Did a member of the* con'dehr *just pledge his loyalty to me? Olwynn was right; I did not appreciate the gravity of the situation.*

# Chapter Thirty-Two

His impromptu discussion with Aeolmar had done little to alleviate Olwynn's concerns about the Prelate's behavior. Not only had Aeolmar all but dismissed Olwynn, the man was clearly drunk. Olwynn sighed; Aeolmar may be a warrior without equal, but as a man, he came up short.

*Of course, I didn't tell him that Sarfek is probably alive.* Olwynn had deliberately withheld that crucial piece of information from the First Hunter, but what was he to do? Tell Aeolmar that Harek hadn't seemed as upset as one should be upon hearing Sarfek's name, so obviously his brother was still alive and was somehow assisting Natraeus? Aeolmar would have laughed him out of The Swan—and with good reason. He needed to find incontrovertible proof about Sarfek's feigned death, and resolved to broach the subject with Aeolmar only when he had such evidence in hand.

If Harek continued to call upon Olwynn as often as he had of late, such evidence would likely be gathered by season's end. Harek's reliance on Olwynn had grown much greater over the past few winters, which in itself was unusual. While Olwynn had held a high ranking position within the *con'dehr* for a good many winters, Harek was not the sort of man to hand off tasks he could accomplish himself.

*No, that's not true, for he often enough turned to Sarfek.* Olwynn wondered if his sudden increase in responsibility was the result of Harek trying to distract him from the truth: Sarfek was quite alive and likely assisting the dark fae.

*But, why fake Sarfek's death?* He had been one of Asherah's advisors, true, but Sarfek and the queen were hardly close. Further, if Sarfek had asked to leave Teg'urnan, his request would have likely been granted. It befuddled Olwynn that the brothers would go to the trouble of faking the sorcerer's demise.

*With Sarfek believed dead, the sorcerer would never be called before the queen to answer for his actions.* At long last, Harek could use his brother to accomplish all those tasks Asherah had long forbidden—namely, infiltrating one's enemies, and no one was more of an enemy to Parthalan than the current *mordeth-gall*. Ehkron's whelp, a beast called Asgeloth, was rumored to be amassing forces in the underworld, as well as wreaking havoc in the mortal realm. Harek had wanted to send a spy to the underworld to learn of the beast's plans, but Asherah had not taken kindly to his suggestion. In fact, she'd railed at her Prelate with such fervor Olwynn worried she'd order his banishment.

She hadn't, but the whole of Teg'urnan had soon learned of Harek's unorthodox request. The Prelate accused Attia of spreading such rumors, and thus began the rift between Harek and the *saffira-nell*. Regardless of who'd said what to whom, the residents of Teg'urnan had been aghast that Harek would suggest sending someone to infiltrate the realm of demons so soon after Sahlgren's pact with Ehkron. It had been a good many winters before the comparisons between the prior king and current Prelate subsided.

"Why would you fake your death?" Olwynn asked Innetha. She and Olwynn had crossed paths upon his return to the palace; the lovely huntress had mentioned that it was her turn to ride along the foothills that surrounded Teg'urnan, and he'd jumped at the chance to accompany her. Having had found nothing out of the ordinary during their first circuit of the palace, they'd paused in a secluded vale to enjoy the unseasonably mild air.

"What makes you think I did?" Innetha countered; there was enough of an edge to her voice to make Olwynn wonder about the nymph's past.

"Not you specifically," he clarified. "Why would anyone?"

"Oh, for a great many reasons." Innetha extended her arms overhead and stretched, then rolled onto her belly to face Olwynn. She'd shed her jerkin and boots as soon as they dismounted and was clad in a dark linen tunic over honey-colored leather leggings. The tunic was sleeveless, and showed off her graceful neck and shoulders. "If you've done something dishonorable, it might be easier to leave your old identity behind than to make reparations."

"You speak as if you have intimate knowledge of such things," Olwynn observed.

"I wasn't always a tracker or a huntress," she said. "Would you believe that I once served a noblewoman?"

"*Dea comora*, I would believe a great many things of you," he replied. "Were you one of her ladies?"

Innetha laughed softly. "Hardly." She fixed him in her gaze, and Olwynn tugged his collar from his neck. "You could say I served in the bedchamber."

With that she sat up and turned her back, busying herself with relacing her boots while she purposefully ignored Olwynn. When his tension grew too great, he shifted close and asked, "Served how?"

Innetha glanced over her shoulder and let him suffer for a few more moments. Then she leaned back, her lips so close to Olwynn's he could feel the heat of her body, and breathed, "Seamstress." Then they both burst out laughing. When they had calmed themselves somewhat, Innetha elaborated about her former employment. "Specifically, I mended worn petti-coats."

"You repaired undergarments?" Olwynn asked with a raised brow. He could not imagine Asherah clad in anything less than the finest silks and never in something frayed or mended. "What sort of noblewoman keeps her ragged clothing rather than having new items made?"

"She was thrifty," Innetha replied.

"Did you also edge her corsets in lace?" he inquired.

"Oh, I wasn't allowed. I'm not very good with a needle, which is why I only worked with her smallclothes."

Olwynn laughed again, imagining the haughty Innetha sur-rounded by the torn and tattered underpinnings of a frugal lady.

"My point, dear Olwynn," Innetha said as she swung her legs about and faced him, "is that as often as not, there is more to one that can be seen at first glance. I'm sure there are things about you that I'd be surprised to hear." Innetha leaned forward; the laces of her tunic had loosened, and even after winter's long confinement the skin of her breast remained rose and gold. "For instance..." She hooked a finger around his belt. "I've heard that many of the guards from those *doja's* were unmanned. Did you, Olwynn, suffer such a fate?"

"You tell me." A quick glance below would reveal that he hadn't. Many of the guards at his *doja* were castrated—it was a favorite punishment of Mersgoth's—but Olwynn had escaped the demon's claws, literally. Never was he more grateful than when Innetha's doe eyes locked with his and her hand strayed lower; then her eyes widened, and she scrambled away from him as if she'd grabbed a poisoned barb.

"What's the matter?" he demanded.

"I...I can see things," she replied, trembling so her voice wavered. "Usually, I only see when I'm healing."

"You're a healer?" Olwynn asked. "Did your parents also have the gift?"

"Gift?" Innetha snorted. "I was cursed with this, cursed to relive the wound's pain even as I healed it..." She drew her knees up to her chest, staring at Olwynn's waist. "I touched your scar, and I saw...I felt." Olwynn felt near his waist and found the scar she'd touched, an old puncture from one of Mersgoth's wicked talons.

"Did... did those things really happen?" Innetha asked, and he understood that she'd seen more than just the one incident. How much, he didn't attempt to learn. He folded her into his arms, rocking her like one would a child.

"They did." He pressed a kiss to her temple. "It's all right. It was a long time ago."

"I should be comforting you. You're the one who suffered," Innetha began, then shuddered as if she'd plunged into an icy pool. He wondered if the visions would stay with her for a time.

"I don't need the comfort. I already know what happened. I have enough for you."

When Innetha was calmed somewhat, and was able to stand without shaking, she rode away without a backward glance toward the vale. Olwynn was disappointed, but he didn't race to catch her; few were able to deal with being told about the horrors of the *doja*, never mind having his memories of pain and humiliation dumped behind their eyes. He assumed that she needed time to herself. He also assumed she'd never want to touch him again, until later that evening when heard a soft knock on his door. Before he opened it, he knew who stood there.

"You said... I heard you say you have comfort for me?" Innetha asked, and they tumbled into each other's arms. They didn't speak that first night together, for words weren't the sort of comfort they sought, but Olwynn felt the edges of his old pain dull a bit. Innetha's touch healed him somewhat, and he wondered if he could do the same for her.

# Chapter Thirty-Three

Aeolmar gritted his teeth, and repeated, "You're just looking for them."

"But not apprehending?" Bron rubbed his chin with a massive hand. "And you say they haven't done anything wrong, so why are we looking for them in the first place?"

A low noise somewhere between a growl and a sigh emanated from Aeolmar's throat. It was Reckoning Day, when Asherah threw open the doors of Teg'urnan and let all of her subjects air their grievances before the court. Asherah felt that this showed her to be a good ruler, a queen who cared for her people first and foremost, and she was correct. However, the dark fae were counted among her subjects, and this would be the perfect time for one of Natraeus' men to infiltrate the palace.

"Think, brother," said Luth. "Aeolmar only wants to know if they arrive. If they do, we'll keep an eye on them until they quit befouling our floor with their boots. If they don't, we'll have an early visit to The Swan."

"Yes," Aeolmar said. "If any of the dark fae arrive, notify me at once." Aeolmar hadn't told the brothers that he would then follow them himself, hoping to catch Harek in an act of treason. While he trusted both Bron and Luth implicitly, he also understood that that the Prelate had many loyal followers. He could not risk speaking his suspicions aloud, not to anyone save Olwynn. He also couldn't risk Asherah hearing some half-whispered facts and jumping to conclusions; no, Aeolmar managed that enough for the both of them.

"As you command," Bron said, then he and Luth trudged off to take their places on each side of the door. As much as their flippant demeanors and copious drinking irritated him, Aeolmar was glad for the brothers' presence. Bron was something of a legend in the westlands, being that he'd once killed a *mordeth* by striking it square in the face with nothing but his fist. Not to be outdone, his wiry brother was renowned for his skill with thrown objects, be they spears or bolts or common stones. His accuracy was lethal at fifty paces, hardly less so at a few hundred. If even a portion of what Olwynn suspected was true, and there was the possibility of fae warring against fae, Aeolmar had truly summoned Bron and Luth to the palace contingent at the right time.

*Gods, please let him be wrong.*

***

Olwynn rapped his knuckles on the heavy wood, silence his only response. Regardless, he pushed open the Prelate's door, intending to leave this most recent account from the northern reconnaissance on Harek's desk for later study. Olwynn hadn't expected to find him here with it being Reckoning Day and Harek due in the great hall while the queen heard complaints. Olwynn shook his head as he placed the scroll amongst the rest. If his suspicions were accurate, Harek was going to great lengths in this latest attempt to win Asherah's favor.

*If it hasn't happened yet, it likely never will.* Not that Olwynn had any intention of offering Harek any sort of counsel on the matter of his infatuation with the queen. Like the rest of the court, he pretended to know nothing of it.

Since no one was there to question his impropriety, Olwynn sat in Harek's chair and absently straightened the parchments and other items scattered across the desk. None of the patrols had detected the slightest threat from the north, or the south, or from anywhere else in the land. By all accounts, it would seem that Parthalan was the safest nation in all the realm, and that her Prelate was pushing his warriors beyond exhaustion as they endlessly searched for enemies that didn't exist. It was a needless squandering of resources, the kind of activity that, if Parthalan's enemies learned of, would seriously hinder the queen.

For that reason alone, Olwynn refused to allow himself guilt about approaching Aeolmar with his suspicions. In truth, there was no one else to turn to; Olwynn outranked the rest of the *con'dehr*, and he certainly couldn't go to the queen without proof. He was mildly astonished that Aeolmar had acknowledged his suspicions, but that was probably due to the First Hunter's dislike of the Prelate. Or, perhaps his drunkenness had made him willing to listen.

Olwynn scrubbed his face as if the action could wipe the thoughts from his mind, then leaned back in the chair. *Hopefully, this will all turn out to be nothing.* His eyes fell upon the key to Sarfek's chambers; ornately wrought of fine copper, it hung on a velvet cord. Since Harek had already given Olwynn permission to examine Sarfek's belongings, he took the key from its peg and set off without a second thought. He would take a quick inventory of the sorcerer's chamber and move on. Hopefully he'd find something to prove Harek's innocence, if only to himself.

# Chapter Thirty-Four

## Asherah Speaks

*The past moon had been nothing if not magical, with Finlay reminding me of my Lormac more with each passing day, though for quite different reasons. When I'd first worn the Sala I wasn't as forthcoming with my affection as Lormac had hoped, so he developed a habit of sneaking up on me, then quickly pulling me behind a door or around a corner for a few moments of passion. Slowly, an embrace at a time, I learned to leave my anxieties behind and let myself love him the way he, and I, wanted. Those stolen moments are among my fondest memories of him, and I never did view the backside of a pillar in quite the same way.*

*Now, I found that I was the one conspiring to steal Finlay's affection, though he complained much more than I ever had. It was a most daunting challenge to catch Finlay unawares, yet I relished the chase as much as any warrior. On this Reckoning Day I had well and truly fooled him.*

*"Have you taken utter leave of your senses, woman?" Finlay demanded. While he walked to his post behind my throne I'd accosted him. Only a thin velvet drape kept the whole of the hall from viewing us.*

*"I didn't think you'd mind," I replied. He glowered at me, his hands firmly on my waist. So firmly, in fact, that when I tried to draw him close he kept me at arm's length. "I meant no harm."*

*"Asherah, you are the queen," he hissed. "I know you don't see yourself as the ruler of this land, but others look to you for leadership and guidance! Have a care with how you present yourself."*

*I was taken aback by his scolding, more so when he dropped his hands and turned away. However, I had to concede his point; I was playing the same games Lormac once played with me, only I hadn't been a queen during that last playtime; at least, I hadn't felt like one. And, I'd only just found someone new to play with.*

*"Finlay." If I hadn't been his queen, I think he would have kept walking. "I'm only trying to draw you out of your shell. You are always so nervous around me, and I want you to be comfortable with my affections."*

*"I cannot be comfortable locked in embraces with you all about the palace," he stated without turning to look at me. "Such things should be done in private."*

*"This is private," I began, but he waved away my explanation.*

*"This is the great hall of Teg'urnan," he corrected, gesturing wildly as he indicated the room beyond the drapery. "This is as far from private as we could possibly be." He faced me, his blue eyes darkened with hurt. "I care for you, Asherah, far too much to play such games with your heart. I'm sorry you don't feel the same."*

*With that he left me, trembling on the edge of tears while Cydia knows how many of my people stood on the other side of that drape, eagerly waiting for me to hear their cases. Somehow, I made it through the day, but I collapsed into Aeolmar's arms once he escorted me back to my chambers. After I told him what had transpired behind my throne, the traitorous bastard took Finlay's side.*

*"Your playfulness is belittling how he feels about you,"Aeol-mar explained. "He's a boy from the desert, full of ideals and notions. To him, you should be a demure maiden, patiently waiting for him to come to you. Instead, you're chasing after him like he's your prey."*

*Gods, I hated nothing more than when Aeolmar made sense. "But I'm not patient," I pointed out. "I never have been."*

*"Then perhaps you should meet him halfway," he suggested.*

*Halfway? I could do that.*

*So there I was, standing before Finlay's door as nervous as I have ever been. I almost didn't knock, but if I didn't then our relationship—if you could even call it that—would never be put to rights, would it? When he opened the door he was more than a bit confused to find me standing there, bearing a carafe of water and two goblets as my peace offering.*

*"May I enter?"*

*He stepped aside, revealing an impressive collection of dag-gers laid out for sharpening. I almost asked about them, but that wasn't why I'd come.*

*"I came to talk. About earlier."*

*Finlay immediately asked for my forgiveness, for one should never scold one's queen, but I wasn't there as a queen. I was only Asherah.*

*"Please, don't apologize. You were right."*

*"I was?"*

*"Yes." I set down the carafe and goblets on a bench, being that the table was otherwise occupied. "The way I have been behaving makes it seem as if when you touch me, it has no meaning...that it's just a brush of skin to skin. That can't be further from the truth."*

*"Can't it?" he asked, I don't think to be argumentative. "You seem...adept at getting your way."*

*Well, that was a polite way to reference my many lovers. "It's only my nature," I went on. "I've seen so much despair that when another makes me happy I delve into games and such." I smiled tightly. "I haven't felt this happy in quite a while."*

*"Truly?" he asked.*

*I reached forward and took his hands in mine. "Truly."*

*He pulled me forward and kissed me, then smiled his bashful smile. "Perhaps a game or two would be acceptable. As long as you let me win."*

*I laughed, for that was where he was wrong. I had most certainly won.*

# Chapter Thirty-Five

As Olwynn crossed the palace from the Prelate's chamber toward Sarfek's former quarters, he noticed that the corridors were uncharacteristically empty. Teg'urnan was a massive edifice with many residents, and its corridors were often crowded at all hours of the day and night. Indeed, one could walk its stone lined halls from first dawn till midnight and not encounter the same person twice. Yet the closer Olwynn got to the sorcerer's rooms the fewer people he saw, until he alone ascended to the Western Tower.

Olwynn recalled how Sarfek had specifically requested those rooms in the Western Tower, halfway to its peak; he may as well have used the whole of the tower, for the rooms above him remained vacant, and those below were relegated to storage. He wondered if the direction was of some magical significance, although the rest of the magic handlers kept their rooms on the eastern side of Teg'urnan. Like as not, Sarfek had desired solitude for his work, whatever such work may have entailed. After those horrible winters Olwynn spent under thrall, he wondered if all sorcerers didn't have some degree darkness to them.

He stood before Sarfek's door for long moments before he entered. The door was old and heavy, as were all the doors in the palace, and looked as if it was hewn from one solid slab of oak. There was a child's tale of Olluhm who, out of spite, felled the mighty trees that had been planted by one of the old gods. Cydia thought it was a tragedy to destroy such things of beauty, and repurposed the fallen trunks as doors for their new home. Truly, the hand of the mother goddess could be felt whenever one touched the ancient wood.

However, unlike the other, rather innocuous doors in Teg'urnan this one nearly stank of foreboding. Olwynn wondered if Sarfek had enchanted it as a way of keeping intruders at bay, though who would be foolish enough to attempt uninvited entry to a sorcerer's den was beyond his ken.

Olwynn turned his attention from the malicious door to the key he clutched, cast of solid copper and so ornate Olwynn wondered at the practicality of the implement. Keys were forged of iron for a reason, and such delicate metalwork was frequently broken off or worn away. Then he moved the key closer to the door and learned that the piece of art in his hand was never meant to work pins and tumblers.

The key warmed in Olwynn's hand and gave off a soft, burnished glow. He would have sworn he heard a low hum, as well, but before he could determine if it emanated from the key or within the chamber, the door flew open. Olwynn glanced about the corridor, then stepped into a room as alien as any he'd ever been in.

There were books everywhere, some bound in leather, some in velvet, and some lettered in gold; one looked to be bound in flesh, and Olwynn stayed clear of it. Not only were there books, but scrolls and parchments and dried up inkpots were scattered about and heaped in corners. Shelves rose on all sides with all manner of flasks and vials filled with only Olluhm knew what. Tapestries and carpets, their vibrant colors long ago stained with greasy smoke, covered the walls and windows. The scent of burnt offerings and incense had seeped into the stones of the room, so much so that Olwynn imagined little puffs of fragrant smoke issuing from the mortar.

Olwynn was fascinated by the room, and his trepidation at entering another's private space quickly gave way to curiosity. He examined parchments and thumbed through the top layer of books, though not the flesh-bound tome, and peered into the varied canisters and vials, careful to leave the contents undisturbed—for who knew what a sorcerer might keep bottled up for later use. Then a hide-covered doorway captured his attention, and he promptly forgot about the canisters and their vile contents.

The hide was covered in strange runic symbols which were scratched into the leather's surface, then rubbed with pitch. The symbols looked familiar to Olwynn, but when he tried to sound them out the rough, guttural words, though somewhat familiar, were no language he could identify. A breeze stirred the hide and, assuming a window had been left ajar, Olwynn pushed it aside to investigate. What he saw was enough to chill his very soul.

A red sphere—an *enthrallment* sphere—lay on a copper altar in the center of the room. What he had assumed was a gentle breeze was in reality pulses of energy falling off the glassine surface of the sphere; Olwynn remembered well how the *mordeth* that imprisoned him in the *doja* would use those pulses to incapacitate those who'd angered him, or just for his amusement as he watched them suffer. The altar was surrounded by bones—whose bones he'd never know, but they were certainly the bones of a grown man—and more of those strange runes. In a burst of recognition, Olwynn sounded out a few more rune, and was rewarded with a stronger, white-hot pulse from the sphere that knocked his feet out from under him. Before he hit the floor, he understood what he had found.

The whole of the room was surrounded in demonic spells.

# Chapter Thirty-Six

## Asherah Speaks

*My terrible morning had transformed itself into a wonderful evening, and I remained in Finlay's chamber until long after the child sun set. Having resolved to do things his way, I left off my games, at least for now, and sat chastely before his hearth whilst keeping my hands to myself. Of course, my good behavior meant that Finlay was more confused than not, which began when he found the carafe filled with only water.*

*"I thought you'd prefer it," I said. "Wine can loosen the tongue, and..." I left off my description of drunken revels (gods, I must remember to never, ever speak of Madoc'na while in Finlay's presence), assuming he'd rather not hear such things. I worried that I'd said the wrong thing yet again, and Finlay confirmed my fears when he set the goblet down with an audible clunk.*

*"Asherah, you act like I'm punishing you," he said. "I don't mind it when you're playful. In fact, I like it."*

*"You do?" I asked, my voice trembling.*

*"I do," he confirmed. "But I also care for you a great deal. This isn't a game for me."*

"It's not for me, either." I looked at my hands, my fingers knotting and unknotting themselves. "I'm only trying to be what you want," I said quietly, but that wasn't quite what I meant. I just... I wanted him to want me, and I was afraid that I'd gone and ruined everything, like I'd nearly ruined things with Lormac. Gods, Argent had never wanted to be solely with me, and Aeolmar had already moved on to some wench at The Swan. A wench who wasn't tainted by demons, like me.

Finlay watched me for a moment, and I imagined the horrible things that must be coursing through his thoughts. How had he fallen in with such a wretch? How can he move on without incurring the royal ire? But he said none of those things; instead, he sat beside me and said the most wonderful words I've ever heard.

"You are what I want." He glided his fingertips across my cheek. "I wouldn't change a thing about you."

Blessed Cydia, did he really mean that? Yes, he must, for Finlay wasn't the sort of man to say a few placating words like Argent would or to wall up his heart as Aeolmar did. He is... He is my Finlay.

I, however, was at a loss for words, so I laid my head on his shoulder and just enjoyed that he was there and that he wanted me so. After a time, he rose and located some wine. He did the pouring, and we sipped from our goblets before the hearth.

"Not that I didn't appreciate the water," he said with a wink and a grin.

"So, if I may not chase you about the palace, how are we to get to know one another?" I asked. "You rarely visit me in my chamber." That comment earned me one of Finlay's wonderful blushes.

"You've a point," he conceded. "I have avoided your chambers, but there is no better place to spend time with my lovely queen."

"Avoided?" I asked, arching my brow. Why would he avoid the one location where he was sure to find me?

*"It's a rather intimate location," he explained. Aeolmar was right, Olluhm damn him, Finlay was full of notions and ideals. Apparently, there was a certain amount of courtship that he and I were meant to endure. Enjoyable torment, that. Remembering Aeolmar's further advice (damn him for his insightfulness!) that I should meet Finlay halfway, an equally enjoyable compromise came to mind.*

*"Why don't you sup with me?" I suggested. "I normally eat alone in my chambers. Or is that too intimate an event?" Finlay smiled, and squeezed my hand. Was that anticipation I saw in his eyes?*

*"I think sharing a meal is an excellent notion, my lady queen."*

*"Tomorrow, then," I said, returning his smile. Yes, sweet anticipation.*

# Chapter Thirty-Seven

When Olwynn came to himself, he panicked, fearing that he'd been returned to the *doja*. But no, the foul reek of demon about him was merely the residue of Sarfek's evil artifacts. He tried to rise and couldn't; if he forced himself to remember such things, he could recall that the sphere's pulse wore off gradually and left little damage.

While he lay on the floor, he examined the copper key and noted that a representation of it was etched on the ceiling above the sphere. *This key unlocks the illusion,* he surmised. *If I hadn't brought it, I wouldn't have ever known that this room even existed.*

As soon as his legs allowed it, Olwynn left the sorcerer's den and returned the key to Harek's study. Later, after he'd burnt his clothes and scrubbed away the unclean magic, along with no small amount of skin, he soaked in a scalding tub and wondered why the Prelate would hold a key to the magic he'd fought so hard to destroy.

# CHAPTER THIRTY-EIGHT

Olywnn entered the hall, and saw the hunters gathered at the smaller hearth. Times past, he'd found it appropriate that the *con'dehr* ate at the front of the hall, and the hunters in the rear. Now, he suspected that Aeolmar was the honorable leader, and Harek something less.

Ignoring stares and grumbles from his fellow soldiers, Olwynn approached the hunters' table. "May I?" he asked Aeolmar.

The First Hunter shrugged, which Olwynn took as an invitation. He sat, and signaled a *saffira* for a plate. "I've learned something," Olwynn said.

"I never took you for a scholar," Aeolmar said without looking up from his food. "Have you proof?"

"You don't even know what I'm about to tell you," Olwynn said, "yet you already demand proof?"

"If I wanted to hear half-wit ideas, I'd speak to Harek."

The *saffira* arrived with Olwynn's plate, and they ate in silence for a time. "What do you know of Teg'urnan's history?" Olwynn asked at length.

"Enough," Aeolmar replied. "Why?"

"Do you know the name Sarfek?"

"Harek's brother?" Aeolmar looked up at Olwynn. "He's dead."

"Is he?" Olwynn countered. "Or is that just what we've been told?"

Aeolmar stood and moved away from the table. After a moment Olwynn followed. "What are you getting at, man?" Aeolmar demanded.

"What I can tell you is this," Olwynn began. "Harek keeps Sarfek's rooms as they were when he was alive. I entered those rooms, and found a secret chamber wrapped in demonic spells."

"You're certain they were demonic?"

"They're the same spells I was subjected to in the *doja*," Olwynn replied. "The same tortures, the same pain...everything." Olwynn leaned closer, and continued, "I believe Sarfek is alive. I believe he is the one helping Natraeus."

"Did you see the man, or just his chamber?"

"Only the chamber, but is that not enough?" Olwynn countered.

"Enough to prove that Harek is a man of questionable loyalties, but not enough to prove his dead brother lives," Aeolmar replied. "I mean to go to the queen, and I cannot do so with only a room of artifacts."

Olwynn frowned, but nodded.

"Why would Sarfek assist Natraeus?" Aeolmar asked.

Olwynn shook his head. "Truly, I don't know."

"That's what I need to know," Aeolmar said. "Whether or not Sarfek lives is a separate concern. I need to know who is assisting Natraeus, and why."

***

"What do you think they're discussing?"

Finlay looked up into Innetha's eyes, dark and luminous. He couldn't say why, but they reminded him of marsh lights. "I've no idea," he answered. "Isn't divining men's secrets your specialty?"

Innetha laughed softly as she straddled the bench. "I have no idea of how to loosen a man's tongue. Usually, they tell me what's on their mind of their own accord."

*They're probably too exhausted to remember which secrets to keep.* Finlay kept his observations to himself and jerked his head toward the First Hunter and the *con'dehr.* "Why does their conversation interest you so?"

"It doesn't. I only asked because I saw you watching them. How is the queen this morning?" Finlay choked on his bread, and Innetha pounded his back while he struggled for air. "As I suspected."

"You suspect what, exactly?" he wheezed.

"That our gracious queen has developed a taste for southern delicacies." With that Innetha sauntered toward Olwynn, the sway of her hips thoroughly distracting him from his conversation with Aeolmar. After giving the couple a scathing, but ignored, glare, Aeolmar left the table and the hall. Finlay abandoned the remains of his meal and followed Aeolmar.

"Is there anything you need from me?" Finlay called after him. Aeolmar halted, his fists clenched as he rounded on Finlay. The Second Hunter stood his ground and waited for Aeolmar's anger to fade. "Something is obviously wrong. Let me act as your second and help."

"What you can do," Aeolmar began, "is determine why a simpering, cowardly king would attempt a war against not one, but two lands more powerful than his own."

"Natraeus?" Finlay asked.

"So, my description's accurate." Aeolmar's mouth twisted into a sardonic, somewhat frightening grin. "Yes, I refer to Natraeus. Learn why he does what he does, why he moved toward a war he cannot win. That will help me."

Aeolmar spun on his heel and left Finlay standing in the corridor, contemplating his next course of action. He considered asking Olwynn about what he and Aeolmar had discussed, but decided against it. Finlay was well aware of Innetha's charms and doubted that Olwynn would give up a morning with her to debate Natraeus' motivations. Instead, he went to the royal archive.

After a day spent surrounded by maps and tomes of all descriptions, Finlay was no closer to answering Aeolmar's question than before. If anything, his research had further confounded him; the dark fae occupied a strange place in the realm, being they were Olluhm's children by Nibika'al and thus unacknowledged by Cydia. Because of that, Cydia refused to let them reside upon the same land as her own children; some thought Cydia spiteful, but not Finlay. If he had a mate who was tricked from his bed, he certainly wouldn't invite the trickster's children into his home.

Nibika'al had found the dark fae a home in the arid region northwest of Parthalan, naming it "night's garden" in the old language. Nibika was once devoid of both resources and farmland, but it was situated between Thurnda and the rest of the elfin kingdoms. In fact, most of the trade routes passed through Nibika, making it an ideal way station for northern merchants, thus bringing needed goods to the region. Finlay recalled a crusty old elf who journeyed to Cadogan every few years, trading ores and gemstones from the north for dried fish and the like...

A shaft of light slanted across the maps, and Finlay feared he'd stayed too long in the archive. Not wanting to be late for his evening with Asherah, he left the parchments where they lay and rushed to her chambers. He fervently hoped that this evening would commence his proper courtship of Asherah, though where that courtship would lead he couldn't guess.

Despite Asherah's insistence that he do otherwise, Finlay knocked before entering her chambers. No matter how close the two had become, he just didn't feel right barging into the queen's private space. Then the door handle turned, and Finlay straightened his back.

"Finlay," Asherah greeted. "I'm so glad you're here."

"How could I refuse," he mumbled, the sight of her taking his breath away. Asherah's pale hair was piled atop her head, a few loose curls grazing her shoulders. Her gown was the colors of sunset, the fabric shifting from peach to red to gold as she moved. Gold embroidery graced the fitted bodice, and the full sleeves and skirt were edged in golden cord. A high collar surrounded her graceful neck, and jewels glinted at her throat.

"You look amazing," Finlay said, acutely aware of his own attire: worn boots, his usual sword belt, and while his tunic and leggings were clean, they were better suited for riding than an intimate meal with the Queen of Parthalan. "Forgive me, I should have dressed differently."

"What you are wearing is fine. After all, it is only dinner," Asherah said. "Now enter, I'm sure you're hungry."

With a wave of her hand, she beckoned him to the inner chamber, where Finlay saw a feast fit for a high celebration. Roast meats, every sort of fruit he could imagine, platters of cheeses and loaves of bread covered the table, along with fine crystal decanters of wine and water. There were even platters of candied berries and other elaborate confections set atop small pedestals. Next to the table stood Attia, Asherah's own *saffira-nell*, along with several other servants, all of them ready to serve food and libations.

"I wasn't sure what you would like," Asherah explained when she saw Finlay stare at the vast amount of food. She gestured for him to sit, and once he had taken his place and availed himself of the wine, Asherah dismissed Attia and the rest of the *saffira*. Then the queen served Finlay herself, piling his plate with assorted delicacies, though she only took a few pieces of fruit and cheese for herself.

"You don't care for meat?" asked Finlay as he sampled the roast duck.

"I've sworn to never again consume the flesh of another," she replied, and Finlay put down the meat. "No, no," she said, waving her hands, "please, eat whatever you'd like. You needn't eat the same as I do."

Finlay tentatively took a bite of the duck, and Asherah smiled as she bit into a ripe berry. He returned her smile with a grin of his own, and they proceeded to enjoy their meal. Time slipped away quickly, and Finlay was surprised when he looked toward the window and saw only darkness; night had long since fallen, the child sun a mere memory on the horizon. Whether his lack of awareness was due to the wine or tremendous amount of food, or perhaps the excellent company, Finlay did not know. What he did know was that he was having the most wonderful night of his life. He and Asherah laughed and talked of many things, and after a time, she noticed that they'd gone and emptied the decanters.

"Shall I send for more wine?" Finlay asked, rising from his seat.

"There is more, in my private chamber." Asherah rose and glided toward the rear door. "Would you like to join me?" she asked, casting a glance over her shoulder that made his heart beat in his ears.

"Of course."

While Asherah located the wine, Finlay took the opportunity to look about the area. They stood in large sitting room, beyond which lay her sleeping and bathing chambers. To the left, large glass doors were thrown open to her garden despite the cool air, and the pleasant scent of winter blossoms wafted in on the breeze. Across from the garden sat the hearth, hewn from a rich green stone, and in front of it was the bench where he and Asherah had fervently kissed, only to be interrupted by Attia. He smiled as he remembered her arms around his neck, her slender fingers as they played with his hair, the hunger that both increased and was sated by her touch. He left off his reminiscence when Asherah returned with the wine and offered Finlay a full goblet.

"Care to walk in the garden?" Asherah asked. Finlay nearly questioned her bemused grin when he realized it was in response to his own smile, born of the memory of her lips on his. Rather than risking an explanation, he extended his arm, and escorted his lady queen to the royal garden. They walked for a time among the blooming plants; when Finlay realized how far they'd walked he looked about in disbelief.

"How big is this garden?" he asked, for they had easily walked the length of the queen's chamber thrice over. More, the garden was in the center of Teg'urnan, but he saw none of the palace's gray stone walls.

"As big as you'd like," she replied, gracing him with that mischievous smile he enjoyed so. "And when you'd like to leave, just turn to the east and my door is five steps away. Anything you'd like is here, from a seashore to a mountain top."

"My queen has a magic garden?" he asked.

"Yes. As far as I know it has always been here, even before Sahlgren." Asherah perched upon the edge of a boulder that was itself at the edge of a meadow. A stream gurgled in the distance, and Finlay wondered if it was stocked with magical fish. "And I have told you, I am no queen in these chambers. Out here, I am not even Asherah, but one with the sky and wind. I am just me."

"Then what shall I call you, O Nameless Beauty?" he asked. "Am I only to refer to you as 'love'?"

"Why ever would you call me that?" she asked.

"You're my love; that's why," he replied. *I cannot believe I just said that. She must think I'm a fool, or worse.*

But Asherah surprised him yet again. "I think I would like to be your love."

Finlay knelt in front of Asherah and brushed her cheek with his fingertips. "Asherah, may I kiss you?"

"You may do more than kiss me," she replied. His hand moved to the nape of her neck as he drew her face to his. That kiss was soft, tender, just the way Finlay wanted to kiss her every morning when he woke, every night before he slept. Asherah wound her fingers in the curls above Finlay's neck and smiled. "And now, I will kiss you." She pressed her lips to his.

The sweet, soft kisses quickly gave way to their passion, and Finlay, needing her closer than he'd ever needed anyone, pulled Asherah from the boulder and onto the ground beside him. Asherah cried out, startling Finlay so that he fell flat on his back with Asherah on top of him.

"Your hands." She rubbed a fresh scrape on her neck. Finlay was well aware of his rough palms, but he hadn't expected them to damage Asherah's delicate skin.

"Forgive me." At the sight of the red mark, he tried to rise, but Asherah had other plans.

"I like you like this." She pushed her palms flat against his shoulders and kissed him again. Finlay couldn't help losing himself in her soft lips, and he forgot that she was the Queen of Parthalan, that they were lying on the ground in her garden; he nearly forgot his own name. Then he forgot himself entirely as he rolled Asherah beneath him and positioned himself between her knees.

Finlay left a trail of kisses along her jaw and on to her throat, while his hands moved to Asherah's breast and plucked open the golden buttons that fastened her bodice. Asherah arched her back as she pulled her arms free of the fabric, then she worked to unfasten his belt. Finlay caressed her bare skin with his hands and mouth as if to worship her, now well and truly lost in her arms.

"Do you want to take me to bed?" Asherah asked, her breath hot against his ear. "Though, this is a pleasant spot for love-making."

Her words roused him, and Finlay raised his head to regard the woman spread beneath him. *What am I doing?* he thought as he sat up, waves of shame rolling over him. He turned his back to the queen and covered his face with his hands.

Asherah sat up as well, and rested her cheek against his shoulder.  "Why did you stop?" she asked. "Do you not like being outdoors?"

"No, it's not that...Well, partly," he replied.

"Then tell me the other part." Asherah's lips caressed his neck. Finlay turned back to her, ready to bare his soul before his love, but found that he could not tear his eyes from her breasts outlined in the moonlight.

"Asherah, you must cover yourself," he said as he pulled the sides of her gown closed. "You...you should not be exposed like this." Asherah looked down, watching his hands as he pulled the fabric together across her torso, then she snatched the thin cloth from his hands.

"Does your queen disgust you?" she demanded as she pulled her gown up to her neck. "Do I not measure up to the girls you are used to?"

"What?" Finlay exclaimed, taken aback by her words. "No, you are beau—"

"Do not lie to me!" she shrieked. "Get out of my sight."

Finlay opened his mouth to protest, but the anger in her eyes kept him silent. He got to his feet and walked a few paces from the queen, and kept his back to her when he spoke again. "I meant no offense," he said softly. "I will be gone before first dawn." He heard her sigh amidst the rustle of fabric.

"You don't need to leave Teg'urnan," she said. "You're a good hunter, and Aeolmar's second. You can do much more good by remaining." Finlay turned around and saw that while she had pulled her gown over her arms, but the bodice remained loose. Asherah noticed where his eyes fell and bunched the fabric together with her fist. She moved to rise and Finlay leaped forward to assist her; he was both surprised and pleased that she accepted his arm. Then she spoke, and her tone told him that she had long ago learned to separate her emotions from her duty.

"You will remain in Teg'urnan, and you will remain a hunter," she continued once she was upright. "We will not speak of this matter again, but carry on as though this night never happened."

Finlay took her hands in his and held them against his heart. "Let me explain," he pleaded. "Asherah, punish me however you wish, take my life if that is all I can give you to atone, but love—"

"Call me that again and I'll have your head," she growled as she snatched her hands away. "Go."

"As you wish, my lady queen," he said as he bowed his head. Finlay turned toward the east, walked the requisite five steps, and left her garden.

# Chapter Thirty-Nine

## Aeolmar Speaks

*I'd been dreaming the most wonderful dream I'd ever had; in fact, it was the first nighttime vision of mine that I wouldn't term a nightmare since before my family died. I was at the sea, lying upon the wet sand just out of reach of the waves. Not another soul was in sight, and yet I'd shed the loneliness that had become such an indelible part of me. As I sat beneath the hot suns, the waves lapping at my feet, I was content.*

*But I wasn't alone. Even though I couldn't see her, I knew she was near. My mate. She who I'd looked so long for, who I'd desired before I ever knew her name, was here on this beach with me.*

*I gazed down the shoreline and saw her in the water, swimming just past the breakers. I called out her name and she smiled, then she made her way back to shore. When she reached the shallows she stood, the water swirling in little eddies about her hips, and I was entranced by her beauty. She was... perfect. Everything I had ever wanted, everything I'd hoped she would be, she was.*

*Then she was in my arms, her lips tasting salty like the sea, her hair floating about her on the gentle waves. I said her name as I covered her face in kisses and told her that I loved her, that I'd never let her go. She gazed up at me with her shining eyes, lovely like crystals set in her perfect face, and she promised that she would love me until the end of time...*

*I drifted in the half-aware state between dreaming and wakefulness, content for I could feel her pressed against me. Her wet hair was cold against my neck but the rest of her was warm and soft. I nestled her against me and burrowed deeper beneath the furs, assuming that her damp hair was the result of our time in the sea and we'd been too eager to get to bed to wait for it to dry. Then I felt her shoulders tremble, and heard her sobs.*

*My eyes finally opened, and I saw Asherah curled up against me, hiding her face as she tried to compose herself. I knew she'd intended to spend the night with Finlay, and her appearance in my bed told me that things hadn't gone as planned. Tears fell against my chest, and she quickly wiped them away. I pretended not to notice as I smoothed back her hair.*

*"Tell me."*

*"It was horrible," she said hoarsely. "Well, not in the beginning. Dinner was wonderful; we were laughing and talking. He was courting me, just like you said. No one had ever courted me in the past, and I liked it. Liked him. I found myself wondering if I could love him." She fell silent as she buried her face against my neck.*

*"What happened to make things not wonderful?" I asked as I wiped away a few more tears. Asherah took a ragged breath before she replied.*

*"We went to the garden to have some wine. He asked if he could kiss me, and I said yes. Before I knew it, we were on the ground together and my gown was unfastened to my waist." She attempted a small laugh, which was more of a stifled sob.*

*"Are you all right?" I demanded as I tilted her chin upward. "Did he hurt you?" By all the living gods, if Finlay had harmed her I would skin him alive in the palace square.*

*"Not intentionally," she replied. My resolve to kill Finlay slowly and with a great deal of pain must have been evident,*

*so she continued, "His hands, they're so callused they scraped me." She guided my fingers across her breast and neck, and I felt the raised welts. His hands must be callused like a smith's to tear at Asherah's skin so. I released her and rolled to the far side of my bed and grabbed a small pot of ointment I used for blood burns. While I rubbed the cool gel on the welts, I asked her what happened next.*

*"He saw my scars, the ones across my breasts, and he turned away from me," she said. "I disgusted him so much he could hardly look at me."*

*I left off my healer's tasks and traced the silver path close to her collarbone. In truth, the scars upon Asherah's breasts were hardly visible, especially when compared with the ones she bore across her back. If I hadn't felt that gash upon her shoulder those many winters past, I might not have ever asked her about the pale marks and just assumed they had been gotten during the many battles she fought. Since that first night we shared, I hadn't paid the scars any mind; if anything, her courage and sacrifice made her more beautiful to my eyes.*

*While I saw her scars as a mere afterthought, to Asherah they were a constant reminder of her enslavement, and she felt each one as if it was newly-gotten. She once shared with me that she held off consummating her love for Lormac for nearly a full turn of the seasons, fearful that he would see her as disfigured, unlovable beast. I've no idea if Finlay knew or cared how Asherah had obtained the marks upon her flesh, but his rejection had confirmed her worst fear: the demons had ruined her.*

*"You know I think you're beautiful," I said. "All of Parthalan speaks of their beautiful queen. You're not—"*

*"I know, I know," she interrupted, "but regardless of what is said, the fact remains that he saw me bare, then pulled away and told me to cover myself." A tear slipped down her cheek; I kissed it away and asked how she'd left things with Finlay.*

*"I shouted at him to leave, but he didn't go. He started offering me words, trying to apologize, but I'd heard enough from him."*

*"He tried apologizing?" That surprised me.*

*She laughed shortly. "He went so far as to offer me his life in penance."*

*"You didn't take it?" Again I was surprised, more so that Asherah didn't accept his apology. Truly, she had the kindest heart of anyone I've ever known. For her to cast Finlay from her presence, he must have well and truly hurt her. Perhaps I'd skin him anyway.*

*Asherah flopped onto her back and sighed. "This has happened before. A man comes to Teg'urnan intent upon bedding the queen so he has a story to share. I daresay it's all Argent saw in me, at least in the beginning. No, a scorned woman isn't worth a man's life."*

*"How can you say you aren't worth it?" I asked as twined my fingers in her damp hair. To me, Asherah was priceless, worth far more than a boy merchant from the desert. "Asherah, how long ago did he leave?"*

*"Shortly after moonrise."*

I glanced toward the windows, saw the lightening sky. "Rih-ka, *it's nearly first dawn. Have you been sitting in your bath, crying, since he left?"*

*"Yes," she choked out as she was again wracked with sobs.*

*"You should have come for me sooner," I said as I folded her against me. I hated it when she cried, hated that I didn't know what would comfort her. No, I knew what she wanted, but it was something I couldn't give her.*

*"I had to wash him off me," she said in a small voice, and I wondered if more had happened between her and Finlay than what she had told me. I left it for the time being and concentrated on offering her what comfort I could.*

*"I would have helped you." My words threw open the floodgates of her despair, and her tears now flowed unchecked onto my chest. "Dea comora, I'm sorry I pushed you to do this." I*

*stroked her back as I held her. "I really thought he loved you. I'm so sorry it happened this way."*

*"It is not your fault. You only wanted what's best." She stared up at me, her eyes molten pools of blackness, and asked me what I knew she wished with all her heart. "What we have...why can't it be love?"*

*I sighed as I tucked her head against my neck. If she only knew how much I really did love her, how I wished I could just claim her as my mate and live out my days with her as the center of my world, how many times I had wanted to say those few words just to make her happy. But I didn't. I'm not the man for her.*

*I remembered my dream and how my mate felt different in my arms, how her laugh had warmed my heart. Already her image was fading from my mind's eye, but I could never forget how she made me feel. As my waking body held Asherah, I felt the need to protect her, to calm her, but I did not feel the same all-consuming passion as I had for the woman in my dream. If I lied to Asherah, I would also be denying her that true happiness, and that I couldn't do.*

*"Asherah, we both know that what we share is not love," I said as I buried my face in her hair. Gods, she smelled good. "We comfort each other and share our pain...but we don't love each other."*

*"I wish we did."*

*"I do, too."*

*Asherah fell silent, lightly tracing her fingertips across my shoulders. We remained wrapped in each other's arms for a time, and I tried to slip back into my dream. I wanted to catch a glimpse of my mate's face, hear her call my name just one more time. My eyes searched the dreamscape for a hint about where she was, when I would meet her...*

*"Aeolmar?"*

*"Mmm?"*

*"You're wrong. I do love you. In time, I hope you'll love me."*

*I kissed her forehead. "I hope so, too,* rihka.*"*

# Chapter Forty

Olwynn arranged a sleeping Innetha in the crook of his arm, and pushed the wild curls back from her brow. As he smoothed her dark, wonderfully rumpled hair, he wondered for the thousandth time if he should tell her what had transpired in Sarfek's chamber. But then again, she may already know.

A quirk of Innetha's mouth had told him that she noticed his red, raw skin after he'd scrubbed away the leftover enchantments from Sarfek's chambers, but she hadn't mentioned anything. She'd also raised an eyebrow at his half-burned clothing in the hearth, but had accepted his explanation that they were old clothes, long past their usefulness. He'd done those things for her, the scrubbing and the burning, to keep her from more of his memories. Now, Olwynn wondered if he shouldn't have told her all along.

"You aren't what you pretend to be," Olwynn said. "You're not what the rest think you are."

She stirred in his arms; apparently, she'd been awake the whole time. "And what do these 'others' think of me?" Innetha raised herself on her elbow, her dark hair falling across her face.

He pushed back her curls, and held the mass of them at the nape of her neck. "You pretend you're only concerned with pleasure," he replied, unsure what polite word was used to replace wanton or trollop. Indeed, many considered her the palace whore. Innetha, however, laughed off his attempted nicety.

"Everyone is concerned with pleasure; I'm just honest about it," she said. "So are you, or I wouldn't be here with you."

"True." Once, he'd wondered about her promiscuity, but she'd slept in his bed every night for nigh on three moons. It was doubtful that all of Innetha's supposed suitors had abandoned her at once. "But you're so much more."

"I'm a woman cursed," she said, rolling over to lie on her back. "I'm fated to endure the pain of those around me."

Olwynn turned toward her, his hand stroking her from throat to breastbone. She'd told him of her curse, but not how it came about, and he didn't press her to speak of things she'd rather leave be. Cydia knew that his own memories were painful enough for her to deal with.

"Do you really see every memory?" he asked. "Of mine, I mean."

"I know something terrible happened to you quite recently, and that you haven't told me about it," she countered. "You've done an admirable job keeping it from me."

"Good." Olwynn pulled a length of dark hair through his fingers. "Can this curse be broken?" She twisted around to face him, her legs tangling with his.

"Yes, but not by you. You've suffered enough," she added. When he still protested she kissed him and did a few other things to change the subject. Olwynn let her distract him, but not as much as she'd intended.

"Is it really only a night's pleasure?" he asked. Innetha's kisses grew more fervent, and by her silence, Olwynn assumed it was. He was surprised by the cold weight in his chest, though he'd been expecting it; why Innetha would feel differently for him he didn't know. He only knew that he wanted her to.

Afterward, their silence remained, and Olwynn wondered if Innetha had said goodbye in her way. As he drifted off to sleep her felt her touch his cheek and whisper her reply.

"I don't want you for only one night."

"Then stay, for all the nights."

"What of the days?"

Olwynn smiled. "Those, too."

# Chapter Forty-One

Finlay stood alone at the Eastern Watchtower, forgoing the windbreak even though the day had proven cold and brisk. He leaned against the post, all but hoping for a stray piece of wood to pierce his skin; if he didn't remove the splinter or clean the wound, perhaps it would fester and poison his blood. If he was lucky, the infection would kill him and end this misery. Nearly four moons had passed since he had offended Asherah in her garden, and while his body completed the daily tasks of living, he was only a shell of his former self.

*If I can survive this long without a heart, then a splinter will surely not kill me.* Finlay pushed off the post and leaned on the railing, his fingers chilled stiff by the frigid wind, but he didn't care. He watched as the child sun broke the horizon and recalled the time he watched the suns rise with Asherah from the same spot. That was before—before he kissed her, before his foolish southern customs made him act like an utter fool, before she hated him with the whole of her being.

"Finlay."

He turned around and saw the First Hunter approaching. Aeolmar, like every other resident of the palace, behaved as if they had no knowledge of his horrible night with the queen.

What Finlay didn't know was if they were truly unaware of the humiliating event, or if Asherah had ordered their silence. "Yes?"

"Natraeus has returned," Aeolmar stated. "Asherah has requested that we be present while she receives him."

"They must have ridden through the night to get here," Finlay muttered, glancing toward the child sun. "Was he expected?"

"No. Nor is he welcome."

They walked in silence to the queen's chambers, and Finlay strove to understand why Natraeus would bother to trek all the way from Nibika without an expressed invitation. Teg'ur-nan was far from the dark fae's land, at least eight days on horseback, and the terrain that lay between the two was anything but hospitable. Finlay opened his mouth to question Aeolmar, but as soon as the two men turned down the royal corridor, they heard shouting. Recognizing the queen's voice, Finlay broke into a run.

"This is preposterous," Asherah shouted as Finlay entered, closely followed by Aeolmar. A quick glance around the room told Finlay that not only were the other three hunters present, but Harek and his *con'dehr* also surrounded Natraeus and his warriors. "Have you taken total leave of your senses?"

"How is reclaiming what is rightfully mine anything but sensible?" Natraeus retorted. "L'hirre stole my lands long ago."

"He conquered you," Harek corrected, his voice rumbling across the room. "You fought a battle. Your force was the weaker, and you lost."

"We were not weak," Natraeus shouted. "We were duped!"

"History says otherwise," Asherah countered, taking her seat again. She glanced toward Aeolmar and Finlay, her shoulders straightening. "If I remember correctly, your five-times grandsire tried to ally himself with L'hirre against another race, all over some imagined affront. Was it the trolls he was angry with? Or perhaps the sylph? I can't keep track of your family's mishaps." Natraeus went red with rage, but Asherah ignored his anger as she continued. "Wisely, in my opinion, L'hirre declined to involve himself in such nonsense. Your ancestor was offended by the refusal and proceeded to attack Tingu." Asherah picked up a quill from her map table, twirling it between her fingers. "Didn't the bulk of your grandsire's force freeze when they attempted crossing the World's Spine in the midst of winter? Yes, frozen faeries are not the best of warriors."

"That is why I need you," Natraeus implored. "Fae united with fae against the elfin menace."

"Menace?" Aeolmar asked. "How are the elves menacing you, Natraeus? They do nothing but mine the earth and manage trade routes, hardly menacing acts."

"That's it," Finlay said quietly. Every set of eyes trained upon the Second Hunter, so he continued, "Since Thurnda became independent of Tingu, Sibeal has controlled all of the trade routes in the north, save the troll roads. Routes that were once controlled by Nibika." Emboldened, he took a step toward Natraeus. "This isn't over elves or past grudges or who rules whom. It's over common gold."

Natraeus clenched his fists, his jaw set as if he'd bitten into iron. Then he exhaled, rearranging his features into a mask of diplomacy. "The fake Lord of Cadogan, is that what you're calling yourself?" he asked smoothly. "Yes, I know of Asherah's lies. The queen's untruths are bound to endanger her people. Clearly, the time for a new leadership in Parthalan is long overdue."

Asherah stood slowly, her voice thinly veiled fury. "Parthalan is mine. Mine! I may bestow a lordship on whomever I choose. Why, just this morning, I considered making you the lord of the dung heap." A few snickers rattled about the chamber, from both Natraeus's and Asherah's retinues. "In light of the fact that you dare to suggest an attack against my heir, I rescind my most generous appointment."

"The Lord of Tingu is your heir?" Natraeus sneered. "A half-elf to lead the fae? Blasphemy!"

"Better a half-elf than one of the dark fae," Asherah retorted. "The last dark fae who ruled here nearly killed the lot of us, fae and elf alike!"

Natraeus' eyes blazed, as did Aeolmar's, but Finlay's voice remained calm when he spoke again.

"Sahlgren's rulership, and his evil deeds, are discussed often here in Teg'urnan, Natraeus," he said. "Painful as these stories may be, we teach our children what has come before, so past mistakes may not be repeated. Apparently, those in Nibika do not share our foresight."

"And I'll hear no more from you!" Natraeus shouted, rounding on Finlay. "Asherah only named you a lord so she may share her bed with royalty! All she's good for, after—"

Finlay moved so fast that neither the dark fae nor Aeolmar could stop him, not that Aeolmar would have. The Second Hunter grabbed Natraeus's ornate tunic and hauled him to his feet. The dark king's guards tried to intervene but Aeolmar blocked them with his body; the dark fae tended toward foolishness, but the guards were wise enough not to test the First Hunter.

"I don't care who you are," growled Finlay. "If you speak of my queen that way again, I'll tear out your throat."

Natraeus, white-faced, nodded.

"I will say this once," Asherah began, her voice taking on a tone of proclamation. She nodded once to the slight man standing at her elbow, and the scribe spread a fresh parchment before him. "If you dare to raise a hand or finger or your cursed, diseased cock toward any elf, I will send the full force of Parthalan's legion to Nibika. If you do anything—anything!—to harm Leran, I will kill you myself." The chamber was silent, save for the scribe's quill as he scratched away. Once the recording was complete, Harek spoke.

"As Prelate, I sentence you to remain within Nibika's borders for the next hundred winters. My legion will escort you to your lands, and guards will remain at your border. If you set foot on Parthian soil, your penalty will be death."

"You cannot," Natraeus shouted.

"I can," Harek replied, "and I have. You have no business here, and we want none with you." The Prelate gestured, and three warriors stepped forward to escort the dark fae from the chamber. Finlay released his hold on Natraeus, his face as hard as stone as he watched the king stumble. Natraeus opened his mouth, perhaps to protest his banishment or maybe complain about Finlay's rough handling, but remained silent as he spun on his heel and left the room, his cloak billowing and his guards following close behind. Harek and the *con'dehr* closely followed, as did the hunters and the scribe, until Asherah was alone with Aeolmar and Finlay. When the door clicked shut, she sank into her chair, her head supported in her hands.

"He's a useless bastard, Asherah," Aeolmar said. "Don't pay his words any mind." He went on, railing about following Natraeus beyond Teg'urnan's gates and sinking a bolt in the back of the dark king's neck. The queen made no comment about Aeolmar's ravings, but remained motionless as she stared at the floor.

Finlay couldn't look away from her. Despite the fact that she had all but ignored him since that evening in her garden, he couldn't bear to see her so distraught. He crouched before her and murmured her name; when she ignored him he gently took her hands from her face. "Aeolmar's right. Letting his words affect you gives him a measure of power over you, and Natraeus is nothing if not powerless."

Asherah continued staring at the floor, but did not withdraw her hands from Finlay's. "Before you came, he said that I'm nothing more than a common wench, a whore even, gifting titles and land to those who would share my bed."

"It would seem that Natraeus covets that honor for himself," Finlay commented, and to his surprise Asherah laughed.

"Do you think so?" she asked, glancing up at him.

"If he merely wanted retribution against the elves, he could have raised an army and fought them long ago. Why come here now, why take the risk? He seeks a greater prize than land or trade routes, my lady queen." She held his gaze for a moment, and in that same moment, Finlay forgot all that had transpired during the past moons and remembered only that he loved her. Finlay squeezed her hand, glad to have taken this first step toward repairing his relationship with Asherah.

"The prize you rejected?" Asherah asked, the words falling from her mouth as a dead leaf falls in autumn. Finlay almost gasped aloud, for those words had cut him as deeply as an obsidian blade.

"Forgive me." Finlay dropped her hands, then he rose and left the chamber, not sparing a backward glance.

"Are you punishing him, or yourself?" he heard Aeolmar demand of Asherah, but Finlay didn't stay to hear the queen's response. He already knew that she hated him.

# Chapter Forty-Two

"Fool," Harek hissed as he shoved Natraeus into the chamber before him. "Of all the stupid things you could have done, you had to threaten Leran."

"I can't help my hatred for the boy," Natraeus spat. "I'd like to impale him before his precious Seat and watch the life drain from him."

"No matter." Harek waved away Natraeus's further descriptions of the Lord of Tingu's demise. "We have accomplished our objective." The Prelate strode to the honeycombed shelves that lined the walls and selected a scroll tied with black cord; it contained the names of those soldiers hand-picked by Harek to escort the dark fae on their return to Nibika. Each had been bound by Sarfek to aid Natraeus in much the same way the sorcerer had once enthralled his own brother.

"You couldn't have just sent warriors to Nibika without all this bother?" Natraeus asked. "Why perpetrate this ruse? You know I care not about trade routes."

"Asherah is a peaceful soul," Harek replied. "Unless she feels that you threaten that which she holds dear, she'll not move against you. And no one is more dear to our queen than Leran."

"Jealous, Prelate?" he asked with a raised brow. "I think you desire the Lord of Tingu gone as much as I."

"I only wish to serve a strong ruler," Harek replied, then poured a measure of wine for himself and Natraeus. "Once you control both Parthalan and Tingu, that ruler will be you."

Natraeus smiled as he quaffed the wine. *He truly is a fool,* Harek thought. *And the fool has played into my hands. Now, I will not only save Parthalan, but that ungrateful Leran as well. Asherah will give herself to me in gratitude.*

"We will dance upon the graves of our enemies, Natraeus," Harek proclaimed, the dark king smiling as he quaffed the wine. *But one of those graves will be yours.*

# CHAPTER FORTY-THREE

Asherah presided over her hunters with her usual poise, but to Finlay her agitation was plain. She picked up her quill only to set it down again and shuffled through her maps as if they were only parchments and not her most prized possessions. Finlay was amazed that no one else seemed to notice her behavior, and resolved to speak with her later.

*But will she let me speak to her?* Only four days ago, Finlay had attempted to comfort Asherah after that unpleasant ordeal with the dark fae, and she had thrown his good intentions back in his face. No, he'd keep his words, well-meaning as they might be, to himself.

"As such, we need to determine how far Natraeus' reach truly extends," Asherah was saying. "Sahlgren once went south to forge a pact with demons, and Natraeus seeks to emulate him in word and deed. Finlay?"

"My lady?" Finlay looked up, startled; Asherah hadn't said his name in so long, he'd assumed that she'd forgotten it.

"You will go to the Southern Contingent. Your purpose will be to ascertain if Natraeus, or any of the dark fae for that matter, have had dealings in the region. You will leave at the next moon." Asherah's black eyes were cold, but not as cold as the lump in Finlay's chest that used to be his heart.

"As you wish, my lady. I'll make the arrangements today." He would have elaborated, and described how he would visit not only the headquarters of that region's hunters but also the trading outposts he knew so well, but he didn't. He knew she wanted to hear nothing further pass his lips, be it an affirmation to follow her orders, a furious scream, or an agonizing sob.

If Asherah had taken note his inner turmoil, she hid it well. Her *saffira-nell* murmured something in the queen's ear, and Asherah dismissed her hunters. Aeolmar brushed past Finlay without so much as a glance, and he wondered yet again if the First Hunter harbored a grudge against him over what had transpired in the queen's garden. Finlay turned a corner and sat on a window seat, his head in his hands; he didn't know how much longer he could endure Asherah's cold treatment of him.

"You need to talk to her."

Finlay looked up as Innetha sat beside him.

"Nothing will change until you do," she continued.

"What do you know of it?" Finlay asked wearily. At last, he had confirmation that others knew of the great rift between him and the queen, yet another reason he should leave Teg'urnan behind.

"I know only what I see," she replied. "Every time you look at Asherah it's like your heart is being torn from your chest. When she turns to you, she looks through you."

"She won't talk to me," he said softly. "I've tried, but all she does is send me away."

"If she's important to you, then you'll try again," Innetha said firmly. With that, she rose and left the Second Hunter alone.

Finlay stared out the window at the great square below. He watched the many denizens of Teg'urnan as they went about their day, the smiths and apothecaries and hawkers, and none of them seemed to have a cold, heavy weight lodged in their chest. They all seemed happy. Content.

*I haven't been content since I was in my shop.* Finlay exhaled heavily and admitted that a life at court was no life for him. He was a simple man from the desert, and wanted a simple life free of intrigue and strife. He wanted the safe, unchanging nature of Cadogan, where he could sweep out the dusty corners of the storeroom and compile inventory lists until the end of time.

Quick movements in the square caught Finlay's eye, and he watched as a woman ran into a man's outstretched arms. He caught her, uttering a great cry of happiness, and spun her about. *So, another rumor is true,* he thought while he watched Olwynn wrap his arms around Innetha as if she were his sole reason for breathing. Since shortly after Winter's Eve, talk was that the two were now mates.

The weight in Finlay's chest was now heavier, for there was only one woman who could make him feel the way Olwynn felt about the huntress. That woman wasn't unchanging like the desert, nor was she safe or simple. She was fire that froze, ice that burned his flesh, and the prospect of living his life without her was worse than an eternity in the underworld.

Abruptly he rose, now seeing the wisdom in Innetha's words. No matter the outcome, he needed to speak with Asherah again, if only for the last time. Finlay strode to the queen's door and found it unbolted, so he pushed his way inside. Her chambers were deserted, with not even Attia there to send a scowl his way.

"My lady?" Finlay called softly. He walked to the garden doors, assuming that Asherah had desired a breath of fresh air, but found them bolted from the inside. He approached her private rooms, assuming the queen sought a brief respite from the stresses of her day.

"Asherah?" he called out, since barging in didn't seem like the best of plans. When he received no response he strode inside and found the sitting room deserted. He swallowed his apprehension and entered her sleeping chamber, which was also empty. Like the door to her garden, her private exit was also locked from the inside.

*Where could she have gone?* Finlay hadn't strayed far from her door and knew that Asherah hadn't entered the corridor. His face went hot as he realized that Asherah was likely in her bathing chamber since that was the only room he hadn't checked. He turned to make a hasty retreat when he noticed something he hadn't during his prior visit: there was a door, which stood wide open, behind the queen's bed. He didn't stop to wonder where the door led as he crossed the threshold. He was determined to explain himself to Asherah, even if it was the last thing he accomplished.

The darkness of the corridor surprised Finlay, as well as its length. He imagined that this passageway was another secret exit, possibly meant to ensure the queen's safety in case of attack, when he spied a soft light, and then heard a woman's moan up ahead. Assuming that the queen was hurt he quickened his pace, but what he saw halted him as surely as a brick wall.

The tunnel ended in a second bedchamber, and the moan he's heard had indeed escaped Asherah's lips, but she wasn't in pain; rather, she was in her First Hunter's arms as he kissed her deeply. Aeolmar had one hand buried in her hair while the other unfastened the buttons at the back of Asherah's gown. He reached the penultimate fastening and peeled the gown from her flesh, leaving the fabric draped about her hips. Aeolmar's hand moved to the front of Asherah's body, and while Finlay could no longer see it her quickened breath left little question as to what he was doing.

Finlay's breath was like thorns in his throat, and he didn't know if he would weep at the loss of her, or choke and die right there in the passageway. He tried to look away, but he couldn't tear his gaze from Asherah's bare skin, so soft and pale. Then Asherah had Aeolmar's jerkin unlaced, and as he shrugged out of the leather he lifted her out of her gown. She laughed as he carried her to bed, and Finlay could not stifle the noise that escaped his lips.

"No," he rasped as Aeolmar laid Asherah on her back. Aeolmar's head snapped up and his gaze met with Finlay's over the top of Asherah's head. The First and Second Hunter's stared at one another over the queen's bare form, each waiting for the other to act.

"What's wrong?" Asherah asked.

Aeolmar looked down and caressed her cheek. "Nothing," he murmured, then he sheathed himself in her. Finlay, who had already begun his retreat down the passageway toward Asherah's chamber, was close enough to hear her cry out in pleasure.

***

When Aeolmar found his second, Finlay was again at the Eastern Watchtower, staring up at the moon. Legend told of Cydia's kindness to unrequited lovers, and Finlay hoped that the mother goddess would heed his prayers, though he himself couldn't decide if his heart's desire was to be the man in Asherah's bed, or to never set eyes upon her again.

"Have you been here all day?" Aeolmar asked.

"Where else do I have to go?" Finlay countered. He did not turn to face his commander, so Aeolmar stood next to him and joined in his contemplation of the moon.

"Did you enjoy watching me pleasure the queen?" Aeolmar asked at length.

"It felt as if you'd ripped open my gut and packed it full of salt," Finlay answered. "At least you can be with her like she deserves. All I've done is make her miserable." Finlay turned to regard Aeolmar, the ruddy moonlight lending sharp relief to his features. "Did she tell you what happened?"

"She did," Aeolmar affirmed without looking at him. "I must say, I fail to understand why you rejected her."

"I want her more than anything, but I can't make love to her," Finlay said.

"Why ever not?" Aeolmar asked. "Are you a eunuch?"

"No," Finlay snapped, unsure if that comment was Aeolmar's lame attempt at levity. "Is that what she thinks?" Aeolmar shrugged, and Finlay leaned his head against the battlement. Asherah not only hated him, but questioned his manhood, as well. "She won't let me explain. Hells, she won't even let me apologize," Finlay mumbled as he scrubbed his face with his hands. "And now, she wants me gone. I carried her in my heart for seven winters. I thought of her and nothing else while I learned swordplay and later while I guarded those pilgrims. I spent that time covered in grit and choking on dust, being beaten bloody by one demon after the next, but I never minded, because it was all for her.  All I wanted was to make myself useful, so I could serve my queen. I thought of nothing but her. Now, all I can think about is her sending me away."

"If that memory is so painful, maybe you should think on something else," Aeolmar suggested.

"Hah," Finlay snorted, and Aeolmar turned a hard gaze on his second. "This, coming from a man who drags his past around like a leaden cloak."

"What do you know of my past?" demanded Aeolmar.

"Only that you won't release it." Finlay half expected Aeolmar to throw him off the watchtower or at least shout for a time. Instead, the First Hunter looked away.

"Despite what you saw, Asherah doesn't want me," Aeolmar said quietly. "She wants you."

Finlay laughed the uneven laugh of one whose mind is close to breaking, and leaned back against the stone wall. "You expect me to believe that? What cruel game are you playing at, man?" Sitting on the edge of the battlement, he let his head loll forward. "She can't bear to look at me. Plague, she can hardly be in the same room with me! When I go south at the next moon, I should just stay there, out of her way. Asherah will be happier without me here."

"No, she won't." Finlay looked up, but the edge was gone from Aeolmar's eyes. For the first time, Finlay suspected that Aeolmar was truly trying to help him, though he couldn't understand why. "Asherah has been alone since she took the throne, and she hoped that you were the companion she sought. She's angry, yes, but more than anything she's hurt. If you care for her, you will stay."

"You would give her away so easily?" Finlay asked.

"The queen's heart is not mine to give." With that, Aeolmar left Finlay and his thoughts alone on the watchtower.

# Chapter Forty-Four

Asherah sighed as she propped her elbows on the table and rested her chin on her interwoven fingers. The queen plainly showed the stresses of the past few days, her weary visage causing a pang of guilt deep in Harek's heart. It was far from the first time Harek had manipulated events around Asherah, but he wondered if Natraeus' last visit to Teg'urnan had gone too far.

"You feel it necessary to send the hunter south?" Harek asked, referring to Finlay's imminent departure.

"Yes," Asherah said decisively. "Sahlgren once found allies in the south, and Natraeus worships Sahlgren's every deed. I can well imagine the fool acting out the old king's treachery."

Harek nodded; he was well aware that Natraeus hadn't contracted with any demon, but he had no objection to sending the desert rat back where he came from. With any luck, Finlay would run into some sort of trouble in the south and die a painful death; then, there would be one less hunter to deal with. He was about to agree with Asherah's plan when her head drooped forward, betraying her exhaustion.

"Rest," Harek said as he stood. "I will handle these matters."

Asherah nodded and, without a word of protest, let Attia lead her to her private rooms. Harek watched his queen walk away from him, jealous of the *saffira-nell* on whose arm she leaned. *No matter, soon enough it will be I escorting her to bed. Our bed.*

Harek rushed through the few remaining tasks and was soon within his own chambers. After filling his goblet with rum—not the harsh elfin brandy, which was little more than swill, but the fine liquor distilled in the mortal realm—he opened a chest carved from pale wood. In it was a glassine sphere, small enough to hide in Harek's palm, nestled upon a velvet bed. He placed the sphere on an intricate copper stand, and the image of his brother swirled to life before him.

"Well?" asked Sarfek. "Has the fool mucked up anything since last we spoke?"

Harek launched into a detailed account of all that had transpired since their last discussion and told his brother of Natraeus's latest visit to Teg'urnan, his subsequent banishment, and which of Harek's men had journeyed to Nibika along with the dark fae. No detail was omitted, for without Sarfek's sharp mind and keen intuition, none of Harek's plans would have come to fruition. Those plans were much easier to execute now, since the queen thought that Sarfek was dead.

He'd timed the news of his brother's demise perfectly. Harek and Asherah had been dealing with some meaningless border dispute in the south, and she was thoroughly aggravated with the local lord. Her maps clearly showed the line of demarcation between his lands and his neighbor's, yet the lord insisted that the mapmaker had been bribed and over half his lands—his birthright, he kept repeating—were now lost due to inaccurate cartography. Asherah loved her maps, but she did not love spending a warm spring day in the dusty archives listening to grown men bicker. She'd had enough of this arrogant dilettante and was about to tell him that he would need to wait for an official ruling at the next Reckoning Day, when Attia entered the chamber.

"My lady," she began, "forgive my intrusion, but there is a messenger."

The *saffira-nell* was visibly shaken, as was the messenger, a young boy who looked as if he'd ridden straight through the night to deliver his news. And well he should have, for all that Harek had paid him.

Once his breathing slowed, the youth launched into a tale of rogue sorcerers who'd taken over a village close to Parthalan's western border. Evidently, they had been attracted to the village by some artifact left over from the old gods and were drawing upon its power. The villagers had become little more than the sorcerers' slaves, and those sorcerers were living like kings while children starved. Sarfek was made aware of their foul deeds and, being a powerful sorcerer in his own right, sought to destroy the artifact on his own. Alas, said the boy, the evildoers proved to be too strong, and Sarfek was gravely wounded. The youth concluded his tale by handing Harek a map detailing his brother's current location. The boy, found in a troupe of thieves masquerading as actors, had well earned his coin.

Harek grabbed the map and raced from the room, hardly sparing a glance in Asherah's direction. He made sure that no one else saw the map, and he sent no word to Teg'urnan for nearly a moon; by that time, rumors began to circulate claiming that whatever had attacked Sarfek had taken his brother as well. But the Prelate did return; with a heavy heart, he advised Asherah that Sarfek had been struck with a wasting sickness and had since died from his injuries.

"He held on until I could reach him," Harek sobbed with his head in Asherah's lap. "But there was nothing to be done. He faded, despite all the healer did for him."

"I am so sorry," Asherah crooned. "To lose one's brother is a terrible, terrible thing." Harek went on, apologizing for taking so long in his return, but Asherah quickly hushed him. "No apology is necessary. You may do as you wish to honor his memory. Sarfek was a good man, loyal to Parthalan. He will be sorely missed."

And so Harek learned that he was an accomplished actor himself, and for the first time he spent the entire night in Asherah's chamber. Of course, he laid his head on the floor before the hearth while she remained across the room in her bed, but he had expected no different. The last—the only—time they had shared a bed it hadn't gone well, but no matter. He was so close to his goal he could taste it, and slept soundly on the cold, hard floor. If Asherah's private door hadn't closed with a bang, he wouldn't have stirred until dawn.

"What's he doing here?" came a rough voice. *Argent,* Harek realized. Why would he come to the queen in the dead of night?

"Sarfek's gone," she replied. "He was stricken with some sort of a magical illness, and Harek was unable to save him. He watched him die."

Argent grunted, then Harek heard the whisper of fabric on fabric. He shifted his position on the hearth and cracked an eyelid, watching as Argent wrapped his arms around the queen, her head upon his shoulder while he comforted her.

Argent, comforting her!

Harek's brother had died; he was the one who needed comfort! By Asherah! But no, that arrogant bastard swept the queen into his arms, then made a crass joke about bedding her quietly so as not to wake the grieving Harek. For good measure, he threw in a few disparaging comments concerning Harek's demeanor. Asherah swatted his shoulder, admonishing Argent for his tactless words, then she and her First Hunter retired to her garden.

*Unbelievable. My brother has perished, yet I lie on the cold floor while Argent receives her attentions.* Harek fumed for the rest of the night, straining his ears and eyes to glean the slightest clue about the goings on in the garden. At last, they returned, and Argent took his leave as the elder sun rose.

Harek heard the latch softly click, then Asherah bustling about her chamber. In a short time, she sat beside her Prelate.

"Forgive me for overstaying," Harek said when he pretended to wake.

"Under the circumstances, I cannot fault you." Harek noted that she had changed her dress; most likely the one from the prior evening was covered in grass stains.

"I thought I heard Argent?" Harek hoped she would tell him that he came to discuss the *sola* or some other matter related to the hunters or to court. He'd heard the First Hunter brag about bedding the queen, but he assumed that the man had been lying or that it only happened once. More than anything, Harek wanted Asherah to deny her relationship with Argent, even if it was a lie. Unfortunately, his queen always spoke the truth.

"Yes, Argent sometimes comes to me in the evenings," she said. "We have, ah, become close."

"I see." Harek rose and thanked Asherah for her hospitality. As he strode down the corridor toward his rooms, one thought rang in his mind: *Argent must die.*

"I hope your plan to kill this First Hunter works out better than the last," Sarfek said, rousing Harek from his memories. "Not only did you not get your woman, Aeolmar is as unbending as stone."

"Demons are difficult to work with," Harek said with a dismissive gesture, though he too missed Argent's complicit, self-serving nature. "If Esguth hadn't attacked earlier than agreed, all would have gone as planned. Natraeus is a man we can control."

"Perhaps you should leave off this quest to obtain Asherah," Sarfek suggested. "Since we've put her on the throne, the wench has done nothing but get in our way. When the dark fae attack, she should be removed along with the First Hunter."

"No!" Harek glared at the transparent image of his brother. "I've waited this long, and I will have her." Sarfek nodded grimly, then the image dissipated. Harek took a long draught of rum, enjoying the slow burn as it slid down his gullet. *Yes, I will have her.*

# Chapter Forty-Five

"Finlay?"

Finlay looked up, and dragged himself out of his bleak thoughts. It was late in the day, this meeting having dragged on since noon, and the strain of pretending his heart wasn't a shredded mass had long since rendered him exhausted. Of course, he had become so adept at pretending he had no interest in the queen that he accidentally ignored Asherah when she spoke to him. "My lady?"

"You're departing tomorrow for the Southern Contingent, yes?" Asherah asked in a neutral tone. That neutrality was what he hated most about their current situation. If only she would behave as if she were hurt or angry. Even if she openly despised him, that would make it easier to bear. Instead, she behaved as if he wasn't sitting before her, and she was staring at an empty chair.

"I am," he replied, but before he could offer any details about his coming journey Asherah turned her attention back to her parchments and began discussing a new topic. Finlay wished he could just leave the room and this anguish behind.

*Why bother with leaving when I'm already invisible?* Aeolmar eyed him as the rest of the hunters turned their attention to the queen. Finlay wondered for the thousandth time if they were merely giving Asherah the respect and attention she deserved or ignoring him as politely as possible. He did not fault them for either, for it was an unusual, uncomfortable situation they were all forced to endure.

*I will remain in the south. I will remain there, and Asherah will be able to live her life free of me and the pain I've caused her.* Despite Aeolmar's assurance that Asherah wanted Finlay as her companion, he was now convinced that his original plan was best. Nearly an entire moon had passed since Finlay had discovered the First Hunter in bed with the queen, since he heard her moans of ecstasy; all Finlay had ever done was made her shout curses as she cast him from her presence.

He exhaled heavily and feigned interest in whatever Bron was saying, something about siege engines and how one or two of the contraptions could easily turn the tide of battle. Aeolmar's words to him that day on the watchtower confirmed that Finlay had hurt Asherah deeply, and as long as she was forced to endure his presence, her wounds would not heal. Once he was at the Southern Contingent, he would find a reason—any reason—for him to remain, and he would send a missive to the queen advising her as such. Surely Asherah would agree to his relocation and be glad to be rid of him.

At last, Asherah ended this endless meeting, and the hunters filed out of her receiving chamber. As usual, Finlay reached the corridor before the rest, but spared a backward glance at his queen. She was seated with her back toward the door, her almost-white hair bound up with black ribbons while a few loose curls grazed her shoulders. She turned slightly, and Finlay saw her ruby lips in profile, the graceful arch of her cheek, and it struck him that if he remained in the south he might never set eyes upon his lady queen again.

Determination overtook Finlay and he strode into the chamber, now intent upon explaining his actions to Asherah, whether she wished to hear them or not. He found his way barred by Attia. "I must speak to the queen," he said.

"My lord, she desires her solitude—" Attia began.

"I must," he pleaded. Attia set her jaw; defying Asherah was not something one undertook lightly, not even by she who had served the queen daily since the beginning of her reign. Something in Finlay's eyes must have spoken to the *saffira-nell*, because she stepped aside.

"I hope she doesn't have me flogged for this," Attia muttered. Finlay ignored her as he approached Asherah, still seated at her map table. She glanced upward, making no attempt to hide her irritation.

"Is something wrong?" Asherah asked with that blank look she always gave him. He hated how she looked at him, as if they had never touched, never shared those precious moments he cherished so. As if they were strangers—no, less than strangers. Strangers were at least polite to one another.

"No," he began, only to fall silent. Asherah stared at him for a moment, then blew out an exasperated breath.

"Then what can I do for you?" she asked coolly.

"I'm leaving," he said. "Tomorrow. At second dawn."

"Yes, I'm well aware of this." Asherah shuffled a few of the maps about, and refilled a crystal inkpot.

"Why are you sending me?" Finlay pressed, refusing to let her rote movements distract him. "I've never been on such a mission before."

"You're from the south," she explained. "You're familiar with the region and therefore the best hunter for the assignment, just as Aeolmar would be sent to the west or Innetha to the north." Now Asherah unwound a scroll and reached for a wax seal, but her ruse did not dissuade Finlay. She portrayed herself as the busy queen who couldn't spare a moment for one lovesick hunter, but it wouldn't work. Not this time.

"I thought..." Finlay's voice trailed off, then he yanked her chair away from the table and knelt at Asherah's feet. "Please, listen to me," he said hoarsely as he stared up at her. "Please, talk to me about that—"

"Finlay," she hissed, her eyes darting about. "We have been over this, and there is nothing to talk about!"

"Yes there is!" His shoulders slumped forward, and his voice cracked when he continued. "Yes there is. After that night, you act as if I'm a stranger to you. I know I don't deserve forgiveness, but I cannot leave without you at least hearing me out. Please, let me explain." Finlay sat back on his heels and took Asherah's hands in his. "Please."

Asherah's face was masked in both anger and pain, her eyes hard as obsidian, her lips an unfurled bud. Finlay had broken the one command she'd given him by mentioning that night, and he worried that he had gone too far. He half expected Asherah to order his true and final banishment, when her eyes softened and she touched his hair.

"Come to my chamber." Asherah rose and grabbed Finlay's elbow, dragging him past the openly shocked Attia. Then she shut the door with a finality that told the *saffira-nell* that they were not to be disturbed. Finlay gazed about the queen's sumptuous rooms, replete with velvet tapestries and silk cushions, far finer than any of the wares sold in his family's shop. He looked down at his faded tunic and worn boots and wondered yet again why the queen had ever bothered with him.

Asherah perched on the bench at the foot of her bed and regarded the Second Hunter. "This once I will allow you to speak freely of that night, although your reasoning confounds me. You made your feelings quite clear at the time."

"How would you know how I feel when you won't let me explain?" he shouted, his frustration getting the better of him. "I tried to explain, but you refused to listen. Now, you won't even look at me! Can't you see that you're killing me?" He dropped to his knees, despair washing over him "And now, you're sending me away. What if I don't return? What if I never see you again? What if I die, never again having seen your smile?" No longer able to bear her hard gaze, he buried his face in his hands.

"It's too bad my smile is all that interests you," she said. Finlay raised his head and gave her a quizzical look. "Yes, I remember your disgusted face when you saw my scars."

"What scars?" Finlay asked, genuinely confused as he cast his eyes over the exposed skin of her hands and neck. "I have a multitude of scars, so many I could scare small children. On you, however, I see none."

It was Asherah's turn to be confused. "I thought that when you saw the marks on my breasts, the state of my body revolted you," she said softly, staring at her hands. Finlay rose up on his knees but she refused to look at him; after a moment, he touched her chin and gently turned her face to his.

"My lady, I assure you that I saw no scars," he proclaimed. "It was dark, and I remember that the moon was waning." Finlay traced his fingertips across her cheek. "This is why you sent me away?" When she nodded, he grasped both her hands in his. "Love, I see nothing in you but beauty," he swore. Asherah offered him a wan smile, then withdrew her hands from his and unfastened her bodice. With trembling hands, she bared the skin beneath her neck and Finlay saw the pale lines that crossed her skin.

"You see? I have many," she said softly, "many more than you think." Finlay traced the fine network of lines near her collarbone, then took the stays from her slender fingers.

"They're so long healed they've become silvery-pale, just like the rest of your skin," he said softly as he refastened her bodice; when he reached the hollow of her throat he fumbled, and Asherah finished the task. "That's all they are by now, just skin." Finlay smiled at her, and Asherah's eyes grew softer yet.

"There are more," she said as she drew up the hem of her gown and revealed the skin above her knees, her once-tender flesh that was now thick and rippled. Finlay frowned, and he dared to touch one of the discolored marks, hardly able to imagine what cruel wound had led to it. When Asherah revealed the scars on her torso he'd assumed that his warrior maiden had acquired them in battle, but these... They radiated from a much more delicate area.

"How did this happen?" he asked.

"When I was a slave," she began, "they...I was their plaything. A toy for demons." Asherah went on to detail the torments she had suffered at the hands of her captors, telling him more than she had ever shared with anyone, things she would never have told Aeolmar or even Lormac, things that only Torim would have known. She described helping broken women bear the demon whelps, how those who were deemed barren and no longer useful were boiled down to a meat soup, and how she finally—mercifully—killed many of her fellow slaves when she made her escape. Her pain poured forth from her, as if the dam that had held it at bay had at last broken under the weight of her memories.

While she spoke, Finlay arranged her skirts over her knees, then he held her hands until she had finished her tale. He understood that Asherah was sharing the most private part of herself with him, and for that he was grateful. His heart cried out for his warrior maiden, his gentle queen, she who had endured so much tragedy and war, but that was not all he felt. Surely, for Asherah to tell him these things she must feel something for him. For the first time since that night in her garden, he felt that most elusive of emotions: hope.

# CHAPTER FORTY-SIX

Asherah clamped her mouth shut and stared at her hands, clasped white-knuckled in her lap. She had never intended to say those things to Finlay; indeed, most men weren't interested in a firsthand account of the torture she'd endured in the *doja*. She sighed, for not only were the words already said, any chance she ever had with Finlay had long since passed. He may as well know everything.

"You see?" Asherah's voice wavered, so she cleared her throat. "They ruined me. All ask me why there is no king, why I have no mate...who would want me, broken as I am?" Asherah kept her eyes downward, certain that Finlay's revulsion of her was finally complete.

"They may have marked your body, but not your soul," Finlay said. "You're still Asherah."

"Asherah," she said shortly, "that's not even my true name."

"I disagree." Asherah raised her head, and in Finlay's eyes she saw not the disgust or pity that she had expected, but something akin to pride. "You're our queen, the she-wolf who defends every last Parthian as if they were her own cubs. Perhaps you weren't called Asherah then, but it's how we know you now." Finlay placed his hand on the nape of her neck, and drew her close. "What of a few scars on your breast? They don't matter to me, not nearly as much as the heart that beats beneath them."

"But on my legs—" she began.

"They matter even less," he said over her. "Much like the scars on your breast, now that they're healed they are nothing more than skin. Lovely, soft skin," he murmured as his thumb stroked the tender skin beneath her jaw. "Love, I swear to you that I was not aware of a single mark on your body before today."

"Then why did you pull away from me?" she pressed.

"It wasn't right, disrobing you as you lay on the dirt like that," he replied. "In the south, only a common wench would allow herself to be handled in such a manner. You are a queen and should be treated as such." Asherah searched his eyes, trying to find a hint of deception but finding only sincerity.

"I thought..." Asherah began as her voice trailed off.

"I know what you thought, and you were wrong."

*I was wrong.* Asherah stared at him for a moment before she burst into laughter, great peals of laughter fueled by the exodus of the shame she'd carried for so long. So many had pitied her, so many had shared in her sorrow, but only Finlay saw her as what she desperately wanted to be: whole. She threw her arms about his neck and rubbed her cheek against his neck; Asherah had missed her sweet boy so dearly, and all over a misunderstanding.

"Forgive me?" she asked. "I...I am so sorry." She pulled back and regarded his sky blue eyes, his dark curls that reminded her of the clear desert nights. . "And I am so very, very happy to be wrong."

"Of course I forgive you," Finlay attempted, only to be silenced when Asherah kissed him. Before they parted, her fingers had traveled to the laces of his jerkin. "What are you doing?" he asked, but she already had the garment unfastened.

"Off with your shirt," she commanded as she pushed the heavy leather from his shoulders.

"I beg your pardon?"

"You claim to have scars that will put mine to shame. Well, prove it." He stared at her, his red face making it clear that he hoped she was jesting. "You've seen me bare to the waist. It's only fair," she teased.

"Fair is in the eye of the beholder," he retorted, but in this Asherah would not be denied. With a sigh, he pulled the tunic over his head and began pointing out some of his larger scars.

"I don't think you have more scars than I, so much as they stand out more against your darker skin," Asherah said as she traced a mark that ran from his shoulder to the middle of his chest. "And you have...hair."

"I do," he replied. "Is that bad?"

"No, not at all," Asherah replied as she touched the curls that covered his chest. They were soft, much softer than the hair on his head. "You're not a full blooded fae?" she asked, for faerie men never sprouted hair on their chests.

"My grandsire was a troll," he replied, so amused by her fascination he forgot to be embarrassed. Asherah leaned close to his face and examined his chin.

"You have no beard," she said, mostly to herself, as she ran a finger along his jaw.

"Would you like me to grow one?" he inquired.

"No, I like your face," she replied with her girlish smile. "How did a troll end up in the hot and dry south?"

"He fell in love with a faerie woman who would not abide the frigid mountains or the endless clang of the smith's hammer, so he made a home where she would be happy. He brought no small amount of relations along with him; most of Cadogan's residents have a fair bit of troll blood." Asherah watched him as he spoke, wondering if he would also go to such lengths for one he loved. She had a feeling he would.

"Come," she said as she rose to her feet. "Sit with me before the fire." She grabbed both of his hands and pulled him up. "We will get something hot to drink, and you will tell me everything there is to know about the ways of trolls."

"I'm not what you would call an expert," he said as he followed. "I care not for the cold, I have no talent for working metal, and I don't hear the earth's call like those full-bloods do." Asherah smiled gaily as she led him to the blazing hearth, before which were two large chairs upholstered in creamy velvet and a tapestry-covered footstool. Finlay took a seat while Asherah darted off to the antechamber, returning in a moment bearing a pot and two bowls.

"Tea," she explained. "It will be ready in a moment." Asherah hung the pot on its hook above the flames while Finlay donned his tunic. They shared a few moments of silence while Asherah stared at the flames and chewed her lip, uncertain if she should ask the question on her mind. *Well, there's only one way to learn the answer,* she thought as she spun about to face her companion.

"Will you stay with me tonight?" she asked. "I hope you don't think me too forward, it's just...I've missed you so," she finished, staring at her hands. *Gods, he's going to think I'm some sort of a whore.* If Finlay thought that, he made no mention of it. What he did do was stand and wrap his arms around Asherah.

"I missed you as well, love," he said against her hair. "To not be able to talk with you, or see you...it was terrible."

"I know," she said, her words muffled by his chest, "I know." They held each other quietly for a time, now both staring at the flames while Finlay stroked her hair.

"Before I agree to stay," Finlay began, "there's something I must tell you, and something I must ask you." Asherah looked into his summer blue eyes and swallowed the lump in her throat.

"Ask away," she said. For long moments, Finlay continued watching the fire, and she did not press him to speak before he was ready.

"Do you still go to Aeolmar?" Finlay asked. Asherah nearly lost her breath in shock.

"Why would you ask this of me?" she countered, then coughed to hide her wheezing. Finlay guided her to a seat on the footstool, and sat beside her.

"I saw you with him," he replied.

"I am with him often," she said. "He is First Hunter, and—"

"No, I saw you *with* him," he repeated, leaving no room for misunderstanding.

"When...when did this happen?" she asked quietly.

"The day you told me I was being sent to the south. I returned to talk to you, and when you weren't in the outer chamber, I looked for you in these rooms. You left the door to that corridor open." He jerked his head toward the doorway behind her bed. "I had no idea where it led. I never would have guessed it ended behind Aeolmar's bed."

"How long were you there?" Asherah asked carefully.

"When I reached the end of the corridor, he was taking off your dress. I know, I should have left immediately, but you were so beautiful I couldn't look away. I wanted to be the one with you, and I wasn't." He fell silent, and took Asherah's hands in his. "After a time he saw me, and I left."

"After a time?" Asherah asked.

"After a time," he repeated, forgoing any elaboration. Finlay continued staring straight ahead, fixated on the crackling flames while he twisted his fingers between hers. "You seemed to enjoy it."

"I did," she replied softly. "What we have is not what it once was."

"He's no longer your lover?"

Asherah laughed shortly, and Finlay at last faced her. "I've called Aeolmar many things, but I've never called him my lover," she stated. "He's wounded, like I am, with scars on his soul that match those on my body. He's my friend, my confidant... He is like Torim. Actually, he is the only one I would deign to call a friend since my Torim was killed. We understand each other in a way that others can't, or won't." She leaned across his body and grasped his other hand. "You know, everything changed between us after you came to Teg'urnan."

"It did?" Finlay asked, taken aback by the comment.

"In ways I never thought it would," she confirmed. "I always thought I would live a solitary life, with neither a mate nor children. Lormac had been gone for so long... Then you were there with me at the jubilee, and the next day when we went riding... I hoped that I had found what I'd always wanted in you: a true companion, someone I could share everything with. Someone I could share my life with. I stopped going to Aeolmar after that day on the Hill, until our misunderstanding."

"How did he react to you rejecting his affections?"

"He practically pushed me into your arms. Yes, he did!" she insisted, seeing his incredulous face. "Aeolmar claimed he could look at you and know that you loved me. He wanted me to give you a chance; no, he forced me to give you a chance, when I was too scared."

"Why were you scared?" Finlay asked.

"What if you didn't want me? I would have been devastated. I was devastated." Finlay put his arm around Asherah's shoulders and tucked her head against his neck, seeming to mull over her words. His questions continued, but Asherah didn't mind. She was ready to tell him everything.

"Why did you go to him that day?" Finlay pressed.

"After that night we had in the garden, I was devastated. I cried for days. I thought that I was wrong, that I had misread your intentions. I thought that you wanted to have your way with me so you could go around claiming to have bedded the queen, only to flee at the sight of my misshapen body." Finlay protested, but Asherah placed her fingers over his lips. "I know now, but I did not know then. So rather than talking to you, rather than listening to what you had to say, I banished you from my presence." She watched her hands clasp and unclasp in her lap, no longer able to meet his gaze. "I was miserable without you, for I had grown accustomed to the time we shared. Then you were gone, by my own bidding you were gone, and in a moment of weakness I went to him in an attempt to forget my pain." She fell silent, and Finlay kissed her hair.

"I'm sorry," he said. She stole a glance at his face; Finlay was so concerned for her pain, when in truth this whole mess was her fault to begin with. *Dearest Cydia, he truly is the best of men.*

"Did you know that we did not finish?" she asked softly.

"Why not?"

"It's rather difficult to make love to a woman drowning in her own tears," was her sardonic reply. "I wanted love, and Aeolmar doesn't love me. I realized this... No, I already knew. I've always known. But that day I wanted—needed— him to love me, and when I realized that he never would..." She blinked rapidly, and cleared her throat before she continued. "It took him the rest of the day to calm me."

"He spoke to me that night, and told me that you wanted me, not him." Finlay laughed softly. "I asked if he was mad."

"I had no idea he'd done that," Asherah said.

"I didn't believe him," he said. "In fact, I thought it was the cruelest joke I'd ever heard. But his words gave me the courage to approach you today."

"Then I am forever grateful to him," Asherah said, then knelt at Finlay's feet. He protested, for in the strictly regimented south, a noble would never kneel before a commoner like himself, but she ignored him. "Can you ever forgive me, really forgive me, for sending you away, for refusing to talk to you...for treating you the way I did?" A single tear rolled down Asherah's cheek, and Finlay crouched down and brushed it away.

"Even your tears are sweet," he murmured as he sucked the tear from his thumb. "My love, there is nothing to forgive. It's over; we can let it be." Asherah grinned at Finlay, her Finlay, and threw her arms around his neck. Impetuous as ever, she pulled him to the floor next to her.

"I am still your love?" she asked. "I worry that I am only Asherah now."

"Always," he replied as he kissed her. "Always." Asherah relished the feel of him against her, the fact that he still smelled of the hot desert, the surprisingly soft curls on his chest.

"Do you dislike floors the same way you dislike the ground?" she asked as her fingers slipped under his tunic and played with the curls over his navel. Finlay pulled back from her embrace and stayed her hands.

"As I said, I also have something to tell you." He looked her in the eye, holding her gaze so intently she could not have turned away if the gods themselves commanded it. "Before I do, I want you to know that I love you, and I would never do anything to hurt you."

"Finlay, you're making me nervous," Asherah said. "If you don't want to stay—"

"It's not that," he insisted. "More than anything, I want to be here with you. If you still want me to stay after you've heard what I have to say, I will." Finlay smoothed her pale hair back from her brow. "You know of my troll blood," he began, and she nodded. "We have certain customs in the south that we still follow. Troll customs."

"I thought you knew very little about the ways of trolls."

"I know enough." He was silent for a time. "Trolls mate for life. We also believe that once you find your mate, there is no other."

"As do the fae," she said, slightly confused.

Finlay's brow furrowed as he searched for words. "But trolls, unlike faeries, believe that you should go to your mate untouched by another."

Asherah's first instinct was to correct him; unlike elves, the fae valued chastity, citing that Cydia held on to her maidenhood for a small eternity until Olluhm claimed the gift that only she could give him. Ballads and poetry across Parthalan lauded Cydia for her ideal, untouched form, a fleeting state of grace and beauty that was now gone forever.

Of course, what had all this restraint earned Cydia? Her mate was seduced by the goddess of night, and if that wasn't horrible enough, he fathered scores of children with his dark mistress. After Cydia cast him from her bed, the temples began the tradition of Olluhm honoring a priestess during each dark moon. Someone, likely an ancient, addle-brained priest, imagined that if the god wasn't continually fathering children, the race's divine blood would become too dilute. What this dilution would cause was never said, but when Olluhm began his visits to the temple, it was assumed that the sun god agreed with the practice. Not that there had ever been any real doubt of his complicity. What man, god or no, wouldn't want his pick of virgins once every moon? Asherah had always wondered if he only came during the dark moon so Cydia would not be forced to witness his latest transgressions.

All of this passed through Asherah's mind, though few followed the strict compacts set forth by the temples so long ago. In times past, when a woman chose her mate and he claimed her, the act was the beginning of the bond that was made unbreakable by binding their souls in the temple. Times had changed, and while mates were still bound, few underwent the ritual while they remained untouched. Life was what it was, and no one begrudged another for seeking a night of comfort.

But that wasn't what Finlay was saying.

"This is what you believe, as well?" she asked.

"This is what I believe," he confirmed. As she looked at his handsome, honest face, Asherah felt that she finally understood his initial reticence to touch her, his clumsiness that night they were together, why her banishment had cut him so deeply. She cast her thoughts back across her own past, from her enslavement to Lormac and the lovers she had taken since his death, and finally to Aeolmar.

And that Finlay had seen her with Aeolmar.

"What must you think of me?" She dropped her gaze from his.

"Love, I'm not judging you," he said as he tilted her chin upward. "How could I expect you to have abided by a custom that you just now learned of? We are somewhat isolated in the south and have many customs not found elsewhere. You followed the path that your life laid out for you, and you were strong and courageous, and I have nothing but love and admiration for you." He took both her hands in his and kissed her knuckles. "I just had to tell you, before things got out of hand again, that I cannot lie with you."

"So that night, it was not being outdoors that made you stop?" she asked.

"It was that as well," he replied. "Not only was I about to claim a woman who was not my mate, I was treating the queen like a whore. I deeply regret that night; not for being with you, that I will treasure always, but for the way I acted. Again, love, I am sorry." She pushed the thick hair back from his eyes and smiled at her sweet boy from the south.

"Surely in Cadogan there were pretty maidens to tempt you," she teased. It felt good to tease him again.

"The south has its fair share of beauties, but there is no one like you," Finlay said as he stroked her cheek. "There is no one with hair like spun starlight and eyes like black diamonds, with a laugh that makes me want to sing with joy. You have thrown open the gates of my heart and will forever reside in it, my most treasured love." He softly kissed her lips, then drew her into the circle of his arms.

"You really have never been with a woman?" Asherah asked, and felt his laugh rumble deep within his chest.

"Nor a man," he replied. "In Cadogan, when a boy reaches his manhood, he swears to hold himself for his mate."

"By holding me and kissing me you're not breaking this oath?" she asked with feigned sternness.

"I hope not," he replied. "I would like to continue doing both." Asherah laid her head against his shoulder, and he stroked her neck. "I would understand if you did not want me to remain, or if you wished to go to him."

Asherah, unsure if she was furious or offended, grabbed his chin. "If I wanted to be with Aeolmar, you would not be able to stop me," she said fiercely. "I don't want him. I want you." Asherah was taken aback by her own words; over the past seven winters, she had convinced herself that she wanted Aeolmar and no other. Now she knew that her First Hunter was right; they had never been in love.

"I want you," she repeated, grateful for the relief that shone in Finlay's eyes. "So, you'll stay?"

"I will stay as long as my queen desires it," Finlay replied, and Asherah felt relief wash over her like a tidal wave. Then, he went and asked her about the future. "What will it be like when I return? Will it be like this?"

"I don't know," Asherah replied truthfully, now faced with a situation she had never imagined: being in love with a man who could not make love to her.  "I don't know."

The lid clattered on the pot, and Asherah rose to prepare their tea. As she shredded the dried leaves somewhat more thoroughly than needed, she considered what Finlay had told her. She couldn't remember her own fleeting state of grace and beauty, thanks to the *mordeth* who'd nearly killed her, and wondered what it was like for Finlay to be so close to her, knowing that they could go no further.

*Well, if it is the path he's chosen, I can only honor his wishes.* Holding the bowl with both hands, she turned from the fire and saw that Finlay had left the floor for a chair. Once he took the proffered tea, she retrieved her own and settled upon the footstool before him.

"This will not do." Finlay took in their seating arrangements. He moved to the side of the chair. "Come, there is more than enough room for you." When Asherah merely stared at him—for how was he supposed to remain chaste if she was always laying all over him?—he added, "Either you come here, or I will shove myself onto that stool with you."

She smiled as she took her place beside him; she'd wanted to be sensitive to his customs and maintain a respectable distance and was once again glad to be wrong. The chair was not quite big enough for two, and her legs dangled over the arm while she leaned against his chest. "You're right, this is better'" She sipped her tea.

Finlay placed his arm about her waist as he breathed in the cool, meadow-green scent of her hair. "I love holding you. I love everything about you."

She leaned back to look at him, gazing into his eyes that were now darkened with emotion. "You're certain that I'm still your love?" she asked again.

"You'll always be my love," he replied as he bent to kiss her. "Now, and always." She stretched to reach him, only to yelp when her tea sloshed out of the bowl. "Careful," he admonished as he took the bowl from her, "or you will have scars to rival mine." Once their tea was safely on the side table, he dragged her onto his lap and kissed first her lips, then the red mark where the tea had spilled onto her neck. "Are you comfortable?"

A thousand words went through her mind—happy, content, loved—but none of them adequately described how she felt.

"Yes, I am," she replied as she laid her head on his chest. Sometimes, a simple answer was best.

# Chapter Forty-Seven

Stiflingly hot, Asherah kicked the furs aside. Northern dignitaries, unaware that the palace was in a much warmer clime and rarely saw snow, frequently sent the queen gifts of fine fur blankets and coverlets, and as a result, her chamber boasted the warmest bed in Teg'urnan. What she wouldn't give for a cool breeze.

But then, the furs were only partly to blame for her warmth; Asherah speculated that Finlay's desert heritage made his blood run a bit hotter than most. She buried her fingers in the soft curls over his heart and smiled, remembering how she had coaxed him into her bed with a promise of just sleeping. Just sleeping! Any other man would have stormed from the chamber, but not Finlay. In fact, he looked more than a little relieved.

And just sleep they did. Asherah, as per usual, retired wearing a thin chemise which she suspected only increased Finlay's anxiety. She convinced him to remove his boots (really, who sleeps in boots?), and unlace his tunic, but that and a goodnight kiss were as far as things went. Asherah didn't mind, she was just glad to have him beside her.

Having pushed aside the bedclothes, Asherah stretched her sleep-stiff limbs, and then pillowed her head on Finlay's shoulder. Her hand found its way back to the soft curls on his chest, and she gently twisted the hairs around her fingers. She traced their path from where it began above his heart, to where they narrowed over his navel, and in the next moment she was toying with the curls below his waist...

"Exactly where are you planning to go with that hand?"

Asherah looked up to find Finlay awake and smiling at her. "I want to know how far this wonderful hair extends," she replied, not moving her hand.

"As far as one would expect," he replied.

"Well, I do not know what to expect, as I have never encountered such luscious curls on a man," she countered as she tugged them harder. Finlay grimaced, then dragged her up his chest so her pale hair fell onto his shoulders.

"Luscious?" he asked with a raised brow. Asherah laughed and hid her face against his neck, wrapping her arms around him and now toying with the curls over the back of his neck. "I like waking up with you," he said as he caressed her back.

"Perhaps you should make a habit of it." Asherah settled herself atop the length of him and felt her toes stretch past his. "You see," she said as she nudged his feet, "I *am* taller than you!"

"An eyebrow's width, no more," he said in mock indignation. "Out there, in the palace, all see you as a serene, graceful queen. Yet here in your chambers you giggle like a maiden and tease all in your company."

"Perhaps I like teasing you best," she said. Finlay's hand moved to capture a loose tendril of her hair, and he scraped her neck in the process. In fact, he'd been scraping her quite a bit, so Asherah grabbed his hand to investigate. "You have no calluses," she said as she ran her fingers over his palm; there were no telltale raised lumps, but his skin felt like it was covered in sand. "Why are your hands so rough?"

"Another aspect of my troll blood. The soles of my feet have the same thick skin, to guard against a forge's heat," he replied. Asherah nudged the bottom of his foot with her toe; yes, it was just as gritty as his palm. In addition to his rough flesh, she felt a small pang of guilt. She had been so upset over what she'd assumed were calluses scraping her, and he could no more alter his skin than she could change her scars. *I'm nothing but a hypocrite.*

Finlay frowned at her silence and offered an apology. "I can speak to the healers if you'd like, see if anything can be done to soften them."

"What? No," she blurted out, horrified that he thought he needed to change the very nature of his skin just to be with her. "No," she repeated in a softer tone, "maybe I like them as they are." Asherah kissed his palm before placing his hand on her hip, then she claimed his lips with all the passion she could muster at such an early hour. Finlay responded with his own ardor, and as he ran those rough palms over her back and arms, his skin catching on the thin fabric of her chemise, Asherah imagined them caressing other areas. She decided that she liked his hands, just the way they were.

Finlay slowly stroked her neck and then her shoulders, acquainting himself with every tiny hill and furrow created by her delicate bones, until at last he reached the edge of her chemise. Asherah let him push down the garment and slide his palms onto her shoulders, only to clench his fists in frustration.

"Am I to assume that sleeping next to a woman is not forbidden by your oath?" Asherah asked. "This oath of yours seems rather lenient," she observed as she kissed his neck. Finlay, apparently having had enough of the queen's continual teasing, rolled until Asherah was on her back and he glowered down at her.

"It is not lenient, it is specific," he corrected. "It says nothing about sharing a bed."

"Then what does it say, Lord Cadogan?" Asherah asked as she wound her arms around his neck.

"'I Finlay, son of Finbarr and Eleni, swear before all the gods and the assemblage of Cadogan to keep myself as my elders prescribed. I will not know a woman, save she who chooses me as her mate, until the end of my days.' That is exactly what I swore." He kissed his bedmate's brow.

"Have you ever regretted it?" Asherah asked, having left the taunts behind and now genuinely curious about his home-land.

"Only for the past seven winters," he replied with a smirk, and Asherah felt him pressing against her belly. She loved the feel of his body against hers, so close she could feel his breath, his heat, every muscle and sinew, as if her chemise and his thin desert clothing weren't the only things separating them. Asherah's breath caught in her throat, for she desired Finlay more than any other man she had yet encountered. She hoped it was an attraction born of love and not of the forbidden.

"I have searched for someone like you for so long... I feared I would suffer eternity alone. But now you are here," she whispered as she traced his cheekbone.

"It's fate," Finlay proclaimed. "I've loved you my entire life."

"That's impossible," she argued "How can you love some-one you've met?

"It's true," he insisted. "Remember the portraits?" Asher-ah smiled as she recalled his father's shop, the walls all but hidden behind portraits of an austere, miserable queen. *Well, miserable no more.* She traced the bridge of his nose, the arch of his brow; no, it was not the craggy brow that existed only in her memory, but Finlay reminded her of a man she loved more than her life.

"My man from the desert." She stared into Finlay's eyes, searching for a streak of gray amidst the blue. There wasn't any, but then she hadn't expected it, just like she had never expected to love anyone as she had loved Lormac.

"That I am." He kissed her fingertips.

"Then I should have travelled to Cadogan centuries ago," she said as she nestled herself against his chest, "I was remiss in my duties." Finlay murmured his assent as he kissed her forehead. "When do you have to go?"

"I should rise soon." He looked toward the window, the lightening sky telling that first dawn was fast approaching. "My gracious queen has ordered that I depart for this mission by second dawn. I will confess, at first I thought she was just trying to be rid of me."

"No." Asherah said, "The queen loves all her people, but you most of all." Finlay tightened his arms around her and they lay together until the elder sun rose. They recited the morning prayer together, but got carried away in the midst of saying goodbye and were still abed when the child sun rose, so they recited Solon's prayer as well. As Asherah walked with Finlay to her private entrance, she decided on a dignified farewell because really, she did want to honor his southern proclivities, only to have him pull her into his arms and kiss her until she was breathless.

"I will count the moments until I'm with you again," he said against her lips.

"You'll only be gone twelve days," she reminded him, but a sudden heaviness in her heart told her that she would count the moments as well.

"It will feel like twelve seasons." He lightly kissed her eyes, then her cheeks, and then her chin, before returning to her lips. "I will only think of returning to you."

"And I will only think of your return."

# Chapter Forty-Eight

## Asherah Speaks

*After Finlay left, I wandered listlessly about my chambers, smiling like a fool. Of this I was certain, for whenever I passed a reflective surface the sight of my lovestruck face made me laugh aloud. Here I was, the Virgin Queen of Parthalan, smitten with a chaste warrior from the desert. Oh, Lormac, what would you think of me?*

*I paused before the mantle and lovingly stroked the Sala. The red heartstone, the symbol of Lormac's love for me, still hadn't paled. Not for the first time since Lormac's death, I wondered what would happen if I placed the Sala against my skin. Would the heartstone revert to white? Would it change based on my heart? I didn't think either of those would happen, since I'm not of Nexa's line, but I refused the attempt. If I did wear the Sala and the stone reverted, Lormac would be truly gone.*

*I sighed and resolved that I should return the Sala to Leran. It was his by rights, and I suspected that he wouldn't have had such strife among the elflands if the Lord of Tingu wore the Sala. That, and it wasn't doing any good on its perch above my hearth, save for my reminiscing. After my night with Finlay, I hoped that reminiscing was coming to an end.*

*The sound of my chamber door opening roused me from my contemplations. "Here," I called, expecting Attia. Like as not, she would have her share of remarks about Finlay, and after she had said her piece, she would demand each and every detail of what transpired last night. Normally I brushed off her inquiries, but today I relished the opportunity to talk with another woman about how Finlay made me feel, his unusual customs, and our maddeningly chaste evening. Imagine my disappointment when the Prelate, not Attia, strode into view.*

*"My lady," he greeted, then his brow furrowed as he took in my disheveled appearance. I hadn't bothered to arrange, or even comb, my hair, and my chemise was more than a little rumpled. "Are you ill?"*

*"No, no," I replied, waving away his concern. "I'm just having a lazy morning."*

*"You'd think Attia would have something to say about that," he began, but I interrupted him before he could recite his list of reasons for Attia's immediate dismissal.*

*"She hasn't yet arrived." He drew a breath, for tardiness was another of her supposed shortcomings, so I continued, "I asked her to arrive after second dawn." That was a lie; quite often, Attia was late of her own accord, but Harek didn't need to know that.*

*Harek shut his mouth so hard I heard his teeth clack, then he stared at the two bowls of tea before the hearth. "Oh, those are from last evening. Finlay and I went over a few details concerning his trek to the Southern Contingent." I prattled on as I gathered up the bowls of long-cooled tea, detailing the particulars of the Second Hunter's journey to the south. Not that I had discussed any of this with Finlay, mind you. Do all queens lie to their Prelates in order to keep them quiet? Between him and Aeolmar, it's a wonder I'm not further from sanity than I already am.*

"Was he here the entire night?" Harek asked when my tale was complete.

"Whether he was or not, it's no concern of yours, Prelate," I admonished. I selected a brush and began the arduous task of unwinding ribbons from my hair (I must remember not to sleep with them) and asked after the reason for Harek's early visit.

"The dark fae," he said gravely. "We have reports that they are amassing close to the border."

"Which side?"

"Theirs." He went on, detailing the numbers sighted, the arms they carried, and the other things soldiers noticed about matters of war. Even after the many battles I'd faced, both as a queen and as a fugitive, I'd never been able to scan a grouping of men and count up their ranks, let alone decide if the enemy was best met with swords or crossbows. But Harek could plan an entire battle and know its probable outcome in the blink of an eye, and for that I was ever thankful.

"Well," I said, mostly to fill the silence. Harek had finished his report on the dark fae's activities, but I was engrossed in a knotted ribbon. I wrestled with my hair for a time, reaching for a small paring knife I that I used for my nails, all while Harek looked on. "We must send word to Leran," I said as I cut the knot free. Luckily, it was all ribbon. "I have no doubt that our legion can ably handle anything Natraeus throws at us, but his ultimate goal is to make Tingu suffer. Leran must be advised."

Harek nodded, still watching me struggle with my mess of ribbons and hair, which now resembled a bird's nest. A mangy, decrepit bird's nest. "Is there anything further?" I asked.

"No, you've heard everything," he replied.

"Very well. If you don't mind, I'd like to prepare for the day." As I stood, Attia entered the room, and ushered Harek into my receiving chamber. Then she took one look at my hair, and declared it such a mess that she'd have to shave my head.

# Chapter Forty-Nine

Harek lingered by the entrance to Asherah's private room, listening for snatches of conversation between the queen and her *saffira-nell*. While he discerned less than half of what was said, he gleaned that Finlay was indeed the direct cause of Asherah's unkempt appearance. Then Asherah giggled like a maiden and told Attia that she could hardly breathe in anticipation of his return.

Unable to bear any more, Harek sat at Asherah's map table, grabbed a parchment and quill, and drew a rough outline of Parthalan and Nibika. *We will approach from here,* he thought as he scribbled, *and I will kill Finlay here.* Harek made a dark, dark mark on the parchment. *Or here. Or here!*

The quill snapped under the weight of Harek's anger, and ink seeped through the thin parchment. He tossed the map and quill into the fire, then leaned heavily on the mantle. *Sarfek is right. I waste too much time on this whore. If she won't have me once Finlay's dead, I'll offer her up to the* mordeth-gall.

Someone knocked on the receiving chamber's door, and Harek gritted his teeth; he assumed that Finlay had returned to bid Asherah yet another sappy farewell. The Prelate's face twisted into a grin as he envisioned the many ways he could kill him, quickly and silently with Asherah being none the wiser. The body wouldn't be a problem; he'd just dump it in the enchanted garden. Asherah still hadn't found the remains of her first lover, whom Harek had thrown off a cliff centuries ago. Of course, he could always burn him...

"My lord?" Harek turned and saw Olwynn standing there, a bundle of scrolls in his hands.

"Gods, at least it's you and not one of those fool hunters," Harek grumbled as he straightened.

"Have the hunters done something?" Olwynn inquired.

"They are always doing something," Harek ranted. "Always in the way, always fouling things up. Why, none of my soldiers have caused half the problems as—"

"Half the problems as what?" Olwynn demanded. Harek regarded him for a moment; yes, he detected a hint of suspicion in Olwynn's eyes. Truth be told, it was more than a hint, and he wondered how much Olwynn had divined of his plans. More, Olwynn was rumored to be mates with the huntress Innetha, an unforgivable act for one of the *con'dehr*.

Harek exhaled heavily; his plans had just become more complicated, and he'd likely have to endure another lecture from Sarfek. It could hardly be helped, what with him now needing to kill two additional men, but these things had to be done. Harek had done too much, come too far, to allow anyone who harbored such thoughts near him.

Pity. He had always liked Olwynn.

# CHAPTER FIFTY

"You now desire to remove the First *and* Second Hunter, and one of your *con'dehr* as well?" Sarfek's image regarded his brother with palpable annoyance. "Too bad Teg'urnan is comprised of stone. Were it a wooden structure, you could set it alight and eliminate all of Asherah's possible mates in one fell act."

Harek glared at the image, and briefly contemplated throwing an inkpot at it. He didn't, but only because he wasn't sure that Sarfek would feel the impact. "Finlay is just as much of an obstacle as Aeolmar," he insisted. "Parthalan will never rise to the power it could be while the queen is surrounded by men who cow to her every whim. The hunters must be eliminated. As for Olwynn, I believe his allegiance lies elsewhere. If I cannot claim his full loyalty, then I've no place for him. "

"Calm, brother, be calm" Sarfek soothed. "It matters not to me whom we eliminate. I only hope your desire for the woman hasn't blinded you to our overall goal."

Harek grunted, and turned his back to the wavering image. Indeed, what was once a plot to conquer the nine realms with Parthalan's legion now seemed simple in comparison. It had all begun three centuries ago, when Harek had complained to his brother that Asherah was a little too peace-loving for his liking; he was a warrior, born and bred, yet there were no wars for him to fight. Hells, even small border skirmishes were few and far between. Sarfek had nodded his understanding and then had inquired if his younger brother fancied himself a warlord.

"Yes," Harek had replied instantly. "A warlord is what I was born to be."

Sarfek had smiled and told his brother that all he had ever wanted was power, though he cared not to sit upon a throne, and demons were the ideal stepping stone for the influence he craved. Since they made their home in the underworld, demons could travel freely amongst the nine realms, which meant that a demonic ally was key in staying one step ahead of one's pursuers. That reason alone was why Sarfek had gone willingly when the *mordeth* captured him, why he had let the demons believe that they controlled him. While he hadn't been pleased about enthralling his own brother, he'd felt that once he gained the *mordeth's* trust he could finagle an audience with Ehkron.

Then Asherah had been dragged, kicking and screaming, to the *doja*, and Harek had fallen in love with the girl the moment he'd set eyes upon her. Sarfek had cautioned Harek against letting himself care for the wretch, since she'd like as not be dead soon, but she had proved strong and cunning. By the time she'd hatched her mad escape plan, Sarfek had grown weary of his life with demons, and he'd assisted as well he could. Sarfek's ultimate plan had always been to use Asherah as a gift for the *mordeth-gall*, but then Ehkron had gotten himself killed by an elf girl while hiding in the mortal realm.

When Asherah had taken Sahlgren's head, Sarfek had thrown his support behind the new queen, and as fate would have it, his brother had been handed the coveted role of Prelate. Sarfek had assumed that Asherah's grief would render her weak-willed and easy to manipulate. Instead, it had made her strong and forthright, determined to keep her borders strong and her people safe. The exact traits Sarfek hadn't wanted in a queen.

Worse, the woman was an excellent negotiator, using her innate wisdom and silken voice to smooth over even the most bristly situations. Within a few winters of her taking the throne, she had resolved every disputed border, quelled squabbles over inheritance, and calmed lords and landowners across the realm. Why, her skills as a mediator had spread far and wide, and her advice became sought in quarrels across the whole of Parthalan and beyond.

Asherah's unfailing righteousness burned in Sarfek's gut, so when Harek begged his brother's aid in removing the queen's lover, he readily assisted. A grieving woman is a compliant woman, he'd said, giving Harek the means to dispose of the man.

Grieve she did, but she did not become the same wretched, quivering woman who had watched the Lord of Tingu's pyre burn. Perhaps toughened by the losses she'd already suffered—Asherah was nothing if not tenacious—she went on ruling Parthalan and taking men to her bed. Finally, Sarfek told Harek that he must remove himself from Teg'urnan altogether if he was to see his plans through to fruition.

"If she remains obstinate after the hunters' deaths, we will revert to my plan," Sarfek stated. Harek nodded; their goal had changed, and they now wished to curry favor with Ehkron's whelp. The beast was called Asgeloth and was said to be both more terrifying and more despicable than his sire. Sarfek could think of no better way to impress the new *mordeth-gall* than by offering him the Faerie Queen.

Harek knew all of this; he and Sarfek had discussed and plotted their future many times over. He had tried to keep Asherah away from the *mordeth-gall*—and for himself—but her continued interest in other men had more than discouraged Harek. Really, Asherah had no one to blame but herself. If she'd just acknowledged Harek as the best man for her, and invited him into her chamber rather than engage in endless dalliances with men so far beneath her, she could have avoided such a fate.

"Agreed," Harek said. "This is Asherah's last chance."

# Chapter Fifty-One

## Aeolmar Speaks

*The messenger bowed and left with alacrity, obviously pleased with himself over a job well done, and thus didn't notice the queen's head droop or me ball my hands into fists. We'd just been informed that Natraeus and his guard had left the Dark Palace of Nibika, and were headed toward Parthalan's northeast border. Oh, and his legion was on the move, as well. How we kept from shouting epithets at the messenger's back was beyond me.*

*"Well, that's it then," Asherah muttered. "Natraeus has long desired a war, and now he has one."*

*Instead of speaking (for Cydia only knows what would have exited my mouth at that moment), I shoved back from the table and stalked about the chamber, briefly contemplating going out to the garden. There I could scream and rail at the plants, bellow about the many ways I would kill Natraeus until my throat burned. I glanced over my shoulder to say as much to Asherah, but the sight of her made the words die on my lips. She held her head in her hands, but even so, they trembled.*

*Knowing that leaving her alone would be a cruelty, I resumed my place at the map table and grabbed a handful of polished pebbles from the basket; there were white stones flecked with blue that represented Parthalan's warriors and others of a dull brown intended to stand in for our foes. It was a technique Asherah and Harek used often, for by arranging the pebbles, they kept from marking up her precious maps.*

*In fact, the Prelate should be here, now, planning all this out, but he was off somewhere with his precious* con'dehr. *Inwardly, I made several sarcastic comments about how we were so much better off without Harek and his foolish notions, but I held my tongue for Asherah's sake. Gods, at this rate I'd bite through it.*

*As I arranged the pebbles in meaningless little patterns, I considered Olwynn's claim, that Natraeus may be receiving assistance in his asinine quest for glory, and that Harek knew who'd been helping him but was keeping such knowledge from Asherah. I'd said nothing to Asherah, or anyone for that matter, but Harek's absences and Natraeus's newfound tactical ability seemed a bit too coincidental.*

*"Do you think someone might be helping Natraeus?" I asked as casually as possible. "Not a demon, but someone else?"*

*"Who would help him?" Asherah countered. "I cannot imagine anyone but a demon contracting with him."*

*I grunted. "He doesn't have the stones to deal with demons," I muttered, envisioning a terrified Natraeus fleeing from one of the small, lesser beasts. In the midst of my tirade about Natraeus's balls shrinking like his courage, Asherah laughed.*

*"Whereas you've balls like boulders?" she teased. "Large and fearsome, giving you the courage to smite any foe?" I'd always enjoyed it when she teased me, though I tried not to let her know. If she did, then the taunts would never end.*

*"Of which you are well aware, my lady," I replied. Vulgarity was uncommon on Asherah's tongue, and a poor way to disguise her fear. "We will keep Parthalan safe, along with Leran," I promised, reaching across the table to squeeze her hand.*

*"I know. I just... I wish Finlay was here."*

*I nodded, and ignored the cold stab in my chest. Not so long ago, Asherah would have come to me for comfort, but those days were over. Instead, I squeezed her hand again. "I can send for him to return at once. He can be here by tomorrow, the day after at the latest."*

*"No, no," she said, "let him complete his mission. If Natraeus does have an accomplice, perhaps they're in the south." She withdrew her hand from mine and began making designs upon the map with the colored pebbles. It was the worst representation of an opposing force I'd ever seen, far worse than the pattern I'd laid out.*

*"I take it you and he got on well that night," I said at length. She hadn't told me what went on between them, and I hadn't asked. As long as she was happy, I had all the information I needed.*

*"Well enough," she said, with that coy glance that could melt a man's heart. Then she put down the stones and asked me something I'd never expected to hear from the Queen of Parthalan. "You know something of the ways of trolls?"*

*"I do."*

*"Do you know how one would claim his mate?"*

# Chapter Fifty-Two

Teg'urnan's corridors teemed with activity, and hardly anyone spared a glance at the Second Hunter as he rushed toward the queen's chamber. Also ignored were the curses he muttered when the gift he'd brought for her stuck him with one of its sharp spines, but no matter. Asherah was worth more than a few drops of blood, though he hoped he wouldn't lose any flesh.

At last, he reached her door and knocked loudly; remembering the early morning hour he knocked again a bit softer, as if re-knocking would somehow erase his earlier thumping. Attia opened the door, her annoyance quickly replaced by amusement.

"May I see the queen?" Finlay inquired of the *saffira-nell*.

"Certainly," Attia replied as she stepped aside. Finlay's entire being brightened when he saw his Asherah, seated as always at her map table, so heaped with parchments and scrolls one could hardly see its surface. Her back was toward the door, and for a moment Finlay just stood there, drinking in the sight of her. She was clad in one of those thin, shapeless garments she liked to sleep in, and her starlight hair was loose and flowed wildly about her.

"My lady queen," he called out. Recognizing his voice, Asherah immediately dropped the scroll she'd been so intently studying and rose to her feet. As she walked toward him, Finlay lost his breath, as he always did when Asherah smiled at him.

"I didn't expect you until tomorrow," she began, but before she could continue he grabbed her by the waist and kissed her.

"I've missed you terribly," he said as he held her. "My horse is none too happy with me, but we made it back a full day earlier than planned. I came directly to you."

She felt the damp curls at the back of his neck and cast an appraising eye over his fresh clothing. "Did you bathe while on horseback?"

*I even missed how she teases me.* "I couldn't present myself to the queen dusty from the road," Finlay replied, then he kissed her again. When they parted, Asherah looked pointedly over his shoulder; he looked as well, and saw Attia wearing a smirk that would have put Innetha to shame.

"You may retire. Thank you, Attia," Asherah said to her.

"It's near enough to first dawn that I might as well remain," Attia said. "Unless you and the hunter desire some privacy?"

Asherah glared at her *saffira-nell*, who ignored the queen and stated she would see to libations for the two. Finlay shook his head; it never ceased to amaze him that the Queen of Parthalan treated her servants like family.

"She likes you," Asherah explained when she turned back to Finlay. "She's done nothing but prattle on about you since the moment you departed."

"And you?" he asked.

"I listened." With that, Asherah led Finlay to the map table and bade him to sit beside her. He frowned as he took in her appearance, for his beautiful queen looked as if she'd been stricken with plague. Her hair wasn't just loose, but disheveled to the point that it escaped the lone clasp that attempted to tame it. Shadows darkened her eyes and the hollows of her cheeks, and her alabaster skin, usually luminous, had gone sallow.

"You look as if you've slept less than me," he observed.

"She's been up every night with those foolish maps," Attia called from the rear chamber. "Perhaps you can convince her to take to her bed?"

Asherah's eyes threw daggers towards Attia's voice, but before she could berate her for such an outburst, Finlay squeezed her hand. "Has something happened?"

Asherah sighed, and leaned her forehead against Finlay's shoulder. He tugged the all-but-useless hair clasp free, and combed his fingers through her starlight waves. "Natraeus," she said at length. "We have learned that he is building forces near the northwest border of Parthalan. Near Tingu."

*Near Leran.* It was well known that Asherah took any threat to the Lord of Tingu as a direct attack against her, and that she would personally eliminate anyone who posed a threat to Leran's safety. Hells, she would incur the wrath of the gods if need be. "What does that fool mean to accomplish?" Finlay asked.

"He wants to make Leran pay for L'hirre's actions," she answered. "Leran's grandsire conquered the dark fae, and they have been subservient to elves ever since. Natraeus also believes that if he can take The Seat, he will then be able to conquer Parthalan as well." She sighed, and nestled closer to him. "That's why he wanted me. He wanted to use Parthalan's legion against Leran, but I went and spoiled his plans."

"Madness," Finlay muttered. Asherah nodded weakly, and Finlay wrapped his arms about her. "Love, he won't succeed." He kissed her now-smoothed hair.

"I know." She straightened her shoulders as she regained a semblance of composure. "I know," she repeated with more conviction. "Did you learn anything while in the south?"

"The Southern Contingent is well and hale," he said. "They cannot recall the last time a dark faerie wandered past them and don't desire to see one, now or ever. I brought you something." Finlay reached behind his back and produced the leather satchel. He set it amidst the heaps of maps and proceeded to roll down the sides, revealing a plant unfamiliar to the queen. Leathery green leaves framed a many-petaled blossom of the deepest red. "It's called a bloodthorn. They grow in the desert, near the sea. I didn't see one in your garden."

"It's beautiful," she breathed as she stroked the soft petals. "Why is it called a bloodthorn?"

Finlay carefully moved the leaves aside and exposed a stem covered in thin, needlelike barbs. "One tends to learn why rather quickly," he explained with a rueful smile.

"I love it," she said as she grinned at him. "Let's find a place for it in the garden."

The queen grabbed the satchel and walked toward the garden doors, heedless of her bare feet and thin chemise as she plunged into the chill night.

"Careful of the thorns," Finlay cautioned as he followed her.

"I'm perfectly capable of carrying a plant without incident," Asherah called over her shoulder. They walked for some time, until they reached the stream at the meadow's edge.

"This is perfect," Asherah proclaimed as she settled the bloodthorn, satchel and all, on the stream bank.

"Shouldn't we dig a hole?" Finlay asked.

"The garden will claim it, if it is given with good intentions." She sat on the mossy bank and breathed deep of the night air. "This is my favorite spot, next to the stream."

"It is a lovely sight." He took in the sight of Asherah as she thoughtfully arranged the plant, turning it this way and that so it would have enough sunlight to grow, but too little to burn. As Finlay watched her, clad in her silken sleeping garment that was likely worth the price of ten strong horses, it occurred to him that he had just gifted the queen a bag of dirt.

"I should have brought you something more appropriate," he muttered, but Asherah shook her head.

"Do you know what people send me?" she asked, and he murmured that he didn't. "Jewels, chalices, cloth-of-gold. Cold, hard things that I neither want nor need." She paused, and fingered one of the bloodthorn's leathery leaves. "But not my Finlay. You gave me something beautiful, something living. You see me for who I am, without all the trappings of royalty. You see only Asherah."

"No," he corrected, kneeling beside her, "I see only my love." Asherah slid her arms about his neck and kissed him, so hard he braced himself against the ground. The price of stability was holding her, so he wrapped his arms around her as they landed on the soft grass. It wasn't a far fall, and he made sure she landed on top of him.

"So, you like the plant?" Finlay asked once they parted.

"More than any other gift I've received as queen," Asherah confirmed.

"We should get up," he said. "You know I don't like it when you're on the ground."

"I like the garden," she retorted, "and I like to lie upon the grass. If you expect me to abide by your trollish ways, you must also follow some of my faerie customs."

"Lying on the ground is a custom?" he inquired.

"Olluhm claimed Cydia in a green meadow," Asherah reminded him. "If the gods don't mind the ground, then neither do I."

Finlay nodded—for who was he to argue with the Faerie Queen about the will of the gods?—when it occurred to him where they were lying. "Is this the meadow?"

Asherah's delicate brows knit together; Finlay wondered if she had never considered that the garden behind her bedchamber might be where her race originated. "I don't know," she said. "I always thought it was beneath the temple. The priestesses claim that the vaults are the most sacred spot in the realm."

"But you say that it's always been here," Finlay pressed, "and it's suffused with magic. Perhaps... perhaps this is where he first saw her."

"Perhaps it is." Asherah sat up and surveyed the area around them, then turned her gaze toward the east. "If Cydia had fallen asleep here, Olluhm would have seen her as soon as he rose." She returned her attention back to Finlay, cocked her head to the side and asked what he was thinking.

"That would be most appropriate to claim a queen where the gods once lay," he responded, amazing both himself and Asherah with his candor. Asherah began saying something about his troll ways, but he couldn't find it in him to care about those archaic southern customs or that they were sitting on the soggy ground or anything but the woman before him.

*We are here, now. I am a faerie man, not a troll; I don't need those customs. I need her.* Finlay grabbed Asherah and kissed her as passionately as he'd kissed her the last time they were in the garden. He was certain of his love for her and meant to make it known to Asherah that he was hers, however she wished to have him. His ardor wasn't even dampened by the cold drops that suddenly ran down his neck.

"Is this rain magical, like the garden?" he wondered.

"No, it is rain from a cloud like all other rain," Asherah said as she got to her feet. "And we are getting drenched!"

# Chapter Fifty-Three

## Asherah Speaks

*That sudden downpour soaked our clothing through to our skin, and Finlay and I stumbled into my chambers looking as if we had hauled ourselves out of the sea. Of course, Attia her flock of saffira were in attendance, ready to witness my latest humiliation.*

*"Don't," I warned, not appreciating her smug face in the slightest. I gestured for Finlay to follow me into the bathing chamber and shut the door, leaving the gaggle of onlookers to talk amongst themselves.*

*"There are robes and towels," I said offhandedly, nodding toward the stacks of carefully folded linen. My attention was focused on getting that wet, clammy chemise off my skin; there is a sound reason why toweling is never woven from silk, since wet silk could easily make a most effective torture device. I cursed and pulled at the rain-swollen laces, well and truly lodged in their individual grommets, before losing my temper, grabbing a small knife meant for trimming nails, and cutting the whole mess apart. The garment made a slapping noise as it fell to the tiled floor. I stretched my cold-stiffened limbs and briefly contemplated a hot bath, when I heard a strangled*

noise behind me. Gods, I had just stripped naked before a man who had taken a vow of chastity.

"I'm sorry," I said hurriedly. I turned to face him, but realized that me facing him probably wouldn't help matters and turned away rather quickly. I also realized that anything I could use to cover myself was behind him, so I picked up my wet chemise and wound it around my hips. "I didn't mean to."

"I know." Then Finlay was behind me, peeling away the sodden silk. I couldn't imagine why he'd done that, but then he wrapped a length of dry linen around me. I felt his fingertips trace a line along my shoulder toward my lower back; it was one of the scars the mordeth had given me. Lormac, being that he was far more interested in my breasts, hadn't gotten around to healing the scars across my back, and I occasionally forgot they were there. Well, forgot is really too strong a word. It was more of an uneasy truce between the scars and me. They stayed behind me, and I didn't rail at them. Much.

I waited for Finlay to ask me why that scar was different from the rest, why it was red and raised and seemed to pulse with its own heat, but he didn't. His gritty fingertips followed it to where it ended over my spine, then he circled my waist with his arms, his forehead pressed against my shoulder. Did he really not care about these horrible marks upon my flesh?

"I spoke with Aeolmar while you were gone," I said.

"About Natraeus?"

"About trolls." I turned to face him. "He spent a great deal of time at Grelk's forge before he became a hunter."

"I thought Aeolmar was from the west."

"He is." Finlay pushed a few soaked tendrils back from my face, and I realized that since the linen was wrapped around my waist that left only my hair obscuring my breasts. My hair is long, yes, but hardly an adequate covering. I tried drawing up the linen, but he was holding me so tightly it wouldn't budge.

"Are you going to tell me what you spoke of?" he asked, his tone betraying more than a slight annoyance.

*"Jealous?" I teased. I twisted out of his arms and let the linen fall away while I searched for a robe; if he could be jealous, then I could be naked. It was only fair. "I asked him if he is familiar with how a troll would take a mate."*

*"Why would the mating customs of trolls interest the Faerie Queen?" he asked.*

*Having located the robe I wanted, I fastened the stays as I weighed my response. Well, there was nothing quite like honesty. "Because the Faerie Queen loves a troll," I replied. Properly covered, I turned to face him once again. "Get out of those wet things, and join me in the front chamber?" He nodded, and I left him to mull things over while I dealt with Attia.*

*"I need a message sent to the Prelate," I told her quietly, once I'd gotten her away from the others. "Tell him that I'm ill and staying in bed."*

*"You were caught in the cold rain," Attia said. My* saffi-ra-nell *loved nothing more than a good conspiracy. She located the copper pot used for mulling wine and set it above the fire, leaving the wine to heat while she saw to my wet hair. "We would not want our gracious queen to catch a chill." She yanked a comb through my heap of tangles.*

*"We wouldn't." I began throwing spices into the wine. "Also, please inform the First Hunter that I'm not to be disturbed today."*

*"Certainly." She extricated few combs from the nape of my neck; they had done such a horrible job of taming this mess I'd forgotten they were there. "Would you like me to give him a reason?"*

*"Tell him... Tell him that Finlay has returned early, and that I wish to spend time with him," I said decisively. Aeolmar, great keeper of secrets that he was, also appreciated honesty. Attia nodded, then peeked over my shoulder into the pot.*

*"You can be heavy handed with the lover's ease," she instructed.*

"*Why do they call it that?*" *I wondered as I added another handful of the tiny leaves.*

"*It makes one more amorous,*" *Attia replied.* "*Thus, the lover may ease his tension with his beloved.*"

"*Gods, Attia.*" *I grabbed a spoon and scooped out as many of the leaves as I could, flinging them into the hearth.* "*I will not make a philter to lure Finlay to my bed! He cannot—*"

*And I fell silent. It wasn't that he* could *not make love to me, he* would *not; in fact, his body had reacted to mine in a few certain ways that left no doubt as to his ability to at least initiate the act. Nevertheless, I would not resort to an aphrodisiac or any other sort of trickery to get Finlay in my bed, not now or ever. Finlay meant too much to me.*

"*What can't I do?*"

*Of course he heard me.* "*Attia was just leaving,*" *I said. Thankfully, Finlay didn't press the matter. My* saffira-nell *rounded up her chattering followers and graced me with another of her smirks as she left. Then, the Virgin Queen and her Chaste Warrior were alone at last. I turned my attention to Finlay, who had forgone wearing one of my robes and instead had a towel wound about his waist.*

"*The robes are too small,*" *he explained the obvious, yet unasked, question.* "*I couldn't get any of them to close.*"

"*Should have worn one anyway.*" *I turned back to the wine. No, I wouldn't trick him into my bed, but I harbored no qualms about teasing him.* "*Would you like some wine?*" *I asked as I ladled it into bowls, then I suddenly felt like an utter fool. Gods, I was always making him tea, asking him to dinner, and now the spiced wine. I was treating him like a pig being fattened up for the slaughter.*

*Well, I'd already offered the wine, and he accepted the bowl as we sat on the thick rug before the hearth, our feet stretched toward the flames. He stared at the red liquid for a moment, then asked,* "*You've heated the wine?*" *Really, from his tone you'd have thought I'd left a mouse floating in it.*

"Attia taught me how to make it," I replied. "She says the herbs will keep away a chill." I decided against mentioning their other uses. Finlay hesitantly took a sip of the warmed liquid and made an excellent effort to hide the disgust on his face.

"I believe I would prefer a chill," he said as placed the bowl to the side.

"It's not so bad," I claimed as I took a small sip; my, but lover's ease is not the sweetest of herbs. "Attia does prepare it better than I." I placed my bowl next to Finlay's and leaned against his chest. "Perhaps we can think of another way to keep warm."

"Perhaps." His lips moved against my hair.

We curled up against each other, Finlay's lack of a robe making it easy for me to toy with the curls above his heart. I enjoyed the warmth of him, the gentle thump of the heart beneath his breast. Worried that I was neglecting the rest of him, I twisted and tugged at the curls around his navel. Surprisingly, he let me. Even more surprisingly, my hand met no resistance when it strayed below his makeshift garment.

"Asherah," he moaned, "what are you doing to me?"

"I told you, I wanted to learn how far this hair extended," I replied. He moaned again, and I eased his torment. "Forgive me."

"No," he said, catching my hand as I withdrew it. "Stay." I smiled, and tucked my arm around his waist. "What did Aeolmar tell you about trolls and mates?"

"He said that troll women look much like troll men, and taking one of them to his bed was the last thing on his mind," I replied. Finlay suppressed a chuckle at Aeolmar's assessment; I wondered if he had any such manly aunts in his family. "He was decidedly unhelpful on the matter." We sat together for a time, silence weighing upon us like a lead weight, until I could no longer bear it. "Tell me the custom?"

"Similar to the fae," he replied. "The woman chooses her mate, and the man claims her."

"And then, the binding is afterward?"

"There is no binding."

"How can that be?" I demanded, sitting up and staring at him. "How can you be mated before the gods without pledging your souls to one another? And how can you have children without the gods blessing?" Even elves, born of the earth rather than any god, begged for Nexa's blessing upon their union. And, unless Finlay was the handsomest troll to ever grace the nine realms, he was mostly fae. That mostly-fae troll laughed softly at my indignation.

"Trolls are simple folk, and their gods are more concerned with the forge and the anvil than who sleeps in whose bed. As for children, my parents are not bound, and neither were their parents. Very few in Cadogan undergo the ritual, since the closest temple is a three-day ride to the north."

Momentarily placated, I settled back against him, and resumed twisting the curls over his heart between my fingers. "I don't think I would feel like I had a mate if I wasn't bound." Then again, Lormac and I weren't bound, and that didn't make him any less my mate. Of course, he'd wanted to bind himself to me, and—

No. This was not about Lormac. I refused to hold myself hostage to his memory any longer. Gods, if he saw me now he'd call me all manner of epithets—coward, fool, other things not half as polite—and he'd be right about all of them. He'd loved me, and would want me to be happy, not subject myself to endless dalliances with men who would never love me.

Lormac would not want me to be alone.

"Are you averse to being bound?" I asked. I wonder if he noticed my hands trembling.

"No," he replied, "I just don't see it as necessary. The bond between mates is born of love. That's what matters."

"True." I still felt Lormac's love for me, saw it whenever I looked at the Sala. But, I wanted to be bound.

"So, you will bind yourself to me?" I asked. Finlay stared at me, hope and disbelief playing across his features. "Although,

*Atreynha has withdrawn into the vaults, so we cannot be bound until the next moon, at the earliest," I mumbled, mostly to myself. "Is that all right?"*

*"What are you saying?" he asked softly.*

*"I am saying that I love you, Finlay of Cadogan, merchant's son, my man from the desert," I replied as my pulse quickened. My hands had gone from trembling to outright shaking, so I sat on them. "You're everything I've always wanted, everything I tried to find with the others. You are my companion, my lover, my perfect mate. I choose you."*

*He cupped my face with his hands and brushed his thumbs across my cheeks. "You always said you couldn't take a mate," he said. "Why now, why me? You could have anyone, a warrior, a king!"*

*"I said I couldn't take a king," I corrected gently, "and you're right, I could have anyone. Kings, emperors, they would all welcome me to their beds." I wasn't being vain; it was the truth, and he knew it. Power and lands and titles those men had aplenty, but I didn't want that. I had never wanted those things. I took Finlay's hand and ran my fingertips over his rough palm, his troll skin that I had once hated but now loved dearly. "I can live without a king. You, I want by my side."*

*"I'm not worthy of a queen's love," he protested. "You need—"*

*"I need you," I said, placing my fingers on his lips. "And how can you be unworthy? I've met your father; he is an honorable man who does honest work. Remember, I began this journey as a slave, not a respectable merchant." I smiled as I spoke, only to have my happiness fade at the continued disbelief on his face. "Of course, I don't command you to choose me. I'll understand if you decline." I refused to lower my eyes, and I hardened my heart against his possible rejection. I was a queen, yes, and Finlay loved me, but he had come to manhood in a land rife with tradition concerning mating. Perhaps he could only claim a woman of troll descent; perhaps she needed to be a virgin, as well. Well, I came up short in both areas, but*

*there wasn't anything to be done. I was only Hillel, a simple woman masquerading as a queen. Nothing more.*

*Mere moments seemed like days while I waited for his response. At last, his eyes softened, and he drew me into the circle of his arms. I didn't know if he had decided to accept me, or if he couldn't come up with a way to decline without breaking my heart. Dreading the latter, I tucked my head against his neck and waited for him to speak. Luckily, I didn't have to wait too long.*

*"Now that you've done the choosing, I suppose all that's left is for me to claim you, and then you'll be mine," he said as he stroked my shoulder. "How is it done, here in Teg'urnan? Are you bound, then claimed, or the other way 'round?"*

*"In times past, you would carry me to the temple and claim me atop the altar," I murmured against his throat. "Mates were bound as they claimed each other. Now, I don't know if it makes a difference."*

*"I don't think I'd like claiming you in the temple," he said as his hand moved to the stays of my robe. "I think I'd prefer claiming you here, in your chamber."*

*So, it was a yes, then.*

*Yes.*

*Yes!*

*I rose up on my knees and kissed him, my almost-mate, as he pushed the thin silk off my shoulders. The robe gone, I yanked the towel from his hips and pulled him into my arms. We probably should have gone to bed for an act of such import, but I didn't want to wait. I couldn't wait; I needed him at that moment. Finlay, as ever, was much more patient than I.*

*"Are you sure?" he asked as he brushed the still-damp hair from my eyes.*

*"I've never been more sure of anything in my life."*

# Chapter Fifty-Four

The elder sun was going toward his rest when Aeolmar entered his chamber, exhausted from a day spent riding. It wasn't often that Asherah granted her First Hunter a reprieve from his duties, and he had taken full advantage of the opportunity.

*But then, I suppose I have Finlay to thank.* Aeolmar wondered how Finlay's day with the queen was faring, and he hoped for a better outcome than their ill-advised dinner. Curiosity overtaking propriety, he strayed toward the passageway that linked his chamber and the queen's. He heard Asherah's soft laughter float across the darkness, followed by Finlay's deep baritone. Aeolmar smiled, and shut the door.

# Chapter Fifty-Five

Aeolmar stood outside the queen's private entrance, his hand crushed into a fist and poised to knock upon the door. He'd never knocked in the past, but then there had never been the possibility of him finding Asherah in another man's arms. He'd almost forgotten this very fact as he'd walked down the passageway that emerged behind Asherah's bed—how he'd greeted her nearly every morning for the past eight winters. Gods, if he had done that, and saw them...Aeolmar squeezed his eyes shut and shoved the door open with such force it banged against the wall. "Asherah," he shouted.

"Here."

Aeolmar looked toward the sound of her voice, and found the queen exiting her bathing chamber, dressed in a robe. A moment later fully clothed Finlay emerged, his wet curls tight against his skull. At least both of them were covered.

"Forgive my intrusion," Aeolmar continued, "but Natraeus's force has moved. By now, they will have crossed half of Sengra."

"Which puts the fool hardly more than a sennight from Leran's keep," Asherah said while she crossed into the public rooms of her apartments, halting before the enchanted map. "They're far enough from The Seat, but still too close to Tingu for my liking."

"The envoy has also returned from Tingu," Aeolmar continued, coming to stand at Asherah's side. "Leran has decided to heed your warning. We have agreed to meet the dark fae here." Aeolmar indicated a point on the map that Asherah knew to be a rocky plain surrounded by the foothills of the World's Spine, where they could easily trap Natraeus' smaller force. "We can approach from here and squeeze Natraeus between our legion and Leran's."

Asherah nodded as she traced their route with her fingertip. "Preparations?"

"Done," Aeolmar replied. In response to Asherah's arched brow, he elaborated, "I saw to them yesterday, along with Harek. We only await your order to march, my queen."

"You worked alongside Harek?" Asherah chided. "Gods, we must be doomed."

"Consider it a gift," he replied. "One that's not likely to be repeated. Now, if you are through distracting my second, we will finalize matters."

With that, Aeolmar turned on his heel and left, mostly so he wouldn't have to endure Finlay and Asherah's goodbye. His second caught up with him in the corridor, and Aeolmar rattled off the final items that were needed for the coming march. Finlay nodded along, offering few words as Aeolmar recited great lists of supplies that he must have committed to memory.

"And if you hurt her, I will kill you."

Finlay stumbled. "I won't. I swear it."

Aeolmar stared at him, his eyes hard as sapphires. "See that you don't."

# Chapter Fifty-Six

## Asherah Speaks

*In an astonishing and unprecedented act of cooperation, Ae-olmar and Harek had planned the northward march with such efficiency that we arrived at our chosen battlefield a full day before Natraeus; I didn't know whether to applaud their dedication, or reprove them for miscalculating how many leagues could be covered in a day. Truth be told, I wished we had remained at Teg'urnan for an extra day, with me enjoying my new mate's attentions. When I said as much to Finlay, he chastised me for such a selfish desire, then proved that we needed no palace. Indeed, our tent proved more than adequate.*

*And Finlay was...wonderful. He was attentive and kind, and sensitive in a way I'd never thought a man could be. I'd expected him to be hesitant, even slightly reluctant as we learned each other, but he was neither. My shy boy from the desert had departed, and in his place was a confident man who knew what he wanted. Me.*

*Inasmuch as I would have preferred experiencing his new-found confidence at home, our early arrival meant that my warriors were well rested with weapons sharp and at the ready. I was saying something to that effect when the elder sun peeked over the horizon on the second day, and the scouts caught the gleam of sunlight on metal. By the time the child sun had joined his father, the full complement of dark fae were assembled in front of us. Unwilling to wait for Natraeus to act first, I rode out and greeted my opponent.*

*"Natraeus!" I shouted. "Come forth and face me!" At first, there was nothing save for a few men shuffling their feet, and I wondered if they realized who I was. Aeolmar, ever concerned for my safety, had convinced me to wear my armor to the imminent battle. It gleamed like quicksilver and boasted a helm shaped like a wolf's head. The metal plate was strong enough to resist a blade, yet light enough to hinder neither me nor my horse. I hardly ever wore it, partly because it had been a gift from Grelk upon my ascension to Parthalan's throne and I was loath to damage it, but mostly because the helm obscured my peripheral vision. Not to mention, if it was damaged it would likely take a century for Grelk to complete any repairs.*

*The damned helm was obscuring my vision even now; I could really only see what was directly before me. Suspecting that Natraeus would slither up from one  side I considered riding the length of warriors, then there was some milling about in the dark fae's ranks and Natraeus, slimy bastard that he is, came forward.*

*"End this now," I demanded. "No blood has yet been shed. Turn around, return to your lands." When he remained silent, I added, "This offer is given once. If you do not accept it, you will die."*

*"Allow me to present a counteroffer, my queen," Natraeus shouted. "Return to Teg'urnan, and once I have conquered the elves, you and I will rule as king and queen of this realm!"*

*His words made the bile rise in my throat, but I swallowed my gorge and laughed. Is it rude to laugh at an opposing king on a battlefield? I couldn't help it; the idea of the dark fae conquering the elves was ludicrous. A herd of field mice would have a greater chance of victory. My obvious amusement unsettled Natraeus, so I laughed some more.*

*"You cannot conquer the Lord of Tingu!" I choked out between laughs. "Leran is descended from the fiercest warriors who have ever walked this earth. He will cut a swathe through the lot of you! He will offer you no quarter, not to you, nor your people." I dismounted, and addressed the warriors fanned out on either side of the dark king.*

*"I implore you, do not let this man sway you," I shouted. "His foolish aspirations will mean your deaths. Leave his ranks, go south into Parthalan. If you abandon this fool's mission, I will grant you asylum."*

*"You would seek to steal my warriors?" Natraeus screeched, with his face reddened and his cheeks puffed out to twice their normal size. He reminded me of a laundress, hot and cranky after a day spent scrubbing his betters' smallclothes.*

*"I offer them life. You way leads only to death." I watched at Natraeus for a moment, then continued. "Your time is nearly up, Natraeus. You have until I reach that boulder," I pointed to a massive stone fifty or so paces off, "to accept my offer. I will warn you, I ride very fast."*

*With that, I turned my back to the dark fae in what was intended to be a show of respect. No warrior worth his sword would strike a retreating foe and thus break one of the unspoken laws of the battlefield. Indeed, such an act would be tantamount to a declaration of war. I had every confidence that I was safe. Queen or no, sometimes I was a fool.*

*I cannot say what caused me to turn. Was it instinct? The gentle creak of a bowstring drawn taut, the soft* thwip *of an arrow as it took flight? Whatever it was, I spun my horse around, drew my sword faster than I ever thought I could, and struck aside the arrow aimed at my heart. My horse reared, but before I could issue the command to charge, the archer who'd loosed the arrow at me crumpled in death.*

*"Natraeus," boomed a deep voice from the rise above. Leran, the Lord of Tingu himself, stood with a bow in his hands.*

*Gods, he looked just like his father, so much so it made my heart ache. "Your fight is with me, not Asherah. I demand you face me."*

*Natraeus, in perhaps his wisest decision yet, fled.*

# Chapter Fifty-Seven

The battle raged around Olwynn, his blood singing with its fervor. *It's been too long,* he thought as he cut down another of the dark fae. He was a warrior, born and bred, and loved to fight like he enjoyed nothing else. Indeed, it had been his prowess on the battlefield that had so quickly earned him a coveted assignment at the Southern Border. Not long after that assignment he had been enthralled by Mersgoth and spent the next few winters watching demons slowly destroy the females of his kind. A living torment worse than the hells philosophers wrote of, worse than an eternity spent in the underworld could possibly be. He'd been helpless to save them, and himself.

Then Lormac and Asherah had arrived, and liberated him and the rest from the thrall; for that act alone, Olwynn would have died for Asherah's sake, but, when she'd become queen, she offered him a position in the *con'dehr*. Any other ruler would have been wary of allowing one who'd had such a close association with demons entry to the elite temple guard. Asherah, for obvious reasons, had looked past his captivity to the loyal warrior that was his core being. For giving him a second chance, Olwynn would die twice for his queen, long may she reign.

When the Prelate had sought to transition the *con'dehr* from guarding the Great Temple to a select few tasked with the queen's protection, Olwynn had been the first he'd turned to. Harek had believed that the old king had placed such emphasis on protecting the temple because of the priestesses' role in his foul plot, and wished to distance his warriors from such a memory. Olwynn knew that the *con'dehr* had been established by Solon's decree, not by any whim or plot of Sahlgren's, but he'd believed in Harek's vision and followed him anyway. Over these past winters, he had assisted Harek in molding the *con'dehr* into the elite and deadly force it was today.

This was why Olwynn could not comprehend the actions of these supposedly noble warriors. His fellow members of the *con'dehr* seemed more concerned with searching bodies and confiscating the dark fae's distinctive curved weapons, which made little sense. Dead men rarely swung swords, and the *con'dehr's* arms were far superior than what Natraeus had supplied to his men. Olwynn's own sword was troll-forged, bestowed upon him by Lormac long ago. He maneuvered himself to a high point and surveyed the battle below, hoping to discern something from his fellow warriors' actions.

From his vantage point, he saw that the *con'dehr* were indeed taking the dark fae's weapons; more, they were mercilessly slaughtering the wounded. *Asherah would never agree to this.* Before he could further consider the plight of the wounded, he spied the hunters in the distance. The brothers, Bron and Luth, fought back to back, but Aeolmar and Finlay were both alone amidst a sea of their dark brethren. Somewhat frantically, he scanned the area for Innetha, and was rewarded with a glimpse of her dark hair just before his fear turned to terror. She was keeping close to the edge of the fray, just as Olwynn had wanted.

*Thank the gods.* He'd been wary of asking her to avoid the thick of it, even though Innetha's skill with a sword was remarkable for a former seamstress. But he had asked, and rather than argue with him, she'd smiled.

"Wouldn't care for a wounded woman in your bed, would you?" she'd teased. Once they'd learned that they were a full day, possibly even two, ahead of the dark fae, they'd accepted the gift of time and spent it in their tent. So far, they'd only emerged once, and that emergence had been brief, indeed. "Messy bandages... fevers... and what if we—"

"Stop." He'd rolled so she was underneath him, and had looked at his Innetha. He'd taken in her green and gold flecked eyes, her smooth skin and graceful neck—trying to memorize every aspect of her appearance. "I don't care if you bleed all over the blankets. I just want you alive."

Innetha had nodded her agreement, and Olwynn had been glad she'd heeded his words. It had been the first time she'd ever heeded him, but it was a start. *A good start.*

Satisfied that his woman wasn't in immediate danger, Olwynn looked back toward Aeolmar and Finlay. He had no worries for the First Hunter's safety—anyone who could take a *mordeth's* sword had little to fear from the dark fae—but Finlay, while a good fighter in his own right, had neither the skill nor stamina of the others.

Olwynn climbed higher, and the pieces of Harek's plan were laid out before him. The *con'dehr* had maneuvered Aeolmar and Finlay far from the rest—but wait, now four of his fellow warriors approached Finlay from behind, effectively cutting him off from any who could protect him. Then a *con'dehr* not ten paces from Finlay was poised to strike a killing blow.

*Why Finlay?* Olwynn remembered Harek's furor over the hunters less than two moons past; that was the morning after Finlay was rumored to have spent the night in Asherah's chamber. And Aeolmar was well known to have been Asherah's lover for many winters, just as it was well known that the

Prelate carried a torch for the queen that blazed as brightly as the elder sun, a torch that the queen had never noticed.

*He means to kill them!* Olwynn immediately cast the thought from his mind, but then he remembered Sarfek's chamber, filled with demonic spells and strange artifacts. Harek was convinced that a dark sorcerer was helping Natraeus, and Olwynn was certain that Sarfek still lived. Sarfek, a powerful sorcerer who had a chamber packed full of evil relics.

*Argent died in battle. As did Brendan before him. And—gods, no!—and Lormac.*

"Hunter," Olwynn bellowed as he ran down the hillside, unsure if he should run to Aeolmar or Finlay. The First Hunter would readily believe his accusations, but Finlay held the greater need; the *con'dehr* were all around him.

Olwynn skidded on the rough, pebbly incline, and used a dark fae's corpse to break his fall. He shouted for Finlay to turn around, to run, but his warnings were lost to the din of battle. Then Finlay fell back, a spear lodged in his gut; Olwynn couldn't see who was responsible, but no matter. The man was dead, so he changed course, now intending to warn the First Hunter. Harek blocked his path.

"Olwynn," Harek said calmly. He was always calm in the heat of battle, seemingly unaffected by the blood and death that surrounded him. Olwynn had always thought that Harek's ability to keep his head was one of the traits that made him an excellent Prelate; now, he thought it marked him as a murderer. "Off to rescue a lowly hunter?"

"I won't let you kill him," Olwynn shouted. "You've created this war, over nothing but your bruised pride! How many have died by your hand, Harek? How many more need to fall?"

"Oh, is Finlay dead?" Harek asked, looking past Olwynn to the hunter's still body. "Good. Only two more to die, now that's not so bad. Is it, Olwynn?"

"No!" Olwynn drew his sword and approached the Prelate. "I challenge you, Harek! I will fight you for their lives!" Olwynn had assumed that the next to die were Aeolmar and Natraeus. At Harek's slow, spreading smile, he realized his error.

"But who will challenge me for your life?" Harek asked, drawing a short sword.

"I do!" Olwynn cried. "Fight me like a man, you coward."

"No." With a flick of Harek's wrist, the *con'dehr* that had surrounded Olwynn descended upon him, bearing the curved daggers and knives they'd scavenged from the dead. When they were done, the body was unrecognizable.

# Chapter Fifty-Eight

The queen fought alone, as was her preference; speed and agility were Asherah's greatest skills on the battlefield. When she was surrounded by foes she didn't have to worry about an ill-aimed strike making contact with a friend. Of course, she was striking to wound, not to kill, but she would shed no tears over the loss of any dark fae. They'd ignored her offer of an honorable retreat, which is more than Natraeus would have offered to his opponents had their positions been reversed.

Asherah spied a shock of oily blackness beneath a foot soldier's cap and laughed to herself. Natraeus, noble king of the dark fae, had shed his cloak and his standard, and was skulking about the battle clad in an ill-conceived disguise. Asherah rushed at him, using a surprised warrior's back as a stepping stone to vault over the fracas and land squarely on Natraeus' back.

"Coward," she hissed in his ear. He opened his mouth, but Asherah shoved his face in the dirt. "Pathetic wretch of a man." She wrenched the dagger from his grip, and pulled him to his knees. "I have your king!" she shouted. Those closest to her dropped their weapons, but a few paces off the fighting continued unabated. "Desist!" she shrieked, now holding Natraeus' own dagger at his throat, but that command was heard no more than the last.

"Hold!" roared a voice, and every warrior obeyed. "Your queen speaks!" Leran strode to Asherah's side, clutching the silver horn that carried his voice across the battlefield. Leran offered her the horn but she shook her head; now, the only sound was the wind over the rocks and a dying man's cries. She would be heard above both.

"I claim this battle," Asherah triumphantly proclaimed. "Your king led you into a war born not of righteousness, but of his own foolish pride! As such, I take his crown, and his land." Asherah snatched the gold circlet from Natraeus' brow and flung it into the dirt. He lunged for it, only to shrink back when the dagger's tip pierced his skin.

"Nibika is no more," Asherah continued. "The dark fae are now, and forever, ruled by Tingu." She let go of Natraeus' jerkin, and he fell to the ground at Leran's feet. "His life is forfeit. Do with him what you will."

"He's your prisoner," Leran stated. "By all rights, his punishment is your pleasure."

"My pleasure is never seeing that man again," Asherah said.

"This son of a whore is not fit to judge me," Natraeus growled. Leran was content to ignore the comment, but Asherah did not allow anyone speak ill of Leran in her presence. She struck the dark king with her metal-gloved hand; dazed, Natraeus dribbled blood and bits of tooth down his chin.

"Sure you wouldn't like to kill him yourself?" Leran asked. Asherah looked sharply at Leran, but her annoyance quickly melted. She had only seen him a handful of times since he'd grown to manhood—and always under less than ideal circumstances. All she wanted was to sit and talk with him, ask after his life, and say those things that couldn't be said on a battlefield. She didn't know if that would ever happen; honoring her promise, she wouldn't set foot in Tingu without his express permission, and Leran had ignored or refused every invitation to Teg'urnan she'd ever sent. In a way, Asherah looked forward to these border skirmishes, since they were one of the few ways she could catch a fleeting glimpse of Leran.

*Gods, I just want him to be my boy again.*

Leran made a cutting gesture, and Natraeus was dragged off toward Tingu's camp. A second gesture brought forth ten elfin warriors who took a protective stance around the Lord and Lady of Tingu while heralds called out the battle's victory and the rest of dark fae were taken as hostages.

"Thank you, for the warning," Leran said. "It was most time-ly."

"Of course," Asherah said with a slight nod. Leran, having said all he'd intended, had already begun to walk toward his camp when Asherah blurted out, "When next I see you, I will return the Sala!"

Leran halted, and slowly turned to regard her. Asherah's continued possession of the Sala had been a point of con-tention with them, for while it was Leran's birthright, Asherah was his father's chosen mate. She would remain the Lady of Tingu until Leran took a mate of his own. "You will?"

"I shouldn't have kept it these past winters," she explained, then launched into a babbling account of how the Sala was his by rights, and how he needed it to keep his borders strong and remind his people that he was Nexa's true and only heir. When she stopped for breath, Leran raised his hand.

"I appreciate your words," Leran said carefully, "but I must ask, why now?"

"Well," she began, then stopped. Leran deserved the truth, but she was loath to share the whole of it with him; for all Asherah knew, Leran would see her mating with Finlay as her final betrayal of his father, call her a traitor, and declare war on Parthalan. Luckily, there were many facets to the truth.

"I need to accept that I'm no longer your protector. You're a warrior grown and can manage your lands as well as I manage mine." Asherah looked over the carnage, and smiled ruefully. "Perhaps, much better than I manage mine."

"You will remain Lady of Tingu," Leran pointed out.

"In title alone," Asherah said. Leran smiled tightly, and bowed.

"As always, I appreciate your generous and magnanimous nature."

Gods! She hated it when he did that! She could never discern if Leran was speaking to her in respect or condescension. She wanted to rail at him, demand that they leave off these court niceties and be who they really were: two people who had both lost the person they loved most.

*No. To do so would only humiliate Leran, and me.* "Lormac would be very proud of you," was all she said. Leran's smile became a grimace, then he turned and left Asherah alone on the battlefield.

# Chapter Fifty-Nine

## Aeolmar Speaks

*I walked across the field, so frustrated and annoyed flames danced upon my palm. I had just fought in the most unsatisfying battle of my life. Had the journey not been as miserable as it was, what with slogging through cold mud and driving rain, I might not have been so irritated. Had I something other than anger to warm me at night, I might not have been so angry. Instead, I'd had Asherah and Finlay on one side of my tent, Innetha and Olwynn on the other, the lot of them making so much noise that I couldn't hope to sleep. To describe my mood as tense would have been a profound understatement.*

*Then Asherah had issued her final set of commands before the battle, the last of which was that we were to keep the casualties to a minimum. I agreed with her in principle, for why should Natraeus' people suffer for his folly? Although, they had made their choice clear when the bulk of them refused Asherah's generous offer of asylum. Still, I made every effort to wound rather than kill. At least I followed the queen's orders.*

*That was more than I could say for Harek and his fool* con'dehr. *They had cut a swath through the dark fae's ranks with such ferocity I questioned Olwynn's certainty of our Prelate assisting Natraeus. It wouldn't make any sense to decimate your ally, not even one as foolish as Natraeus, or for someone as foolishly prideful as Harek.*

*I wanted to speak with Olwynn, but he was nowhere to be found. That didn't bode well; if Harek had acted in collusion with Natraeus, the time to call him out was now. Leran had custody of the dark king, and unless the Lord of Tingu had suddenly become as soft-hearted as a maiden, Natraeus would meet his ancestors before nightfall. My mood was quickly degrading from aggravated to aggressive; gods, if I found Olwynn holed up with Innetha I'd strangle the both of them.*

*Also missing was my second. I'd assumed he was with Asherah until the queen herself asked after his whereabouts. After reassuring Asherah that her mate would turn up soon, I inquired as to when he and Olwynn were last seen; I was convinced that Olwynn was off with Innetha, but asking after the two disguised my concern for the one. When no one remembered having set eyes on either, I ordered a search of the entire field, leaving no stone or corpse unturned.*

*"Here's your second!"*

*I walked toward the voice, not bothering to rush until I saw the furrowed brows of those staring at a corpse. The corpse's hand clutched a sword that the queen had once bestowed upon a merchant in Cadogan. I shoved the others aside and dropped to my knees beside Finlay's body, held fast to the ground by a pike run through his belly.*

*"Hells," I muttered. I uttered a few more curses, more distraught over Asherah's coming reaction than Finlay's death. I doubted that she would recover quickly from the loss of her mate; indeed, the loss of a second mate may be too much for her, or anyone, to bear. "Find the queen," I said to the one who'd found Finlay. "Tell her nothing, but bring her directly—" I fell silent, having been interrupted by a soft, gurgling cough. Incredibly, Finlay struggled for air.*

*"He lives," I shouted. "Get me bandages! Water! And find a healer!" Those around him remained rooted in place; clearly,*

*they all thought that Finlay would be dead in a few moments and have no need of such things. Only, I was not about to let him die.*

*"Move!" I bellowed. "Or I'll impale the lot of you! Bron!" I shouted into the air. The hunter appeared in an instant. "Search the bodies. Bring me every cloak and spear you can find."*

*"Are we making a litter?"*

*"A tent." We were far from our camp. I didn't know if Finlay would survive being moved, and I meant to save him, not kill him while bumbling about the field. I took the small knife I kept in my boot and cut away Finlay's jerkin, exposing the wound. The pike was all the way through him, but there was very little blood. Of course, when I removed the pike the blood would pour out like a waterfall. Unless...*

*An image of my sister Linnea and her sewing basket, flashed behind my eyes. No healer was present to offer advice (or call me an uneducated imbecile), and since I had no way of knowing if our healers had survived the battle, or if another was within a day's ride, I took matters into my own hands.*

*"Give me your rum," I said to Bron.*

*"Rum?" Bron repeated.*

*"I know you have a flask on you somewhere." Gods, he and his brother drank so much of the stuff it was a wonder they remained upright. My eyes burned into Bron's back until the man handed over his prized possession. He mumbled that it was an odd time for libations when I poured half the contents over Finlay's wound. Bron briefly mourned the loss of his drink, but muttered that he'd not like it if Finlay died, and resumed his search for cloaks and spears. He'd begun assembling the tent when one of those who'd found Finlay reappeared bearing bandages and water.*

*"Get a horse, go to the village at the base of the rise and get a needle and thread. Fine thread, the kind used for ladies' gowns." He nodded as he stared at Finlay's limp form, unmov-*

ing. "Now!" I shouted. Olluhm's Balls, did no one understand that time was of the essence?

Wisely, the soldier didn't need to be told again. I wadded up the bandages and pressed them around the pike. The wound was oozing a little, and I'd yet to learn how much blood had seeped into the ground below him. I didn't take my attention from my charge until I heard soft footfalls behind me, and a muffled gasp of horror.

"No," Asherah gasped as she knelt in the mud, "no no no." She reached toward him with shaking hands, recoiling when his eyelids fluttered.

"He lives," I said, "barely." I grasped her hand and placed it on his; his flesh was so cold he may as well have been dead. Asherah's black eyes glittered, and she slowly looked over the length of his form.

"Why is that still in him?" she asked, meaning the pike.

"If I take it now, he'll bleed out. I've sent someone for thread."

"You'll sew it?" she asked, and I nodded. "Can't you heal him?" I didn't understand her question, but Asherah's eyes were fixed behind me.

"If I absorb a wound like that, it will kill me," Innetha replied. She dismounted and crouched by Finlay's head, then tilted a waterskin to his lips.

"Then die!" Asherah shouted. Innetha ignored Asherah as she railed, and kept tending to Finlay. I, however, needed to concentrate. I grabbed Asherah's chin and yanked her face before mine.

"Keep shouting rather than helping and he will die!" Asherah did not speak, but her lower lip quivered and tears rolled down her cheeks. "Talk to him, hold his hand," I implored, my tone now soft. "Give him something to live for."

"He can't... he can't die," Asherah sobbed.

"He won't," I promised. I kissed Asherah's hand, then pressed it against Finlay's cheek. "He won't."

*Then, a hundred things happened at once. Bron finished assembling the makeshift tent, the soldier returned with quite a fine sewing kit, and Finlay began retching. I thought the retching must be a good sign, for why would one near death need to clear his windpipe, though he lost much of the water Innetha had so carefully dribbled down his throat.*

*Asherah whispered soothing words in her mate's ear, and he calmed quickly. Most likely, Finlay had little strength to fight; he looked worse than before, his skin having gone ashen, and a thin sheen of sweat covered his flesh. I had to get that pike out and quickly, lest an infection lodge itself in his gut. That, not even I was willing to face.*

*"Hold his shoulders, but stay where he can see you," I instructed Asherah. "Once it's out, we need to cover the front of the wound, and turn him over so I can sew his back."*

*Asherah nodded as she put her weight on Finlay's shoulders, and as Bron and Innetha held his legs I yanked the pike free. Fortunately, the pike was little more than a sharpened length of wood and didn't have a barbed tip, so it withdrew cleanly. Not fortunately, the removal sent Finlay's body into violent convulsions. Asherah shrieked and Bron bellowed an ancient charm that warded against necromancy. I ignored the both of them and rolled Finlay over, doused the gaping hole in his back with the last of the rum, and hurriedly stitched his flesh closed.*

*"Lay him flat!" I shouted. Innetha, the only one with any wits left, thrust a slightly cleaner cloak under Finlay's body, then handed me a second needle. I'd left the other underneath him, but I managed to sew up his belly just as quickly as I had his back. The worst of it over, we sat him up and wound bandages around his torso, then I lifted my second and brought him inside the makeshift tent, and settled him on a bed of scavenged cloaks.*

*"What can I do?" Asherah asked, her earlier hysteria now gone. Being covered in your loved one's blood is a singularly sobering experience.*

*"The blood loss will chill him," I explained. "Lay with him, keep him warm. When he wakes, give him water."*

*"Aeolmar," she began, "if you hadn't..." Her voice wavered, and I pulled her into my arms. Gods, if she cried or thanked me or did anything, I truly would go mad.*

*"Hush," I said. "See to your man. There will be time for talking later." Asherah nodded and let me guide her to Finlay's side. I watched her arrange herself against him, carefully avoiding the wound, and left the mates to what might be their last bit of privacy.*

*Outside the tent, I stretched and looked down to find my tunic and jerkin soaked in Finlay's blood. I tore them off without thinking, then crumpled to the ground in an exhausted heap, my breath white puffs in the frigid air. After a few moments, Innetha sat next to me and wrapped a blanket around us both.*

*"You're more of a healer than I," she said. "Where did you learn to sew wounds?"*

*"Nowhere. I've only ever mended my boots."*

*"Do you think he'll live?"*

*"Gods, I hope so, for Asherah's sake."*

*We sat in silence for a time; I imagine that we both hoped to hear a sound from the tent, a moan or gurgle, some sign of life. But, there was nothing. Innetha laid her head on my shoulder, and I had neither the strength nor desire to push her away.*

*"Do you remember when I healed your hand?" she asked at length.*

*"How could I forget?" I replied with a sidelong glance. I gazed into her doe eyes, and wondered how I would feel about Innetha if we'd met under different circumstances. She was lovely, as all nymphs were, and a good huntress. Hells, she was a far better tracker than I, better than any tracker I'd ever met. I wrapped an arm about her shoulders; she was soft and warm, but more importantly she was there. I was glad she was there.*

*A herald called for the queen; somewhat hoarsely, I yelled out our location and, because I wasn't going to disturb Asher-*

*ah for anything less than the end of the world, asked for the message. After he'd caught his breath the herald recounted a list of the wounded and then the dead. The latter was short, but contained a name I hadn't expected.*

*"Olwynn?" I repeated, and the herald nodded. "How did he die?"*

*The herald explained the multitude of wounds on Olwynn's body, all of which seem to have been gotten at close range, all of which were delivered with the curved daggers used by the dark fae. In the end, he was only identified by going through the lists of who was accounted for, and who was not. I asked if any other bodies were mutilated, and the herald replied that three in total were nearly hacked to bits. All were* con'dehr.

*"Makes no sense," I muttered. "Dark fae don't disfigure the dead any more than we do. And how could they manage such carnage on members of the* con'dehr?*" Perhaps Harek's elite force wasn't as elite as he'd bragged. It was only then that I noticed Innetha's silence and realized that I'd been discussing the death of her lover as if he was a man she'd never met. Although, if anyone could be described as stone-hearted as I, it was certainly...*

*A drop of wetness splashed onto my chest. That stone-hearted woman was weeping in my arms.*

# Chapter Sixty

A sputtering cough shattered the silence of the tent. Asherah blinked as she woke, having forgotten where she was, then recognized the noise as Finlay coughing beside her. She was momentarily relieved, for coughing meant breathing. Then she panicked as she realized he was also choking and rolled him to his uninjured side. Once he had cleared the congealed blood from his throat, she offered him a sip of water; he drank greedily and succumbed to another fit of coughing. After it passed, he drank again, slowly, and grimaced. Asherah saw that dried blood had sealed his eyes shut, so she dampened her fingers and gently stroked his eyelids.

"I didn't think I'd ever see your eyes again," Asherah murmured once he opened them.

"You're all bloody," Finlay croaked. "Are you hurt?" He tried to rise and check her for wounds, but the pain in his gut held him immobile.

"It's your blood," Asherah whispered. "All of it is yours."

"Good," he said as he managed an arm around her shoulder. "It would kill me if anything happened to you."

"You nearly were killed," she said, her voice catching in her throat. "If they hadn't found you..." Her words trailed off, but he knew what she was about to say: that he would have been just another one of her loved ones to die on her.

"You really think I'd leave you?" he asked as he pushed her hair, now stained red with his blood, behind her ear. "I'm not so easy to get rid of. However, I imagine that I finally will have greater scars than yours."

Asherah stared at him, then hid her face against his neck and laughed at the sheer absurdity of his words. Finlay laughed with her, but it quickly degraded to yet another wet, hacking cough. Once he had steadied himself, Asherah lovingly glowered at him. "Sustain another mortal wound, and I'll kill you as penance."

"I love you, too."

# Chapter Sixty-One

## Asherah Speaks

*We had been watching the waves crash against the rocks for the better part of the day, me growing more and more impatient with every break and swell. Aeolmar, however, was as content as I'd ever seen him. As he stared at the crashing surf, however, I got the feeling that he was staring at a far-off memory, or perhaps a dream that had never been.*

*"You got your wish." When he looked at me quizzically, I continued, "You've brought me to the sea."*

*"So I have." The salty air blew back his hair as he fingered a shell in his palm. Earlier, we had walked along the beach, the tide swirling around our bare ankles, and Aeolmar had amassed quite a collection. At first his behavior had befuddled me, and I was befuddled yet again when he readily answered my unasked question.*

*"Once, when I was a boy, my father brought us to the sea," Aeolmar began. "My mother had always wanted to see the vast expanse for herself."*

*"Was your village far from here?"*

*"No. Not far." He cradled the shell in his hand, tracing the curved edge with a fingertip. "My sisters collected piles and*

*piles of shells, baskets full that we dragged all the way home. We had no place to store them, so we fixed them to the wall above my mother's hearth. We made her a great archway of shells, always there to remind her of the sea."*

*I shook my head at the irony of my life. For all the years Aeolmar had been my lover, I had wanted him to share his past with me, to open up his heart for I felt that until he did, there would be no place for me in it. Now he finally had, when we were waiting for my mate to arrive so we could begin our seclusion.*

*"I never would have taken you as sentimental," I commented.*

*He laughed to himself. "Most times, I don't know what to make of myself."*

*He may not, but I certainly did. Aeolmar was an expert at building fortifications around his true self, at keeping others at bay, and—again, too late—I had at last discerned the reason why. He'd been wounded so terribly that he kept everyone out, those he cared for along with the rest. Regardless of his attempts to keep me out, I saw the man within.*

*I threw my arms around his neck and kissed him, not as passionately as I once would have but intense nonetheless. I feared he would push me away, but he didn't and kissed me back.*

*"What was that for?" he asked once we parted. "I don't think Finlay would approve of me kissing his mate."*

*I ignored his statement and answered his question. "All those nights I had you in my bed, I desperately wanted you to be like Lormac. You were the only one since him who cared for me, the only one who saw me as a woman instead of a queen... I just wanted you to love me and be my mate, as he was." He moved to speak, but I placed my fingertips over his mouth and gently stroked my thumb over his lower lip. So many times he had kissed me, made me forget, made me feel as if what I was doing mattered, that I was a good queen and a better woman. Gods, I was going to miss him.*

*"I now realize that you've never been like Lormac," I continued. "You, my dearest friend, are like Torim." Aeolmar squeezed my hands and said nothing for a time; while it was not unusual for him to be silent, I had the impression that he might be too overcome to speak.*

*"I can agree with that," he said at length. "And, like Torim, I care for you a great deal, but not in the way a mate should. I wish I did."*

*"I know." I worked my way to the crook of his arm, resting my head on his shoulder, and thought about how lucky I was. With a man like Finlay as my mate, and Aeolmar as my friend, I finally felt more like Asherah than Hillel.*

*Eventually, Finlay arrived, apologizing for his lateness but blaming the still-tender wound on his gut that was less than a season healed. He probably shouldn't have been riding at all, but he'd insisted that if we were to be bound, then we should have a proper seclusion. And the only way we could remain undisturbed would be if we left Teg'urnan altogether. Aeolmar was our ready accomplice, though he'd had his misgivings.*

*"Are you sure this is how you want to handle it?" he had asked. I had just told him that Finlay and I were to be bound in secret, with only a select few privy to the knowledge.*

*"Yes," I answered without hesitation. When he gave me those damned searching eyes, I threw up my hands in frustration. "How would you feel if you were me? Whenever I let myself get close to someone, they die. Torim... Lormac... Argent... All dead. Lovers I had taken before Argent, dead as well. Only you still live, and you were the most discreet." I turned away, suddenly uncomfortable speaking with my former lover of my imminent binding. "And Finlay nearly died. He would have died, if not for your help. It's enough to make me wonder if those I love are being targeted."*

*"Then I will help you," Aeolmar said simply, and I let out my breath in a great exhale. I hadn't realized just how much his approval meant to me. I turned back to him, and the set of*

*his jaw told me that the questioning was not done. "You're not even telling Harek?"*

*I sighed again, and debated my answer. It wasn't that I didn't want to share my suspicions with Aeolmar, but if I said aloud that I feared Harek may be the cause of my lovers' deaths... No. I would not. "I don't think he wants to be involved in these matters."*

*Aeolmar had accepted my explanation and helped me arrange two journeys from Teg'urnan. Aeolmar and I would depart for a mission to the west, and Finlay would be sent to the south. The ruse was to have the appearance of Finlay and I being apart, when in reality, he and I would be enjoying our seclusion, while Aeolmar remained by the sea, waiting for our emergence. I'd thought the plan was unfair to Aeolmar, being left alone, but he claimed he would enjoy a bit of solitude. As First Hunter, solitude was certainly hard to come by.*

*And now Finlay, my mate, my one true mate, was here, and we were leaving Aeolmar alone with his thoughts. I tried to be compassionate towards my First Hunter, but all I could think of was my coming time with my love, and how I never wanted that time to end.*

*I am Asherah the Ruthless, virgin queen no more. Long may I reign!*

# Chapter Sixty-Two

## Aeolmar Speaks

*I watched the two of them ride off, my hand over my heart as I felt the small bump created by my mother's pendant. It was there as a silent reminder of her, and of her final wish for my happiness. So many times I'd nearly put the pendant around Asherah's neck, but as I watched her depart I understood how wrong it would have been. I loved her—gods, how I loved her!—but I could never care for her as well as Finlay. If anyone deserved such unconditional devotion, it was Asherah.*

*And why couldn't I love her properly? My all-consuming vengeance towards Mersgoth. He had killed my family so long ago, yet every breath he took meant that he was still ruining my life. Why had I let the need for his death consume me so? I considered my gentle mother and my stoic father; they wouldn't have let themselves be endlessly tormented by a demon,* mordeth *or not. They would have lived their lives, taking whatever happiness had been offered them and enjoying each moment they shared. It was what they had done, right up to the end.*

*I stared at the waves, those very same waves where I once had a vision of my mate. I'd hoped that it was Asherah in my vision, but it hadn't been she. No, it was a woman I had yet to meet, and if I had yet to meet her, I had time to make myself into the sort of man she deserved—not a surly hunter who cared only for death and demons, one who spent weeks at a time following fruitless trails and half-whispered rumors... No. She deserved better than that. She deserved to be treated better than I had treated Asherah.*

*I resolved to leave off my hunt for Mersgoth and to spend more time at Teg'urnan. I hated the way those stone walls closed in around me, choking the breath from my lungs, but when I found her I would need to give her a home, wouldn't I? I would be a good man, and a good mate, and I would give her the sort of life she deserved. The sort of life my father had given my mother.*

*A wave crashed closer to shore and the salt water splashed onto my face. I saw once more my earlier vision of her playing in the surf, and...were those our children alongside her? I nearly laughed out loud, never having realized how much I had desired a family, though I acknowledged how alone I felt without my own. Yes, there were children, and if I squinted just so I could make out their features. There was a boy who took after me, and girl who looked like her mother. Gods, if she wasn't beautiful. I felt that I loved her already.*

*I only had to find her.*

***

The story continues in...

Rise of the Deva'shi

Book Three of The Chronicles of Parthalan – turn the page for a sneak peek!

I hope you enjoyed reading about Parthalan as much as I enjoyed writing it. Click here to leave a review.

Join my mailing list here (and receive a free ebook as a gift): https://authorjenniferallisprovost.com/contact/

*Here's your sneak peek from Rise of the Deva'shi. Enjoy!*

***

"Will there be women in this village?"

Aeolmar's gaze slid toward Luth. "Missing Innetha already?"

Luth snorted. "Hardly. She refused to become my mate. Again!"

"Of course she said no," said Luth's brother, Bron. "What self-respecting woman would have you?"

Aeolmar almost bit through his tongue; he thought Innetha was many things, but respectable was not one of them.

"*I* hope there will be women," Adhaire said, bringing his horse alongside Luth's. "After I complete my Trial by Stealth, I'll want to celebrate!"

Aeolmar glanced at the young *nuvi*, doubtful of his chances. Adhaire recently won the Trial by Combat for a third time, but had only recently mastered calling fire. Aeolmar assumed it would take Adhaire a few tries to master stealth, as well.

"Have faith," Finlay said. "Adhaire will be a fine hunter."

"Of course," Aeolmar agreed, unwilling to say more until Adhaire actually failed. Once that happened, he would petition Asherah to have the useless *nuvi* removed from the *sola* and sent far, far away from Teg'urnan.

Not that Aeolmar intended to witness Adhaire's failure himself. Aeolmar had chosen to hold this exercise outside a village close to his birthplace. Once the Trial was underway, Aeolmar planned to slip away and visit his home. Nothing remained of his childhood home but a charred patch of earth, but it was home nonetheless.

Aeolmar touched the small bump over his heart. He'd taken his mother's pendant with him, rather than leave it behind in Teg'urnan. He hoped his mother's spirit rested close to her grave, since he needed her advice now more than ever. He was tired of his life as First Hunter, tired of being alone, of palace life... Gods, he was just tired.

The hunters arrived in the village of Brennus and found the inn. It was overseen by Ingvarr, a man known throughout the west for his hospitality as his mate, Elma, was for her fine cooking. While Finlay spoke to Ingvarr about boarding the horses, Aeolmar investigated the stables. He'd never left Myrnnhe anyplace he wouldn't sleep himself, and needed to see his horse's accommodations for himself.

As Aeolmar approached the stables he spied movement at the far corner; a small form clad in a tunic and leggings, a flash of bright hair. Intrigued, he followed the person toward the back of the yard...and almost bumped into a girl coming the other way. She gasped and dropped the saddle she was carrying, scooping it up an instant.

"May I pass?" she asked, balancing the saddle on her hip.

Realizing that this girl was the one he'd followed, Aeolmar took a long look at her. Her hair was flame red, bound up in a braid that did a poor job restraining her curls, her eyes were pale blue, and her skin was golden and a bit burnt across her nose and cheeks. What amazed Aeolmar most was her size; she was hardly larger than a child, yet she had a woman's curves. And she held that saddle as if it were weightless.

"May I pass?" she repeated, tapping her foot. Aeolmar stepped aside, then she stalked past him and placed the saddle on the workbench. After watching her for a moment, Aeolmar joined Finlay and the innkeeper.

"Who is that?" Aeolmar asked, indicating the stable.

"My stable girl, Latera," Ingvarr replied. "She has a way with horses, you know. Some of my patrons only stop by for her services."

"We'll need her to accompany us," Aeolmar said. Finlay raised an eyebrow, but Aeolmar ignored him. "If we stable our horses here and walk to the location, it will add days to our journey. I'd prefer to take the horses as far as we may."

"Of course," Ingvarr said, looking at Latera. She saw the innkeeper's gaze, then busied herself with the saddle. "Latera is a willful girl, and may refuse just for the sake of refusing. Let me send my mate to speak with her, my lord."

"No need. I'll ask her myself," Aeolmar said, striding toward the stable. Finlay and Ingvarr followed.

"Do we really need to bring her?" Finlay asked.

"How long do you want to be out here, days from Asherah?" Aeolmar countered. When Finlay grunted, Aeolmar assumed his second agreed. Aeolmar entered the stable and confronted the girl behind the workbench.

"I am Aeolmar, First Hunter of Parthalan," he announced.

"I'm Latera, and I brush the horses," she replied, her gaze on her work.

"Please excuse her, my lord," Ingvarr said. "She's a human who was lost here and is still learning our ways." Ingvarr glared at Latera and added, "She claims she was royalty in her homeland."

Aeolmar looked at Latera, noting her slanted eyes and pointed ears. "Why do you look like one of us if you're human?"

"I didn't always," she replied. "I'm told it's the effect of the realm."

Aeolmar had known many humans, and none had taken on fae characteristics. In the midst of wondering who had told Latera such lies, he realized he was frowning at her. He lightened his expression and continued. "My hunters and I will make camp a short distance from here for two nights. We will need someone to care for our horses. Ingvarr tells me that you have a way with them."

"Hunters or horses?"

His eyes narrowed. "The latter."

"Yes, I do," Latera replied. "Will you stable them here?"

"No. You will travel with us."

Understanding dawned in her pale eyes and she glanced at Ingvarr. "Won't I get in the way of your hunt?"

"We aren't hunting," Aeolmar replied, "This is a training mission. My hunters have scouted the area, and there are no demons nearby. You won't be in any danger."

Latera was silent for a time. It was an unusual request to take a young woman into the forest with five hunters, but Aeolmar believed it was a necessity. Her presence meant that the hunters wouldn't need to worry about their mounts, and therefore get the Trial over with sooner. Then the hunters would return to Teg'urnan, and Latera would be safe in her stable.

"Very well," Latera said. "When do we leave?"

***

After she packed Latera joined the hunters in the inn's small courtyard, and they rode into the wood. While the hunters rode warhorses Latera was astride Elma's elderly pony, Petal. Latera didn't know if she envied or hated the hunters.

Aeolmar rode at the front while Latera was at the rear, flanked by Finlay and Adhaire. The *nuvi* regaled Latera with his exploits; Aeolmar noted that he left out that they'd all happened while in training yard. After Adhaire's fifth such tale, Finlay took over and told stories about Queen Asherah. He said that she was called Asherah the Ruthless, and by some the Assassin, and could destroy any demon she faced.

"What of him?" Latera asked, nodding toward Aeolmar.

"Our First Hunter?" Finlay asked. "He's only the most feared warrior in Parthalan. Some say he's even more fearsome that Asherah."

"That's a lie," Aeolmar called over his shoulder. "Asherah is the finest huntress ever to grace Parthalan's soil."

"You think I tell lies about the queen?" Finlay countered.

Aeolmar looked back and saw Finlay smiling, while Latera studied her pommel. "I think you say whatever nonsense comes to mind."

Finlay laughed. "Nonsense, is it? When we return to Teg'urnan I'll throw myself at Asherah's mercy and appeal to her good heart."

Aeolmar suppressed a smile as he faced forward. Though their binding remained secret, all of Parthalan knew how Finlay loved the queen. Few suspected that she loved him in return.

It wasn't long before the hunters found a clearing with room for the horses and tents, bordered by a stream on the western edge. While Latera saw to the horses and the hunters set up the tents, Adhaire resumed boasting.

"I'm glad we brought the girl," Adhaire said. "After I complete my Trial, I'll take one of the wineskins and—"

Aeolmar's hand closed around Adhaire's throat. "You'll do nothing of the sort," Aeolmar said. "Latera is not a woman to woo. She is here to care for the horses, nothing more. Furthermore, she is under my protection. Understood?"

"Understood," Adhaire croaked, and Aeolmar released him. As the *nuvi* gasped for breath, Finlay took Aeolmar aside.

"Wasn't that a bit harsh?" Finlay whispered. "Latera's a pretty girl. Adhaire merely noticed."

"I promised her she would be safe," Aeolmar replied. "How would you feel if you were a girl surrounded by five men twice your size? I cannot have him making her uncomfortable."

Finlay frowned but didn't argue. A short time later, Adhaire set out into the forest to begin the Trial by Stealth with Luth, Finlay, and Bron following close behind. Aeolmar lingered at the camp, assembling a fire in the center of the clearing.

"You're not part of the game, my lord?" Latera asked. She sat across the firepit from him, repairing a stirrup.

Aeolmar's mouth quirked. He liked that she was interested. "I'll follow once the fire is set."

"Are you sure you'll find them?"

"Yes, I'll find them," he replied. "Ingvarr said you're a princess?"

"I'm the first born of King Harold and Queen Ladyslava, heir to Gannera," Latera replied. After a moment she added, "My lord."

"How did you come to be in Parthalan?"

"I don't really know. I was with my sisters in the courtyard when a wind rose from a pond and brought me here. That was six winters ago, and I've been here since."

Aeolmar blinked. Had she really arrived in Parthalan by way of a magical vortex? Instead of questioning her about the vortex, he asked, "Do you like it here?"

"Ingvarr and Elma are good to me." Latera looked up from her work. "Why do they all talk about how scary you are? You don't seem scary to me. My lord."

Aeolmar laughed. "I can be scary, when I need to be."

Latera watched him for a moment. "You should laugh more often. Then no one would be frightened of you." She bent to pick at her stitching. Aeolmar whispered the words to call fire, and in another moment, it was crackling away.

"I'll set out now. We'll try to return before dark. Remain close to camp where it's safe." Aeolmar entered the forest, tracking the hunters instead of moving toward his childhood home. He didn't want to stray too far from the camp, or from Latera.

***

Continue the story here.

# Acknowledgments

I've said it before and I'll say it again: writing a book is not for the faint of heart, and no one—no one—can go it alone. Following is a list of people who helped me, helped this book, and helped me stay sane-ish.

First of all, thank you to everyone who read and enjoyed the first book in this series, *Heir to the Sun*. I was blown over by how well received it was, and by all the great comments and reviews. Thank you! And don't worry, the third installment, *Rise of the Deva'shi*, is available now.

Let's talk about this amazingly beautiful cover, courtesy of Cover Villain. There have been many representations of Asherah over the years, but this image captures her as she truly is: a bad ass warrior queen. Asherah never looked so good!

Speaking of awesome writer/editor/friends, the print edition of this book was assembled and beautified by Jennifer Carson. Jenn's an amazing artist in her own right, and everything she creates is made of magic. They call her the Dragon Charmer for a reason!

So many people have beta read this manuscript that I don't want to thank anyone individually, for fear of leaving someone out, but thanks none the less. And to the good folks at Bellatrix Press, who believed—and still believe—in Parthalan, you have my gratitude.

And a big, big thank you to the Wonder Twins, Ember and Robby, and Robb. Without you three, I don't know what I'd do. Love you guys.

# About the Author

Jennifer Allis Provost is a native New Englander who lives in a sprawling colonial along with her beautiful and precocious twins, a dog that thinks she's a kangaroo, a parrot, a junkyard cat, and a wonderful husband who never forgets to buy ice cream. As a child, she read anything and everything she could get her hands on, including a set of encyclopedias, but fantasy was always her favorite. She spends her days drinking vast amounts of coffee, arguing with her computer, and avoiding any and all domestic behavior.

Find Jenn on the web here: http://authorjenniferallisprovost.com/

For up to the minute sale notifications, follow her on Bookbub here: https://www.bookbub.com/profile/jennifer-allis-provost

For exclusive content, follow her on Patreon: -https://www.patreon.com/jenniferallisprovost/

Friend her on Facebook: http://www.facebook.com/jennallis

Follow her on Twitter: @parthalan

Happy reading!

# Also By Jennifer Allis Provost

**The Chronicles of Parthalan, a six volume epic fantasy
(and one short story collection)**
Heir to the Sun
The Virgin Queen
Rise of the Deva'shi
Pieces of Parthalan: Six All-New Stories From The Land Of
Parthalan
Golem
Elfsong
Sunfall

**The Copper Legacy, a four book urban fantasy:**
Copper Girl
Copper Ravens
Copper Veins
Copper Princess
**A duology based in the Copper world:**
Redemption
Salvation
**Poison Garden, an urban fantasy filled with seers,
witches, and one seriously hot detective:**
Belladonna
Oleander
Bleeding Hearts
Thornapple

**Gallowglass, an urban fantasy set in Scotland and New York:**
Gallowglass
Walker
Homecoming
**Winter's Queen, an urban fantasy set in Scotland and Elphame:**
Touch of Frost
Giant's Daughter
Elphame's Queen
**Changes, a contemporary romance:**
Changing Teams
Changing Scenes
Changing Fate
Changing Dates